**THE BALFOUR INVESTIGATIONS
BOOK 1**

Blood And Birthright

James Black

Copyright Notice

BLOOD AND BIRTHRIGHT

Copyright © 2025 James Black. All rights reserved worldwide. No part of this book may be reproduced or copied without the express written permission of the Author.

This book is a work of fiction. Characters and events in this novel are the product of the author's imagination. Any similarity to persons living or dead is either purely coincidental or a tribute to the writer's skill.

First Edition

Published by James Black

For more information: www.jamesblackauthor.com

ALSO BY JAMES BLACK

The David Balfour Investigations

Coming December 2025

The Callander Murders

Visit www.jamesblackauthor.com for updates

Dedicated To:

My Wife
Who thought this was a good idea.

Prologue

Yes, it was a mess. A twisted labyrinth of lies, weakness, cruelty, and greed that would surely ruin the family's reputation if it ever came out, but she could see a way through, clear as moonlight and stark as day—and she would guide them safely across.

Because that's what family was, and that's what love requires. Sacrifice, forgiveness, strength in the face of darkness—without those simple qualities they would have nothing, and she would not be slow to remind them of that. Not this time.

The light flickered gently, casting shifting shadows across her hands as she worked, her movements precise and focused. It was soothing, rhythmic, each action a silent promise, every moment tightening bonds she hoped would hold firm despite the impending chaos.

The winter darkness pressed close against the windows, a quiet reminder of her isolation, but the flickering glow offered gentle comfort, and the faint scent of warmth lingered in the room, stirring memories of better times, past joys long kept hidden.

She smiled briefly, a quiet sigh of satisfaction slipping past her lips, as she envisioned the path ahead.

Perhaps it was because the warm room was too full of her own thoughts, maybe she was too distracted by the emerging hope weaving bright paths through the tangled shadows, but either way, she didn't hear the quiet footfall behind her, didn't sense the presence slipping in from the dark.

The first blow came without warning, a savage burst of violence that fractured her skull, sending her sprawling forward. She felt a sickening crunch as her head collided with the hard surface beneath her, her vision flaring white-hot, pain radiating outward, blotting out all rational thought.

Slipping into oblivion, disbelief tugged weakly at the edge of consciousness, the faint whisper of betrayal fluttering across her mind so shocking that she barely registered the second blow, or the third, or the fourth.

Each struck with merciless precision and escalating savagery as it broke bones, shredded skin, and echoed through the dull haze of her dying senses with a brutal finality.

As the darkness gathered, and as warmth fled her shattered body, she clung briefly, helplessly, to a single, fleeting thought: that the family could endure. That love forgave—even now.

And then everything faded, consumed by the encroaching void.

Chapter 1

Highland Perthshire, 1860

Clattering, shrieking, its lanterns piercing the nighttime blackness, the late train cut into the Perthshire mist like a knife.

Shooting towards the purple shrouded hills, their steep rocky hillsides wreathed in a lingering fog lit by a ghostly full moon, the engine crew sweated in the exposed cab, oblivious to the lingering winter chill that still hung grimly over the Scottish countryside, as if determined to keep the anaemic spring at bay.

Holding court in the guard's van, conductor Hector MacGregor—staunch advocate of the beneficial medicinal effects of adding a wee drop of whisky to your tea when a chill was abroad—held court to his assistant Donald Murray.

'He's bringing bad news to someone, Donald. I'm telling you now. In twenty years I've never seen the night train stop at the Callander halt. Not once in all that time. I cannae recall carrying a gentleman in first-class overnight before the fishing and shooting starts neither.

'You mark my words son - it's a black night for someone up the line.'

Donald, a firm believer that the comings and goings of the gentlemanly classes were a mystery best ignored (and that any involvement or notice in such goings on could bring only trouble) said nothing but nodded sagely.

If old MacGregor could be encouraged to keep pontificating, and his tea kept judiciously topped up from the bottle kept hidden at the bottom of his knapsack, there was every chance that he could keep to his cosy perch—nestled atop two sacks of mail beside the guards' van stove—all the way there and back again.

But he couldn't ignore the truth of what he said. There was something about the first-class passenger. Something about the way he smiled, the way he looked through you—like he already knew everything you were ever going to say or do or know—that made Donald shiver down to his boots.

He was right.

Sitting alone in the first-class carriage, David Balfour watched as the nighttime landscape slipped past the window, a dozen degrees of darkness pockmarked by the occasional pool of moonlit water or glistened leaves as they clattered past.

Gazing across the scurrying landscape and reflecting on the many changes it would soon undergo, he watched as the night slipped past, thinking of the lights that would pop into existence across what was now inky black. Where tonight empty hillsides and lonely lochsides stood silent, over decades to come the solitude would be replaced by a thousand pinpricks of light cast out from household windows, streetlamps and the constantly rolling roads.

If Donald had known what Balfour knew, his fireside perch would not have seemed so comfortable tonight—because he really did know so much more than Donald would ever see.

He knew that within a few years the Dunblane, Doune and Callander Railway livery Donald was wearing tonight would disappear, swallowed up by the galloping expansion of the Caledonian Railway Company as progress continued to race forward.

He knew that Hector MacGregor would retire within five years, the presentation of his congratulatory pocket watch moment captured forever in black and white on a faded inside page of the Stirling Observer, and that within seven the grizzled conductor would be dead of pulmonary tuberculosis.

He knew that by the end of the decade a telegraph cable between Britain and North America would span the Atlantic sea. That financial panic in London would see unemployment soar, sending discontent and unrest racing like an inferno through the British working classes, and that an outsider called Thormanby would win the country's most important horse race that summer.

Most of all, he knew that in 19 years time, on a rain-lashed December night, Senior Mail Guard Donald Murray would still be riding the rails when a bridge spanning the River Tay collapsed, sending him and 74 passengers and crew of the service from Burntisland plummeting to an icy death.

Because when he had time to properly prepare, Balfour really did know everything.

***

The weather worsened, great wet drops of snow beginning to slap against the windows of Callander train station's waiting room as it swirled and eddied beneath the icy crags that dominated the small town.

Inside the squat sandstone building, struggling to warm his hands at the barely lit stove, Solomon Shaw shivered.

It had been less than an hour since he was woken by the local constable hammering at his door, bringing orders to hitch up his carriage and prepare to collect a gentleman from the overnight mail train, but already the warmth of his bed felt a long, long way away.

'For two pins I'd have boxed his ears and kicked his arse back down the road Mr Rennie. Battering at a man's door in the middle of the night and handing out orders like he's God almighty.

'If it wasn't for my wife being present, and for it being a question of obliging Mr Young himself, he'd have gone home a sorry beggar tonight.'

Privately, Callander Station Master James Rennie wondered if the glowering Shaw—thick-set and naturally belligerent but standing five feet five in his best boots—would have made much impact upon the strapping frame of local Constable Arthur Buchan, but a man unexpectedly awoken on a night like this was entitled to a wee bit of a moan, so he nodded gravely, and agreed that tonight was indeed a lucky one for the fortunate PC Buchan.

'Aye Solomon, you've the patience of a saint. I doubt there's a man in Perthshire who would have blamed you either, but as you say, a summons from Mr Young is a matter of some importance.'

As chief prosecutor for the region, and the starting point for justice throughout the county, Procurator Fiscal John Young was not a man to be ignored. Rennie had himself received a telegram from the law officer that evening warning him that the unexpected service would be making an unscheduled stop, and it was something about the tone of that brief message—making it clear that the single passenger disembarking from the train was to be afforded every possible assistance—that was reason for him attending the arrival in person, rather than deputising his hapless assistant.

Glancing at his pocket watch, Rennie shifted slightly uneasily in his seat, glancing out the window and across the snowy platform into the blackness beyond.

'Well, he'll be here soon enough Solomon. What were your instructions?'

' They're simple enough Mr Rennie. Just collect the first-class passenger arriving on tonight's train and take him to Mount Stewart Farm on the road to Strathyre - no matter what the weather, no matter what the hour. Mr Young will already be there by all accounts, having come overland from Perth, and will be waiting for him.'

Grimacing, Rennie wrapped his greatcoat tighter and shuddered slightly in response. Any event that had brought Fiscal Young to a windblown farm on the edge of the area at this time of night was unlikely to be good news, but whoever or whatever he had summoned to join him there, with the power to redirect to railway itself and roust people from their beds the length and breadth of a line still being built, was clearly a force to be reckoned with ... and perhaps even one to be feared.

***

The driver, unaccustomed to making the stop at Callander, braked a little too sharply, a little too late - the engine's massive iron wheels squealing against the rails as the train slid rapidly into the station. Its momentum carrying the first wagons past the point at which Rennie and Shaw stood waiting, bracing themselves against the twin onslaught of the arriving train's backdraft and the rising winds, the first-class carriage ground to a halt just beyond the pool of illumination cast by the platform's final lamppost.

Straining to see through the thickening snowfall swirling in the downcast light, they heard a carriage door slam before the guard's whistle pierced the night once more and the train began to move off again, quickly gaining momentum in a cascade of soot, sparks and steam.

The silence returned as quickly as it had been shattered, only to be cut once more by the sound of heavy footsteps accompanied by the click of a brass tipped walking cane, coming closer through the dark, rapping out a staccato beat as the waiting functionaries peered into the blackness.

Neither of them was sure why, but they both held their breath as the the steps grew closer - tap, tap, tapping towards them with a steady tread until the figure of a dapper, dark eyed young man, immaculately clad in a tweed suit and overcoat of the latest city cut, finally stepped into the lamppost's struggling light and stood for a moment, silently surveying the hunched welcoming party before him, a half smile playing on his lips.

'Mr Rennie I presume?'

Striding forward, the figure took Rennie's hand in a firm grip.

'I'm David Balfour, Justice of the Peace, and you'll be my driver?,' he said, nodding at Solomon as he did so, his hand moving instinctively to the antique pocket watch beneath his waistcoat as if its weight offered comfort in the uncertain night.

'You have my thanks for coming out on a night like this, gentlemen, but I'm afraid there's little time for pleasantries. We must leave for Mount Stewart immediately,' he grinned, tossing a leather bag to the hapless coachman and setting off towards the station exit with a confident stride.

'Come now Mr Shaw. Death awaits us.'

Chapter 2

MIT-13 Office, Edinburgh, 2025

'Where the fuck is Balfour?

'Davey? Stop dicking about with that computer and set up coffees for the team.'

Detective Chief Inspector Kirk Munro, head of Police Scotland's roving Major Investigations Team 13, better known internally as Department 404—the force's unofficial dumping ground for officers whose careers had encountered 'complications'—strode into the headquarters incident room like a whirlwind, booming instructions at his surprised team as he swept through, his flapping coat tails scattering papers, files and empty coffee cups in his wake.

A dominating, well built man in his early forties, standing above the rest of his team at well over six foot two with a physique to match and the unbreakable self-belief that often came with his stature, Munro surveyed his domain with easy confidence and brimming expectation.

'Meeting room one in five minutes, folks. That's if Balfour can get his shit together and manage a round of coffees without screwing it up, of course, so let's call it 15.'

Grinning widely, he threw a wink at his second in command DI Fiona Campbell, an attractive blonde in her early thirties, who responded with half a smile before returning to the reports spread across the computer screens cluttering her desk, delivering a passing punch to the shoulder of DS Stuart McGinty, who barely grunted, his head buried deep in the morning's newspapers.

A taciturn Highlander, 'Shinty' McGinty was a hard man to read—seldom responding to Munro's breezy charm in quite the way he'd become accustomed to. Not that it mattered. He was solid, hard working, meticulous and dependable without appearing to be particularly over-ambitious, and that suited his DCI down to the ground.

'Nice one boss.'

Detective Constable James Mulholland, a slightly florid young man in his twenties with a mop of curly black hair swept back from a faintly receding hairline, grinned enthusiastically at Munro. Brimming with unrestrained self confidence and ambition, the admiration he held for his DCI fell short of hero worship, but not by much.

Racing to join Munro as he headed into the meeting room to await the rest of his team, Mulholland skipped past DC Rhona Murdoch as she finished picking up the files scattered by Munro's barnstorming entrance off the floor, blowing a stray strand of red hair from her face as she restored order to the chaos. Automatically cataloguing inconsistencies in the case files - the details others missed and the patterns they ignored -

she threw a wry smile in Campbell's direction and headed in to join the morning briefing.

***

'Right. Let's get started and Balfour can catch up when he decides to grace us with his presence,' said Munro as the last of the team shuffled in to take their seats, barely minutes after first barking for the meeting to start.

'Fiona. Kick off with the series of rapes in Carnoustie and we'll take it from there.'

Stepping up to the head of the room and clicking on a remote control, DI Campbell pointed to the large interactive whiteboard screen as the display flickered to life with images of six young women and a single mugshot of a heavyset male.

'Ok. We're pretty much wrapped up here. The gorilla on screen is Mark Strachan. He's got previous for sexual assault, four of the victims have positively identified him as their attacker and forensics have been able to tie his DNA to all but one of the women attacked over the last 18 months. We also have witnesses prepared to identify him as being near the attack locations at or around the time of three of the rapes and items belonging to two of the victims were recovered from his home when we searched it.

'To date, he's continued to claim total innocence, but his lawyer looks a little green around the gills and I reckon we're a matter of days away from him pleading guilty in the hope of getting a reduced sentence. Either way, the Fiscal's office is confident of securing a conviction and Rhona and David have done a great job of packaging up the paperwork ready to go.'

As if on cue, Campbell was interrupted by the door crashing open as Balfour attempted to negotiate his way through the doorway without spilling the six steaming coffee mugs balanced precariously on a tray.

There was something about Balfour that set Munro's teeth on edge—the quiet confidence, the expensive clothes, the way he never seemed rattled by anything. He reminded him of the entitled pricks who'd made his own rise through the ranks twice as hard as it should have been.

'Nice of you to turn up Davey,' sighed the DCI with a theatrical roll of his eyes. 'Hope we haven't dragged you away from anything important?'

Grimacing, DC David Balfour briefly considered retorting, but decided against it. Everyone present knew that, located as far from MIT-13's temporary offices as it was possible to be and at its busiest in the early morning, making a coffee run through the Headquarters canteen was, at best, a 20 minute job. And nobody knew it better than Munro, who had set him the same impossible task every day since joining the Major Investigations Team six months ago.

In less robust workplaces such behaviour would be cast as bullying, but as the most junior member of a team in a tough environment, sometimes it was better to just serve your time and take your lumps.

McGinty glanced at Balfour's expensive suit and handmade shoes with mild curiosity. For a junior DC supposedly posted here due to some kind of HR fuck-up, the lad certainly didn't dress like someone struggling financially.

In the meantime, as he distributed the drinks and tried to avoid eye contact with the smirking Mulholland, Campbell resumed.

'So as I was saying, the Procurator Fiscal's office are very happy with the package Balfour and Rhona have put together and are confident that Strachan will be going down for a very, very long sentence. David - could you summarise the position for us please?'

Happy to be back on firmer ground, Balfour ran through the meticulous package of scientific evidence, witness statements and interview transcripts he and Rhona Murdoch had assembled over many months of careful investigation under Campbell and McGinty's supervision, a painstaking search for the perpetrator of a series of violent rapes that had terrorised the small seaside town for over a year.

'So in summary, the PF is happy that we've got more than enough to put him away for a thirty year stretch as a minimum, although the prosecutor is going to push for a whole life sentence,' he concluded. 'So everyone is happy except the six young women whose lives he destroyed before being caught.

They've all been offered support and counselling, but I don't think any of them will ever really recover fully.'

'Save that guff for the social workers,' interrupted Munro. 'I shouldn't need to remind anyone that MIT-13's major focus is on clearing the national caseload of problematic or crimes, so as far as we're concerned the most important factor here is that the case is now closed, and my—or should I say our—clear up rate remains high enough to get me out of here. So good work Fiona, and Davey, leave the bleeding heart stuff for the university debate team or wherever you spend your spare time … victim support is someone else's problem.

'Fiona? What's next?'

Shrugging, Campbell clicked the remote and the screen refreshed with a new set of mugshots.

'That pretty much wraps it up. Just two more things to note today. First, you'll have read the press reports from yesterday's High Court proceedings regarding the Kilmacolm house invasions …'

She paused as the rest of the team broke out in cheers, thumping the desk in front of them loudly as the front page of that morning's Daily Record newspaper - complete with a full length photo of DCI Munro addressing the press pack from the courtroom steps - appeared on the big screen.

'Full ten year sentences for the entire gang and an extra five for the main ringleader Shug Mackay. A pretty satisfactory result all round ladies and gents, and a real feather in our caps given the amount of fear and publicity the original violent robberies generated when they started.

'Considering our unofficial remit is to be the binning ground for political hot potatoes and HR nightmares, our stats aren't bad,' Fiona commented dryly, earning a few wry chuckles around the table. 'We keep solving the unsolvable - someone upstairs might start asking questions.'

'And finally, the powers that be,' she winked, nodding in Munro's direction, 'are very keen on us tidying up the betting shop robberies as soon as can be done. Most of the hard graft has been done on this guys, so if I can ask you to prioritise getting the paperwork for these wrapped up in a neat ribbon and off our desks ASAP that would be ideal.'

'Anyone got anything else to add?' She asked, glancing at the DCI—now fully absorbed in something on his smartphone—before gathering up her things from the desk and dismissing the team with a brisk nod.

'Good. Now let's get to work.'

***

As anyone paying attention could have told you: Munro's empire was built on bluster and it was Campbell's quiet competence that kept things actually functioning—juggling McGinty's cynical experience, Mulholland's desperate ambition, Murdoch's analytical precision and Balfour, the unknown quantity who didn't quite fit anywhere else.

They were barely through the meeting room door when the phones began to ring in unison, signalling a call from central command and blowing the starting whistle on a race back to their desks and a frantic scrabble for pens, notepads or whatever scraps of paper came to hand.

With the help of a sharp elbow delivered expertly to Mulholland's ribs, Rhona Murdoch won by a length, scooping up her handset and sending the rest of the phones silent as she commanded the caller to proceed.

Scribbling notes in a hurried scrawl, the words on the page obscured from the rest of her team by a cascade of red locks, her pen suddenly paused, and she looked up at Balfour with a raised eyebrow, urgently signalling for him to summon the DCI.

Completing the call in a rapid fire series of staccato one word questions and answers, she slammed down the handset and looked up at the team gathered expectantly around her desk.

'You're never going to believe this. Uniform have just attended reports of a very messy murder in Heriot Row. They've identified the body ... and it's Rowena James.'

His eyebrows shooting skywards, Munro's customary look of self assurance briefly vanished. Ruling matriarch of one of Edinburgh's oldest families, Rowena James not only socialised with half of the city's ruling elite, but she owned a significant chunk of it too. No matter where or how or why she had met her end, the demands for answers were going to come fast and loud, and if he didn't provide answers quickly enough, pretty soon the pressure would mount to replace him with someone who could.

'Right. Fiona, you're with me. Shinty, get on to uniform and tell them to touch nothing until I get there, understand? Then take Mulholland and Murdoch and get ready to coordinate house to house enquiries - I want an officer knocking at every door in the district before the body's even cold.'

Outside, the last stubborn patches of snow clung to Edinburgh's streets, winter refusing to release its grip despite the calendar's promises of approaching spring.

Grabbing his overcoat and swinging it around his shoulders, sending another avalanche tumbling from the nearest desk, Munro paused momentarily to watch the team burst into activity. Exploding through the door as he swept out of the office, he halted briefly, casting an unfriendly eye on Balfour before he turned.

'I suppose you may as well come too. You can hold my jacket and fetch the tea.'

Chapter 3

Mount Stewart Farm, Callander, 1860

The snow was slackening as the carriage crested the final rise, and the full moon, now visible between the clearing clouds, bathed the vista below them, illuminating the glen's white covered expanse in a pale light.

Stretching out before them stood a patchwork collage of snow-covered fields, punctuated only by a frozen grid of hedgerows leading to the sole visible house standing in the middle distance, light blazing from every window like a beacon calling through the still of night.

'Nearly there then, Mr Shaw,' said Balfour, slipping out of the carriage door, pivoting on the running board and swinging up beside the coachman on the exposed driver's bench. 'And quite a prosperous spread too by the looks of it.'

A growl that might have been 'Aye sir it is,' issued from deep within the layers of voluminous overcoat enveloping the hunched figure. 'Mount Stewart is the biggest farm in the area by a long way. Five hundred acres if it's an inch, some of the most fertile pastures in the county, and the best quality livestock this side of the Highland line.

It's not always been that way. When my wife was a girl these were the worst run holdings in Scotland. The old owner, a terrible slave to the drink, let the place run wild until they found him dead in the river one New Year's Day, and then Mr Henderson's father bought the place at auction and turned it into the place it is today.

'They say he cleared and planted the first hundred acres himself, and didn't hire a single hand until the silver from the first crop came in. That may or may not be true, but there's many that say Mount Stewart is the richest farm in the county today, and I'd not bet against it.'

It was, Balfour reflected, a perfect example of how some families maintained wealth and status across generations while others - like his own - saw everything slip away through tragedy and circumstance. The unfairness of it still rankled, even after all these years. Even after he'd fixed it.

'He's done very well for himself then. Is he well liked to match?'

'I wouldn't say he's everyone's cup of tea sir. A wee bit too fond of his own worth, if you take my meaning. But he's an elder of the church and widely respected by the middling folk. Good pals with Dr Geddes and Mr Arburthnot the lawyer, and the only thing you could say he's wanting is a wife.

'That's not for lack of opportunity. Half the daughters of the parish have beaten a path to his door over the years, but he's never seemed to be in a hurry to march to the altar... not that any sane man would judge him for that,' he glowered, burrowing deeper into the depths of his overcoat and falling silent, lost in his own thoughts.

Smiling to himself, Balfour wrapped himself tightly in his tweeds and sat back, enjoying the last of the starlit icy silence as the journey trotted towards its inevitable end. The Highland landscape tugging at memories he usually kept buried - of childhood adventures before his father's disappearance had shattered everything.

***

As the carriage clattered into the farmhouse courtyard, a constable standing ready stepped forward to offer Balfour a steadying hand as he climbed down onto the frozen cobbles as the figure of John Young emerged through the red painted door to greet the arrival.

'Now there's a sight for sore eyes! You're so damned elusive that I wasn't at all sure that my telegram would find you, but good fortune smiled and here you are sir, here you are.'

Vigorously pumping Balfour's hand, Young slapped his shoulder heartily as his bellowed greeting bounced around the courtyard buildings. A solid, conservatively dressed man who looked more like a country squire than the county of Perthshire's most prominent legal officer, his bluff, honest countenance broke into a grin as he welcomed a man he regarded as one of his closest friends and confidants - as much as anyone could claim to know the elegant investigator.

'Seriously though, I'm glad you could come so quickly, Balfour old chap. This is an ugly one, and I don't mind admitting that it has me stumped.'

Gently extracting himself from Young's grip, Balfour stepped back to take in the scene. Lit by the blazing farmhouse windows behind him, and behind his obvious delight over reconnecting with an old friend, Young's usually sanguine features looked unusually pale, the Procurator Fiscal's normally bright countenance clouded by a slightly sickly pallor.

'Well then. Let's start at the beginning and see what we can do to unravel the mess together. Why don't you tell me the whole story as you know it so far and then we'll take it from there?'

'There's not an awful lot of it to go on,' said Young with a shake of his head. 'The landowner Henderson travelled to Perth on business yesterday, leaving his sister Janet in charge of the house. When he returned he found the entire place firmly locked, the windows barred and the doors bolted, and no amount of knocking could raise a reply. Eventually he summoned some of his hands to break down the door, and gaining access, found his poor sister murdered most horribly.

'He sent me this letter by the next available train and I travelled up immediately, arriving a few hours ago,' he continued, drawing a single sheet of paper from the pocket of his waistcoat and handing it to Balfour.

Unfolding the proffered paper, Balfour scanned the brief communique, scrawled in an untidy but not uneducated hand.

'Dear Sir, Please come out here immediately, as my sister has been murdered whilst I was in Perth. Your obedient servant, William Henderson.'

'And the building was completely sealed?' he asked, examining the now brightly lit windows on the farmhouse's second floor.

'Locked as tight as a drum,' Young confirmed, 'and barely touched since the discovery was made. Henderson prides himself on reading the latest scientific and learned journals whenever he can so is familiar with some aspects of modern detection, and insisted that nothing was disturbed until I arrived.'

'And anything moved since?' queried Balfour.

'Not a thing. I brought two constables with me from Perth and they briefly checked the building to ensure nobody remained hidden within, but nobody has been in or out since that moment.'

***

Balfour could tell that the murder scene was going to be a messy one just by the sickly complexion of the young policeman standing guard inside the farmhouse door.

It was.

In the middle of the simple but well appointed kitchen, the murdered woman was lying face down in a pool of blood, her arms outstretched and hands covered with gore. The flagstone floor around her was spattered with bloody foot marks, while the furniture lay scattered about the room in a confusion of upturned chairs, tables and scattered household implements, while the whitewashed walls and tin bath beside the fireplace were thickly spotted with blood, as though they had been sprinkled liberally with a brush.

    The body, stretched out before a fireplace from which Balfour could detect the smallest hint of lingering warmth, was roughly covered with a rumpled set of bed clothes, although as these remained virtually spotless, with not a drop of blood staining the white linen, he suspected they had been thrown over the lifeless corpse after the bloody deed had been done, in a poorly conceived attempt to conceal the evidence.

    Peeling back the crumpled sheets to reveal that the woman was fully clothed - right down to the stiff enveloping apron commonly worn by housewives and maids to protect their gowns during domestic chores and the woollen cap upon her head - Balfour glanced back up at Young and the shaken looking Constable watching on.

    'Did anyone touch the body after it was discovered?'

    'Just once when we arrived, sir. It was clear she was dead but I thought it best to make certain,' confessed the young PC, his neck blushing a rosy pink beneath the smartly starched collar. 'She was still a little warm when we found her, though her hands and feet were cold.'

    Nodding, Balfour continued his examination of the body. Although fully clothed, he could see no evidence of any scratches or injuries except the back of the head, reduced to a pulp of matted hair and skull fragments still glistening with blood and brain matter. A second wound, in the form of a large, deep and irregular hole, lay just below the murdered woman's ear.

    As to the murder weapon there could be little doubt. Beside the body lay a bloody axe or hatchet, of the type typically kept in kitchens to assist in tending the ever present fire, its blade covered with gore and clumps of dark hair.

Standing, Balfour glanced around the room again before addressing Young.

'I'd like a doctor to examine her in due course, but there seems to be little doubt about how she died. I suspect that further examination will conclude that after falling or being knocked down, her murderer struck her with the hatchet two or three times – landing one blow behind the right ear, and one or more to the rear of the head.'

'Exactly what transpired before she died is impossible to say at this point, but judging by her attire, the scattered bed clothes, the lit fire and the laundry implements close by, it seems obvious that she was surprised and brutally butchered in the middle of her domestic duties.

'That much is straightforward. Now all we have to do is find out by whom... and why.'

Chapter 4

Heriot Row, Edinburgh, 2025

'Murder is dead easy', Munro boomed as the team walked up the steps to the smart townhouse. 'Nine times out of ten the perpetrator is a member of the victim's closest family and the motive is either jealousy or anger, built up over years of bullshit,'

'Twenty quid says that's exactly what's happened here. Mark my words.'

Heriot Row, a sweeping expanse of Georgian townhouses that had been built specifically to create Edinburgh's most prestigious residences and some 220 years later was still doing the same job, was already alive in a festival of high visibility jackets, chequered police tape and blue flashing lights. Uniform had sealed off the street at each end, and the usually sedate street was packed with a mass of liveried and unmarked vehicles representing everything from the Ambulance service to what seemed to be the city's entire forensic crime scene team.

The March morning carried winter's bite, a sharp wind whipping between the Georgian terraces, sending pedestrians hurrying with hunched shoulders and turned-up collars.

In the porch of number 22, one of a handful of buildings on the row still preserved intact as a palatial four storey home and not converted into stately apartments for Edinburgh's upwardly mobile professional classes, Munro's team were met by a sheepish crime scene manager brandishing an array of full forensic suits over one arm and an officious-looking clipboard in the other.

'Sorry folks, but nobody sets foot in here without being fully suited, booted and signed in. Melville's orders. We've had three Chief Superintendents and a Commissioner demanding progress reports already and he says that if even the slightest thing goes wrong on this one, he wants a comprehensive list ready of who to throw under the bus.'

Munro, unaccustomed to being addressed so directly by the lower ranks, briefly looked like he was going to protest, but shrugged and reached out for a forensic suit, gloves and boots.

'Myself, Detective Inspector Campbell and DC Balfour signing in. McGinty, Murdoch and Mullholland on the house to house. Shinty, you know the score - if there's been so much as a delivery driver in the street this morning I want to know who it was, where they were going and what colour their mother's underwear is, understand?

'You heard the man people, this one's already getting more unwelcome attention than a drunk girl on prom night, so let's get out in front of this one before it runs away from us.'

***

Clad head to toe in forensic suits, Munro, Campbell and Balfour stepped into the townhouse's elegant entrance hall, where Jim Melville, head of the city's forensic services, stood consulting one of his team at the foot of a sweeping set of mahogany stairs.

'What's happening, Jim?' barked Munro, glowering upwards at the phalanx of SOCO team members buzzing around the upper landing. 'Pretty sure I gave specific instructions that I didn't want anything done before I got here. Did you not get the memo?'

Melville, a rarity in the department for seemingly remaining completely unmoved by Munro or his reputation, grimaced in response.

'And what memo was that, Kirk? The one hidden under the standing order detailing that forensic teams need to secure the integrity of crime scenes before DCIs start blundering around them like a bull in a china shop? Or the note from my mother saying that I'm excused from bullshit mind games? Never thought I'd see your lot handling one of the Crown Jewels anyway - I thought Department 404 stuck to gutter cases.'

'Orders from above,' Munro snapped back irritably. 'Apparently we're expendable enough if it goes sideways, so now, has anything actually useful been done yet?'

Apparently oblivious to the acerbic SOCO's sarcasm, Munro pressed on as if nothing had happened.

'So, what have we got then?'

With a glance over the DCI's shoulder at Campbell and Balfour and a barely audible sigh, Melville summarised what they knew so far.

'Uniformed officers were called at 09:30 hours by Gavin James to report finding his wife Rowena dead in the study upstairs. According to what he told the responding officers, he arrived home together with his brother-in-law George Cockburn to find the premises locked. They let themselves in, headed upstairs to the study to discuss some deal they're working on and discovered the body.

'That's pretty much all she wrote for now. We haven't found any obvious sign of a break-in so far and everything seems in order apart from the dead woman upstairs, but I won't be in position to file a complete report till close of play today at the earliest.'

'And the pair who reported discovering the body?'

'They're waiting in the kitchen with a uniformed officer. Both of them seem pretty badly affected, which is hardly surprising, but they should be up to a brief interview if you tread sensitively.'

Waggling his eyebrows suggestively at his team, Munro grinned broadly.

'Looks like someone owes me twenty quid! Davey, you can have the first chat with Gavin and George - henceforth known as prime suspects one and two - shortly. There's so much top brass crawling over this case already that they won't let us do much at this stage anyway, so you might as well fumble about. In the meantime, let them stew in their own juices while we have a look at the crime scene.'

Rowena James, latest in a long lived dynasty that had loomed large on Edinburgh's horizon for more than two centuries, lay slumped across the vast leather topped antique desk sited prominently in the study's magnificent bay window, her brains sprayed liberally across the large computer screen sitting in its centre. Smartly dressed, in an outfit that looked like it cost as much as the elegant room she had died sitting in, her head lay twisted with one cheek lying on the expensively tooled leather work surface, green eyes stuck wide open as if in a state of perpetual and everlasting shock.

On the screen, behind spots of blood and gristle, sat the flickering plans of what looked like a property development, with an artist's impression of a luxury apartment and shopping complex sitting alongside what was obviously a large and extremely detailed architect's blueprint.

Packing his bag beside the bloody tableau, Medical Examiner Dr Randolph Cliff looked up as the detectives entered the room, a furrowed brow replacing his habitual sardonic expression.

'No quips or witty observations this time please,' he said, casting a warning glance in their direction. 'Rowena James was well known to me. She is—was—a formidable businesswoman, an active charity patron and a great benefactor to this city, so you'll forgive me if I dispense with the usual cynical banter on this occasion and get straight to the point.

'Death was, clearly, a result of multiple blunt force injuries to the back of the head. I will resist the temptation to say too much until I've had the opportunity to carry out a full post-mortem examination at the morgue, but judging by the spread of blood, tissue and skull fragments we're still recovering from the desk, walls and window frames, it is safe to say that her assailant struck her repeatedly and with great force.'

'Any indication as to the murder weapon?', Fiona Campbell enquired.

'Not as yet Detective Inspector. Initial examination suggests something hard and heavy, but she's been hit with such ferocity that it will require a full autopsy to identify the weapon used and even then it may not be possible.

'Christ,' sighed the usually unshakeable medical examiner, sadly shaking his head. 'They must have really hated her. What an absolute bloody waste.'

Tight lipped and visibly moved, Cliff snapped his bag shut, and with a final sad glance back at the dead woman, hurried out of the room.

***

Padding into the kitchen, his plastic bootees making a whispering, shuffling sound on the polished antique floorboards, Balfour found Gavin James and George Cockburn seated at an expansive oak kitchen table, grasping steaming mugs of the extra sweet tea that Family Liaison Officers across the land issued as a matter of course to the relatives of murder victims in the immediate wake of their shocking destruction.

A glance at the glowering expression on the uniformed Superintendent hovering at the back of the room and the tear stained, rumpled faces of the two primary witnesses confirmed Munro's initial assessment instantly - this first encounter was going to be very, very short.

Realising too late that the plastic forensic overall that he was wearing was doing nothing to soften the experience, he slid onto a chair opposite the pair and nodded as sympathetically as he could.

'I'm Detective Constable David Balfour gentlemen. Please do accept my sympathies for your loss. I'm extremely sorry to intrude on this moment and realise that this is the worst possible time to be asking questions, but I do need just a couple of minutes of your time. Anything we learn at this moment could be crucial to finding out who did this to Mrs James, and timing is always critical in these matters.'

Gently squeezing his brother-in-law's shoulder, it was Cockburn who leant forward to take the lead.

'We understand you have a job to do Constable, and will answer any questions we can, but please understand that this is an incredibly difficult time for us and we're both in a state of shock.'

Nodding sympathetically, Balfour drew a notebook from his jacket pocket and smiled as disarmingly as he could.

'Thank you sir. I think I have all the basic details, but could you begin by confirming the circumstances in which you discovered Mrs James' body?'

'There's not much to tell. We were both in London yesterday meeting potential partners for a new development deal we're working on, and shared a taxi here straight from the airport this morning. We let ourselves in and Gav deactivated the alarm system with his code as usual. We walked straight upstairs to make some follow-up calls, opened the study door, and that's when we saw it... her. Just lying there.'

Cockburn paused while his brother-in-law sobbed, gulping in breathfuls of air as he struggled to remain composed.

'Everything has been like it was in slow motion ever since. Gavin ran forward to check if there was anything we could do and I called 999. It seemed to take forever but I suppose it only took minutes, really, and then suddenly the house was full of policemen.'

'And did either of you notice anything about the house? Anything different?'

'Apart from the body of my murdered sister you mean?' Cockburn spat back in a sudden flash of anger. 'No. Everything was exactly as it normally is.'

Pausing to allow the man a moment to regain his composure, Balfour glanced at the still heaving shoulders of Gavin James and briefly considered asking a direct question of the grieving widower before thinking better of it, acutely aware of the Superintendent's looming and increasingly impatient presence.

'I won't keep you much longer sir. Detective Chief Inspector Munro will want to speak to you both in due course, but if I could ask one last question for now: can you think of anyone who might want to harm your sister?'

As James collapsed face down on the table, sobbing hysterically, Cockburn looked back at him through bewildered eyes and shook his head emphatically.

'You didn't know her Detective Constable, but you'll soon learn why that sounds so ridiculous. Rowena was an angel - an absolute angel - and the idea that anyone in this world or the next would want to do her harm is beyond belief.'

Chapter 5

Mount Stewart Farm, Perthshire, 1860

'It's the damnedest thing, Balfour,' Young mused, his breath forming small clouds in the crisp morning air as they stood together in the farmhouse courtyard. 'I've learned to take popular opinion with a pinch of salt, but by all accounts, Janet Henderson was something of a paragon—well thought of by everyone who knew her, and the least likely person in the glen to be making mortal enemies.

The Procurator Fiscal shook his head with bewildered frustration. 'That's precisely why I telegraphed for you, old fellow. When the obvious explanations fail, it takes your particular type of mind to unravel the truth.

Balfour smiled grimly, unconsciously touching the scar that marked his left cheek as he surveyed the imposing stone facade. 'And the second puzzle?'

'How in the blazes did he get in?' Young grimaced, gesturing towards the splintered oak door with his walking stick. 'Henderson and his men were obliged to break down this door to gain entry. Every window latched from inside, every entrance secured tight as a fortress. Yet somehow, someone murdered her and escaped—leaving the building sealed behind them.'

'Then we'd best examine every possible entrance,' Balfour smiled, moving purposefully towards the damaged doorway. 'Shall we begin?'

A first fruitless hour was quickly followed by a frustrating second as the two men conducted a methodical examination of Mount Stewart farmhouse, their investigation carrying them from room to room as they tested every window latch, examined every door frame, and scrutinised every conceivable point of entry—only to find secure iron bolts that showed no signs of tampering and heavy wooden frames swollen tight with winter moisture that had clearly been unopened for months.

'Nothing,' Young muttered, as they stepped back into the courtyard, a combination of frustration and the effort spent clambering into the farmhouse's numerous store cupboards and box rooms colouring his face a bright salmon pink and noticeably increasing the severity of the limp he'd carried since his service in India.

'Every blessed entrance is as secure as the day it was built.'

Not for the last time, it was Solomon Shaw who provided the breakthrough.

Summoning Balfour and Young's attention with a deep, guttural eruption that was half polite cough, half venomous growl, Shaw beckoned them to follow with a swing of a lit hurricane lamp and led the pair through a narrow passage and into a small service yard where a low stone archway revealed steps descending into darkness.

'You'll have had a wee look into the coal cellar from the door next to the scullery, but a lot of these farmhouses have separate hatches for deliveries to save trailing a load of dirt and stoor through the lobby. I ken for a fact that you can get in and out of a lot of places that way no bother.'

With a grin, Young patted the scowling coachman's shoulder. 'By George, you're absolutely right, Shaw. I confess I've never given a thought to the practicalities of coal delivery.'

'Aye, well. Different worlds, sir,' Shaw intoned with barely a flicker as he handed the lamp to Balfour, stepping back into the morning gloom as the investigator descended the steps with the hint of a smile on his lips.

After a few minutes of searching, the sounds of careful footsteps, the scrape of coal and the whisper of fabric against stone occasionally echoing softly upwards, Balfour emerged brushing coal dust from his tweeds.

'It is possible, but if anyone had actually used this route to enter the kitchen, there would be clear evidence—footprints, disturbed coal piles, traces on the hall floors or on the axe. The cellar is covered in soot, but there's not a trace of it anywhere in the house.'

His shoulders sagging as their final possibility evaporated, Young huffed in frustration. 'So we return to our impossible puzzle—a beloved woman murdered in an empty house locked tighter than a bank vault, with no means for entry or escape and no rational solution to the crime.'

Balfour's thumb traced the edge of his pocket watch, his eyes unfocused as he stared somewhere into the distance, far beyond the immediate scene. 'Strange how often the impossible becomes familiar, isn't it? As if the same riddles echo across…' He paused, still lost in thought. 'Well. Time will tell.'

***

The return journey to Callander unfolded beneath a steel grey sky, the earlier snow having given way to a bitter wind that cut through even the thickest tweeds and set the bare branches of the roadside birches rattling like old bones.

Huddled together on the driver's bench beside the smouldering presence of the taciturn Solomon Shaw, Balfour and Young maintained a companionable silence as the carriage's wheels ground steadily through the frozen ruts, each man deep in contemplation of the grisly scene behind them.

What troubled Balfour—even more than the obvious brutality of the murder—was the peculiar contradictions of the crime scene itself. The locked house and the undisturbed rooms beyond the kitchen spoke of precision and calm, while the ill concealed corpse and the lack of any apparent effort to hide the murder weapon or the resulting gore of blood suggested passion or rage. A combination of cold calculation and unhinged emotion? That didn't really make any sense.

'A penny for your thoughts?' Young enquired as they curved through the village of Kilmahog, a mere mile from the outskirts of Callander, its first cottages appearing through the morning mist like ghosts materialising from the grey landscape.

'There are too many discrepancies for my liking,' Balfour responded. 'Our killer was methodical enough to secure every door and window, yet careless enough to leave the hatchet beside the body. Thorough enough to leave no trace of anyone else being there, yet so hasty that he left bloodstains throughout the room. Desperate enough to butcher an innocent woman, but uninterested in even a cursory look around the valuables left in the house.'

Balfour paused, watching as Shaw guided the horses around a particularly treacherous patch of ice. 'What do you know of William Henderson's character? Shaw here mentioned he was broadly well regarded, but sometimes local reputation and private reality diverge considerably.'

Young shifted uncomfortably, drawing his greatcoat tighter against the biting wind. 'I've encountered Henderson at various agricultural fairs and such local gatherings, though we don't move in quite the same circles. Dr Geddes knows him better—they're old friends, from what I understand, along with Arbuthnot the lawyer. Henderson's certainly prosperous, and by all accounts successful, though there's something… reserved about him, which might have occasioned some speculation over the years, but nothing that ever became more solid that local gossip, to be fair.'

As they clattered through Callander's main street, past the familiar sandstone buildings and the station where Balfour had arrived what felt like a lifetime ago, Young directed Shaw toward a row of substantial houses set back from the road behind expansive and well-maintained gardens.

'Dr Geddes took Henderson back with him after completing his examination at the farm. The poor fellow was in such a state of shock that Geddes felt it necessary to provide immediate medical attention.'

Dr Geddes met them at his front door, a tall, angular man in his fifties whose professional bearing could not entirely conceal his obvious concern for his patient.

'Gentlemen, please come in. I've given Mr Henderson a mild sedative and brought him here directly from Mount Stewart. The shock of discovering his sister in such circumstances has left him quite undone, as you might imagine.'

'Your initial examination, doctor?' Balfour enquired as they stepped into the warm hallway.

'Several blows to the skull, and death would have been instantaneous from the first,' said Geddes, his tone brisk and professional. 'The poor woman could not have suffered much, if that provides any comfort, but beyond that, the brutality of the injuries are such that you would need to enquire with an expert at the University in Edinburgh to learn much more.'

***

They found William Henderson seated beside a blazing fireplace, obviously still wearing the same crumpled clothes he had travelled in the previous day. His appearance dishevelled and his face bearing a greyish pallor, he rose shakily as they entered, offering a weak handshake before sinking back into his chair and staring deep into the flames.

'Mr Henderson,' Balfour began gently, settling into the chair opposite. 'I realise this is an extraordinarily difficult time, but if you could manage just a few questions, it would help us enormously in our investigation.'

Henderson nodded slowly, his eyes focusing with obvious effort. 'Of course. Anything that might help catch the monster who did this to poor Janet.'

'Dr Geddes and the Constable have explained the circumstances of the discovery. When you returned from Perth and found the house locked, what exactly did you observe?'

'Everything was sealed tight. Every door bolted, every window barred from the inside. I called out, knocked, even threw pebbles at Janet's bedroom window, but there was no response. That's when I summoned the farm hands to break down the kitchen door.' His voice trembled. 'I should have acted sooner, but I thought perhaps she had taken ill and couldn't hear me…'

'When you left for Perth yesterday morning, was your sister in good health and spirits?'

'Perfectly normal. She saw me off at the door, reminded me to take my coat as the weather was turning, and asked me to collect an order from the draper's shop in town…' he tailed off as the words choked him, pressing a handkerchief to his eyes.

Balfour leaned forward slightly. 'Mr Henderson, I hope you'll forgive the delicate nature of this question, but were there any recent difficulties in the household? Any dismissed servants, unpaid debts, or disputes with neighbours that might have created ill feeling?'

Henderson's response came with surprising vehemence, his grief momentarily replaced by anger. 'You want to know who could have done this? Look no further than John Crichton, my ploughman. The man's a brute, a violent drunk who's been nothing but trouble since the day I hired him. I should have dismissed him months ago.'

Dr Geddes shifted uncomfortably. 'William, surely you don't mean…'

'I mean exactly what I say,' Henderson barked, his voice rising. 'The man has a vicious temper when he's been drinking, which is most evenings. He's threatened violence before when I've had to correct his work or dock his wages for slovenliness, and Janet was always nervous around him.'

Young and Balfour exchanged glances. 'These threats, Mr Henderson, were they specific?' Balfour asked.

'Specific enough. Last month the brute told me he'd see me 'get my comeuppance' after we quite fairly accused him of stealing a set of keys from the house. The man's dangerous, I tell you.'

Dr Geddes cleared his throat diplomatically. 'Of course, there was also the matter of Christina Miller. That little harlot might bear some consideration…'

But Henderson raised an abrupt hand to interrupt him. 'So you've listened to the local gossip, have you? Aye, it's true the stupid minx had got herself pregnant and Janet had to let her go, but whatever her moral failings, the lassie didn't… would never… could not have been involved. You need not waste any time considering her, sir, none at all.'

Balfour frowned, glancing up at the doctor's sceptical expression. 'And do you know where Miss Miller might be now?' Balfour asked.

'Crichton's wife of all people took the girl in, as far as I know, but don't waste any time on that little hellion. It's Crichton you want. Mark my words.'

Dr Geddes stepped forward before Balfour could respond, his hand moving protectively to his patient's shoulder. 'Gentlemen, I really must caution you against prolonged questioning. Mr Henderson has suffered a profound shock, and excessive interrogation could seriously compromise his recovery.'

Casting a warning glance in Balfour's direction as he rose from his chair, Young agreed. 'Perhaps you could send word to the manse when Mr Henderson is a little recovered? Reverend MacLeod has kindly offered accommodation so we'll be his guests for a day or two, should either of you think of anything else that might be helpful in the meantime.'

With Geddes already ushering them toward the door with professional determination, as they cast a last glance back into the room Henderson nodded a vague farewell in their direction.

'Reverend MacLeod is a good man. He'll see you're properly looked after.' He paused, his eyes flitting away from Balfour's and back into the fire. 'You must see to it that Crichton… that whoever did this, is caught and punished. Janet is… was the only connection to my family I had left, and the matter must be wrapped up clean.'

Chapter 6

Heriot Row, Edinburgh, 2025

Having swept the length of Heriot Row, knocking at each door in turn, Murdoch and Mulholland met at the doorstep of the final house and stared at the weathered brass nameplate.

Balfour

'So what I don't get is, how can he afford a place like this on a DC's salary?' queried Mulholland, scanning the handsome sandstone edifice of number 46. 'I mean even the Chief Super probably couldn't stretch to it, right? Must be worth what, a million? Maybe two?'

Nodding, Murdoch absently leaned forward and ran her thumb across the grimy brass plate.

'I think he said he inherited it, along with the other places, the lucky bastard. They're all owned by some family trust. Real old money stuff.'

'Really?' snorted Mulholland, scowling as he stepped back to inspect the large corner property. 'You see, every summer when I was a kid we'd go on holiday to the Trossachs, and we stayed at Davey's house every fucking year until his Mum died.

'His dad had been some big name DCI up in the sticks but he was out of the picture, so his mum rented out their house as a B&B and they didn't have a pot to piss in. Drove about the place in a clapped out old Mini Metro, and they never looked like the kind of family with filthy rich relatives and landed gentry lurking in the background to me.'

'I guess it must have been some distant relative they never knew existed until they died or something like that,' shrugged Murdoch. 'You hear stories about that sort of thing all the time. Anyway - how did you get on with the house-to-house? Turn up anything?'

'Nah. Most of them are out of work at this time of day,' Mulholland sighed, idly kicking a discarded cigarette butt into the gutter. 'One old biddy next door said she saw the husband and brother getting out of a taxi sometime after nine, but that was pretty much it. You?'

'Nothing. Not a thing. A handful of retired folk and a couple of cleaners who didn't see anything, but apart from that everyone must have been out trying to pay their massive mortgages,' she grinned. 'Want to guess who's going to be back here doing overtime tonight?'

Scowling, Mulholland ran a hand through his oily curls. 'Shite. I was meant to be going on a date.'

***

Better known across the rest of Police Scotland as Department 404 - 'file not found' - MIT-13 was the organisation's unofficial dumping ground for troublesome or politically inconvenient officers.

Officially a major incident team, unofficially a graveyard for careers, it represented the last chance saloon for every soul in it, although not all of them seemed to be completely aware of that fact.

Balfour was. Acutely so.

Rubbing at the bridge of his nose in a vain attempt to ward off the stultifying effects of their makeshift office's stuttering fluorescent lighting, he knew they had the Rowena James murder precisely because it was so important.

No one else wanted the political heat: elite families, media vultures, and whispered scandals meant the case was a ticking time bomb, and despite Munro's oafish confidence, he knew that from the moment news of the Edinburgh matriarch's death had broken, it had been earmarked for the attention of the force's most disposable assets.

Around him, the squad room thrummed with low, uneasy energy. Chairs scraped on linoleum tiles long overdue replacing, keyboards clicked insistently, whispered conversations hovered like flies over a bloated corpse.

Despite being less than 24 hours in, fatigue had settled thickly into every corner, mingling with the stale scent of burnt coffee and ink-warm paper.

He was dragged roughly from his thoughts by Munro, who burst into the room and slammed both hands down on the slightly uneven conference table temporarily serving as the team's central hub, slopping coffee across its surface as it wobbled wildly beneath the onslaught and the usually cocksure DCI's knuckles pressed white against the stained laminate.

'First, the bloody betting shop hits. Mulholland, update the team.'

DC Mulholland straightened his tie eagerly. 'Six independent bookmakers hit in four months, boss. All small operations, no corporate backing. Latest was Bilsland's on Easter Road - £12,400 taken plus damage to the till systems.'

'Suspects?' Munro asked impatiently.

'We've got one charged and remanded to Saughton jail - Jamie Sinclair, 19, caught with marked notes from the McKenzie job after an anonymous tip. He's got previous for shoplifting, minor fraud and possession, but nothing like this.'

McGinty looked at the map plotting out the hits on his monitor and raised an eyebrow. 'Kid's barely old enough to shave, let alone plan six professional heists. Who's in charge?'

'He's not talking,' Mulholland continued. 'Won't give up his accomplices, claims he just found the money. But the forensics team recovered professional lock-picking tools and electronic jamming equipment from his flat.'

'Professional?' Munro scoffed. 'They're robbing bookies, not the Bank of Scotland. Sinclair had the cash and the gear - case closed. No corporate pressure, no media interest, no political heat. Just small-time bullshit nobody cares about.'

Balfour, tapping on the map, interjected. 'Sir, the geographical pattern and the equipment level suggest …'

'Pattern?' Munro cut him off. 'The pattern is opportunistic theft. Stop looking for conspiracies where one scared teenager will do.'

McGinty muttered under his breath. 'Scared of what, though? Kid won't even ask for a lawyer.'

'Good lad, Mulholland,' Munro continued, ignoring McGinty. 'Now, onto something that actually matters…'

Pausing, Munro theatrically scanned the room until the faint hum of chatter wilted completely. 'It's simple enough. The scuttlebutt is that Gavin James has debts up his arse and a cock that won't stay in his trousers. The brother, Cockburn, is notorious full stop. A filthy rich, evil-tempered, entitled little bastard.

'Personally I don't care which one it is, but lock them both down now.

'Focus solely on them. Run their financials, trace their call records, and go through their sock drawers. I want the whole nine yards, and I want it done fast. Don't get distracted by anything else. We know one of them did it, so pick one and nail them to the table, understood?'

Around the table, heads dipped as a mutter of compliance rippled through the team while Munro, barking a quick order for DI Fiona Campbell to co-ordinate efforts, turned to head back to the small private office he shared with the team's broken photocopier.

Balfour interrupted.

'Um, we haven't actually finished the house-to-house enquiries from last night, sir,' he said, drawing an uncomfortable glance from Mulholland. 'There's still a good few residents we haven't spoken to yet, and somebody might've seen something…'

Munro's warning glare shot towards Balfour, impatience tightening his lips.

'For Christ's sake Balfour. How many times do I have to say this? Modern policing is about the clever and efficient use of resources, not bumbling about chatting up the public and hoping for the best.

'We don't have time for door-knocking. This isn't 1952. You're not PC Merrybollocks out for a lovely stroll, and if you go off on one of your random side quests I'll nail YOUR bollocks to the table, understand?

While the rest of the team almost imperceptibly shifted quietly away from him, Balfour met Munro's stare steadily, refusing to flinch. 'Sometimes old-fashioned works, sir.'

A heavy silence hung in the air, like the chest tightening pressure you feel just before the first crack of thunder breaks the storm, as the team waited for a response.

Munro broke it first, his irritation hissing through gritted teeth and an unconvincing forced calm.

'Listen closely, everyone. Everyone from the Chief Constable to the First Minister is breathing down my neck, so make no mistake - they're breathing down yours. This needs to be quiet. It needs to be cheap. And it needs to be done fucking NOW. Step out of line and mark my words: if you thought you'd fucked up getting posted here, wait until you see where I send you next.'

Watching as Munro turned away barking further instructions, the pressure of a dozen tasks reshaping the room as the team dissolved into clusters, Balfour settled back into his chair.

Glancing towards Campbell, who offered him a tight, understanding nod and a roll of her eyes, he knew that the best thing he could do now was to keep his head down, his opinions to himself, and to follow instructions.

Trouble was, he never could get the hang of that sort of thing.

***

The walk from the car park to the mortuary building gave Balfour and Murdoch their first real chance to talk without Munro's bombastic presence dominating every conversation, and Murdoch was making the most of it.

'I mean, what's that about?' she said, tucking a wayward strand of red hair behind her ear as they approached the stark facade of the city mortuary, sitting uncomfortably in the Cowgate's medieval shadow. 'Hell, the man hardly ever leaves headquarters himself, but in six months working for him, I've never known Munro send anyone other than Campbell to an autopsy.

Balfour glanced sideways at his colleague, noting the slight tension in her shoulders. 'First one?'

'Christ, no. I've been to plenty. Just never for MIT-13. Munro usually keeps me chained to a desk doing background checks and financial analysis while everyone else gets the proper detective work.' She paused at the entrance, looking up at the institutional signage. 'So why us? Why now?'

'Maybe he's finally recognised your analytical skills are wasted on spreadsheets,' Balfour offered diplomatically, though privately he suspected Munro's motives were far less charitable. More likely, the DCI was calculating that if the autopsy revealed anything inconvenient to his preconceived theories about Gavin James and George Cockburn, it would be easier to discredit or ignore the findings if they came from his two most junior officers.

'Bollocks,' Murdoch snorted, pushing through the glass doors with more force than necessary. 'He's covering his arse. If Cliff finds something that doesn't fit his neat little domestic murder theory, he wants someone expendable to take the blame for missing it.'

The reception area of the mortuary was a study in functional bleakness: beige walls, fluorescent lighting that cast everything in a sickly pallor, and the distinctive smell of industrial disinfectant failing to completely mask something far less pleasant beneath. Behind the reinforced glass partition, a middle-aged receptionist with steel-grey hair looked up from her computer terminal.

'MIT-13 for Dr Cliff's post-mortem examination,' Balfour announced, producing his warrant card.

The receptionist didn't look up from her computer. 'Suite 3. He's expecting you. Gown up first - changing rooms are down the corridor to your left.'

Chapter 7

The Manse, Callander, 1860

The Reverend Alexander MacLeod's dining room accommodated six guests around its substantial oak table that evening, the manse's finest china gleaming under the warm yellow glow of the wall-mounted oil lamps as the massed ranks of previous Ministers gazed down from their portraits in vague presbyterian disapproval.

Seated opposite Young, Balfour found himself flanked by Dr Geddes on one side and the slight, angular figure of Mr Arbuthnot the lawyer on the other, while across the table Miss Amelia Sterling occupied the place of honour to the minister's right.

The young schoolteacher presented a striking contrast to the sombre gathering of professional men. Her dark hair was arranged in a neat style that spoke more of practical efficiency than feminine vanity, while her apparently simple grey dress was not only expensively cut in the latest style but imbued with a degree of ruggedness that suggested it had not been designed for flower arranging and embroidery.

'I must apologise for the somewhat unusual nature of our gathering,' MacLeod began as he carved the roasted fowl, his tone and expression equally concerned. 'Miss Sterling is our schoolteacher, gentlemen, currently residing at the manse while repairs are made to the schoolmaster's house. I fear your business is hardly suitable for such refined company, but she has expressed an interest in your investigative methods and declined to take supper in her room.'

He paused, regarding the young woman with the expression of a man who found himself in an unprecedented and dangerous social situation.

Miss Sterling looked up with a slight smile that managed to be both polite and faintly amused. 'How kind of you to say so, Reverend MacLeod. I confess I find the practical application of investigative methods far more instructive than mere theoretical study.'

'Quite so, quite so,' Dr Geddes interjected warmly, his weathered face brightening. 'Miss Sterling has proven most helpful in my botanical studies. A keen eye for detail and a methodical approach to classification that would do credit to any natural philosopher.'

'Speaking of scientific methods,' Young interrupted, helping himself to vegetables, 'I've received word from Edinburgh regarding our investigation. The post mortem examination will need to be conducted there by Professor Littlejohn at the University. Dr Geddes here has done excellent preliminary work, but the severity of the injuries requires more specialist attention.'

Visibly brightening, Miss Sterling's attention was now fully engaged. 'Might not the pattern of blood distribution at the scene also provide additional evidence? In my reading of German scientific journals, I've encountered fascinating studies on the analysis of such physical traces.'

As Arbuthnot nearly choked on his wine, the minister's face assumed the expression of a man who had recently been subjected to one of the Doctor's more intimate examinations.

'My dear young lady,' he began faintly, 'surely such matters are far beyond the scope of your educational responsibilities...'

'On the contrary,' Balfour interjected smoothly, his dark eyes fixed on the schoolteacher with new interest, 'such observations could prove invaluable. What specific studies do you reference?'

Her dark eyes flashed as she warmed to the subject. 'Largely Professor Uhlenhuth's work at the University of Greifswald documenting how the pattern and trajectory of blood spatter can indicate the position of both victim and attacker at the moment of impact. Most fascinating, although I admit the applications are rather, um, specialised.'

Young's eyebrows shot upward. 'Good Lord. How does a schoolteacher in Callander come to read German forensic studies?'

Miss Sterling's smile became slightly enigmatic. 'My late father was a physician in Edinburgh, Mr Young. Our family has always valued learning above convention - he believed knowledge should not be constrained by expectations of what a lady ought to know. I inherited both his extensive library and his conviction that truth is better served by facts and examination than it is by opinion or circumstance.'

'Well I never,' muttered Dr Geddes, regarding the young woman with newfound respect. 'And here I thought your interest was limited to botany and chemistry.'

'All sciences are connected, Doctor. The same principles of careful observation and logical deduction apply whether one is studying plant specimens or... 'other forms of evidence.'

MacLeod, by now a delicate maroon, cleared his throat with the air of a man determined to restore proper order to his dinner table. 'While Miss Sterling's... unusual accomplishments are no doubt admirable, perhaps we might focus our attention on more practical matters. Dr Geddes, Mr Arbuthnot, you both know the local community far better than our visiting investigators. Surely you can shed light on the characters most likely to be involved in this terrible business?'

Arbuthnot set down his fork with the deliberate precision of a man trained to choose his words carefully.

'Indeed, Reverend MacLeod raises an essential point. There are two individuals whose circumstances make them objects of particular suspicion.'

'Quite right,' Dr Geddes nodded gravely. 'John Crichton, Henderson's ploughman, and that unfortunate young hellcat Christina Miller. Either separately or in concert, they present the most obvious explanation for this tragedy.'

'Crichton first,' Balfour said, leaning forward with professional interest. 'What makes him suspect?'

Dr Geddes exchanged glances with Arbuthnot before speaking. 'The man's a brute, I'm afraid. Known throughout the district for his violent temper, particularly when he's been drinking, which is most evenings. Henderson should have dismissed him long ago, but good hands can be difficult to find.'

'And Henderson mentioned that he had specific grievances against the Henderson family?' Balfour enquired.

Arbuthnot nodded his confirmation. 'I witnessed the incident myself. Henderson consulted me about dismissing Crichton after he suspected him of stealing a set of keys from the house, along with a sum of money. The man's response was... most threatening.'

'And Christina Miller?' Balfour asked.

The three local men exchanged meaningful looks that spoke volumes about their shared assessment of the girl's character.

'A different sort of problem entirely,' Dr Geddes said with professional delicacy. 'Although she was first to be accused of stealing the missing keys, Henderson dismissed her after she was found to be in a condition that made her continued residence impossible.'

'The child's parentage?' Young enquired bluntly.

MacLeod's expression grew stern. 'It's well known locally that the father is none other than Crichton himself. Which explains why the brute was so angry about the girl's dismissal - and why both of them had cause to seek revenge against poor Janet Henderson.'

Miss Sterling's intelligent eyes moved from face to face as she absorbed this information. 'How very convenient,' she murmured so softly that only Balfour caught the words.

'I beg your pardon, Miss Sterling?' MacLeod asked.

'Nothing of consequence, Reverend MacLeod. Merely observing how the various elements of the case seem to align so... neatly.'

Dr Geddes leaned back in his chair with the satisfied air of a man who had solved a complex puzzle. 'When you consider it logically, gentlemen, the conclusion is inescapable.' Henderson mentioned that the Miller girl had actually returned to the house after her dismissal - supposedly to collect her remaining belongings, but more likely to settle her grievances.

'She would have retained keys or known how to gain entry, and her rage over the public disgrace would have festered. The murder follows naturally from such circumstances. Crichton may well have encouraged her or provided assistance, given his own grievances against the household.'

'And he has taken the girl in now?' Balfour asked.

'Right under his wife's nose, if you can believe it,' Arbuthnot replied with obvious disapproval. 'The woman claims to be offering charity, but more likely she's terrified of what her husband might do if she refuses to harbour his... responsibility.'

There was something in Amelia's expression - a slight furrow of concentration, a tightening around her eyes - that suggested she was cataloguing every detail with unladylike precision.

'It seems remarkably straightforward,' she observed quietly. 'Two suspects with clear motives, opportunity through stolen keys, and convenient explanations for any potential witnesses. Almost too straightforward, one might say.'

As one, the three local gentlemen turned to regard her with expressions ranging from mild surprise to outright disapproval.

'My dear young lady,' Arbuthnot said with the patient tone one might use to correct a child, 'in legal matters, the simplest explanation that accounts for all known facts is generally the correct one. Complicated theories serve no one but novelists and sensation-mongers.'

'Of course,' Miss Sterling replied with perfect politeness, rising as she prepared to exit the room. 'How foolish of me to suggest otherwise.'

***

The Crichton cottage presented a stark contrast to the comfortable warmth of the manse, its smoky walls and rough furnishings telling Balfour everything he needed to know about a household where life was one long running battle to get through the long Highland winter.

Seated on a hard straight-backed chair before the smouldering fire, Christina Miller was a slender young woman barely sixteen years of age, her dark hair pulled severely back beneath a plain cotton cap, her brown eyes glinting with a sharp intelligence and a strong hint of defiance. Despite the loose-fitting dress, her pregnancy was advanced enough to be obvious, despite having some months to go.

'Miss Miller,' Balfour began, settling himself on the rough wooden chair that Mrs Crichton had offered before withdrawing to her cooking at the far end of the small room. 'I hope you'll understand that I must ask some questions about your time at Mount Stewart Farm. I know this is difficult, but anything you can tell us might help us find who killed Miss Henderson.'

Although surprised by Balfour's gentle tone, her chin lifted slightly, the spark in her eyes flaring brighter. 'Aye, I ken why you're here, sir. You've already decided it was me, haven't you? You fine folk in the big houses, whispering about the wicked servant girl who got herself into trouble, aye?'

'I've decided nothing, Miss Miller. I'm here to learn the truth, whatever that might be.'

'The truth? Ha!' She spat. 'The truth is that the Henderson house isn't as prim and proper as they make out, and that I had nothing to do with any of it, but the truth doesn't suit the story you all want to tell, does it?'

Balfour leaned forward slightly, his voice remaining gentle but taking on a more businesslike tone. 'Tell me about the circumstances of your dismissal from Mount Stewart.'

Christina's expression darkened. 'Mr Henderson called me into the parlour one morning, said my condition was becoming an embarrassment to the household and that my services were no longer required.'

'He didn't mention the missing keys and money when he dismissed you?'

'Not a word. It was all about my belly and how it wouldn't do to have such a spectacle under his roof.'

'And had you taken anything from the household?'

The question brought a flash of genuine anger to her features. 'I'd never steal from them that treated me right. Not so much as a crust of bread, sir.

'Then how do you account for the missing items?'

'I cannot account for them, but I know I didnae take them.'

Balfour made a note, then looked up again. 'What was your relationship with Miss Janet Henderson?'

Christina shrugged, though Balfour caught a flicker of something softer in her expression. 'She wasn't a bad sort. She could be particular about how things should be done, and I've never held my tongue when I thought differently, but she was fair, mostly, and she never held a grudge when the dust settled.'

'And Mr Henderson?'

The hardness returned immediately. 'Miss Janet kept the house so there was not much occasion to speak directly. I minded my business.'

'But you must have formed some impression of his character?'

Christina hesitated, choosing her words carefully. 'He's got a harsh tongue and a lot of regard for himself, sir. Quick to remind others of their place, slow to forgive insolence or disrespect.'

'And so apart from the day you were dismissed, his behaviour was always proper toward you, Miss Miller?'

The young woman's cheeks flushed deep red, but her gaze never wavered. 'Mr Henderson is a gentleman, sir.'

Balfour nodded, sensing there was more to be learned but recognising that pursuing it now would be fruitless, moved to conclude. 'One final question for now - do you know of anyone who might have wished Miss Henderson harm?'

'No sir, I do not. If someone killed her, it couldnae have been because of something she did. It must have been because of something she had, or something she knew.'

***

A cottage that had seemed sparse during his conversation with Christina Miller felt positively oppressive as John Crichton filled the small space with his smouldering presence.

A powerfully built man in his thirties with the calloused hands and weather-beaten face of someone who'd been earning a living from the reluctant Highland soil since boyhood, he had greeted Balfour and Young politely enough when they arrived to speak with Miller and himself, but his eyes hid a simmering anger that seemed barely held in check and almost impossible to conceal.

'So you're the gentleman investigator they've brought in from Edinburgh,' he said without preamble, his voice blending the broad accent of the region with an undertone of barely concealed hostility. 'Come to find which of the poor folk you can blame for the troubles of the rich, aye?'

'I've come to find the truth, Mr Crichton, wherever that might lead.'

'Aye, well, the truth's simple enough. I was working the fields from dawn till dusk the day Miss Janet died, never went near the farmhouse, and saw no soul approach it either. But I doubt that's the answer you're looking for.'

Crichton settled his bulky frame onto a wooden stool that creaked ominously under his weight, his massive hands clenched into fists that rested on his knees like weapons waiting to be deployed as he answered Balfour's opening question about his time with the Henderson family.

'I work their land. They pay my wages. There's not much more to tell.'

'I think there's a bit more to tell Mr Crichton, Mr Henderson suggests there have been disputes between you, and he has some very credible witnesses who claim to have seen it.'

A bark of harsh laughter escaped Crichton's lips. 'Disputes? Aye, you could call them that. The man's got ideas about how a working man should behave - touching his cap, speaking only when spoken to, accepting whatever treatment he's given like a whipped dog. I've never been very good at that sort of performance.'

Young interjected. 'He mentioned the threats you made against him.'

'Did he now?' Crichton's eyes narrowed dangerously. 'And what threats would those be?'

'He claims you threatened to see him "get his come uppance" after being accused of theft.'

'I said he'd get what was coming to him eventually, aye. Men like Henderson always do. But I never threatened to be the one delivering it, and I certainly never threatened harm to Miss Janet.'

Balfour leaned forward slightly. 'You were accused of stealing keys and money from the household.'

'Accused, aye. But never proved, was I? And notice how quickly they found someone else to blame when it suited their purposes.'

'You mean Miss Miller?'

The change in Crichton's demeanour was immediate and startling. The anger remained, but it was joined by something approaching pain, a vulnerability that transformed his harsh features into something almost gentle.

'She's a handful right enough, but that lassie never stole anything in her life. She's as honest as the day is long, and who says different is either a fool or a liar.'

'She's staying here with your family now.'

'Aye, she is. My wife insisted, and for once I agreed with her completely. The girl needed help, and Christina's always been good to us.'

'Always?'

'She lodged with my wife when she first came to the school here. A bright lassie, eager to learn, never afraid to speak her mind. When she needed work, the Mrs spoke for her to Miss Janet, and she's been grateful ever since.'

Balfour made careful notes, then looked up again. 'The child she's carrying - do you know who the father is?'

The question brought such a swift and violent change to Crichton's expression that Balfour instinctively shifted back in his chair. The big man's hands clenched tighter, his jaw worked silently for several moments, and when he finally spoke, his voice was thick with barely controlled rage.

'Aye, I know. And so does the bastard who did it to her. But she won't name him, and I won't break her confidence.'

'People are saying it's you.'

'People say a lot of things. Doesn't make them true.' Crichton's voice was steady, but his knuckles had gone white. 'I'm married to a good woman, Mr Balfour. Whatever my faults, I don't go about ruining young lassies.'

'Then who?'

'Ask Christina. If she wants to tell you, she will. If not, then it's not my place to speak for her.'

Crichton was already moving toward the door, his interview clearly at an end. 'Ask the right questions of the right people, Mr Balfour. And maybe you'll find answers that don't involve hanging some poor soul for the convenience of the gentry.'

As the door slammed behind the departing ploughman, Balfour sat in the sudden silence, considering the contradictions he'd just witnessed. A man quick to anger, certainly, and one with clear grievances but also someone whose rage seemed directed at injustice rather than revenge, and whose protective instincts toward both Christina Miller and the memory of Janet Henderson appeared entirely genuine.

The question now was whether those protective instincts might have driven him to perjury or worse... to murder.

Chapter 8

Cowgate Mortuary, Edinburgh, 2025

Dr Randolph Cliff was already deep into his examination when they entered the autopsy suite, his normally sardonic demeanour replaced by the focused professionalism that had made him one of the city's most respected pathologists.

The room was starkly functional: white tiles, stainless steel surfaces, and banks of equipment that hummed quietly in the background. Unlike the dramatic depictions favoured by television crime shows, there was no music, no theatrical lighting, just the clinical precision of medical science applied to violent death.

Rowena James lay on the examination table under the harsh fluorescent lights, her body stripped of the grandeur provided by the opulent surroundings they'd first encountered her in. Washed in the unforgiving illumination, the injuries to her head were enough to make them stop and pause momentarily as they approached.

'Ah, the cavalry arrives,' Cliff said without looking up from his work, his voice muffled slightly by the surgical mask. 'I was beginning to think Munro had decided my findings weren't worth hearing.'

'He sent us instead, sir,' Murdoch replied, her apparently irrepressibly straightforward nature apparently unaffected by the grisly clinical environment. 'DC Murdoch and DC Balfour.'

'Really?' Cliff's eyes crinkled slightly above his mask in what might have been amusement. 'Well, no matter. Irrespective of how your DCI may feel, dead people don't care about rank and neither do I. So pay attention please - I'll only go through this once.'

He gestured to the victim's head with a gloved hand. 'Multiple blunt force trauma injuries, as we established at the scene. What's interesting is the pattern and sequence. The killer struck her at least three times, probably more. Judging by the angle of impact to the occipital bone, the first blow came from behind while she was seated and certainly would have been enough to render her unconscious, if not immediately dead.'

Balfour leaned closer, studying the confused, pulped wound pattern. 'But they didn't stop.'

'Far from it. The strikes continued long after she was clearly dead, so it's safe to assume that this wasn't functional violence - it was emotional,' said Cliff as he indicated the different areas of trauma. 'The pattern suggests someone in a state of absolute fury or blind panic, but that's speculation on my part.'

'Any indication of the weapon used?' Murdoch asked, her pen poised over her notebook.

'That's where it gets interesting.' The pathologist moved to a nearby board, across which several close up photographs of the victim's wounds were arranged. 'The wounds are consistent with a heavy, blunt object - something with significant weight and mass. The injury patterns are quite distinctive, actually.'

He pointed to one of the photographs. 'See these impact marks? The shape is unusual - not your typical hammer or crowbar. Something spherical or rounded, but with considerable heft behind it. The damage pattern suggests the weapon had significant momentum when it struck.'

Balfour studied the images, his brow furrowed. 'Any idea what could cause that sort of injury?'

'Nothing immediately obvious. The weapon would need to be heavy enough to cause this level of trauma, but the impact pattern is... well, it's unlike anything I've seen in thirty years of forensic pathology. We've tested for trace materials - metal fragments, rust particles, that sort of thing - but the results won't be back for another day or two.'

'Time of death?' Murdoch asked.

'Based on rigor mortis and body temperature when she was discovered, I'd estimate between 11 PM the previous night and 3 AM the morning she was found. The central heating in that house makes it difficult to be more precise, but that's your window.'

Cliff began removing his gloves, his examination apparently complete. 'Apart from that there's nothing more to tell. No evidence of sexual assault, no defensive wounds on her hands or arms, and no signs she was restrained.'

'A surprise attack then,' Balfour observed.

'That would be my conclusion,' Cliff nodded. 'Presumably poor Rowena was so focused on whatever she was working on at the computer that the killer was able to approach from behind and strike without warning. She never had a chance to defend herself or even turn around.'

'I'll have a full written report ready by tomorrow morning, and I'm requesting additional forensic tests on the trace evidence,' he said as he washed his hands at the deep stainless steel sink. 'If there's anything more to be found, we'll find it.'

***

'There's nothing to find,' Balfour announced to the assembled team, his voice carrying the flat disappointment of a man who had spent the better part of two days pointlessly staring at security footage to confirm nothing.

'We've been through the recordings with a fine tooth comb and there's nothing. The angle of the shot is covering 95% of the room but once she's sat behind the desk you can't see her, but from the moment she enters the room to the moment James

& Cockburn arrive the following morning, there isn't a trace of another living soul entering the place.'

Standing before the incident room's whiteboard, where photographs of Rowena James's study were arranged in meticulous sequence, he clicked through the relevant frames on his laptop, the images projecting onto the wall behind him as the team hunched forward in their mismatched office chairs.

'CCTV confirms the other stories too. Kemp leaves the basement flat at 18:47, walks to the bookies, returns at 19:23 and doesn't budge until the following morning, then James & Cockburn pull up in a taxi at 09:31, exactly as they reported.'

'For fuck's sake,' Munro exploded, his chair scraping violently against the linoleum as he pushed back from the conference table. 'So what you're telling me is that our victim was murdered by the invisible bloody man? That's your contribution to this investigation?'

'I'm just telling you what the evidence shows,' Balfour replied evenly, his dark eyes meeting Munro's glare with self-possessed cool. 'The footage is comprehensive - every entrance, every corridor, every possible approach to that study. If someone had entered that room, we would have seen them.'

McGinty, who had been methodically working his way through the morning's newspapers while listening, looked up with a grunt. 'Unless they were already inside.'

'That's exactly what I was thinking,' Campbell interjected, leaning forward with renewed interest. 'What about the basement flat? Could someone have accessed the main house from there?'

Balfour shook his head. 'Separate entrance, separate alarm system. Apparently the internal door between the basement and main house has been sealed shut for years, but even if it wasn't, it would be impossible to get from there to the study without passing multiple cameras.'

'Right then,' Munro barked, his patience visibly fraying. 'Murdoch, please tell me your financial analysis has turned up something more useful than Balfour's technological dead end.'

Murdoch stood up from behind a thick folder of printouts, her red locks dishevelled following two straight shifts scrolling through row after row of financial information. 'Actually, sir, the financial picture is quite complex. Rowena James wasn't just wealthy - she was the controlling shareholder in a business empire worth approximately £47 million.'

She connected to the projector and pulled up a prepared chart showing the intricate web of companies and property holdings. 'James Holdings Limited, the main company, owns blue-chip commercial properties across Edinburgh, Aberdeen, and Glasgow - all profitable, all stable. But here's where it gets interesting - her husband Gavin has been developing his own separate venture.'

'What kind of venture?' Campbell asked, making notes.

'A luxury housing development in the Borders called Riverside Gardens. Forty-three executive homes, planning permission secured, but it's been haemorrhaging money for eighteen months. Cost overruns, contractor disputes, weather delays, even a protest campaign by some of the local residents. If you can name a problem that can happen to a property development, it's happened to this one.'

Munro's eyes lit up with interest. 'And where does Rowena come into this?'

'That's just it sir - according to the loan agreements, Gavin had persuaded his wife to provide personal guarantees for bridging finance while they sorted the project funding, personally underwriting £8.3 million in debts.'

'Christ,' whistled Mulholland. 'So if the project collapsed...'

'She'd lose a lot. Maybe not everything, but her blue-chip empire would have to be broken up to cover Gavin's debts.

As it was she'd made moves to convert her liabilities back into standard commercial loans under his name, but she died before the transfer of guarantees were finalised.'

'And the banks can't pursue a dead woman,' McGinty observed grimly.

'Exactly. And here's the kicker - the final documents requiring her signature were scheduled to be signed at 10 AM the morning her body was discovered.'

A heavy silence fell over the room as the implications sank in. The overhead fluorescent lights hummed insistently, casting their harsh glare across the assembled faces while the distant sounds of headquarters' daily routine continued beyond the thin partition walls.

'What about the brother?' Campbell mused. 'What's Cockburn's financial situation?'

Murdoch consulted her notes with a slight frown. 'That's proving more complicated. Multiple offshore accounts, investments through shell companies and various family trusts - it's going to take time to untangle, but from what I can see so far, he's not exactly struggling.'

'Right then,' Munro said finally, his voice carrying a note of satisfaction mixed with renewed urgency. 'Now we're getting somewhere. Our grieving widower had every reason to kill his wife before she could sign papers that would have made him liable for millions in debt. It's time to turn the thumbscrews - Gavin James just became our prime suspect.'

***

The unmarked CID car sat in the gathering dusk in Heriot Row, its engine ticking quietly as it cooled, while Murdoch and Balfour waited for the formal interview time that Campbell had arranged with professional precision - late enough to unsettle, early enough to suggest urgency.

'So you grew up near here then?' Murdoch asked, glancing sideways at her colleague as she adjusted the rear-view mirror to keep an eye on the townhouse's elegant front door. 'Mulholland mentioned you used to holiday in the Trossachs when you were a kid.'

'Grew up there, actually,' Balfour replied curtly, his attention fixed on the movement of curtains in upper windows as residents prepared for evening routines. 'Callander.'

'Right, but I mean, with both your parents gone, how'd you end up with…'

'Time to go,' he interrupted, checking his watch and opening the car door as Campbell's text arrived, summoning them inside.

The evening air carried the distinctive Edinburgh blend of sea salt and expensive dinners being prepared behind Georgian windows.

Murdoch caught sight of a sleek black BMW parked outside as they approached the townhouse. 'Christ. Anderson & Associates. James has lawyered up with the big guns.'

'Can't say I blame him,' Balfour replied, pressing the brass doorbell.

The drawing room of number 22 had been transformed into an informal interview suite, with Campbell positioned professionally at a mahogany side table where her digital recorder sat beside crystal decanters that nobody was touching.

Gavin James sat hunched forward on a cream leather sofa, his expensive suit rumpled and his face bearing the grey pallor of a man who hadn't slept properly since discovering his wife's body. Beside him, Douglas Anderson KC, a sharp-featured man in his fifties whose reputation for dismantling police cases was matched only by his fees, maintained the watchful stillness of a predator calculating distances.

'Mr James,' Campbell began, her tone professional but not unkind, 'we need to discuss some financial matters that have come to light during our investigation. I realise this is difficult timing, but these questions are necessary.'

Anderson's pen hovered over his legal pad. 'Given my client's recent bereavement, Detective Inspector, I trust we're proceeding with appropriate sensitivity.'

'Of course.' Campbell consulted her notes with deliberate care. 'Mr James, we've examined the financial records for your Riverside Gardens development. Our analysis shows the project has encountered significant difficulties over the past eighteen months.'

James's hands trembled as he reached for his water glass. 'Property development is unpredictable, Detective Inspector. Setbacks are normal, expected in this business.'

'Eight point three million pounds in cost overruns?' Murdoch interjected quietly. 'All personally guaranteed by your wife, with final documentation scheduled to be signed the morning her body was discovered.'

The silence that followed was broken only by the distant hum of Edinburgh traffic and the measured scratch of Anderson's pen across paper.

'That's quite a substantial financial exposure for Mrs James,' Campbell observed, her voice maintaining its professional neutrality. 'Can you help us understand the timing of these arrangements?'

James finally looked up, his eyes red-rimmed and desperate. 'Rowena understood the business. She knew developments could be challenging, but she believed in the project. We both did.'

'I kept thinking if I could just get one project right, just prove I wasn't completely useless, she'd forgive everything. The personal guarantees were supposed to be temporary - bridge funding until I could secure proper investment. But every delay cost more money, every problem needed more cash, and Rowena kept signing because she believed in me.

'Even when George was telling her I was bleeding the family dry, she still signed. I couldn't tell her about the affair because losing her trust would have meant losing everything.'

'Let's talk about George,' Campbell continued, barely glancing at her notes. 'We understand he had concerns about the Riverside Gardens project.'

Something shifted in James's expression, a flicker of discomfort that he tried to conceal. 'George is... George has always been protective of Rowena. Sometimes too protective.'

'In what way?' Balfour asked from his position near the window.

James hesitated, glancing at his lawyer before continuing. 'He never thought I was good enough for her. Made that clear from the beginning. The business with Riverside Gardens... he was opposed to Rowena's involvement from the start.'

'Opposed enough to prevent it?' Campbell pressed gently.

'George can be... forceful when he feels his family's interests are threatened,' James admitted reluctantly. 'He had words with Rowena about the guarantees. Said I was taking advantage of her generosity, that the family money shouldn't be used to bail out my failures.'

'How did your wife respond to that?'

James's hands clenched into fists. 'She told him it was none of his business. That she was perfectly capable of making her own financial decisions.'

Anderson leaned forward slightly. 'Detective Inspector, are you now suggesting that Mr Cockburn might have had motives?'

'We're suggesting nothing, exploring everything,' Campbell replied diplomatically. 'Mr James, we also need to discuss your personal relationships outside the marriage.'

As the room's elegant Georgian proportions seemed to contract in around him and the dust spinning in the fading winter light slowed to a crawl, James realised where the questioning was heading, and the colour drained completely from his face.

Chapter 9

Royal Infirmary, Edinburgh, 1860

Stepping out of the early afternoon sun casting long wintry shadows across the cobbled courtyard, the first thing that hit them as they crossed the Royal Infirmary of Edinburgh's imposing stone facade was the smell.

Led by a young medical student through corridors permeated by the distinctive smell of carbolic acid failing to completely obscure the sweet cloying odour of death, Balfour and Young found Dr Henry Duncan Littlejohn in a spacious, well-lit room designed for forensic examination. A tall, composed man in his mid-thirties with neatly parted dark hair and modest mutton-chop sideburns, he wore the formal attire of a Victorian professional: high-collared white shirt, waistcoat, and cravat.

Methodical and precise, with the calm intensity of a man accustomed to extracting truth from the rawest of circumstances, in five years since being appointed Police Surgeon to the City of Edinburgh Littlejohn had already established himself as one of Scotland's foremost authorities on forensic medicine. With a reputation for wide ranging scientific excellence and innovation, his testimony was increasingly sought in the most complex cases.

'Mr Young, Mr Balfour,' he stood, greeting them with firm, formal but not unfriendly handshakes. 'As per your request I have completed my examination of Miss Henderson, and I must say, the case presents some rather unusual features.'

Even in death, Janet Henderson maintained an air of quiet dignity. Laid out on a marble examination table, covered with a clean white sheet, her face somehow seemed strangely peaceful, despite the violence that had ended her life.

'I have conducted a thorough examination,' Littlejohn continued, indicating his notes with precision, 'and the cause of death is quite clear - multiple blunt force injuries to the skull. This was perhaps clear from the outset, but the pattern of these injuries does tell us a great deal about both the weapon used and the circumstances of the attack.'

He moved to the head of the table, his manner briskly professional but respectful. 'Miss Henderson sustained no fewer than four separate blows to the skull, three to the occipital region and one to the right temporal area. The first blow would surely have been immediately fatal, and so the subsequent strikes were delivered post-mortem.'

Littlejohn carefully turned Janet Henderson's pale face to reveal the head wounds. 'The primary impact fractured the occipital bone extensively, driving fragments into the brain tissue, and the force was sufficient to cause immediate unconsciousness and rapid death through massive intracranial haemorrhage. The temporal wound, though less severe, penetrated the skull to a depth of approximately one inch.'

He indicated the cleaned wounds with a pointed instrument. 'Observe the irregular shape of the impact sites - consistent with the pitted surface of an axe blade rather than a smooth implement - while the wound edges show characteristics of a sharp blow followed by a tearing motion, typical of hatchet injuries.'

Young leaned in, his face grave. 'So she would not have suffered?'

'She would have lost consciousness immediately,' Littlejohn confirmed. 'Death would have come within moments if not instantaneously.'

Balfour studied the doctor's careful notes. 'Can you tell us anything more about the weapon used, Doctor?'

'As you might have expected, the weapon was undoubtedly the kitchen hatchet found at the scene. I have examined it thoroughly and found traces of blood and hair consistent with the victim's injuries.'

He indicated the detailed ink sketches spread out across the desk. 'The angle of impact indicates the attacker was standing behind the victim, likely while she was seated or bent over some task. Interestingly, the subsequent blows were delivered with less force and from slightly different angles, suggesting the attacker's state of mind may have changed during the assault.'

Littlejohn moved to a side table where the murder weapon lay cleaned and examined. 'I have measured the blade dimensions against the wound patterns. The cutting edge is approximately three inches wide, consistent with the temporal wound, while the blunt back edge of the hatchet head created the crushing injuries to the occipital region. Blood patterns on the handle also indicate the weapon was gripped firmly throughout the attack.'

Balfour, deep in thought, looked up at the surgeon. 'Could these injuries have been inflicted by a woman?'

'An excellent question,' Littlejohn nodded approvingly. 'The force required for the initial blow would be considerable, but not beyond the capabilities of a strong woman in a state of extreme emotion. The kitchen hatchet would be familiar to any woman of the lower classes, certainly, and the angle of the wounds could be consistent with an attacker of either sex.'

'And the time of death,' Young enquired.

'Based on the condition of the body and his letter to me, I see no reason to dispute Dr Geddes' estimate that death occurred between six and eight hours before discovery. The degree of rigor mortis in the facial muscles and the temperature of the extremities on a cold day would have provided reliable indicators, so I must concur with his finding that the event occurred during the period she is reported to have been in the house alone.'

Littlejohn paused, consulting his notes once more. 'There is one additional detail that may prove significant. Miss Henderson's clothing was undisturbed, and there is no evidence of any struggle prior to the attack. Her fingernails were clean, showing no skin or fabric that might have been torn from an assailant.'

'So again, she was taken by surprise while she thought herself alone,' Balfour muttered.

'Or by someone whose presence in the kitchen would have seemed routine or unthreatening,' Littlejohn confirmed, glancing at him. 'Certainly, the evidence suggests the victim was completely unsuspecting when the first blow fell.'

'Dr Littlejohn,' Balfour said as they prepared to leave, 'in your professional opinion, does this crime suggest careful planning or impulsive violence?'

The police surgeon considered the question carefully. 'It can only be speculation, but while the attack itself was brutal and frenzied, the circumstances suggest at least some degree of premeditation or planning. This was surely not an act of pure impulse, but neither was it the work of an accustomed killer. Something in between, perhaps...

'A grievance nursed? An opportunity presented? The whys and wherefores therein are a speculation too far for a simple surgeon,' he said, escorting them to the door. 'But I am certain that I don't envy you the task.'

It was not until their train entered the Carse of Stirling, and the unmistakable crags of Ben Ledi stood above the purple shrouded hills welcoming them back into the Trossachs' frosty embrace, that Balfour spoke again.

'Dr Littlejohn's examination confirms what the scene suggested,' he said, looking thoughtfully into the onrushing view. 'This must have been personal. Someone who knew Janet

Henderson, who had access to the house, and who harboured sufficient motive to commit murder. So our question now is - who truly fits that description?'

'You have doubts about Christina Miller?' Young queried. 'There are plenty of those that believe I should have ordered her arrested already.'

'I have doubts about everything,' Balfour smiled. 'There is a light in which the evidence points toward her, certainly, but something feels wrong. Littlejohn's observations all suggest an element of cold hearted consideration that I just don't see in her character.'

'You think we should examine the farmhouse again?'

'I think we should examine everything again,' Balfour replied, gazing into the distance. 'The truth is often lurking in the details that everyone has overlooked.

***

The second search of the farmhouse proceeded with methodical precision, Young and Balfour painstakingly alert for any detail that might have escaped notice during the confusion of the day of the murder's grisly discovery.

Constable Buchan, a tall, raw-boned man whose ungainly frame seemed to bump against every doorway and low beam, followed in their wake with the patient resignation of someone accustomed to being directed by his superiors, his heavy boots echoing hollowly on the wooden floors as they worked their way through the building.

'Nothing in the kitchen beyond what we observed yesterday,' Young muttered, running his hands along the whitewashed walls with practised thoroughness. 'The parlour's undisturbed, the scullery shows no sign of tampering, and the main bedroom appears exactly as Henderson claims he left it before departing.'

They had saved the smallest chamber for last - a narrow, cheerless room tucked beneath the farmhouse's sloping roof that had clearly served as quarters for domestic staff, its single window offering an oblique view of the courtyard below and a vast swathe of grey morning sky.

'This would have been Miller's room during her employment,' Balfour observed, noting the sparse furnishings: a narrow iron bedstead, a plain wooden chair, and a small chest of drawers whose paint had long since faded to an indeterminate colour somewhere between brown and grey.

As Young examined the meagre contents of the chest, Balfour found himself studying the floorboards with growing interest, his keen eyes noting how the wood near the window had been worn smooth by years of foot traffic, while the planks closer to the bed showed a different pattern of wear entirely.

'Constable Buchan, could you bring that oil lamp closer? There's something here that requires better illumination.'

Kneeling beside the bed, Balfour ran his fingers along the edge of one particular board, feeling how its surface had been worn smoother than its neighbours, the wood polished to an almost silky finish that spoke of repeated handling.

'Young, look at this. The edges here have been rubbed nearly round - not the sort of wear you'd expect from normal foot traffic.'

Drawing his pocket knife, Balfour worked the blade carefully along the board's edge until he found the spot where the wood gave slightly, allowing him to lever the plank upward with a soft creak that seemed to echo through the small room like a confession.

Beneath the loose floorboard lay a small cavity, and within it a collection of items that made Young whistle softly through his teeth: a roll of banknotes bound with string, several pieces of jewellery including a delicate gold locket, and a small leather purse containing coins that clinked softly as Young lifted it into the lamplight.

'Well, well,' Balfour murmured, examining the locket with careful attention. 'J.H. - Janet Henderson, unless I'm very much mistaken. And this amount of money... far more than a servant could save from her wages, I'd venture.'

Constable Buchan, peering over their shoulders with professional interest, nodded grimly. 'Aye, well I think we all ken fine how that came to be hidden here. There's been talk in the village for some time now, with small things going missing from households on the regular.'

'What sort of things?' Balfour enquired, his tone carefully neutral.

'Food items mostly, sir. A loaf of bread here, some cheese there, maybe a few eggs or a piece of ham. The sort of thievery that suggests someone who's hungry rather than someone who's wicked, if you take my meaning. But there've been other incidents too - a silver thimble that went missing when the Miller girl was visiting, a set of sleeve buttons that vanished from a house where she'd been helping with the washing.'

Young frowned, considering this information. 'And nobody thought to report these suspicions to the authorities?'

'With respect sir, what was there to report? No one ever saw her actually take anything, and most of the items were all so small and insignificant that it seemed more trouble than it was worth.

Balfour examined the worn edges of the floorboard once more, noting how the wood had been polished smooth by repeated handling. 'This hiding place has been in use for years, I should think. The wear pattern suggests regular access over a considerable period.'

'So we're looking at a systematic pattern of theft rather than a single incident of desperation,' Young observed grimly. 'Stealing from her employers as well as from her neighbours.'

Balfour said nothing as they prepared to leave the small chamber, taking one final look around the sparse furnishings. The cheerless atmosphere spoke of a life of service and deprivation that might well drive someone to theft, and yet there was something about the neat arrangement that troubled him.

'So Constable Buchan,' he said as they descended the narrow staircase, 'in your experience, are the petty thieves around here usually so organised and adept?'

The constable considered this carefully before shaking his head firmly. 'No sir. People rarely plan anything very carefully at all - they just take their chance and hope for the best. If you ask me, this looks more like someone who's been making thievery a regular part of their life.'

***

'It seems clear enough to me, Mr Young,' the Reverend MacLeod declared, his voice carrying the full weight of its moral certainty as he poured whisky in the manse's snug parlour. 'The evidence speaks for itself, and my congregation's elders are becoming increasingly vocal in their concerns about allowing such wickedness to go unpunished.'

Hardening along its customary lines of stern disapproval, The minister's countenance took on a sense of purpose as he distributed glowing amber tumblers to the guests scattered around his crackling fireside.

'Indeed,' Young agreed, accepting his drink with a grateful nod. 'The stolen items, the systematic nature of the thefts, the clear motive for revenge against her former employers - everything points to Christina Miller as our culprit. I confess

I'm inclined to have Constable Buchan arrest her first thing tomorrow morning.'

Dr Geddes, settled comfortably in his favourite armchair, raised his glass approvingly. 'Quite right too. The girl's been a source of scandal and disruption for months now. Better to have the matter resolved quickly and cleanly before it festers further. Particularly for poor Henderson himself, who's most anxious that matters are brought to a conclusion at the earliest opportunity.'

Balfour, who had been staring thoughtfully into the warm depths of his whisky, looked up with a slight frown. 'Gentlemen, I find myself troubled by a rather significant inconsistency in our reasoning.'

'Oh?' MacLeod's eyebrows flicked up with irritation. 'And what might that be?'

'If Miller possesses the cunning everyone suspects, why would she leave such damning evidence to be discovered? A person with that degree of native intelligence would surely have removed or destroyed anything that might incriminate her.'

'Perhaps she simply didn't have the opportunity,' Young suggested although, deeply trusting of Balfour's instincts, his tone carried less conviction than before.

'Or perhaps,' Miss Sterling interjected quietly from her seat near the window, 'we're making assumptions that don't bear scrutiny.'

The men turned to regard her with expressions ranging from surprise to disapproval, MacLeod's face darkening at the latest in a series of unexpected feminine interruptions he was struggling to become accustomed to.

'Miss Sterling,' he began with strained patience, 'while your educational background is admirable, criminal investigation requires…'

'It requires an understanding of character, Reverend MacLeod. And I know Christina Miller's well.' Her eyes flashed with quiet defiance. 'She's impetuous, certainly, with a sharp tongue and a quick temper. But she's also clever and cunning enough to survive on her wits - she would never leave stolen items lying about to be discovered, nor could she bear a grudge longer than a few days.'

'You speak as though you know her personally,' Dr Geddes observed with the slightly befuddled frown of a man torn between reason and whisky.

'I do know her personally. Christina was one of my pupils before circumstances forced her to seek employment. She has keen native intelligence matched by an explosive tendency to speak her mind, and I can tell you with absolute conviction that if she had killed Janet Henderson, it would have been in a fit of chaos and rage, not through cold calculation.'

MacLeod set down his glass with considerable emphasis. 'An explosive temper? That hardly speaks in her favour!'

'On the contrary,' Miss Sterling replied steadily, 'it suggests that if Christina were guilty, the crime scene would tell a very different story.'

Balfour regarded the schoolteacher with growing appreciation. 'You believe someone else placed those items in her hiding place?'

'I believe,' Miss Sterling said carefully, 'that the evidence is rather too convenient to be entirely believable.'

Chapter 10

Heriot Row, Edinburgh, 2025

'I believe,' Mulholland said flatly, 'that the evidence is always pretty much what it appears to be. A guilty person is caught red-handed, and then all of this, Davey boy, is just a massive waste of fucking time.'

Standing in the elegant morning room of 22 Heriot Row, waiting for the caretaker to emerge from the basement flat for questioning, Mulholland's latest pronouncement carried the lazy authority of someone who had already done more than enough thinking for his own satisfaction.

'The husband had motive, means, and opportunity,' he continued, counting off each point with his fingers one by one. 'The business was going under. She was about to sign papers that would have made him personally liable for millions. He had unrestricted access to the house. Back of the net. Case closed.'

Balfour, who had heard the identical speech from Munro at the morning briefing and was idly examining the room's Georgian skirting boards instead, looked up with a slight frown. 'Right. So you've no problem with the security footage clearly showing he wasn't in the building when she was killed?'

'Doctored,' Mulholland replied without hesitation. 'Or there's a blind spot we haven't found yet.'

A sudden cough made both detectives spin round to find Douglas Kemp standing behind them, his slightly hunched frame flinching as their focus whirled onto the live-in handyman.

'The policeman said you wanted to see me,' he said, more of a statement than a question. 'Sorry. I was just... I came up from downstairs.'

'Christ almighty,' Mulholland muttered, his heart racing from the sudden intervention. 'Where the hell did you come from?'

Balfour's eyes flicked toward the door, which he'd been watching from the corner of his eye, waiting for Kemp to emerge, and wondered briefly how he'd failed to see him enter.

'Whatever,' Mulholland sighed, pulling out his notebook with obvious disinterest. 'So, Dougie. You were in the building on the night Mrs James was murdered. Tell us what you did that evening.'

'I had fish fingers for my tea and then I went to McKenzie's. I go there a lot,' Kemp began slowly.

'That's the bookmaker on Elm Row, aye?'

'Yes, Jojo lets me play on the machines whenever I want.'

'I bet he does,' grinned Mulholland, waggling his eyebrows in Balfour's direction. 'And then what?'

'Jojo uses his key to give me credits so I played the big one with the lights. But Tam and Eddie came in and I don't like them so I came back again.'

Cutting off the leering Mulholland with the flash of a scowl, Balfour smiled softly at the increasingly upset man in an attempt to quell his rising panic. 'What time was this Douglas?' Balfour asked gently.

Kemp's brow furrowed with concentration, like a child struggling with a difficult sum. 'It was... it was seven o' clock. Or Eight o'clock. Maybe a bit after. Mrs Patterson was putting her bins out.'

'And you stayed in your flat all evening? Didn't go out again or go upstairs again until the next day?'

'I don't go outside or into the big house at night. Mr George doesn't like it. He says I have to stay where I'm safe.'

Balfour, studying the man's mounting anxiety, lowered his voice still further. 'Could you help me with something very important please Douglas? Do you know about the security system?'

A visible tremor ran through Kemp's slight frame. 'Oh yes. I know where all the cameras are. Better than everyone. The new ones AND the old ones.'

'Old ones?' Mulholland's expression telegraphed its first flicker of genuine interest.

'I don't think I meant to tell you that, but it's hard to think,' Kemp said in a mildly confused tone. 'Most people don't know about the old system but they never took it all out when they put the new one in. Some of the old cameras are still there. Hidden. I'm good at hiding things.'

The two detectives exchanged glances.

'Where exactly?' Balfour asked carefully.

'One's up on the landing,' Kemp began. 'Built into the chandelier. And there's another in the front hall, behind the mirror.'

His voice trailed off and he flinched again, as though regretting the words.

'So would these cameras still be working?' Mulholland asked, stepping in front of Balfour and pressing closer in on Kemp as he sensed the prospect of a Munro pleasing curfew.

'I... I'm not sure. Maybe. The old system was different, with boxes, not digital like the new one.'

With Mulholland looming over him, the caretaker finally cracked, tears streaming down his cheeks as his shoulders shook with giant, racking sobs.

'She was kind to me,' he sobbed through the tears. 'Rowena was the only one who ever… who didn't…'

The raw, visceral grief in his voice was so genuine, even the emotionally retarded Mulholland instinctively stepped back, recognising the depth of the uninhibited animal sorrow on display.

'I'm sure she valued you too, Mr Kemp,' Balfour said quietly.

***

'The tech boys reckon they might be able to recover something from those old drives,' Mulholland announced to the assembled team, his voice barely concealing his smugness as he consulted his notepad. 'The geek I spoke to reckons they could still have been recording - they're running specialist recovery software now.'

Around the conference table, the team displayed varying degrees of interest. McGinty continued combing through the day's newspapers with studied indifference, while Campbell leaned forward with professional attention.

Murdoch scribbled notes, while Balfour wore his customary expression of polite scepticism.

'What exactly did these old cameras cover?' Campbell asked.

'Front hall and the first floor landing,' Mulholland replied, practically bouncing in his seat. 'Kemp was dead chuffed about how cleverly he'd hidden them - built right into the chandelier and behind the mirror. Been there for years until I found them.'

Munro's eyes lit up as he leaned back in his chair. 'Excellent work. When will we have results?'

'They're saying it usually takes 24 to 48 hours for a preliminary assessment, but not to hold my breath sir. Depends on how much data they can salvage.'

Balfour shifted uncomfortably. 'That's all well and good, but even if they do recover footage from the front hall and landing what's it going to show? We still have the fundamental problem - the footage we do have already shows nobody entering or leaving the building during the relevant time period. These cameras won't change that.'

'But that's exactly the point!' Munro exclaimed, his voice rising with sudden enthusiasm.

The DCI stood up abruptly, his chair scraping against the linoleum as revelation dawned across his features. 'Christ, I've been looking at this all wrong. This isn't just a murder case - it's a bloody locked room mystery!'

McGinty finally looked up from his newspaper with a grunt of interest, while Campbell exchanged glances with Murdoch.

'Think about it,' Munro continued, beginning to pace behind his chair. 'Gavin James kills his wife, but he needs an alibi. So what does he do? He creates a false timeline.'

'How d'you mean, sir?' Mulholland asked, leaning forward eagerly.

'Simple,' Munro grinned, warming to his theory. 'James enters the house earlier than he claims - probably hours before he and Cockburn arrive together. He kills Rowena, slips out through a window or back door, grabs a taxi back to the airport and then returns with his brother-in-law as if arriving for the first time.'

Campbell frowned. 'But the current cameras show no one entering earlier.'

'Exactly! That's why he needed to study the camera angles first. He found the blind spots, used them to get in undetected. But the old system covered different angles - I guarantee those drives will show him sneaking in when he thought nobody was watching.'

'You think he found a way to bypass the security system?' Campbell asked sceptically.

'I think he studied it for months, mapping every camera position, timing every rotation. And once these recovered drives show us exactly how he did it, we'll have him bang to rights.'

Mulholland nodded eagerly, sensing his moment for recognition. 'The tech team are treating it as priority one, sir. I've already told them to call me directly with any updates.'

'Good lad,' Munro beamed. 'See? This is what proper detective work looks like. Sometimes the most puzzling cases have the simplest solutions. James thought he was being clever with his locked room trick, but he didn't reckon on me turning up.'

Balfour remained unconvinced. 'Sir, with respect, if someone can get in and out without being seen on any camera system, old or new, that suggests something more sophisticated than simple misdirection.'

'Bollocks,' Munro dismissed with a wave. 'Now, I need you and Murdoch to take a trip up to the Trossachs to interview Cockburn. He's staying at their weekend place while our boys crawl over the house, so you pair can toddle off up there, tick the boxes and see if you can get him to undermine James' alibi. Not that it matters - I've already got this sewn up, but we need the paperwork watertight.'

'Mark my words. Within 48 hours, we'll have Gavin James explaining exactly how he pulled off his little vanishing act from a custody cell.'

***

The drive to Callander took just over an hour, Murdoch taking control of the comfortable cruise towards Scotland's most romanticised landscape while Balfour studied the case files, only occasionally glancing at the familiar countryside rolling past the windows.

They crossed the wide Carse of Stirling, that fertile expanse of ancient farmland stretching between the central belt and the Highlands, and rolled up the gentle climb towards the gateway to the Highlands. Rounding a final curve, the town emerged before them against its dramatic mountain backdrop, the purple bulk of Ben Ledi and its neighbouring peaks rising like sentinels behind the neat Victorian houses and modern tourist amenities.

'So you really grew up around here then?' Murdoch asked as they passed the sign for Callander, her casual tone not quite masking her curiosity. 'Must be strange coming back for work.'

'Strange enough,' Balfour replied diplomatically, closing the file and focusing on the approaching town. The main street looked much as it always had, though the proliferation of outdoor gear shops and coffee houses spoke to its continued evolution from working Highland community to tourist destination.

'Just seems odd, you know? Growing up in a place like this and ending up in MIT-13. Most people with your background would be fast-tracked somewhere more prestigious.'

Balfour glanced at her sideways. 'What background would that be?'

'Come on. The houses, the trust funds, the way you carry yourself. You're not exactly typical police material, are you?'

'Neither are you, from what I've observed.'

Murdoch conceded the point with a slight smile as they pulled up outside a substantial Victorian villa set back from the road behind well-maintained gardens, its commanding position and brass nameplate speaking of comfort and privilege. They sat for a moment, studying the imposing facade and the expensive cars in the driveway, before walking up the gravel path to an ornate front door that opened before they could ring the bell.

George Cockburn received them in a drawing room that managed to be both expensively furnished and somehow devoid of personality. Seated beside him, Patricia Fraser KC - a sharp-featured woman whose reputation for dismantling police cases was matched only by her fees - maintained the watchful stillness of a predator calculating distances. Everything from the antique furniture to the oil paintings suggested old money deployed with clinical precision rather than genuine taste.

'Officers,' Cockburn said, gesturing to chairs arranged before a marble fireplace. 'I trust this won't take long. Ms Fraser has advised me to cooperate fully, but there are funeral arrangements to consider.'

'We appreciate your time, Mr Cockburn,' Murdoch began. 'We need to clarify a few details about your relationship with your sister and brother-in-law.'

'Relationship?' Cockburn's eyebrows rose slightly. 'Rowena was my sister. Gavin married into the family. What more needs clarifying?'

'Your opinion of the Riverside Gardens development, for instance.'

Cockburn's expression hardened. 'My opinion was that it represented precisely the sort of reckless speculation that destroys generational wealth. Rowena had responsibilities to the family legacy that transcended her husband's entrepreneurial fantasies, but the doe-eyed cow simply forgot about them whenever her low-rent lothario was involved.'

'Strong words,' Balfour observed quietly.

'Accurate words. The James family has preserved its position for over two centuries through careful stewardship, not wild schemes dreamed up by people with no understanding of genuine wealth management.' His voice carried the casual disdain of someone discussing inferior livestock.

'Do you think Mr James killed your sister?' Murdoch asked bluntly, blissfully unaware of the sharp look her sudden switch of subject drew from the hovering KC.

The question appeared to genuinely surprise him, a supercilious smirk briefly dancing across his lips. 'Gavin? Good God, no. The man lacks the backbone. He's weak, he's stupid, and he's criminally underbred, but certainly not violent.'

Cockburn paused, his lips curving in what appeared to be rising amusement. 'No, for all his many, many faults Gavin loved my sister and is devastated by what's happened, the poor slob. It's all rather touching, even though given that the family interests are now properly protected, I must confess I'm not personally entirely devastated by the timing of events.'

'Meaning you now control the trust?'

'Meaning the assets remain where they belong, with someone who understands their significance.'

Balfour leaned forward slightly. 'What about Douglas Kemp? Do you believe there's any possibility he could have been involved?'

For the first time, Cockburn's composure flickered, and Fraser's pen hovered warningly over her legal pad. 'Douglas? That's... Douglas wouldn't hurt anyone. He's a moron and a simpleton, but harmless. I've never heard such nonsense.'

'He had access to the house. Knew about the security systems.'

'Douglas has been with the family for years. Rowena was fond of him, protective even. The idea is preposterous,' said Cockburn in a tone warning that he considered the subject closed.

'Let's discuss your trip to London,' Murdoch continued, switching tacks as she took up the reins. 'You flew back with Mr James yesterday morning?'

Fraser leaned forward slightly. 'Mr Cockburn, you needn't elaborate beyond what you've already told the police.'

'We met at arrivals. We took different flights - I flew BA, Gavin chose some budget airline - but we shared a taxi from the airport.'

'Different flights?' Balfour's voice remained impassively neutral, but something in his tone made Cockburn's shoulders tense almost imperceptibly nonetheless.

'Different travel preferences, different schedules. We're not joined at the hip, Detective Constable.' His voice carried a new edge. 'Though I'm curious why MIT-13 is handling this case. One might have expected something this high-profile to go to more... competent hands.'

Fraser's slight smile suggested she knew exactly which strings her client could pull if necessary.

'Just following standard procedure, sir,' Murdoch replied smoothly.

Irritated, Cockburn stood abruptly, moving to the window. 'I think we've covered everything relevant, haven't we? Unless you're planning to arrest someone, I have arrangements to make. Ms Fraser, I believe we're done here.'

'My client has been most cooperative,' Fraser interrupted, closing her portfolio with deliberate finality. 'I trust any further enquiries will be properly channelled through appropriate levels of command.'

As they walked back to the car, Murdoch glanced back as Cockburn remained silhouetted against the window, his gaze fixed Northwards on the afternoon light dancing across Ben Ledi's weathered slopes.

'Charming fellow,' she muttered. 'Did you catch how he got all spiky when we pushed on the alibi details?'

'I did,' Balfour replied, as she started the engine. 'I think we need to have a closer look at that particular chain of events.'

'The flights?'

'The flights, the timing, the whole London trip.' He paused, considering. 'George Cockburn is clearly a man who's very good at protecting his interests. The question is what exactly he considers worth protecting.'

Chapter 11

Dr Geddes' House, Callander, 1860

Ben Ledi's purple shrouded crags, brooding beneath a fitful sky casting wandering shards of light across its crags, formed a dramatic backdrop visible through the windows of Dr Geddes's well-appointed sitting room.

The weak spring morning required the assistance of oil lamps to properly illuminate the room's expensive and rather new-looking furnishings, their warm glow casting long shadows across the mahogany table where a gleaming silver tea service had been arranged with ceremonial precision.

Dr Geddes looked on as quietly as his parlour maid moved between the guests filling cups with practiced efficiency, while beside the fireplace, the Reverend MacLeod's black clerical dress made him appear even more austere than usual. The lawyer Arbuthnot sat with the same careful precision that characterised all his movements, gold-rimmed spectacles catching the lamplight.

Occupying the leather armchair at the table's head, the transformation in William Henderson's appearance since discovering his sister's body was remarkable.

Gone was the grey-faced, hollowed out figure of the previous interview. In his place sat a man who carried himself with the assured bearing of the landowning classes, his posture and demeanour reeking of the confidence derived from a lifetime of privilege and the unquestioned acceptance of the three pillars of local authority gathered to his aid.

'Mr Henderson,' Balfour began, settling into the chair opposite, 'we are grateful for your continued cooperation. With a day's reflection, we hoped you might recall additional details about the circumstances preceding your sister's death.'

Acknowledging the fresh cup of tea placed in front of him by the parlour maid with a slight nod, Henderson breathed in deeply before responding. 'Of course, Mr Balfour. Though I must confess that discovering Janet in such circumstances has made it difficult to focus on anything else at all, much less small particulars that might be significant.'

'Naturally,' Balfour said, 'What troubles me most, however, is the question of how her killer gained entry to a house secured from within. Your sister Janet suspected Christina Miller of stealing a set of keys from the household - could she have used these to gain access?'

A flash of something - discomfort, perhaps, or irritation - crossed Henderson's features before being quickly suppressed. 'I hardly think it necessary to dwell on that particular matter, Balfour. Janet's suspicions regarding the girl were... perhaps hasty, given her condition and the circumstances of her departure.'

Dr Geddes leaned forward supportively. 'Indeed, Henderson showed remarkable Christian forbearance throughout that unfortunate affair. A less charitable employer might have involved the authorities directly.'

'Nevertheless,' Young interjected, 'if Miller possessed the stolen keys...'

'I can assure you, gentlemen,' Henderson interrupted firmly, 'that the girl's involvement is most unlikely. Janet may have suspected her initially, but I am now certain the real culprit was John Crichton, my ploughman. The stolen keys were never recovered, and I suspect it was Crichton who took them, allowing poor Miller to bear the blame for his crime.'

The Reverend MacLeod nodded gravely, though his expression carried a hint of puzzlement. 'Indeed, Crichton is a troublesome individual, though I must confess I had rather expected our discussion to focus on... other suspects.'

Dr Geddes cleared his throat diplomatically. 'With the greatest respect to your charitable nature, Henderson, we must consider all possibilities. The Miller girl's circumstances - her dismissal, her condition, her obvious desperation and quarrelsome disposition - would seem to present rather compelling motives.'

Henderson's jaw tightened almost imperceptibly. 'Gentlemen, I appreciate your concern, but I believe you underestimate Crichton's capacity for violence. The man has displayed increasing insolence in recent weeks - a failure to show proper respect, a reluctance to accept correction, a general air of barely contained hostility that I now recognise as far more dangerous than I initially appreciated.'

'In what specific ways?' Balfour enquired, noting the subtle exchange of glances between the three local worthies.

'It was subtle at first - neglecting to remove his cap when spoken to, a surly manner when given instructions, deliberate slowness in completing tasks. But I now believe he was nurturing grievances and resentments, working himself up to some act of vengeance against his betters.'

Mr Arbuthnot adjusted his spectacles with careful precision. 'While such behaviour is certainly concerning, my dear Henderson, we must acknowledge that the evidence against the Miller girl remains substantial. Her access to the household, her obvious motive for revenge, her knowledge of your sister's routines...'

'Moreover,' Dr Geddes added gently, 'with the stolen keys in her possession, she would have had unrestricted access to the farmhouse. And women in her condition are known to experience violent fluctuations of temperament.'

His voice growing more insistent despite his audience's scepticism, Henderson shook his head in flat refusal. 'I understand your reasoning, gentlemen, but you fail to appreciate Crichton's true nature. The man has always harboured a jealous grudge against the family's position in the community. I suspect he saw Janet's murder not merely as revenge, but as a way to strike at the heart of everything he most resented about his station in life.'

The Reverend MacLeod exchanged a meaningful look with Dr Geddes before speaking. 'Your Christian charity does you credit, Henderson, but surely we cannot allow sentiment to cloud our judgment. The girl's guilt seems... rather evident.'

Balfour made careful notes, though his expression remained neutral. 'And you're quite certain that Miss Miller could not have been the one who stole the keys originally?'

The question brought an immediate stiffening to Henderson's posture, his knuckles whitening slightly as he gripped his teacup. 'I see no benefit in pursuing that line of enquiry, Mr Balfour. The girl's departure from our household was handled with appropriate sensitivity to her... condition... and I would prefer not to compound her existing difficulties with unnecessary scrutiny.'

Henderson straightened in his chair, his voice taking on a note of bullish authority as he warmed to the task. 'Gentlemen, I trust I make myself clear when I say that John Crichton possesses both the means and the malice necessary for this terrible crime.

'Waste no effort on the maid or anybody else. The matter is clear to me, and if you would have the good grace to heed the word of someone who truly knows the man, you will find that ultimately, all of the evidence will point in his direction.'

***

The Reverend MacLeod having departed to attend a wealthy elderly parishioner in the county, the manse parlour had settled into a comfortably quiet evening as Balfour, Young and Miss Sterling sat arranged around a cheerfully crackling fire.

Regarding the schoolteacher with careful interest, the lamplight casting a warm glow across her thoughtful features as she read the book that never seemed to be far from her hand, Balfour seized the advantage of a moment away from their well meaning chaperone to strike up the kind of conversation he was fast learning would have made the devout presbyterian blush to his boots.

'I confess myself curious, Miss Sterling,' he said, settling back in his chair. 'Yesterday evening you mentioned Professor Uhlenhuth's work on blood spatter analysis. Could such techniques actually be usefully applied to our present circumstances, do you think, or is it largely theoretical?'

Miss Sterling's dark eyes brightened immediately, and she leaned forward with the enthusiasm of someone finally given permission to discuss a cherished subject. 'A concept is only theoretical until somebody tries it out, Mr Balfour; after that it's a fact, and the only thing stopping its application are dull wits and stupidity. But yes, the German research has identified distinct patterns that I believe could reveal remarkable detail about our own sorry incident.'

Young raised his eyebrows, his port glass paused halfway to his lips. 'Surely you don't mean to suggest that mere bloodstains can provide reliable evidence in a criminal investigation?'

'Far from mere, Mr Young. The pattern, velocity, and distribution of blood droplets can indicate the position of both victim and attacker, the force of blows, even the type of weapon used.'

Warming to her task, she suddenly stood, dipped her fingertips into the astonished Young's glass and sent a spray of ruby red droplets across the stone tiled hearth, gesturing enthusiastically at the resulting splatter. 'When blood strikes a surface at an angle, it creates an elongated pattern that points directly toward its source. The degree of elongation reveals the angle of impact with mathematical precision.'

Balfour, grinning, leaned forward. 'And you believe this could assist in determining what occurred in the Henderson kitchen?'

'Without question. The spatter pattern on the whitewashed walls should provide a clear reconstruction of events - whether Miss Henderson was standing or seated when struck, the approximate height of her attacker, even the sequence of blows.'

'Additionally, the absence of blood in certain areas would indicate where furniture or the killer himself stood during the attack.'

Young set down his glass, his legal mind evidently wrestling with the implications. 'Such evidence would carry weight in a courtroom?'

'I would propose examining the scene with a magnifying apparatus to document every droplet, measuring angles with mathematical instruments, and creating detailed sketches showing the distribution patterns,' she smiled, meeting his gaze directly. 'It might take a little effort to persuade a judge of its merits, but such evidence would be far more reliable than mere supposition or witness testimony motivated by superstition or prejudice.'

'Ultimately, science is undeniable.'

Balfour laughed, slapping his old friend firmly on the shoulder as the redoubtable Young paused, momentarily befuddled by the clarity and directness with which his science lesson had just been delivered.

'So Miss Sterling, What other techniques might prove applicable?'

Again, the response came with startling authority. 'Fingerprint analysis, for one. It's been almost 80 years since Mayer's studies demonstrated that no two individuals possess identical fingerprint patterns. The hatchet handle, door latches, even the stolen items we discovered should bear the distinctive marks of whoever handled them.'

'Fingerprints?' Young sputtered, nearly choking on his port. 'You propose to solve murders through examination of... grubby finger marks?'

'The Chinese have used thumbprint identification for centuries, Mr Young. European science is merely catching up to ancient wisdom,' she smiled, turning to Balfour with growing excitement. 'We could dust surfaces with fine powder to reveal latent prints and compare the patterns under magnification to establish definitively who handled which objects. I have some cosmetic powder that should suffice.'

Studying her closely, a faint smile on his lips, Balfour grinned at his colleague and continued. 'What of the physical evidence itself? The sequence of wounds, the force required?'

'Bone fracture patterns reveal the direction of impact forces. Brain tissue distribution indicates the victim's position when struck. Blood coagulation timing can establish precise chronology,' the schoolteacher listed off with clear-eyed enthusiasm. 'Even the victim's clothing might retain microscopic evidence - blood droplets, fabric fibres, hair fragments that could be matched to the victim.'

As the two men absorbed this information, Balfour found himself studying the young schoolteacher with entirely new appreciation and, were he to admit it, an undeniable buzz of trepidation.

Uncertainly, Young cleared his throat. 'Miss Sterling, while your learning is... impressive, surely such methods are too new, too radical for the scope of a rural investigation?'

'On the contrary, Mr Young. If you truly seek justice for Janet Henderson, then you are obligated to employ every tool available,' Sterling responded with a note of steel. 'Science cares nothing for social convention - it only wants the truth. So should you.'

In the sudden silence that followed, broken only by the crackling fire and Young's audible intake of breath, Balfour leaned forward and, ignoring his friend's now thoroughly confused countenance, asked the only question on his mind.

'At the risk of seeming somewhat inappropriate, Miss Sterling,' he said carefully, his eyes sparkling, 'would you be willing to assist in conducting such an examination?'

***

Beneath the watchful gaze of portraits depicting a range of classical Highland scenes, Young and Balfour settled at a corner table where the murmur of conversation and the gentle clink of cutlery against china would provide a civilised backdrop to their deliberations without risk of being overheard.

Occupying the ground floor of Callander's most substantial establishment, its tall windows offering views across Main Street to the hills beyond, The Dreadnought Hotel's dining room clattered through a busy luncheon service around them.

'I confess myself quite astonished by Miss Sterling's contributions last evening,' Young was saying, carefully buttering his bread as a serving girl placed steaming plates of mutton and vegetables before them. 'Her observations regarding the evidence were remarkably astute, though I'm not entirely certain how to account for her... um, directness in addressing such matters.'

Balfour smiled, tasting his wine with obvious appreciation. 'Times are changing, John. Miss Sterling represents something of the future, and the scientific methods she spoke about will become increasingly important in the years ahead. We'd be foolish to dismiss such insights simply because they come from an unexpected source.'

'Scientific method?' Young raised an eyebrow, his fork poised halfway to his mouth. 'Spinning magnets, bottled lightning, chemicals that fizz and all that hocus-pocus?'

He chuckled, shaking his head with bemused affection. 'Well, your predictions about the future have proven remarkably accurate thus far, old fellow. That tip about the Great Western Railway stock did jolly nicely for me in any case.'

'Speaking of which,' Balfour replied with a slight grin, 'I'd suggest keeping a close eye on developments in telegraph technology…'

Their companionable conversation was interrupted by the approach of a well-dressed gentleman whose expensive tweeds and confident bearing marked him as a member of the commercial classes.

'Gentlemen, forgive the intrusion,' he began with the polished courtesy of someone accustomed to conducting business over good dinners. 'Charles McKenzie of McKenzie & Sons, grain merchants. I understand you're investigating the terrible business at Mount Stewart?'

Young set down his wine glass, glancing across at Balfour with the easy familiarity of old campaigning companions. 'Indeed we are, Mr McKenzie. A shocking crime.'

'Aye, a dreadful affair - we've been supplying Henderson for years, and poor Miss Janet was always most courteous in her dealings with our representatives.

'Quite so. I mention it because when my man Reid returned from his rounds that day, we were discussing the terrible news of Miss Henderson's murder, and he remarked that it must have been the day for misfortune, as he'd passed that thieving vagabond Jon Fox on the road heading South.'

Balfour leaned forward with quiet attention. 'And he encountered this Fox character on the day of the murder?'

'Yes, in the late afternoon. Reid observed him walking along the Strathyre road, looking even more dirty and unkempt than usual - covered in filth from head to foot,' McKenzie said, lowering his voice slightly. 'I wouldn't normally trouble you with such a minor observation, but given the local gossip about thefts at Mount Stewart and Fox's reputation I thought it might be of interest to your investigation.'

Balfour shot a sharp glance in Young's direction.

'Mr McKenzie, would it be possible to arrange a meeting with your Mr Reid? We should very much like to hear his account directly.'

'Certainly. He's due back in town tomorrow evening from his rounds in Balquhidder. Shall I have him call upon you at the manse?'

As McKenzie departed with promises to arrange the introduction, Young turned to his companion with raised eyebrows.

'Another thread to follow, it would seem. I must say, old chap, that our investigation is becoming rather more complex than I initially anticipated.'

Chapter 12

MIT-13 Office, Edinburgh, Present Day

'This is going to be easier than we thought,' Munro barked, striding into the incident room with his customary theatrical flourish, coffee mug in one hand and a stack of camera stills in the other. 'We've got developments on multiple fronts, and I want everyone singing from the same hymn sheet before we start making arrests.'

The familiar chaos of MIT-13's makeshift headquarters buzzed around him as the team abandoned their various morning tasks - McGinty folding his newspaper, Campbell closing her laptop with a decisive snap, Murdoch and Balfour exchanging glances across their cluttered desks as Mulholland practically bounced in his chair with anticipation.

'First, the good news,' Munro continued, slapping the photographs down on the conference table with enough force to rattle the dirty collection of mismatched coffee mugs scattered across its scarred surface. 'Mulholland's discovery of those hidden cameras has paid dividends. The tech boys have recovered partial footage from the old system - grainy as hell, but it shows movement in the front hall during our window.'

A ripple of interest passed through the assembled team as Mulholland preened visibly, straightening his tie and shooting a triumphant glance in Balfour's direction.

'So we've got our killer on camera then?' Campbell asked, leaning forward with professional attention.

'Not exactly,' Munro admitted, his enthusiasm dimming slightly. 'The quality's shite and we can only see the suggestion of a figure. Forensics are going to try and enhance it enough to determine approximate height and build. They reckon it's highly unlikely we'll get anything more out of it, but it confirms someone was moving through the house during the relevant timeframe.'

McGinty looked up from the grainy still shots of the footage with a grunt. 'So no chance of actually identifying who it was?'

'Doubtful, but it doesn't matter. We know it's James, and once we establish that, the enhanced footage will only provide corroboration,' Munro replied with the satisfied air of a man who had everything under control.

Murdoch raised her hand tentatively. 'Sir, I've been reviewing the street-level CCTV footage and found something odd. A white transit van appears twice on murder day - once outside the James house at 8 am, then on Cockburn Street at 3 pm.'

She consulted her notes. 'Registration matches an ANPR flag from the betting shop robberies, but it was never followed up. Van's registered to Jojo Menzies - runs the only bookmaker in a three-mile radius that hasn't been hit.'

Munro barely looked up from his phone. 'What's the connection supposed to be? Elite families like the Cockburns don't associate with small-time criminals.'

Mulholland smirked from his desk. 'Probably just a coincidence boss - half the vans in Edinburgh are white transits.'

'Exactly. What's some two-bob loan shark got to do with Edinburgh's landed gentry?' Munro shook his head in exaggerated confusion. 'Chalk and fucking cheese. Come on Murdoch, use that famous brain of yours - that's why you're here in the first place.'

'The Cockburn family moves in circles where people get their money from trust funds and offshore investments, not from lending cash to punters in betting shops,' Munro continued, warming to his theme. 'Suggesting there's some meaningful connection between them and street-level scum like Menzies is exactly the sort of overthinking that bogs down investigations and wastes everyone's time.'

Balfour interjected calmly, his measured tone cutting through Murdoch's obvious discomfort as she retreated into her notes. 'Sir, with respect, sometimes the most unlikely connections…'

'Sometimes, Balfour, a simple domestic murder is exactly that - simple,' Munro cut him off with growing irritation. 'Gavin James needed his wife dead before she could sign those financial documents. He had access, he had motive, and now we have evidence placing someone in the building during the crucial period. End of fucking story.'

Campbell cleared her throat diplomatically. 'What about the brother? Cockburn certainly had his own financial motivations.'

'Possible, but less likely,' Munro conceded. 'James had the immediate pressure - bankruptcy looming, personal guarantees coming due. Cockburn could afford to wait and see how things played out. But either way, we're looking at one of them, not some elaborate conspiracy involving loan sharks and basement dwellers.'

The DCI paused, scanning the assembled faces with the satisfied expression of a general surveying troops finally brought into line. 'So here's what happens next. Campbell, I want you coordinating with forensics on that camera footage. McGinty, background checks on both James and Cockburn - travel records, phone calls, anything that might contradict their stated movements. Murdoch...'

He fixed the red haired analyst with a stern glare. 'Stop faffing about and focus on the financial timeline - when exactly did James realise he was facing personal bankruptcy, and how long did he have to plan his solution.'

'But first… Mulholland, you're leading the scene search,' Munro continued. 'Get back to Heriot Row with forensics and map every possible entry point. If James pulled some sort of vanishing act using blind spots or camera angles, I want every inch of that house checked against the footage. Every door, every window, every potential access route.'

Mulholland straightened visibly, clearly pleased to be entrusted with such an important assignment. 'Absolutely, sir. Should we focus on the main house or include the basement flat as well?'

'Both, but don't waste time on the basement connection - we've already established that the internal door between Kemp's flat and the main house has been sealed shut for years. Focus on the likely possibilities.' Munro's dismissive wave suggested the matter was closed. 'Balfour, you can assist with the systematic search. Make sure every camera angle is properly documented.'

'Remember - we're not here to solve every crime in Edinburgh or uncover some grand conspiracy. We're here to nail Gavin James for murdering his wife, get the case wrapped up clean, and move on to something that doesn't have half the city council breathing down my neck. This systematic search will give us exactly what we need.'

'The beauty of this approach,' Munro continued, warming to his theme, 'is that it's methodical, scientific, and foolproof. James thinks he's been clever with his locked room trick, but once we map out exactly how he did it, we'll have him dead to rights. No jury-confusing conspiracies, no elaborate theories about mysterious outsiders - just good modern detective work proving that the obvious suspect did exactly what we thought he did.'

***

The Georgian elegance of number 22 looked strangely clinical under the harsh glare of police arc lights as the smaller forensics team conducted their second sweep of the premises, their equipment now focused on the detailed mapping Munro had demanded.

Standing in the entrance hall, Balfour could see Mulholland directing the team in the drawing room with theatrical authority, his voice ringing out clearly as he assigned tasks to an increasingly disgruntled gaggle of SOCO officers who'd clearly have rather been left to get on with their jobs.

'Check that window frame again - look for any signs of tampering with the locks,' Mulholland instructed, like a determined school prefect drunk on the power of the day. 'The killer had to get in somehow, and it's our job to work out exactly how he did it.'

While the systematic search continued around him, Balfour had only one interest. Following the narrow service stairs down from the main house, he found himself in a cramped utility area full of discarded furniture that clearly hadn't been used for decades. The internal door that should have connected to Kemp's flat was immediately obvious - not just sealed, but bricked up completely, with modern plasterwork covering the blocking.

'Definitely no access there,' the SOCO confirmed, running his hands along the smooth wall surface. 'That's been permanently sealed for years. You'd need a sledgehammer to get through.'

Balfour studied the wall carefully, noting the quality of the workmanship and the age of the plaster. But something nagged at him - a question about perspective, about which side of a wall you examined and what you might miss.

Satisfied he'd learned what he could from this angle, he made his way back upstairs where Murdoch was consulting her tablet near the front door.

'The basement connection,' he said quietly, approaching while Mulholland remained occupied directing the bedroom search. 'That's the only question that really matters.'

Murdoch looked up, catching the serious undertone beneath his casual words. 'You've checked it yourself. Completely sealed.'

'From this side, yes.' Balfour glanced back toward where Mulholland's voice echoed from the drawing room, then fixed Murdoch with a steady look. 'But all of this - the camera mapping, the blind spot analysis, the systematic search - it's a waste of time. Someone needs to examine Kemp's side of that wall properly, and finish the door-to-door enquiries. That's where the answer is.'

Understanding flickered across her features, quickly followed by concern. 'If Munro finds out you've ignored direct orders while he expects you here...'

'Someone saw something,' Balfour said simply with a shrug. 'They always do. Sometimes the answer's just about asking the right people the right questions.'

With a shake of her head, Murdoch produced half a smile and sighed deeply. 'I'll cover as much as I can, but be careful - Mulholland is desperate to kiss Munro's backside. He'll grass you up in a heartbeat if he gets the chance.'

Apparently unconcerned, Balfour was already checking the time on his phone, pulling up the list of unrequited house-to-house calls and glancing back into the building, where he could see Mulholland revelling in his role as dictator for a day.

The systematic search would continue for hours, mapping every camera angle and potential entry point.

But he knew they were looking in the wrong places entirely.

***

The incident room felt different after hours, stripped of its daytime urgency and left with only the persistent hum of computer screens and the occasional distant clatter of footsteps snaking through the echoing hallways.

Campbell sat at her desk, working through the forensics coordination notes, while Murdoch and Mulholland occupied opposite ends of the conference table, their laptops casting blue glows across tired faces.

'So where'd your boyfriend disappear to then?' Mulholland asked, not looking up from his screen as he typed his report on the house search. 'One minute he's there documenting camera angles, next minute he's vanished like a bloody magician.'

Although irritated, Murdoch's fingers barely paused as they danced across her keyboard. 'He's not my boyfriend, and I don't know where he went.'

'Course you don't,' Mulholland smirked, finally looking up with a leer. 'Look, I get it. He's got that whole mysterious thing going on - sits to one side watching everyone, got that scar on his cheek like he's been in some proper fights. Very romantic, I'm sure.'

'What's that supposed to mean?' Murdoch's voice carried a slight defensive edge she immediately regretted.

'Come on. I've seen you looking,' said Mulholland, leaning back in his chair and bursting with obvious satisfaction at her discomfort. 'The way you watch him when he's doing his thoughtful detective routine. All the times you've backed him up in briefings. Fancy him, do you? Hoping for a quick and dirty bunk-up in the canteen after hours, hey?'

Campbell's pen froze, although she didn't look up.

'You're being ridiculous,' Murdoch replied, although her cheeks had coloured slightly.

'Am I? He's weird though, isn't he? Looks older than he should for someone who's supposedly our age, never joins in with the rest of us for beer nights, or golf, always fiddling with that daft antique pocket watch like he just stepped out of the last century.' Mulholland's pace gathered as he revelled in her embarrassment. 'Only reason he got this job is because his dad was some big shot DCI up north before he fucked off. Everyone knows that.'

'Really? You might have got away with that sort of thing 50 years ago, but it's hardly going to happen today is it?'

'Isn't it? Bloke thinks he's smarter than everyone else, especially me. Well, he can think what he likes, but if he keeps pulling stunts like today - disappearing when Munro's given him direct orders - he'll be back in uniform before Christmas. Prick.'

Campbell set down her pen with deliberate precision, her chair creaking as she finally looked up. 'Mulholland.'

Something about her tone made him straighten slightly. 'Yes, ma'am.'

'That's enough.' Campbell's voice was quiet but carried an edge that suggested she was not someone to be tested. 'Whatever personal issues you have with DC Balfour are irrelevant to his work performance.'

'I'm just saying, ma'am, that…'

'You're gossiping like a schoolboy,' Campbell said as she stood and moved over to the coffee machine with measured steps. 'And you're making DC Murdoch uncomfortable in the process. Is that really the kind of colleague you want to be?'

Mulholland's confident smirk faded rapidly. 'I was just making conversation. Having a wee bit of banter.'

'No, you were being a dick.' Campbell poured coffee with steady hands, not looking at either of them. 'I've seen enough workplace harassment to recognise it when I see it, and that's what this is heading toward.'

The room fell silent except for the slight scratching noise emanating from the walls as the elderly building's rodent population went about its business and Murdoch, clearly uncomfortable with being the centre of attention, stared resolutely into her screen.

'Look,' Campbell continued, turning back to face them both, 'MIT-13 isn't exactly a prime career destination, is it? We're all here because someone, somewhere, decided we were problematic. Maybe we asked too many questions, maybe we didn't play the political game well enough, maybe we just had the bad luck to be in the wrong place when someone needed a scapegoat.'

She returned to her desk, coffee mug in hand. 'But that doesn't mean we have to make it worse for each other. Balfour's a good detective - thorough, intelligent, and he gives a damn about getting things right. That's more than I can say for most people in this building.'

Mulholland shifted uncomfortably. 'I didn't mean anything by it.'

'You didn't mean anything by it ma'am. And yes, you absolutely did. You meant to undermine a colleague and make Murdoch feel awkward about working with him with a stream of juvenile bloody innuendo,' said Campbell, her eyes fixed on him with steely intensity and a unaccustomed hard edge to her voice. 'The question is why.

'What's Balfour done to you that's made all that ok, in your opinion?'

The silence stretched until Mulholland finally shrugged. 'Nothing, I suppose. He just... rubs me the wrong way.'

'Then that's your problem to solve, not his.'

Campbell's tone softened slightly. 'We're stuck with each other in this place. We can either work together professionally, or we can make everyone's life miserable. What's it going to be?'

Mulholland nodded sullenly, his bravado now completely departed. 'Professional. Yes, ma'am.'

Chapter 13

Callander Church Hall, Callander, 1860

'Professionalism and thoroughness. That, gentlemen, is what separates proper investigation from slander, supposition and superstition.'

Working with quiet authority, Balfour smiled as the assembled constables in Callander's church hall gazed back at him. The obvious discomfort of men more accustomed to wrestling drunks at closing time or quietly handing out rough justice to pickpockets unblemished by the freshly polished brass buttons gleaming in the morning light.

Standing before a detailed map of the region pinned to the whitewashed wall, he traced potential routes with the systematic precision that was fast making him invaluable to embattled legal authorities across Scotland's most challenging counties.

'Constable Buchan, you'll coordinate with the station master. Based on Reid's testimony yesterday evening, we know Fox travels illegally by rail - hiding in goods wagons or between carriages. The line South is his most likely route, so I want every station between here and Edinburgh alerted.'

Scribbling furiously on his pad, the telegraph operator sent in readiness from the local Post Office struggled to keep up as Balfour composed messages with military efficiency.

'Edinburgh Central - Priority. Jon Fox, vagrant, tall angular with a distinctive limp. Suspected Mount Stewart involvement. Likely illegal rail transport. Detain immediately.'

'Stirling Station - Fox travelling south from Trossachs. Check goods wagons, alert platform staff. Physical description follows.'

'Inspector Crawford, Perth - Railway vagrant proceeding your direction. Previous form illegal travel methods. Coordinate station surveillance.'

'Constable Maclaren,' he continued without pause, 'you'll cover the road network. Fox knows every bothy and shelter in the county, but he'll need supplies if he's running long-term.'

Young, observing with calm satisfaction, had seen this approach before - the same systematic coordination that had broken the notorious Blackwood poisoning case, the same attention to detail that had exposed the Dysart smuggling ring.

'Um... begging your pardon sir,' the youthful Maclaren ventured carefully, blushing deeply as Buchan scowled at the impertinence of his interruption, 'but Fox has always been a petty thief, sir. Never known for violence or serious crime. Are we certain he's our man sir?'

A heavy silence settled over the small room, the two constables rigid with concern that questioning a gentleman investigator's methods might have overstepped their bounds.

Balfour's expression softened immediately. 'An excellent question, Maclaren. Never hesitate to think critically about evidence - that's precisely what good police work requires.'

'You're right - we're not certain of anything yet, but that's precisely why we need him found. Fox may be guilty of murder, he may be guilty of theft, or he may simply have been passing at a most inconvenient time. I don't believe in coincidences though, so let's chase this down.'

He paused, studying the map with the same intensity he'd once applied to battlefield intelligence during his years of service.

'A known thief, covered in filth, carrying stolen goods, spotted fleeing the area on the day of a murder at a house accessible through a coal cellar? That's either our killer, our closest witness, or the most remarkable coincidence in criminal history.'

***

The manse parlour felt smaller with five men gathered around its polished mahogany table, the afternoon light filtering through tall windows that looked down across the mature gardens towards the River Teith.

Young sat at the foot of the table, feeling rather like the accused as he gazed at the grave faces of the local authorities who had summoned them with an urgent message delivered during another lunch in The Dreadnought Hotel. Balfour, wearing his customary expression of mild detachment, remained standing, his back against the wall.

The Reverend MacLeod occupied the chair at the table's head, his clerical dress lending an air of moral officialdom to the proceedings, while on either side of him sat Dr Geddes and Arbuthnot, their faces variously arranged into expressions of concern, approbrium, and unblinking reptilian determination.

'Gentlemen,' MacLeod began, with all of the measured authority mustered by years in the pulpit, 'we have requested this private meeting because the current situation has become untenable. Mr Henderson's health continues to deteriorate under the strain of this prolonged investigation, and the good name of our community suffers with each passing day.'

Young shifted uncomfortably in his chair, his legal instincts already warning him of the direction this conversation would take. 'Reverend MacLeod, I understand your concern, but proper procedure requires...'

'Proper procedure?' Dr Geddes interrupted, his tone sharp with professional frustration. 'Procurator Fiscal, I have examined Henderson personally. The man is on the verge of complete nervous collapse. Every additional day of uncertainty pushes him closer to a condition from which he may never recover.'

Arbuthnot leaned forward, his lawyer's manner somehow managing to blend courtesy and subtle threat. 'Moreover, Mr Young, we must consider the broader implications.

'This is no simple farmer. Henderson is not without influential connections in Perth and Edinburgh, and his business dealings involve men of considerable standing and quite remarkable levels of influence. They, also, are beginning to ask uncomfortable questions about the conduct of this investigation.'

Balfour, who had remained silent throughout the exchange, finally spoke. 'And what remedy do you gentlemen propose?'

'The remedy is obvious,' MacLeod replied with pompous certainty. 'Arrest Christina Miller immediately. The evidence against her is overwhelming, and the community's peace of mind demands swift justice.'

'If not the girl,' Dr Geddes added pragmatically, 'then Crichton will suffice. Either would serve to end this intolerable situation and allow Henderson to begin his recovery.'

Young's voice carried a note of warning. 'You're asking me to arrest someone without sufficient evidence.'

'We're asking you to act upon the evidence you have,' Arbuthnot corrected smoothly. 'The stolen items discovered hidden in her former room, her obvious access to the missing keys that would have granted her entry to the house, her motive for revenge, her knowledge of the household routines. Any reasonable man would consider that sufficient grounds for prosecution.'

The lawyer paused, allowing his words to settle before continuing. 'Of course, if you feel unable to proceed, there are other authorities who might take a different view. My own connections extend to the highest levels of the legal establishment in Edinburgh - into the chambers of the Lord Advocate himself, indeed, and I should be most reluctant to burden such distinguished gentlemen with concerns about provincial... irregularities.'

In the silence that followed, Balfour studied the three local worthies with growing irritation. Justice was not their concern. Maintaining the established order, preserving Henderson's reputation and ensuring their own positions within the community's carefully maintained hierarchy remained unblemished - that clearly was.

It was a situation with which he was becoming depressingly familiar.

'Gentlemen,' he said quietly, his dark eyes moving from face to face, 'you speak of evidence against Miller and Crichton. But I must observe that the same evidence - access to the household, knowledge of routines, opportunity for grievance - applies equally to others. Including, I'm afraid, both Mr Henderson himself and even yourselves.'

The effect of his words was immediate and electric. Dr Geddes flushed deep red, MacLeod's jaw tightened visibly, and Arbuthnot's careful composure cracked just enough to reveal the anger lurking beneath his usual sallow composure.

'That is an outrageous suggestion,' MacLeod said, his voice vibrating with clerical indignation. 'William Henderson is a pillar of this community, an elder of the church, a man whose character - along with my own - is beyond reproach.'

'That's good,' Balfour replied evenly, 'because character is precisely what we are investigating.'

***

Even if the Very Reverend Archibald MacLeod, MA, DD, FRSE, Minister of the Parish of Callander and Clerk to the Presbytery of Stirling, had intended to say more - the explosion put an end to it.

A single, concussive BOOM shook the manse to its ancient stone foundations, followed by the unmistakable crack of glass and a burst of unnatural white light that flared against the tall parlour windows. For one stunned second, no one moved, and then every man in the room leapt into action.

Balfour was the first to the garden door, moving with determined briskness, followed closely by Young and Arbuthnot. While Dr Geddes, calmly professional, called for his medical bag, Reverend MacLeod, pale with outrage, paused only to snatch up his clerical hat before striding out in a fit of episcopal indignation.

They emerged into the lower garden, the summerhouse now visible across the lawn and wreathed in thick whitish smoke while the manicured south-facing grounds - normally serene beneath the gaze of the River Teith - were now scattered with scorched papers, broken glass, and one very startled and slightly singed squirrel.

From within the smoke, the summerhouse door creaked open.

Amelia Sterling stepped calmly out into the daylight, a faint trail of magnesium residue curling after her like a theatrical flourish. Her long skirt was lightly singed at the hem, a dark streak of soot marked one cheek, and a single strand of black hair had worked itself loose from its usual immaculate arrangement to trail diagonally across her face. She exhaled once and tucked her notebook under one arm with composed precision.

'Well,' she said, mostly to herself, 'that was informative.'

The men stared.

'What in God's name...' MacLeod began, coughing more violently than may have been necessary as the acrid smoke reached his lungs. 'Miss Sterling! Have you gone completely mad?'

'I don't believe so, Reverend,' she replied, dabbing at the soot with a lace handkerchief that had clearly not been manufactured for chemical cleanups. 'Although the chlorate proportions I chose were evidently a little optimistic.'

In what had been a challenging week for the Minister, the lady's cool aristocratic indifference to his stress proved to be the final straw.

'You've ignited something in the manse grounds! On consecrated land!' He was nearly shouting now. 'The very air itself smells of brimstone! This is not some German academy for disorderly women - this is a manse! A seat of moral example!'

Amelia blinked at him, entirely unmoved. 'It's also currently the centre of an unsolved murder investigation, and flash photography, as you may not know, is extremely effective for capturing forensic details - blood traces, fibre textures, impact splatter. I would have preferred to carry out the experiment in a proper laboratory, but you don't appear to have one Minister.'

She turned slightly and gestured back toward the summerhouse, visibly blackened around the window frames. 'Besides, I made rather a breakthrough.'

Geddes cleared his throat meaningfully. 'She might have blown herself up.'

'Yes,' Amelia agreed. 'But I didn't.'

Arbuthnot, brushing soot from his coat sleeve, spoke for the first time. 'Be that as it may, Miss Sterling, I hardly think...'

Amelia cut him off with a perfectly arched eyebrow. 'I assure you, Mr Arbuthnot, there is no aspect of your opinion I fail to find indispensable.'

MacLeod turned in desperation to Balfour, who had been watching the exchange with a glint of amusement. 'You must see that this is intolerable.'

Balfour shrugged mildly. 'Miss Sterling's methods are... unconventional. But I've found that truth rarely emerges politely.'

MacLeod opened his mouth, then shut it again. His glare moved from Amelia to Balfour to the scorched grass, then back to Amelia, now noting something in the margin of her notebook with visible satisfaction.

With the smoke continuing to drift lazily over the gardens, curling past the riverbank and into the tree-lined perimeter of the manse grounds, the men drifted back toward the house while Amelia remained alone in the garden, soot-streaked and smiling faintly to herself as she took a seat on the garden bench and bent humming over her work.

As is the nature of these things, the blast that shook Callander grew in scale and intensity as the story spread like wildfire through the village. Mrs Macfarlane the housekeeper would swear it rattled the parlour teacups, apprentices claimed to have seen lightning bolts shoot high into the skies, and horses were said to have bolted from Main Street to Aberfoyle. The gardener suggested, without humour, that he might apply for hazard pay.

Within the troubled manse itself, Balfour knew that the incident would mark a turning point: A woman with gunpowder on her skirt and steel in her blood had just lit a fuse, but not everyone intended to wait for the bang.

Chapter 14

MIT-13 Office, Edinburgh, 2025

'Right then, sunshine. This is what's going to happen. You sit yourself down, I'm going to shove a lit rocket up your arse, and you're going to sit there and like it while it goes off.'

His voice laced with the poisonous calm his team had learned to fear more than his regular explosions, DCI Munro's bulk filled the doorway of the small conference room where Balfour found himself seated across from Campbell and a smirking Mulholland.

'Yesterday I gave you specific, direct instructions to remain at the Heriot Row scene and assist with the systematic search. Clear instructions. Unambiguous instructions. Instructions that a bloody trainee constable could have followed without breaking a sweat.' Munro's voice began to rise as he warmed to his theme. 'And what did you do instead?'

Balfour met his superior's glare steadily, his hands folded calmly on the scarred conference table, his watch chain just visible beneath an immaculately pressed shirt cuff. 'I completed some of the outstanding house-to-house enquiries that hadn't been finished, sir.'

'Some of them?' Munro's eyebrows shot upward with theatrical incredulity. 'So not only did you fuck off on a solo mission because you thought you knew better than your commanding officer, but you didn't actually manage to finish the job?'

'I contacted about half of the missing residents, sir. Unfortunately, none of them had observed anything relevant to our investigation.'

'Brilliant. Absolutely fucking brilliant.' Munro turned to Mulholland with an expression of exaggerated amazement. 'So our boy wonder here abandons his assigned duties, wastes an entire afternoon knocking on doors like some Victorian constable, and comes back empty-handed. Meanwhile, you had to cover his absence while the forensics team waited for his input on camera angles and access points.'

Mulholland practically glowed with satisfaction. 'The SOCO team leader was asking specifically where DC Balfour had gone, sir. I had to make excuses about radio problems.'

Campbell, shooting a warning glance at the still-smirking Mulholland as she attempted to inject some balance into the proceedings, shifted uncomfortably in her chair. 'Sir, while the timing wasn't ideal, sometimes a thorough approach to completing all potential witness interviews makes sense...'

'Thorough?' Munro cut her off with a snort of derisive laughter. 'Is that what we're calling insubordination these days? Christ, Fiona, look at him. That stupid antique pocket watch, the boots — even his brand new coat somehow manages to look like it was made a century ago.

'I've got no idea what he's meant to be, but I'm pretty fucking sure it's not here.'

He turned his attention back to Balfour with renewed venom. 'Well, here's some modern policing for you, Detective Constable. Since you're so fond of the simple, methodical approach, and since you clearly can't be trusted with high-profile cases, the betting shop robberies are now entirely your responsibility.'

Balfour's eyebrows rose slightly, the first crack in his composed facade. 'Sir, I thought DC Mulholland was handling that investigation.'

'Mulholland was handling it brilliantly, but he's needed for proper detective work on the James case. You can spend your time chasing small-time thieves around — assuming you can manage that without going off-piste and starting your own private investigation.'

The DCI leaned forward, his knuckles pressed white against the table surface. 'Let me be absolutely clear about something, Balfour. This department operates on efficiency, cost-effectiveness, and results. We don't have the luxury of unlimited resources or the time to indulge your romantic notions about "thorough" detective work. Management want cases closed quickly and cleanly, not drawn out into expensive exercises in academic curiosity.'

'Sir,' said Campbell, launching a final attempt at intervention, her voice carefully diplomatic. 'Of course we need to balance thoroughness with efficiency, but sometimes…'

'The only thing we need to balance is keeping this investigation on track,' Munro interrupted. 'And if Balfour demonstrates that he can actually follow orders and close the betting shop case without any more freelancing adventures, then maybe — maybe — we'll consider letting him back into proper detective work.'

'Until then, get the fuck out of my office.'

***

The modernist bulk of HMP Edinburgh squatted against the sky like a monument to poor decisions and bad luck, its glass and stone facade slick with horizontal rain as McGinty guided their unmarked pool car through the outer security gates.

The morning mist clinging to the Pentland Hills on the horizon had been lifting fitfully all day, revealing glimpses of brightening sky before settling again, as if the weather couldn't decide between winter's grip and spring's promise.

'Munro wants this betting shop nonsense wrapped up yesterday,' he said, showing his warrant card to the uniformed guard on duty. 'Says we're spending too much time on small-time shite when we should be concentrating on proper crimes... whatever they are.'

'Hasn't changed in years. He was the same in Govan - all about the quick wins and the headlines. Never changes.'

'You've worked with him before?'

McGinty's jaw tightened slightly, but he said nothing.

Studying the prison's imposing facade through the passenger window, Balfour shrugged as they rolled up. 'So, what's your take on this Sinclair character?'

'Kid's nineteen, got previous for shoplifting and minor fraud. Mulholland reckons the job's done and the Procurator Fiscal is happy so long as she gets her scalp, but he's hardly master criminal material.' McGinty parked in the designated police bay, switching off the engine with a resigned grunt. 'Either way he was caught red-handed with the marked notes, so he's up to his scrawny wee neck in it and there's nobody else to take the fall.'

Inside, the interview room smelled of disinfectant and desperation, its yellow walls scarred by years of difficult conversations. Jamie Sinclair looked even younger than his nineteen years, his skinny frame swimming in the regulation tracksuit as he hunched forward across the metal table, hands clasped tightly and knuckles gleaming white.

'Right then, Jamie,' McGinty began, settling his solid frame into the plastic chair with the careful precision of a man who'd learned not to trust institutional furniture. 'Let's start with the easy stuff. Bilsland's bookies on Easter Road — you were there, you took the money, you got your prints on the till, and now you're completely fucked.'

'Aye, naw, but...,' Sinclair mumbled, his Edinburgh accent thick with nervousness. 'I never really done nothing man. I just... um. Aye, eh, no comment.'

Balfour leaned forward slightly, his voice gentle but persistent. 'We already know that Jamie. Shoving a sawn off shotgun in some poor woman's face isn't really your style now, is it? But we do know that someone a lot bigger than you organised these hits...'

'Aye,' grinned McGinty. 'Six different bookmakers in under four months? That takes planning, knowledge of security systems, inside information about cash holdings — the works. We ken that wasn't you, Jamie, just like we know the guy who did is out there wetting himself laughing while you rot in here.'

'Just give us his name, wee man, and maybe we can help get you out of this mess.'

If he'd been showing signs of softening, the transformation in Sinclair's expression was immediate and unsettling as the defensive sullenness vanished — replaced by a look of genuine terror that made his hands tremor as he pulled them back from the table.

'I cannae tell you that,' he whispered, glancing toward the door as if half the Edinburgh underworld was listening outside. 'You don't understand — these aren't people you cross.'

Despite his reputation for toughness, McGinty's mask slipped slightly, briefly revealing a flash of sympathy as his brow furrowed in the face of the boy's obvious dilemma. 'Son, if someone's threatened you we can arrange protection, but you need to give us something to work with.'

'Protection?' Sinclair scoffed. 'You think prison or anything else is going to keep me safe from them? You think your protection's going to help when my maw's still at home and they've got people fucking everywhere? You're having a laugh pal. No chance.'

Recognising the bone-deep terror in the young man's voice, Balfour shifted to a fresh approach.

'The equipment we found at your flat,' he said carefully. 'Electronic jamming devices, professional lock picks. That's not something you buy at the corner shop Jamie. By the time the court looks at that, considers the planning needed for a job like yours and throws in a conspiracy charge you'll be looking at 20 years to Life. No question.'

'But I never bought nothing,' Sinclair insisted, his voice rising with panic. 'They gave me everything, told me exactly what to do, when to do it. It was just meant to be easy money man. A couple of hours work for more cash than I'd see in months.'

'And when they approached you, where was that?'

The question hit like a smack in the mouth as Sinclair physically recoiled, pressing himself back against his chair as his breathing became shallow and rapid.

'I never said nobody approached me... I just... I just found the stuff, and then I did the McKenzies one and that was it. Aye, that was it, I um... no. I didn't...' he stammered, before thrusting his face in his hands. 'Oh fuck.'

The damage was done. Balfour had seen that same progression countless times — the moment when someone realised that the lie was uncovered and the truth revealed. Everyone in the room knew the reality of Sinclair's situation now. The only question was whether he could muster enough courage to front the lie out.

'Jamie, you're looking at serious time here,' McGinty said, his tone becoming almost fatherly. 'Conspiracy charges, organised crime enhancement, the lot. But if you're being used by bigger fish, that changes things.'

'No, it doesn't,' Sinclair whispered, and for the first time his voice carried absolute certainty. 'Because they don't care if I go down, long as I keep my mouth shut. And if I don't keep my mouth shut...'

He didn't finish the sentence, but he didn't need to.

The drive back to headquarters passed in contemplative quiet, McGinty navigating Edinburgh's afternoon traffic while Balfour stared out at the familiar streets with new eyes.

'The Kid's terrified of someone,' McGinty observed as they slowly edged through the Gorgie traffic towards headquarters. 'There's no way in hell this was his operation — a nineteen-year-old shoplifter who suddenly became a master criminal with access to professional equipment and inside knowledge of six different security systems? Give me strength.'

'No doubt,' Balfour agreed, remembering the genuine terror in Sinclair's eyes at the thought he might have let something slip. 'So we're really looking for someone with enough influence in the housing schemes to make him believe prison's safer than talking.'

'Aye mate, and that narrows the field a good wee bit. We're not looking for your average Edinburgh hard man — we're looking for someone with a bit of reach and some real connections.'

***

The warmth of the pub was a welcome contrast to the raw Edinburgh evening, the wind blowing off the Forth and up through the ancient city's streets apparently unaware that according to the calendar, spring was only a few days away.

A soft, low murmur of conversation hummed through the cosy interior, punctuated by the occasional burst of laughter from the corner tables. Balfour and Murdoch had claimed a small booth near the back, nursing their drinks with the subdued exhaustion that inevitably followed confrontations juggling paperwork, Munro, and a multitude of investigative dead ends.

Murdoch took a sip of her gin and tonic, eyes fixed on the swirling ice cubes as though seeking some hidden revelation. Finally, she broke the silence.

'You know, it wouldn't kill you to play along with the boys a bit. Pretend to appreciate Munro's infinite wisdom, hit a few golf balls badly, laugh at his dreadful jokes now and then. That sort of thing.'

Balfour shook his head, a weary smile briefly appearing before dissolving into seriousness. 'I've tried that before, Rhona. It never works. I've got a fundamental incompatibility with bullshit and guys like that can always tell. Easier never to fall in with them if you're inevitably just going to fall out again.'

Despite herself, Murdoch gave a short laugh, chuckling into her glass. 'Fair point. But you do realise that sticking out like you do makes you an easy target for the likes of Mulholland, right?. They spend their lives hiding amongst the herd and absolutely live for people who won't fall into line.'

'True enough,' Balfour acknowledged, staring into his whisky glass. 'But conformity never suited me. Too many foster homes, too many people telling me how to fit in while shoving me right back out the door. Eventually, you realise the only way to keep true to yourself is to steer clear of everyone and avoid getting too close. Much easier in the long run.'

Murdoch squinted at him quizzically, curiosity lending directness to her tone. 'You know, I've heard bits and pieces about you, but never the whole story and never from you. So spill — How does someone like David Balfour end up at MIT-13?'

Balfour hesitated briefly before smiling, shaking his head as if surrendering to inevitability. 'Alright. You win.' He took a breath, eyes focused on a distant memory. 'My dad was a DCI — good reputation, well-respected. Disappeared when I was six, under circumstances no one ever explained properly. Rumours of corruption, affairs, you name it.

'My mother passed when I was ten — something curable, something that shouldn't have happened. Then came foster homes, orphanages, placements — all temporary — before I left at 16 and never looked back.'

He paused, taking a sip of his whisky. 'Then there was University, a bit of travel, and basic training at Tulliallen. It all seemed to be going alright... and then suddenly I got fast tracked into MIT-13 — the latest in a long line of places I don't quite seem to fit. It's fine though. I've got other interests.'

'And all the money? You must be rolling in it.'

Balfour hesitated briefly, as if caught unawares by the directness of her question, before continuing.

'Yeah, well it turns out that a lot of things in my childhood could have been better, but anyway, the long and the short of it is that someone bothered to invest in mining and railways back when they were a thing, and so now it turns out I have a family trust. Not a big deal really. Just a means to an end.'

Murdoch watched him thoughtfully, absorbing the rapid-fire revelation.'Fair enough. Sorry Balfour. You don't have to talk about it more than that.'

Balfour met her gaze, grateful. 'And you?'

She paused, swirling the ice in her glass. 'Actually, speaking of which - this team is dysfunctional as all hell, isn't it? Campbell - why's she here? The senior team seem to know, but anybody who does just shuts up and refuses to talk. Whatever she's done, nobody will breathe a word about it.'

She took another sip, her analytical mind working through the puzzle. 'But Munro? Nobody seems to know. Nobody. Even McGinty just shrugged when I asked him. Whatever he did to end up here, he's the only one who seems to know it. Constant source of canteen gossip and speculation, but nothing concrete.'

'So we've got nearly everybody with a few years under their belt knowing exactly why Campbell ended up in Department 404, but they won't say a word. Meanwhile, nobody knows why Munro's here even though everyone's dying to find out. Backwards, isn't it?'

She leaned back, swirling her drink again, clearly debating something internally before finally deciding to share. 'And me? Well, I get it, you know? I'm a bit weird about details. I have obsessions, I see patterns, and I know people think I'm pedantic, and nosey, or even rude. But I'm just trying to get everyone to see what's true.'

She paused, eyes fixed on some distant point beyond the pub's interior. 'At my last department, the pressure to deliver quick wins was intense. It destroyed a lot of good officers and me along with them. The DCI there used shortcuts, skipped crucial steps and ignored evidence that didn't fit into the chosen narrative — a bit like Munro, but with charm and charisma.'

'And you spoke up,' Balfour surmised.

Her smile was bright and instant. 'Loudly. I thought I was going to make a difference, but they just laughed, branded me 'difficult,' then transferred me here. The boss got promoted to Superintendent, I got Department 404, the place where careers go to die.'

'Yet here you are,' Balfour noted quietly, 'still pushing back.'

'Here we both are,' Murdoch corrected firmly, raising her glass slightly. 'Still pushing back.'

Balfour, meeting her gaze, lifted his whisky and touched her glass lightly. 'To the details then, Rhona.'

'To the details,' she echoed, her eyes holding his for an instant before they both drank.

Chapter 15

The Manse, Callander, 1860

Solomon Shaw burst through the grey pre-dawn mist clinging to the River Teith in a thunder of sparking carriage wheels and urgent hoofbeats, clattering through the village streets as he careered towards the manse gates.

Balfour, already dressed and standing beside the window with his morning tea, watched as Solomon Shaw's familiar carriage materialised from the swirling haar, his horses lathered with sweat and his usual grimly unflappable demeanour replaced by scowling agitation as he leapt down from the driver's bench.

'That's Shaw arriving in some considerable hurry,' Balfour observed dryly, setting down his cup as Young hurried down the stairs from his chamber, hastily pulling on his waistcoat. 'And at this hour, I rather suspect it's not good news.'

The carriageman barrelled through the front door before the Reverend MacLeod's housekeeper had time to cross the hall, his boots echoing hollowly on the polished tiles of the entrance as he strode directly toward the breakfast room door, where an expectant Balfour waited.

'She's away," Shaw announced without preamble, steam rising from the folds of his enormous greatcoat and his breath forming small clouds in the chill air. 'Christina Miller - vanished from the Crichton cottage sometime during the night. Mrs Crichton found her bed empty when she went to call her for the morning milking.'

Young set down his coffee cup with a sharp clink. 'Gone where, man? And how do we know she hasn't simply stepped out early to run an errand or attend to some chore?'

'Because she's taken everything with her,' Shaw replied grimly from the depths of his attire. 'Mrs Crichton sent word that every stitch of clothing she had to wear and every penny she had to spend is gone. Not that it amounted to much sir, but do you ken many folk that take their worldly goods out for a walk in the morning?'

Amelia Sterling, who seemed to have slipped into the room through the garden doors and now stood by the fireplace - red cheeked and coat still buttoned - interrupted. 'Were there any indications of a struggle? Any signs that she left under duress rather than by her own choice?'

Shaw shook his head emphatically. 'No miss. Nothing disturbed, nothing broken. But Crichton's beside himself with worry, and his wife's convinced something terrible has befallen the poor girl. She was that fond of the lassie - treated her like her own daughter.'

Balfour moved to the window, gazing out across the mist-shrouded gardens at the purple-tinged braes stretching away towards Strathyre.

'The timing is remarkably inconvenient,' he muttered, more to himself than to the assembled company. 'Just as we appear to be closing in on an answer that satisfies all parties, our primary suspect disappears into a Highland wilderness a dozen search parties could comb for weeks without finding so much as a trace.'

Young stood abruptly, his chair scraping against the wooden floor as the full implications of the situation dawned. 'We must organise our pursuit immediately, Balfour. Every constable, every toll house, every inn must be alerted. The girl cannot be allowed to escape justice.'

'Justice aye?' Shaw interrupted, his weathered face hardening rapidly. 'Setting the dogs on a frightened wee pregnant lassie and dragging her back in chains to face the hangman's noose?'

Oblivious to the Reverend MacLeod's background spluttering as he reeled beneath the unfiltered opinion of the working classes, the carriageman's voice gathered a cutting edge as he glowered at his genteel audience. 'You gentlemen won't have spent much time or thought watching how that girl is with the Crichton children, how gentle she is with the animals, or how kind she is to the older folks.

'I have. And anyone with a set of eyes could tell you she's no more capable of bashing in poor Janet Henderson's skull than I am of flying to the moon.'

'Shaw,' Young began, his tone attempting diplomatic authority, 'your sympathy does you credit, but we cannot allow personal feelings to -'

'Personal feelings?' growled Shaw, his eyes flashing dangerously. 'Like the personal feelings of every gentleman in this county who's already decided she's guilty? Aye sir. Very good. She must be a dangerous one right enough.'

As Balfour caught the simmering Shaw in his gaze and delivered a slow, deliberate nod of acknowledgement, Amelia broke the momentary tension with a decisive snap.

'Guilty or not - and I rather think not - the girl must be found and cared for. Christina was one of my pupils before circumstances forced her to seek employment - I know her family circumstances rather well, and I suspect that her instinct would be to hide in a very different sort of wilderness than the one you assume.

She moved to the window beside Balfour, her dark eyes curiously intense. 'Her mother worked in the textile factories before coming to the Trossachs, and Christina mentioned cousins still employed in the Gorbals. A young woman in her condition, with limited resources and every reason to fear discovery - she would seek somewhere she already has connections.'

'Glasgow,' Balfour said quietly, nodding as realisation dawned. 'She's headed for Glasgow, where a pregnant serving girl could lose herself amongst the mill workers and factory hands, where no one asks questions so long as you can work.'

Shaw nodded grimly, his leathery countenance reflecting the same conclusion. 'Aye, that's my thinking. She'd take the train from here to connect with the Scottish Central at Dunblane, then straight through Stirling to Glasgow.

'If she managed to catch the early morning service… she could be in Buchanan Street Station any moment.'

***

The telegram arrived during the quiet hour before luncheon, delivered by a breathless boy from the post office who had clearly run the entire length of Main Street to reach the manse with what he gleefully knew was momentous news.

Balfour read the brief message twice before handing it to Young, who studied the cramped handwriting with growing satisfaction while the assembled dignitaries of Callander waited with barely concealed anticipation.

'CHRISTINA MILLER DETAINED BUCHANAN STREET STATION. PREGNANT FEMALE MATCHING DESCRIPTION. AWAIT YOUR INSTRUCTIONS. INSPECTOR LAUDER, GLASGOW CONSTABULARY.'

'Excellent news,' proclaimed the Reverend MacLeod, his clerical countenance brightening considerably as he reached for the crystal decanter at his elbow. 'The Lord's justice moves in mysterious ways, but it moves nonetheless.'

Arbuthnot nodded gravely, accepting a generous measure of the Minister's finest brandy with the ceremonial gravitas of a man marking a significant victory. 'Indeed, Reverend. The community's peace of mind will be greatly restored by this development.'

'More than that,' Dr Geddes added, 'Henderson's health will improve immeasurably once this sordid business is concluded. The strain of uncertainty has been most damaging to his constitution.'

Balfour accepted his glass but did not drink, studying instead the amber liquid catching the afternoon light streaming through the tall windows overlooking the River Teith as Spring began to assert its arrival. Although he could not immediately identify the source of his discomfort, he was struggling to share in the eager satisfaction of these pillars of local society.

'We must arrange for her immediate return to Callander,' Arbuthnot declared, raising his glass. 'A proper identification, formal charges, and swift proceedings before the Sheriff. Justice must be seen to be done, and done expeditiously.'

'Quite right,' MacLeod agreed, his voice resonating as he unconsciously adopted his habitual stance in the pulpit. 'The longer such matters drag on, the more they corrupt the fabric of decent society. Better to excise the poison quickly and allow the community to heal.'

Dr Geddes leaned back in his chair with professional satisfaction, swirling his brandy as he contemplated the resolution of what had been a most trying episode. 'I know you had your doubts Balfour, but I confess myself unsurprised by this development. The girl's flight was itself an admission of guilt - innocent persons do not flee in the night like common criminals.'

'It would certainly seem so,' Young concurred thoughtfully with a glance at his friend. 'Much as I have learned to place great faith in your instincts, Balfour old chap, her behaviour does follow the classic pattern of criminal guilt -

initial defiance, followed by panic and attempted escape when the evidence mounts against her.'

The warm parlour filled with a contented murmur as another glass was poured while outside, the brisk midday sunshine casting long shadows as the congratulations continued.

In the end, it was Arbuthnot who proposed the theatrical gesture that would mark Christina Miller's return to face justice.

'We should arrange a special train,' he announced, his legal mind gleefully calculating the symbolic impact of such a proceeding. 'A formal escort to bring her back to Callander under proper authority, demonstrating that justice in this county operates according to the highest standards of civilised procedure.'

MacLeod's eyes brightened at the prospect. 'An excellent suggestion. The community deserves to witness the proper conclusion to this unfortunate affair. Nothing furtive or secretive - everything conducted in the full light of public scrutiny.'

'Indeed,' Dr Geddes added with growing enthusiasm. 'A demonstration that law and order prevail in our district, that those who transgress against their betters cannot simply disappear into the anonymous masses of the cities.'

As the conversation continued around him, Balfour found his attention drifting to the distant peak of Ben Ledi, an array of unanswered questions bombarding his thoughts. The convenient placement of evidence, the timing of Miller's flight, the apparent simplicity of a case that had initially seemed impossibly complex...

None of it made any sense.

And Shaw's assessment, delivered in the yard earlier that morning with characteristic bluntness, was still ricocheting around in his memory: 'They've already hanged the lass in their minds, sir. There's not one of them that would hesitate to personally put the rope around her neck.'

His thoughts were interrupted by the sound of approaching footsteps in the hall, and moments later Amelia Sterling appeared at the door, her usually composed features marked by undisguised concern.

'Gentlemen,' she said, slowly taking in the flushed cheeks and empty glasses, 'I understand Christina has been found.'

'Indeed, Miss Sterling,' MacLeod replied with satisfaction, gesturing with clumsy gallantry toward an empty chair. 'The wheels of justice turn, and the guilty cannot escape their fate indefinitely.'

Amelia's dark eyes flicked across the faces of the assembled men, noting their obvious satisfaction before settling on Balfour with an expression that conveyed both urgency, frustration, and something deeper.

'Indeed they cannot, Reverend MacLeod. Indeed they cannot.'

***

The tolbooth's strongroom, which doubled as an impromptu gaol when occasion demanded, felt deathly chill despite the brazier crackling in the corner.

Her dark eyes darting between the faces surrounding her like a cornered animal, Christina Miller sat on the rough wooden bench with her back pressed against the wall. The special train from Glasgow had deposited her at Callander Station barely an hour ago, bewildered and frightened after the long journey under guard, and her wrists still bore the red weals left by the chafing manacles the railway superintendent had demanded she wore for the uncomfortable ride.

'Miss Miller,' Balfour began, settling onto the single chair while Young remained standing near the barred window, 'we need to understand why you left Callander so suddenly.'

'I never killed nobody,' she said flatly, her jaw set in stubborn defiance despite the tremor in her voice. 'And I'm not saying nothing else till you tell me what's to happen to my bairn when you hang me.'

Young cleared his throat diplomatically. 'No one has spoken of hanging, Miss Miller. We simply need to understand how you managed to travel to Glasgow. Such a journey requires resources.'

'I had money.'

From his position just outside the open door, Solomon Shaw shifted his weight, the leather of his coat creaking in the damp air. 'Aye, well, that's the question isn't it? Where'd a lassie like you get the coin for rail tickets and lodgings?'

Christina's eyes flashed with their old fire. 'Maybe I'm better with money than you think, old man.'

Shaw's weathered face remained impassive, but his tone carried the authority of someone who knew the price of everything. 'A ticket to Glasgow costs near a month's wages for folk like us, lassie. And you've been sending money home to your family since you started working.'

'You don't know nothing about my affairs.'

Amelia Sterling, who'd insisted on chaperoning the young prisoner since she'd stepped off the train and into the jeering crowd awaiting her arrival, stepped forward from the shadows near the brazier, her voice quiet but precise. 'You were one of my most promising pupils, Christina, and you have a keen mind for figures, so you must know exactly how unlikely this sounds. I want to help you, but the mathematics simply don't support your claim.'

The young woman's defiance wavered as she realised the logical trap closing around her. Her hands moved protectively to her belly, and for the first time, tears threatened at the corners of her eyes.

'I never asked for help," she whispered. '

Balfour leaned forward slightly. 'But someone offered it?'

'I can't say." The words came out strangled, desperate. 'You don't understand... I...'

She stopped abruptly, pressing her lips together as if physically holding back the words that wanted to spill out.

Balfour watched her carefully, noting how her gaze kept flicking toward the door as if expecting someone to appear. 'Someone gave you money to leave Callander. Someone who knew you'd be suspected of Miss Henderson's murder.'

It wasn't a question, and Christina didn't treat it as one. Her silence stretched until Shaw, unable to contain himself, growled under his breath.

'Christ almighty, they've played you like a fiddle, haven't they? Given you just enough rope to hang yourself with.'

'I don't know what you mean,' she said, but her voice had lost its fight.

Amelia's analytical mind was already working through the implications. 'Someone with means. Someone who knew the timing would look suspicious. Someone who wanted you gone before...' She paused, studying Christina's face. 'Before anyone could question your guilt or the accepted version of events.'

The tolbooth fell silent except for the hiss and crackle of the brazier. Christina Miller sat hunched on her bench, no longer the defiant hellcat of local legend but a frightened girl who had finally grasped the iron trap closing around her.

Balfour exchanged a glance with Young, seeing his own growing certainty reflected in the Procurator Fiscal's troubled expression. Shaw's gargoyle features had hardened into grim resignation, while Amelia Sterling stood perfectly still, her pale face a clear indication of the inevitable conclusion they all now faced.

'Christina,' Balfour said quietly, 'in two days' time, you'll appear before the Sheriff. The evidence against you - the stolen items in your room, your flight from Callander, your inability to account for your travel funds - it will be more than sufficient for a conviction.'

She looked up at him with eyes that had aged years in the space of minutes. 'And then?'

Young cleared his throat, his legal training demanding honesty even when kindness would be easier. 'The penalty for murder is death, Miss Miller. The Sheriff will have no discretion in the matter.'

'Unless,' Shaw said gruffly, stepping into the room, 'you tell us the truth.'

Christina's hands trembled as she pressed them against her belly. 'You don't understand. They told me... they said if I kept quiet, they'd make sure the bairn was cared for. But if I talked...'

She didn't finish the sentence, but the implication hung heavy in the damp air.

Amelia stepped closer, her voice gentle but urgent. 'Christina, whoever promised you that protection has already abandoned you. You're here, facing the gallows, while they remain safe in their home. What loyalty do you owe to someone who would let you hang to protect themselves?'

'Easy for you to say, Miss Sterling,' Christina replied with a flash of her old spirit. 'You're not carrying a child that'll need feeding whether its mother's alive or dead.'

The brutal honesty of it silenced them all. Outside, the sound of voices could be heard - townspeople gathering to catch a glimpse of the murderess, their excitement barely contained as word spread that justice would finally be served.

Young moved to the barred window, his face grave as he observed the growing crowd. 'The community has already decided your fate, Miss Miller. Unless you can give us evidence pointing elsewhere, I fear no amount of legal argument will save you from the verdict they expect.'

Shaw spat into the fire, the spittle hissing angrily on the hot coals.

Christina looked from face to face, seeing sympathy but no hope, understanding finally that her silence was a luxury she could no longer afford. The question was whether she had the courage to break it before courage became irrelevant.

'I need time to think,' she whispered.

'Time is the one thing we don't have,' Balfour replied quietly. 'By tomorrow morning, formal charges will be filed. After that...'

He didn't need to finish.

Chapter 16

Heriot Row, Edinburgh, 2025

As if determined not to give way to Spring too soon, the rain had been falling steadily for hours, turning Edinburgh's elegant Georgian streets into a maze of slick pavements and reflected streetlights that shimmered like watercolours on wet stone.

Pulling his coat tighter as he approached number 18 Heriot Row, the very last destination in his fruitless door-to-door search, Balfour noted the immaculate brass nameplate that read 'Marchmont' in understated engraving above a bell push that looked as though, if pressed, it would alert the inhabitants with a discreet cough rather than an uncouth jingle.

The woman who answered the door was a study in Edinburgh propriety - silver hair swept into an elegant chignon, pearls at her throat, and a cashmere twin-set that had probably cost more than most people's monthly wages. Everything about Mrs Marchmont, from her perfectly applied lipstick to her polished brogues, suggested someone for whom maintaining appearances was no mere preference but a sacred feudal duty.

'Detective Constable Balfour, Police Scotland,' he smiled through the wet, producing his warrant card. 'I'm conducting enquiries regarding the incident at number 22. I wonder if I might have a few minutes of your time?'

Mrs Marchmont's expression flickered between distaste at the subject matter and the ingrained courtesy of her upbringing. Her fingers, adorned with understated but expensive rings, gripping the door frame as she weighed up competing obligations.

'Such a dreadful business,' she murmured, her cultured Edinburgh accent carrying notes of genuine distress. 'Poor Rowena. Though I must say, Constable, this is hardly the sort of matter one discusses on the doorstep.'

The pause stretched as breeding warred with discretion, until finally, inevitably, good manners prevailed.

'Perhaps you'd better come in.'

The drawing room that Mrs Marchmont led him into was a masterpiece of Georgian elegance - tall windows framed by silk curtains, oil paintings in gilded frames, and furniture that had clearly been chosen by ancestors with impeccable taste and unlimited budgets. A fire crackled in the marble fireplace, casting warm light across Persian rugs that had probably graced these floors since the house was built.

'I should arrange tea,' she announced mistily, as if discussing murder without proper refreshment might pose a serious breach of civilised conduct. 'Do sit down, Constable. That chair belonged to my great-grandfather - he knew Sir Walter Scott, you know.'

Balfour settled carefully onto the antique chair, acutely aware that he was probably the first police officer ever to occupy it, while around him, the accumulated weight of Edinburgh's social hierarchy pressed down like a physical presence, wrapping up several generations' worth of privilege in a symphony of gilt, silver and polished walnut.

Mrs Marchmont returned with a tea service that belonged in a museum - bone china painted with delicate roses, silver teaspoons that caught the firelight and shortbread biscuits fanned out neatly across an outrageously elegant plate. Her movements as she poured were graceful and automatic, the product of a lifetime's practice in the rituals of class.

'Now then,' she said, settling into her own chair with careful dignity, 'I must confess myself rather conflicted about this entire matter. One does not wish to gossip, particularly about such tragic circumstances, but I suppose civic duty must take precedence over personal distaste.'

She paused, studying the steam rising from her teacup as if seeking guidance in its curling patterns.

'I'm terribly sorry I wasn't available when your colleagues called previously,' she said, settling back into her chair. 'I was visiting my sister in Perth that evening. Such a dreadful shock about poor Rowena - one simply cannot imagine.'

She shook her head sadly, sipping her tea with practised delicacy.

'I do wish I could be of more assistance, but I'm afraid I noticed nothing out of the ordinary that morning. Just the usual comings and goings, you understand. In fact, I actually saw Mr James and his brother-in-law getting into a taxi together that very day - I presume on their way home to discover that terrible scene.'

Balfour looked up from his notebook. 'Where exactly did you see them getting into this taxi, Mrs Marchmont?'

'Oh, it was near Charlotte Square. I was on my way to meet Lady Maybury at Jenners - Tuesday is our usual day, you see. They were just getting into the same vehicle as my taxi passed.'

***

'Your alibi is bullshit, Mr James.'

'You can keep hiding behind the fancy lawyer and expensive suit if you like, but we both know you're lying through your teeth.'

Watching through the one-way glass as Munro loomed over Gavin James like a predator circling wounded prey, Balfour's gaze flitted between the occupants of the interview room as the DCI lurched triumphantly towards his breakthrough moment. While Campbell maintained her poised, professional exterior in the face of the bombast and his KC exuded the settled calm of a man whose exorbitant fees would be paid no matter the outcome, the quailing suspect had looked on the edge of tears for the entire interview.

'I don't know what you mean,' he whispered, his voice barely audible through the intercom system, as his brief shifted uncomfortably in his chair, raising an eyebrow at the dangerous territory they were now entering.

'Course you don't.' Munro slammed a CCTV still on the table between them with enough force to make everyone in the room flinch. 'Mrs Marchmont from number 18. Pillar of Edinburgh society, member of the Ladies' Golf Club, observant old cow. Does she ring a bell, Gavin?'

A sausage-like finger stabbed down on the black and white shot, showing a busy street view in the centre of town, timestamped 09:47 on the morning of the murder.

'Because she saw you and your brother-in-law getting into the same taxi that morning. Not at the airport like you claimed, but already in town and only a few minutes from the murder scene.' Munro's voice dropped to a menacing whisper. 'Do you want to 'fess up now, Gavin - while there's still time to make a difference to your sentence? Or would you rather wait until you're completely fucked?'

Through the glass, Balfour watched as the last vestiges of James's composure crumbled. The man's shoulders sagged, his hands trembling as he pressed them against his face, and when he looked up, his eyes were bright with tears.

'It's not what you think,' he said, his voice breaking. 'George and I... we just needed to... I mean... we just... we arranged to meet.'

Douglas Anderson leaned forward urgently. 'Mr James, I must advise you not to…'

'No.' James cut him off with surprising firmness. 'They'll find out anyway.'

He looked directly at Munro, something almost like relief flickering across his features. 'We weren't in London. We made that up because we were both... doing things Rowena wouldn't have liked. Seeing people we shouldn't have been seeing.'

The room fell silent except for the hum of the recording equipment. Balfour leaned forward, studying James's face through the glass, noting the way his grief seemed to intensify rather than diminish as he spoke.

'I've been involved with someone. Rowena found out but I promised I'd stopped. And George...' James's voice caught. 'He has his own interests, but Rowena swore she would shut off the money if he brought shame on the family again...'

Munro's eyes lit up with predatory satisfaction. 'So you coordinated your return journey to hide your adultery from your wife. Made sure you had each other as alibis for the imaginary trip to London while you were both screwing around behind her back.'

'It wasn't really like that,' James protested.

'It was exactly fucking like that!' Munro thundered.

'Do you hear him Campbell? Another chinless rich boy who thinks he can have his cake and eat it too. Aye, well not on my watch. Not when Kirk fucking Munro is on the job.'

'So how did it go down? Did she find out, threaten to kick you out into the street? Or was it really just about the money?'

Through the intercom, Balfour could hear James's breathing becoming shallow and rapid.

'She never knew,' he croaked. 'Rowena never knew about any of it. That's why we arranged to meet and come back together. To maintain the pretence. To protect her.'

Munro leaned back in his chair, satisfaction radiating from every pore. 'Protect her? By murdering her before she could sign the documents that would have made you personally liable for millions in debt?'

'I loved my wife!' The words exploded from James with such force that even Munro seemed momentarily taken aback. 'Whatever my faults, whatever mistakes I've made, I would never have hurt Rowena. Never.'

But Munro, satisfied, was already rising, gathering up his papers with brisk efficiency. 'Right then. We're just awaiting phone records for both of you and a completed financial analysis to wrap this up. You, Gavin, are royally fucked - we've got motive, means, and a coordinated attempt to pervert the course of justice.'

He paused at the door, turning back with a savage grin. 'Your KC can explain to you how conspiracy charges work. But I reckon you'll be lucky to see daylight again this side of your seventies Mr James. Sleep well.'

As the interview room emptied, Balfour remained in the observation room, staring at the monitor where James sat slumped in his chair – oblivious to his KC's entreaties – his body shaking with genuine, wrenching sobs that echoed through the empty space.

Something was wrong.

Despite the lies, despite the deception, despite the convenient timing of Rowena's death - something about James's grief felt authentic in a way that didn't fit with premeditated murder. Clearly the man was weak, an admitted liar and almost certainly an adulterer. But a killer?

Somehow it didn't seem to fit.

***

Quite deliberately, Balfour's study could have been furnished at virtually any point since the builder, John Paton, had handed over the keys to its very first owner back in 1808 - a fresh faced young stranger with an upstart fortune built on textiles and steam.

Apart from the debris of modern investigation scattered across the leather-topped desk - forensic photographs competing for space with a glowing laptop screen revealing row after row of detailed records - in the low lamp light the room managed to look exactly as it had done for more than 200 years, apparently unconcerned with the passage of time.

Despite the breakthrough that had led to James's afternoon revelation about his extramarital activities, Munro had dismissed his contribution with characteristic bluntness. Pointing out that James's mobile phone records would ultimately have unearthed the truth anyway - a fact that had somehow enabled Mulholland to claim credit for the development - the DCI had delivered his verdict with customary venom.

'At the end of the day, you've brought me information that you disobeyed my direct orders – twice – to go get,' he'd said on his way out of the office. 'I don't know why you think that would change my assessment of your capabilities or your future job prospects.'

Recalling Campbell's calm advice to remain patient, keep himself busy prepping the betting shop robberies for trial and try and stay out of Munro's way – solid counsel emphasised in more industrial tones by the down to earth McGinty – Balfour knew that the smartest thing to do now would be to keep his head down. To play the political game and toe the line until the boss found someone or something else to use as his personal punching bag.

The advice was sound, sensible, and entirely impossible for him to follow.

James's tears during the interview had seemed genuine enough, the shame and grief raw and unfiltered as he'd admitted to an affair that would have destroyed whatever remained of his marriage. It was all there: the timing, the evidence and the motive all combined to spin a narrative that satisfied everyone's need for resolution, and yet somehow, it didn't feel like enough.

He leaned back in the wingback chair he'd bought from Trotter of Ballindean and studied the room's familiar details.

He didn't have much to remind him of his family, but what there was of it was spread around this room. Retrieved from the chest of assorted pictures, documents and curios that his father's old Superintendent had brought to Balfour's last children's home shortly before his 18th birthday, they lined the mantelpiece like a parade of distant memories.

Faces from generations past gazed down as he mused with knowing smiles, the similarity of features across time striking as the same dark eyes and angular cheekbones looked out from sepia prints and faded colour snapshots alike.

How many times had investigations followed this same pattern? Convenient suspects, condemned by evidence that aligned too neatly with preconceived notions of guilt. The powerful protecting their interests while the vulnerable bore the weight. It happened in every era, in every jurisdiction, in every possible context, with depressing regularity.

Sometimes the convenient suspect was guilty, of course. Often, even. But when they weren't, how many innocents had paid the price for other people's crimes? How many had faced judgment with truth on their side but power arrayed against them?

His gaze drifted to a formal portrait of a man in police uniform as, almost without conscious thought, his hand moved to the pocket watch that he always carried, its familiar weight both a comfort and a reminder of happy times. The antique timepiece felt warm against his palm, its elaborate engraving catching the lamplight as he drew it forth, the battered case worn almost smooth by years of handling.

The mechanism's gentle tick seemed louder in the evening quiet, each second marked with mechanical precision while somewhere in the building's depths, the old heating pipes gurgled and sighed like sleeping giants. He found himself winding the watch with slow, deliberate turns, counting under his breath as he watched the hands rotate towards their appointed positions.

If there was a way to prevent an innocent person from facing judgment based on misaligned evidence, if there was a pattern to be understood, a truth to be exposed, then surely that was worth pursuing regardless of the personal cost?

His dogged determination now threatened to hang one victim. Perhaps it could remove the noose from the neck of another.

As the watch hands revolved the room's atmosphere began to shift subtly, shadows deepening, while outside the sounds of Edinburgh's evening traffic grew muffled - and the world began to turn.

Chapter 17

Callander Railway Halt, Callander, 1860

The early morning train from Edinburgh carved through the mist-shrouded Carse of Stirling like some firebreathing creature of legend. The relentless rhythm of its wheels matching the urgent pulse that pounded at Balfour's temples as he pressed his face against the cold window glass and watched the familiar mist wreathed slopes of the Trossachs rising from the grey dawn ahead.

As ever there was little comfort in the homecoming - only the crushing weight of time slipping away like water through cupped hands, each passing mile bringing Christina Miller closer to the formal charges that loomed on the near horizon. Just one misstep away from seeing her dragged away in chains to await trial at the Perth Circuit Court for a crime he felt in his bones was not hers.

One circuit judge, fifteen jurors and a welter of evidence already stacked against her. In a world where the right to a legal defence depended largely on the size of your purse, there was not a lot standing between one lonely girl and the hangman's noose.

His carriage hitched and steaming in the chill air, Solomon Shaw was waiting at the halt in Callander Station as Balfour stepped off the train, his weathered features wreathed in sullen introspection. Ignoring the usual formalities and gesturing urgently towards the conveyance, he launched into a breathless update before his passenger's boots had left the ground.

'The postmaster tells me the Sheriff arrives tomorrow morning to make his decision on formal charges,' Shaw announced without preamble as he climbed into the driver's seat and gathered up the reins. 'A telegram came down from Perth that the arrangements have already been made, and his lordship intends to take the lassie back with him to Perth jail to await the next circuit court.'

Swinging himself up onto the driver's bench with hasty agility, Balfour paused as he considered the scale of the challenge ahead. A single day was all he had to find something that could stop the inevitable in its tracks, yet the Highland landscape stretched before them like a vast puzzle where any one of a thousand remote corners could - and had - sheltered secrets for generations.

'Sixteen miles to Strathyre and back, and that's just the main road,' he muttered, his chest tightening as the implications crashed over him like a Highland avalanche. 'Add in every cottage, every bothy, every farm scattered across the braes, and we've only got a single day to find what everyone else has missed.'

Shaw's weathered hands worked the reins as he cast a sideways glance at his passenger as he mused. 'Did you manage to sort out whatever business was keeping you in Edinburgh, sir? You were hardly gone before you were back again.'

'I found what I was looking for, not that I think it helped,' Balfour replied tersely, his jaw tightening as he considered the legal machinery already grinding into motion. 'Once she's in Perth awaiting the Lord Advocate's indictment, new evidence will become worthless. The system works on the assumption that local investigation was thorough, that the Sheriff wouldn't have signed charges without sufficient proof…'

'And nobody there will know her from Eve,' Shaw added darkly. 'They'll just see a slut of a servant girl accused of murdering her betters.'

'Exactly.' Balfour's voice carried a bitter edge. 'The legal machinery grinds forward, not back.'

The silence stretched between them as the carriage rolled through the awakening village, past windows where candlelight flickered behind drawn curtains and chimneys began to release the first tentative wisps of morning smoke. Balfour's mind raced through the possibilities ahead - hundreds of isolated dwellings, thousands of potential witnesses, all scattered across terrain that could swallow secrets whole and keep them hidden for decades.

'Someone must have seen something,' he said finally, his voice carrying a note of desperate certainty. 'Christina Miller didn't simply vanish from existence during the hours when Janet Henderson was murdered. She was somewhere, doing something, with someone who could vouch for her presence. We just have to find them.'

With a grunt, Shaw's grizzled visage creased into something that might have been optimism as he locked Balfour in a steady gaze.

'Well sir, that doesn't leave much choice to pick from then, does it? If there's truth to be found we've got to find it, and we will - even if we have to kick down every door between here and Strathyre to shake it loose.'

***

The sun had barely cleared Ben Ledi's gnarled peak when Shaw's carriage began its desperate circuit, striking out from Callander along the military road that ran North through a string of scattered settlements and lonely farmsteads stretching upwards into the towering glen.

Their first stop was Corriechrombie, a small farmstead perched on a windswept brae across the River Teith from Mount Stewart, where an elderly woman emerged from one of the collection of cottages wiping flour-dusted hands on her apron as the carriage clattered into her yard.

'Christina Miller?' she repeated, her weathered face creasing with concentration as Balfour explained their urgent mission. 'Aye, I ken the lassie well enough, but I've not seen hide nor hair of her since autumn. Been too busy with my own troubles to go visiting, what with my husband laid up with the lung fever and the spring planting to see to.'

One down, dozens to go, and the day already slipping away like sand through an hourglass.

The second farm yielded nothing but blank stares and shaking heads. The third produced a young farmhand who claimed his mother had seen Christina Miller dancing naked with the fairies on Midsummer Night last year, an observation that Shaw dismissed with a string of oaths that would have made a sailor blush. The fourth dwelling stood empty, its residents away to sell their Highland cattle at the Lowland markets.

By midmorning, as they wound their way through the increasingly remote settlements scattered across the braes like distant stars, Balfour could feel mounting anxiety clawing at his chest with icy fingers. Every minute that passed brought Christina Miller closer to her appointment with the Sheriff's formal examination, and still they had nothing more to offer her than their sympathy.

'There's the Campbell place,' Shaw announced, pointing his whip toward a substantial cottage nestled on a rocky outcrop, smoke rising from its chimney in a lazy spiral. 'Big family, lots of comings and goings. If anyone would know about the lassie's movements, it'd be them.'

But the Campbells too shook their heads with genuine regret. They'd heard the terrible news about poor Janet Henderson, and the shocking accusations against Christina Miller, but could tell them nothing.

The sun was climbing toward its zenith when they finally struck out along the rough track that led to one of the journey's most isolated dwellings. Here, in the shadow of the towering crags that guarded the entrance to the deep Trossachs, lived the last of the folk who still clung to the old ways, measuring their wealth in cattle and their neighbours in miles.

'That's the Morrison place,' Shaw said with a hint of finality as he gestured toward a low-built cottage that seemed to huddle against the hillside for protection from the winds. 'Old Morag Morrison is the local howdie - brings most of the bairns into the world for miles around. If anybody kens anything, she's our best hope.'

They found the old midwife bent over her herb garden, her grey hair escaping from beneath a practical woollen cap as she tended the neat rows. A woman of more than sixty years - it was difficult to tell - she carried herself with the quiet authority of someone who had seen more of life's mysteries than most, a front row spectator at the arrival of nearly every soul in a thirty mile radius.

'Christina Miller?' she repeated, straightening slowly as Balfour explained their desperate search. 'Aye, I ken lassie. What do you men want of her now?'

Something in her tone made Balfour lean forward intently. 'Mrs Morrison, Christina needs our help. Have you seen her recently?'

'Recently?' The old woman's brow furrowed. 'Depends what you mean by recent, I suppose. She's been helping me with a difficult case this past week or so.'

Shaw and Balfour exchanged quick glances. .'We need to speak with you about a most serious matter,' Balfour said carefully. 'Janet Henderson of Mount Stewart Farm has been murdered, and Miss Miller stands accused of the crime.'

The effect was both immediate and dramatic as Morag Morrison's hands flew to her mouth, her face draining of colour as she staggered backward against the cottage wall.

'Murdered? Poor Janet? When? How?'

'Last Tuesday evening,' Shaw responded grimly. 'Killed in her own kitchen with a hatchet while her brother was away in Perth..'

The old woman's eyes widened in horror. 'And they think Christina did this terrible thing?'

'The Sheriff arrives tomorrow to examine the charges,' Balfour said urgently. 'The evidence against her appears overwhelming.'

'But Tuesday?' The old woman's voice took on a sharp pitch of disbelief. 'Last Tuesday evening? That's impossible!'

Balfour felt his pulse quicken. 'What do you mean, impossible?'

'Because Christina Miller was here with me from dawn Tuesday until well into Wednesday morning,' Morag declared with absolute certainty. 'She never left my sight for more than a few minutes at a time.'

For a long moment, the only sounds were the sighing of wind through the heather and the distant cry of a golden eagle circling the crags above. Then Morag Morrison seemed to reach a decision, and nodded firmly at them both.

'I sent for her at dawn that day - the woman's condition had taken a turn for the worse during the night, and I needed another pair of hands. Someone with sense and experience of these matters.'

Shaw leaned forward eagerly. 'And the lassie came?'

'Directly. Arrived before the morning was properly begun and stayed through the day and all that night. The labour was long and difficult - near on twenty hours from start to finish, and touch and go for both mother and child.'

'Christina was at my side the entire time. We worked together through the day, through the evening, and well into the next morning when the bairn finally came.'

Both men grasped the implications immediately. If Christina Miller had been attending a difficult birth from dawn on the day of the murder through the entire night and into the following morning, she couldn't possibly have been at - or anywhere near - Mount Stewart Farm when Janet Henderson was killed.

'If she was with you all that time,' Balfour said, his voice tight with urgency, 'why didn't Christina tell us? Why didn't she offer this as her defence?'

Morag Morrison's expression hardened with protective resolve. 'Because the woman came here in secret to birth her child away from prying eyes and wagging tongues. Christina gave her word to keep the matter private, and she's not one to break such promises lightly.'

'You'll testify to this before the Sheriff and the Procurator Fiscal?' Balfour asked.

'Aye, I will. I'll swear to Christina's presence here and name two other women who saw her here too, but you can tell those gentlemen plain - I'll not be revealing the mother's name unless the law compels it.

'Now, water your horses and give me a moment to gather what I need. We've a lassie's life to save.'

***

'All's well that ends well,' Young declared with considerable satisfaction as he settled into the Reverend MacLeod's best armchair, accepting a generous measure of whisky with the relieved air of a man who had narrowly avoided presiding over a miscarriage of justice.

'The Sheriff has departed for Perth, the charges against Miss Miller have been formally dismissed, and we can all sleep soundly knowing that justice has prevailed.'

The manse parlour glowed warmly in the fitful spring evening as the assembled polite company congratulated themselves on their collective wisdom, barely pausing to acknowledge the role their previous certainty had played in nearly condemning an innocent woman to the gallows. There, clearing his throat, the Reverend MacLeod focused the room's attention on the more pressing matter - apportioning blame where it now clearly belonged.

'Of course, the real villain of this piece has been obvious from the beginning,' he pronounced with the thunderous authority that made his Sunday sermons so effective. 'John Crichton - a man whose violent temperament and ungodly resentments have been the talk of the parish for months. We should have listened more carefully to Henderson's warnings about his character.'

Arbuthnot, consulting his pocket watch with the fastidious precision that characterised all his movements, allowed himself a thin smile of legal satisfaction. 'You're quite right Minister, the witness testimony from the Sheep's Head inn is particularly damning - Mrs MacPherson's account of seeing him pass that bundle to the girl the day she ran to Glasgow can surely leave little room for doubt about his involvement in the original crime.'

Dr Geddes nodded gravely, swirling his whisky as he contemplated the satisfying resolution of what had been a most trying professional challenge. 'Indeed, the evidence against Crichton is overwhelming now - providing Miller with the stolen keys and money for her escape, his known grievances against the Henderson family, his violent disposition when drink is upon him. Everything points in his direction.'

Balfour, standing by the tall windows where the evening light cast long shadows across the polished floor, once again found himself wrestling with an array of evidence that seemed almost too convenient in its completeness. Although, having personally interviewed the innkeeper who'd witnessed the ploughman handing over the clinking bundle shortly before

Miller's poorly considered flight himself that afternoon, he had little doubt over what the man claimed to have seen.

'Gentlemen,' he said quietly, his voice cutting through the satisfied murmur of conversation with the sharp edge of professional scepticism, 'I confess myself troubled by how neatly all the evidence aligns against Crichton. The stolen keys, Miller's "escape" money, the witnessed handover and his established motive - it's all remarkably comprehensive and logical for a crime supposedly committed in the heat of passion.'

Amelia Sterling, who had been examining the minister's impressive collection of theological volumes with apparent scholarly interest, turned from the bookshelf with her dark eyes reflecting the firelight, her voice carrying just a hint of devilment.

'It is remarkably convenient that, within hours of our suspect's acquittal, all of the evidence seems to point so swiftly and clearly in Henderson's direction,' she observed sardonically, her gaze moving from face to face with uncomfortable directness. 'Must we always look downwards, or is it not possible that guilt could equally reside in more elevated quarters?'

The effect of her words was immediate, MacLeod's countenance darkening as he responded. 'Miss Sterling, surely you understand that the lower orders are naturally inclined toward such base impulses. Violence, theft, deception - these are the inevitable products of ungodly living and moral dissolution. It is precisely why Divine Providence has ordained the natural hierarchy of society.'

Nodding gravely, Dr Geddes voiced his support. 'Indeed, my dear young lady. In my professional experience, the labouring classes possess neither the moral restraint nor the spiritual guidance necessary to resist their baser instincts when provoked. Crichton's behaviour follows a pattern as predictable as any medical condition.'

Amelia's response came with the cool authority of someone whose aristocratic education had included rather more worldly instruction than the assembled gentlemen might have expected.

'With respect, Reverend MacLeod, my own family have gambled and whored their way across the centuries with a creativity and thoroughness that would astonish your ploughmen. You might not move in such circles very often, but in my experience, vice and criminality are hardly the exclusive province of the humble.'

The seismic effect was immediate. Dr Geddes nearly choked on his whisky, Arbuthnot's spectacles slipped down his nose in shock, and even the redoubtable Young raised an eyebrow at such unprecedented directness from a lady of supposedly gentle breeding.

'Miss Sterling!' MacLeod sputtered, his moral foundations visibly shaken. 'Surely you cannot be suggesting that persons of breeding and education are capable of the same... the same base criminality as the working classes?'

'I'm suggesting, Reverend MacLeod, that human nature operates quite independently of social rank,' she replied with dangerous calm, a ribbon of cultured steel running through her voice. 'Indeed, in my experience, it is those with the most to lose that often prove the most desperate in their methods of preservation.'

Chapter 18

MIT-13 Office, Edinburgh, 2025

'They're all the same, these posh pricks,' Munro declared as he glowered at the incident board—arms tightly crossed and marker pen in hand—reviewing the deranged web of red string, photographs, post-it notes and financial printouts with malevolent satisfaction.

'Dirty bastards, every last one of them.'

The morning briefing had an edge of desperation about it, case files scattered across every available surface while McGinty nursed a steaming mug of tea with the weary concentration of a man who'd clearly been up half the night. Doing what, nobody knew.

Campbell sat perched on the edge of her desk watching Munro's manic board work with barely concealed concern, while Murdoch and Mulholland hovered near the percolating coffee machine like vultures circling roadkill.

Balfour, staring into the middle distance, looked a million miles away.

'Right then,' Munro announced, stepping back from his handiwork with obvious relish. 'James has finally shown his true colours. The lying bastard admits he was never in London, admits to shagging around behind his wife's back, admits to coordinating a fake alibi with his brother-in-law.'

He jabbed the marker at James's photograph. 'Motive, means, and - now we know the alibi was complete bollocks - opportunity. The only question left is how the sneaky little shit pulled it off.'

Mulholland, stirring the coffee he'd elbowed Murdoch aside for, chipped in. 'I'll keep on at the nerds but the security footage still shows no one entering or leaving during our window boss.'

'Exactly!' Munro's eyes gleamed with manic energy. 'Which means that what we're dealing with here, son, is a classic locked room mystery. James might think he's Sherlock bloody Holmes, but every locked room has a solution - it's just a question of finding the misdirection.'

As he warmed to his theme, he began pacing up and down the room, threading between scattered archive boxes. 'See, this is what separates the proper detectives from the amateurs. When faced with the impossible, we don't throw up our hands and start theorising about mysterious strangers. We ask ourselves - what's the trick? How did he make us think he wasn't there when he absolutely fucking was?'

Campbell frowned. 'So you think he found a way to bypass the cameras?'

'Has to be. Camera angles, blind spots, timing - there's always a way if you're clever enough and desperate enough.' Munro snapped back. 'The question is - which method did he use?'

'Could be any number of things, boss.' said Mulholland, slopping coffee onto the already stained municipal carpet as he shrugged, clueless.

'Which is why we need to explore every possibility,' Munro declared, consulting his notes. 'We've already confirmed the basement connection was sealed decades ago, so it's not alternative entry routes. Has to be camera positioning, timing tricks, some technical misdirection we haven't spotted yet. Has to be.'

He turned to Balfour with barely concealed malice. 'Right. You can start by going back to Dr Cliff. I want that time of death window questioned properly. Could he have got it wrong? Was there anything about the central heating, the body position or room temperature that might have thrown off his calculations?'

The suggestion drew sharp looks from around the room. Even by MIT-13 standards, questioning Cliff's professional competence was the stuff that epic and spectacular career suicides were made of.

'Sir,' Campbell began diplomatically, 'suggesting the chief pathologist made a fundamental error...'

'Is exactly what we need to do if James killed her outside our assumed window,' Munro cut her off. 'Maybe he's not fucking about with cameras - maybe he's playing games with the timing. Maybe he did it earlier or later than we think, giving himself the perfect alibi while we chase our tails looking at the wrong bloody hours.'

With a resigned smile, Balfour held Munro's eye, nodding cheerfully, as the DCI faltered briefly before continuing.

'It's his breakthrough, so Mulholland's taking point on the interview with James' mistress,' he said. 'Balfour, you can tag along as his assistant so we don't have to waste anyone useful on helping with the note-taking, fetching coffee and all that sort of thing. Should be very educational for you.'

'Since you've still got that betting shop case going nowhere fast anyway,' Munro added, determined the humiliation should be deliberate and complete, 'you should have plenty of time for the support work.'

Mulholland, ecstatic, glowed with satisfaction. 'Happy to show Balfour how proper interview technique works, boss.'

'The rest of us,' Munro continued, 'will be working the angles. Camera positioning, building schematics, security system vulnerabilities - all the technical aspects that require actual grown up detective work.'

As the team began to disperse, Munro's voice followed Balfour toward the door. 'Remember, these aren't complex assignments. Question Cliff about his timing, let Mulholland handle the woman, write up your notes.

'Even you should be able to manage that without overthinking it.'

***

The Cowgate mortuary's corridors smelled of disinfectant and… something else. Maybe it was just the underlying scent left by the many generations who'd walked their lengths, or perhaps it was a figment of the imagination triggered by the unavoidable presence of death, but either way Balfour's footsteps echoed hollowly on the polished lino as he made his way towards Dr Cliff's office, each step feeling like a small betrayal of professional courtesy.

Entering after his tentative knock was met with a sharp greeting of 'Enter,' he found the pathologist hunched over a microscope in his cramped office, surrounded by the accumulated detritus of thirty years spent extracting truth from the dead. Medical journals competed for space with coffee-stained case files, while certificates and commendations hung slightly askew on walls that had seen better decades.

'DC Balfour,' Cliff said without looking up from his microscope. 'Let me guess - our esteemed DCI has sent you to ask whether I might have made an error in my findings regarding Rowena James.'

Balfour paused in the doorway, caught off guard by the pathologist's directness. 'Sir, I...'

'Oh, don't look so uncomfortable.' Cliff finally raised his head, his eyes crinkling with sardonic amusement. 'I've been expecting this visit for two days. Munro's desperate to find something - anything - that will close the case, but he quite simply hasn't got the bollocks to come down here and question my professional competence himself.'

Enjoying the impact of his uncustomary profanity, the older man leaned back in his chair, studying Balfour with the level of decidedly clinical interest he usually reserved for autopsy subjects. 'Interesting though, that he sent you rather than Mulholland or one of his other boot-lickers. I'm afraid that it says something rather telling, Mr Balfour, about how he views your expendability.'

'With respect, Dr Cliff...'

'No offence taken, lad. It's actually rather refreshing to meet someone from MIT-13 who has the decency to look embarrassed about their orders.'

Cliff gestured to the chair opposite his desk, chuckling. 'Let me tell you something about your beloved DCI. You don't judge a man like Munro on what you see - you judge him on what you don't.'

Balfour shot a look across the desk, his notebook balanced on his knee. 'What do you mean?'

'When did you last see Munro conduct a difficult interview personally? When did you last see him leave the office for anything more challenging than a quick glance at the crime scene?' Cliff's voice carried the weight of long observation. 'The man's career is built on delegation and bluster, but he's terrified of any situation where his authority might be challenged by his equals or superiors - of which he has many.'

The pathologist stood and moved to the window overlooking the Cowgate, his reflection ghostlike in the glass. 'He'll bully subordinates all day long, throw his weight around with junior officers who can't fight back. But send him to question a KC or a consultant pathologist? Not a chance.'

Ignoring the almost intoxicating temptation to join in with some eviscerating observations of his own, Balfour paused, steadied his thoughts, and pushed himself into following the disciplined professional path. 'I wouldn't necessarily disagree, Dr Cliff, but despite the source of the question, it always pays to look at every possibility - however remote.'

Cliff sent back a smile of genuine appreciation. 'There's the logic I was hoping for. Well played Mr Balfour. Ok then - let's examine the evidence properly.'

He moved to a filing cabinet and withdrew the James case folder, shuffling the autopsy photographs and crime scene notes across his desk with practised efficiency. 'Time of death estimation depends on multiple factors - body temperature, rigor mortis, livor mortis, stomach contents, environmental conditions.'

'The central heating in that house was set to 22 degrees,' Balfour noted, consulting his notes.

'Exactly the problem. Stable high temperature interferes with natural cooling patterns. Add to that her position at the desk - blood pooling was affected by the chair's support - and the calculation could potentially become less precise than I'd prefer.'

Cliff traced his finger across a temperature chart, his expression thoughtfully professional. 'My original estimate of eleven PM to three AM was conservative, based on the most reliable indicators. But if Munro wants a broader window...'

He paused, making quick calculations. 'Ten PM to four AM would be defensible, though I wouldn't stake my reputation on the extremes. Does that help his case?'

'Not particularly. Even with the extended window, he'd need to have been in that building during the critical period. The lack of CCTV footage remains unchanged.'

Cliff began returning the materials to their folder, then paused thoughtfully. 'You know, I lived in an identical Georgian townhouse for years - same period, same builder, same layout. But the acoustics in the James place struck me as odd when we were working the scene.'

Balfour looked up from his notes. 'Odd how?'

'Different sound patterns than you'd expect. My old place had predictable acoustics - voices echoed through it in a very particular way. But in number 22, it seemed to be... I don't know. Something different.'

Cliff sealed the folder and returned it to the cabinet with a slight shrug. 'Probably just my imagination. Though I suppose none of that helps your boss's misdirection theory anyway.'

'Probably not,' Balfour agreed, standing to leave. 'Thank you for your time, Dr Cliff. And for your patience about... the circumstances.'

'Think nothing of it. Just remember what I said about Munro and be careful - a man who sends others to fight his battles usually has a good reason for staying out of range himself.'

***

The flat on Morningside Road was respectable, expensive, and discreet - exactly what one would expect from someone who valued both privacy and professional presentation - occupying the ground floor of a converted Victorian villa with an understated facade that gave not the slightest hint of the exclusive services provided within.

Catherine Stewart answered the door with the assured composure of someone accustomed to sizing up visitors quickly. An attractive woman in her early thirties with rich chestnut hair pulled back in a sleek French twist, she wore a figure-hugging black dress that showcased her curves with a sense of class and elegant precision.

'Police Scotland,' Mulholland swallowed, his brandished warrant card drooping in the face of the woman's confident physical presence. 'We need to, um, discuss your relationship with Gavin James.'

Leaning against the doorframe as she examined their credentials, everything about her presentation - from the confident tilt of her head to the way she commanded the space around her - spoke of someone who had turned a potent blend of sensuality, poise and business acumen into a very comfortable living.

Catherine's expression remained carefully neutral, though her lips curved in the faintest suggestion of amusement as she made them wait just a little longer than most, slowly twisting the proffered card back and forth between two perfectly manicured fingers. 'I was expecting this call. You'd better come in then.'

The sitting room was tastefully furnished with antique pieces and original artwork, the morning light streaming through tall windows to illuminate what was clearly a carefully curated environment.

'Right then,' Mulholland began without invitation, taking a seat before it was offered. 'Gavin James has already told us about your little arrangement, so let's not piss about. We need to verify his whereabouts on Tuesday night when his wife was murdered.'

Catherine's composure remained unruffled as she settled into the chair opposite, crossing a pair of elegant legs. 'What specifically do you need to know?'

'Timeline. When did he arrive, when did he leave, was he actually here when he claims?' Mulholland's pen was already poised over his notepad. 'Because right now, your boyfriend's looking at a murder charge.'

'He was here from Monday afternoon through Tuesday morning,' Catherine replied without hesitation. 'He left around nine on Tuesday morning, saying he had to meet his brother-in-law somewhere in the centre of town.'

Mulholland looked up with obvious scepticism. 'So - the entire time he was supposed to be in London. That's very convenient. The grieving widower who just happens to have a ready-made alibi from his bit on the side.'

'It may be convenient, constable, but it also happens to be the truth.'

'Course it is, hen. And if that was coming from anyone other than a whore, I'd maybe even believe you too,' he sneered with casual disdain. 'What's your game then? He's obviously paying you for sex. How much do you charge for an alibi too?'

The insult landed, and Balfour watched Catherine's expression harden. 'I don't need to be paid to tell the truth, Detective Constable.'

'Don't you? Because from where I'm sitting, you're just another tart providing convenient testimony for a guilty man.' Mulholland, showily consulting his watch. 'Happens every bloody week.'

He snapped his notebook shut abruptly and stood. 'Look, I've got what I need here. You're lucky I can't be arsed doing the paperwork for a perjury charge, and if I were you I'd start looking for somebody else to pay the fee for getting into those knickers - lover boy isn't going to be around much longer.'

'You're making a mistake,' Catherine said evenly.

'The only mistake would be believing a word you've said.' Mulholland paused at the door, shooting a dismissive glance back. 'Balfour, just get the formal statement wrapped up. This slapper's word is worth about as much as a three pound note.'

As the door slammed behind Mulholland's departing figure, Catherine briefly paused before switching her gaze back to Balfour.

'Your colleague's made up his mind,' she observed dryly.

'He has his theories,' Balfour replied diplomatically, remaining in his chair. 'But I'd like to hear your account properly - if you don't mind ma'am.'

Catherine studied him carefully, cautiously, before nodding. 'You're different from him.'

'Different how?'

'Well you're better looking for a start,' she smiled easily. 'But more importantly you seem to have manners - and you're actually listening.'

She gestured toward an unnoticed security camera camouflaged discreetly in the corner. 'The nature of my business can sometimes be... uncertain, so for safety reasons I installed a system that records everything in every room. High definition, audio, timestamp - the works. I can prove exactly when Gavin arrived, exactly when he left, and exactly what happened in between.'

Balfour carefully adjusted his expression to ensure it displayed only professional interest. 'And, um, what did happen ma'am?'

'He came here because his world was falling apart. The business was failing, his marriage was under strain, and his brother-in-law was breathing down his neck about the family money.' Catherine's voice carried genuine sympathy. 'He wasn't plotting murder - he was having a breakdown. We ordered takeaway, watched Netflix, and he cried like a child about how he'd ruined everything.'

'That hardly sounds like the behaviour of someone planning a premeditated murder.'

'Gavin James couldn't plan a trip to the corner shop, let alone coordinate a killing,' Catherine said with absolute certainty. 'He's weak, Detective Constable. Weak and scared and completely overwhelmed by the sort of people he married into. But absolutely incapable of carrying out a violent crime.'

Balfour, jotting down notes, looked up with an encouraging glance.

'If you want to find a killer in that family,' Catherine continued, her voice dropping to a warning tone, 'I'd start looking at George Cockburn. I've heard stories about him through my professional network, and trust me - he's the dangerous one.'

'In what way?'

'Let's just say his tastes run to the extreme, his temper runs to the violent, and I wouldn't leave my worst enemy alone in a room with him,' she said, her eyes flashing with genuine concern.

'James might be weak, unfaithful and a liar with money, but Cockburn? He's something else entirely.'

Chapter 19

Heriot Row, Edinburgh, 1860

The grandeur of Heriot Row had taken on an ominous quality in the grey afternoon light as Balfour approached number 17, the Cockburn family townhouse rising like a monument to generations of accumulated prosperity.

At sixty-two, Cornelius Cockburn possessed the assured bearing of old aristocracy, his pale eyes pinning down his prey with the unblinking certainty of someone whose right to authority had never been questioned, receiving Balfour in a drawing room dripping with the accumulated treasures of three generations, the patriarch of the Cockburn dynasty smiled thinly as he pressed on with the interview.

'I must confess that it seems quite improbable that it has taken so long for us to finally meet sir, our families having been near neighbours for so long, but we have all become rather accustomed to seeing number 46 shuttered,' he said with silken courtesy that somehow managed to sound like a threat.

'I understand that you are often abroad on business?' His smile was perfectly calibrated - warm enough to satisfy social convention, cold enough to establish hierarchy. 'I confess myself intrigued by the reports of your activities in Callander. Such dramatic events for such a peaceful district.'

Before Balfour could respond, a servant appeared at his elbow with a steaming cup, having materialised so silently that he found himself glancing towards the door through which he presumed the man had entered. But the doorway remained empty, no movement visible in the corridor beyond, and the servant's footsteps had been inaudible on the thick Persian carpets.

'Excellent service you maintain, Mr Cockburn,' Balfour observed, accepting the delicate china with interest.

'Indeed,' Cockburn replied with evident satisfaction. 'The house was designed to allow the staff to attend to their duties without disturbing the family's comfort. One doesn't wish to see servants constantly traipsing through the main rooms, after all.'

As if summoned by their conversation, another figure appeared bearing a tray of elaborate pastries, setting them carefully on the side table before retreating with the same ghostly silence.

'My family has always understood that civilised living requires proper arrangements,' his host continued, the temperature in his voice dropping several degrees despite his unchanged smile. 'My grandfather commissioned architects who understood such refinements when he acquired this property from a rather unfortunate textile merchant who'd overextended himself.'

Cockburn grinned with reptilian satisfaction. 'I've recently made a similar investment in Callander. It's a charming spot - quite the fashionable retreat for Edinburgh society these days.'

'A sound investment, no doubt,' Balfour replied carefully. 'The district seems to attract a great many discerning visitors.'

'Precisely. One must diversify one's holdings, and property in the Trossachs represents both pleasure and profit, though I confess the recent murders have rather dampened the romantic appeal of the region.'

'Your grandfather sounds like a man who understood the requirements of his position,' Balfour deflected diplomatically.

Outside, Edinburgh's weather remained changeable and unpredictable. Sudden squalls of rain followed by brief, teasing intervals of watery sunshine that promised better things before clouds gathered again.

'Oh, he understood a great deal more than that,' Cockburn replied with silken satisfaction. 'Built the family fortune from absolutely nothing, you know. Started with just one ship trading to the Caribbean, ended up with a fleet of twelve vessels and interests across three continents.'

His smile took on a predatory quality as he gestured towards a display case containing various maritime instruments and exotic curiosities. 'That collection represents his more... educational ventures. The goods that established our position, the tools that maintained proper order. Grandfather always said that success required understanding how to manage difficult situations with appropriate firmness.'

Balfour's attention was caught by one particular exhibit - a set of iron shackles connected by heavy chains and an iron ball, their metal surfaces worn smooth by handling yet somehow retaining a brutal gleaming quality that suggested recent cleaning and maintenance.

'Grandfather's ball and chain set,' Cockburn replied with casual indifference, though his pale eyes watched Balfour's reaction with interest. 'Tools of the trade, you might say. One must maintain certain standards, after all.'

'Grandfather used to say that understanding human nature was the key to business success. He said that people are remarkably predictable once you grasp their fundamental natures - the weak require guidance, the rebellious require correction, and the profitable require... management.'

The implications slithered through Balfour's mind with savage clarity as he studied the pitted metal restraints sitting so incongruously in their velvet-lined case. Slave ships, human cargo and systematic brutality - and all of it proudly exhibited in one of Edinburgh's finest drawing rooms, celebrated without shame or concealment.

'The trade must have been quite... demanding,' he managed, his voice carefully impartial.

'Enormously profitable, once one understood the proper methods,' Cockburn replied, his smile becoming positively serpentine. 'Grandfather possessed quite remarkable insights into handling... resistance.'

His pale eyes fixed on Balfour with calculating interest. 'I imagine your investigative work has taught you similar lessons? The necessity of firmness when dealing with the lower orders? The importance of maintaining pragmatic distance despite temporary disruptions or social fads?'

As another servant materialised without warning to clear their empty cups, Cockburn smiled without warmth as he swept a dismissive hand in the parlour maid's direction.

'Grandfather always maintained that proper architecture should make unpleasant necessities disappear entirely. Rather like good government, one might say - the less one sees of the actual mechanisms, the more comfortable everyone remains.'

His unflinching gaze glittered with cold amusement as he added, 'Of course, the same could be said of delicate discussions, business conversations, the majority of family matters and the occasional need to address... disciplinary issues without disruption.'

***

The clatter of iron-shod wheels sparking across the cobblestones echoed through Heriot Row's genteel tranquillity like gunfire, shattering the late afternoon calm as Solomon Shaw's carriage careered around the corner from Dundas Street, sending respectable pedestrians scattering in all directions for the safety of doorways and railings.

Balfour, emerging wrapped in thought from the Cockburn townhouse, looked up to see his faithful carriageman hauling on the reins with desperate urgency, the horses' flanks steaming with sweat and their breath forming white clouds in the brightening Edinburgh air.

'Mr Balfour!' Shaw bellowed before the wheels had stopped turning, flushed with exertion beneath the battered derby that seemed to permanently frame his gnarled features. 'Thank Christ I found you, sir. Been to your house three times, hammered on every door in the street, and nobody could tell me where you'd gone.'

Leaping down from the driver's bench with agility, Shaw strode across the cobblestones with his greatcoat billowing behind him like a battle standard, his expression thunderous enough to make passing gentlemen cross to the opposite pavement rather than risk colliding with what appeared to be a localised whirlwind of spitting rage.

'Shaw, what in God's name...' Balfour began, but the carriageman cut him off with a dismissive wave that would have scandalised any observer familiar with proper social hierarchy.

'It's gone to hell, sir. Complete bloody disaster while you've been away doing whatever it is you get up tae,' Shaw fulminated. 'Your man Young sent me to fetch you urgent like after the telegraph boy couldn't raise anybody at your house. Said to tell you they've arrested Crichton and are ready to indict him.'

Balfour, arriving back to the moment with an unceremonious jolt, looked momentarily bemused as the coachman grabbed his attention with all the subtlety of a Highland avalanche.

'Arrested? On what charges?'

'Drunk and disorderly to start with, then assault on a constable, then murder when they dragged him before the magistrate this morning,' Shaw spat, his hands clenching into fists as he recounted the rapid sequence of events.

'The stupid bastard got himself into a fight in the public bar of The Crown last night - three sheets to the wind and mouthing off about Henderson being a lying toff who deserved what was coming to him.'

His features twisting beyond even their usual disorderly state as he continued his account, Shaw's voice dropped to a more confidential level as he squinted suspiciously at passers by. 'Course, half the bloody parish was there to hear him make threats, and when PC Buchan tried to calm him down, Crichton took a swing and laid the poor lad out cold.

'It was a cracking punch Sir. Near took his head off.'

'And the murder charge?'

'That came courtesy of your three fine friends - Dr Geddes, Arbuthnot, and the Reverend MacLeod. Soon as they heard about the fight, they were onto the magistrate like vultures,' Shaw's eyes blazed. 'Had him charged, processed, and ready for transfer to Perth jail before anybody even knew what was happening.'

'But surely Young tried to stop it?'

'He didn't get a chance to,' Shaw replied grimly. 'He'd travelled through to Aberfoyle that day to attend some business, and by the time he got back they were stuffed full of duty and community safety and clear dangers to public order, and Crichton was trussed up like a bird for the oven.

Shaw spat contemptuously into the gutter, his expression thunderous even by his own remarkable standards.

'It's an open and shut case, according to Mr Arbuthnot. They've got witnesses to the threats, witnesses to the assault, and a man neatly wrapped up in chains waiting for transport to Perth. He says the community can sleep safely knowing that proper order's been restored.'

Squinting as the sun angled down from just above the distant castle walls, Shaw indicated the carriage seat with a determination that didn't seem to make Balfour's place in it optional.

'Begging your pardon sir, but Mr Young says he needs you back there tonight if there's any chance of you asking any more of your inconvenient questions.'

The urgency of it crashed over Balfour like ice water as he grasped the full implications of what Shaw was describing.

'How quickly can we reach Callander?'

'There's a train leaves Waverley Station for Stirling shortly - gets us into Callander by eight o'clock if we're lucky with the connections,' Shaw replied, checking his battered pocket watch. 'My cousin Jimmy can sort his horses and rig while we catch the evening service.'

Trotting sharply along the length of Princes Street, Shaw scattering errand boys before them with a fucilade of rich and earthy oaths, Balfour looked at his travelling companion as they rounded the entrance to Waverley Station.

'And what do you think Solomon?' he asked , 'Tell me honestly - do you think Crichton could have killed Janet Henderson?'

The carriageman was silent for a moment, his brow creased with thought, before finally shaking his head with slow certainty.

'Could he have done it? Aye, the man's got a wild temper and no love for his betters. Did he do it the way it was done? That's a different question entirely, sir. I couldn't be sure one way or the other, but if there's one thing I've always liked about him, is that rather than sneak about with in the dark, Crichton's the type to punch you in the face and then tell you why you deserved it.'

***

The evening train had deposited them at the Callander halt just as the last light faded behind Ben Ledi, the familiar silhouette of the Highland peak's long slopes standing against an empty sky filled only by the early full moon.

Delivered by one of the sullen army of small boys that seemed perpetually available to run errands for him, Shaw's carriage clattered out from the yard and through the village streets with urgent purpose, past windows where oil lamps were beginning to flicker to life and chimneys were releasing the first tentative wisps of evening smoke.

His usually robust countenance clearly troubled by the haste in which they'd found themselves drawn to this point, Young met them at the tolbooth door.

'Thank God you're here, Balfour,' he said without preamble, gripping his friend's shoulder with obvious relief. 'They've got him locked up tight as a drum, formal charges filed, and transport arranged for dawn. I've managed to delay the transfer for proper questioning, but only just.'

'What's his condition?'

'Belligerent, although he's sobered up enough to understand the gravity of his situation,' Young replied grimly. 'Still claims he never touched Janet Henderson, but his denials aren't exactly convincing given the circumstances.'

In the tolbooth's strongroom John Crichton sat on the rough wooden bench with his massive frame hunched forward, his wrists bound by iron manacles and his face and clothing clearly bearing the evidence of the previous night's altercation.

He looked up as Balfour entered, his dark eyes blazing with the same defiant fury that had marked their previous encounter, though beneath the surface anger there was something new - presumably the growing recognition that his situation was hurtling beyond mere inconvenience and into genuine mortal peril.

'So, come to see your handiwork have you?' Crichton growled, his voice hoarse from a night of shouting and a day of interrogation. 'Come to say your piece?'

'I've come to hear what happened at the Crown last night,' Balfour replied evenly, settling onto the single chair while Young remained standing near the barred window. 'The charges against you are serious, Mr Crichton. Murder, assault on a constable - even the least serious of them could see you transported or hanged.'

'Aye, well, that's what you want, isn't it?' Crichton spat, his massive hands clenched despite the shackles. 'Tie up all the loose ends neat and tidy.'

'You did threaten Henderson publicly. Multiple witnesses heard you.'

'I said he'd get what was coming to him eventually, aye,' Crichton replied without hesitation, his voice carrying the dangerous edge that had made him notorious throughout the district. 'And I meant it. The man's no saint, whatever airs he puts on for the kirk.'

'Strong words from someone whose livelihood depends on his favour.'

'Some things matter more than wages,' Crichton growled, though his eyes shifted away briefly. 'I'll not watch idly while others do whatever they please.'

Balfour leaned forward slightly, studying the ploughman's face in the uncertain light.

For a moment, Crichton seemed on the verge of saying more, his jaw working silently as he weighed his words. But then his expression closed off again, the defensive walls slamming back into place.

'I'm saying that some men think they can do as they please and never face consequences and with good reason too. That's all.' His voice grew carefully evasive.

'What about Christina Miller? The community still believes you were... involved with her.'

The change in Crichton's demeanour was immediate and telling. His shoulders tensed, colour rising in his cheeks as anger and something that might have been shame warred across his features.

'I told you before - the community believes a lot of things,' he said finally, his voice thick with emotion. 'Still doesn't make them true.'

Crichton's hands trembled slightly as he spoke. Whether from guilt, anger, or simple exhaustion was impossible to determine, but the man was clearly struggling.

'Did you kill Janet Henderson, Mr Crichton?'

'No.' The word came out flat and final, although Crichton's eyes didn't quite meet Balfour's as he said it. 'I never laid a hand on Miss Janet. She was decent folk.'

'Yet the indictment will say you had access to the keys, knowledge of the household routines, and we know you harboured resentment against the family.'

'I've heard Janet herself say that half the country has reason to hate Henderson,' Crichton shot back, some of his fire returning. 'And what about that vagabond Fox? A known villain seen skulking about the area. Why aren't they asking questions about him?'

It was a fair point.

It was also one that had been troubling Balfour since Fox's mysterious disappearance. The tramp's presence in the area, his suspicious behaviour and his convenient vanishing act all suggested the potential for involvement, even if it did feel more coincidental than sinister.

'Fox is being sought,' Balfour replied carefully. 'But he lacks your intimate knowledge of the household, your personal grievances, or your demonstrated capacity for violence.'

'So because I'm not afraid to use my fists, I'm a murderer?' Crichton's voice rose dangerously. 'Because I speak my mind, I must be guilty of butchering an innocent woman?'

The passionate denial carried conviction, but Balfour had learned not to trust emotion alone when evaluating guilt or innocence. Men could lie with remarkable sincerity when their lives hung in the balance, and Crichton's relationship with Christina Miller clearly involved secrets he was at pains to protect.

Balfour shook his head. 'Your threats against the family, your connection to Miller, your access to the home - the evidence forms a clear pattern, Mr Crichton.'

'Evidence?' Crichton barked out a bitter laugh. 'What you call evidence, I call a convenient story. I could tell another, but all that matters now is who's telling it.'

As Balfour prepared to leave, studying the massive figure hunched on his bench like a caged bear, he found himself genuinely uncertain about the man's culpability.

Crichton had motive, means, and opportunity, along with a violent temperament that made him a credible suspect. He could easily have done it, and he certainly wouldn't be the first or last workman to harbour dire thoughts about his employer, but the lack of any concrete

Outside, as they walked back through Callander's quiet streets toward the manse, Young voiced the question that had been troubling them both.

'What do you think, Balfour? Guilty or innocent?'

'Capable of the crime? Certainly. The circumstantial evidence against him is substantial and compelling.' Balfour paused, glancing back toward the tolbooth. 'But something feels incomplete. Whether that's because crucial evidence is missing, or because I'm allowing sentiment to cloud professional judgement, I simply cannot say.'

Chapter 20

Elm Row, Edinburgh, 2025

The rain had finally stopped, leaving Edinburgh's streets gleaming under the streetlights as Balfour and Murdoch made their way up Leith Walk towards Jeremiah's Taproom, the broad street's curious blend of homebound commuters and outbound revellers swishing by in a series of shimmering amber reflections.

Murdoch had been thinking about the craft beer and burger Balfour had proposed after another thankless day, but as they approached a neon-lit bookmakers' shopfront, he suddenly slowed his pace.

'Actually, quick detour,' he said, nodding towards the betting shop's grimy windows. 'Won't take long.'

Murdoch stopped walking, her red hair catching the light from the flickering 'OPEN' sign as she ran an eye over the scruffy exterior and the sign above the door saying Menzies - Turf Accountants.

'What kind of detour?'

'Just want to have a quick word with the owner.'

She studied his face suspiciously, noting the careful neutrality in his voice. 'About what exactly?'

Balfour held up his hands defensively. 'I'm following up on the betting shop robberies, exactly like Munro ordered...

'But while we're here... I do keep thinking about that white transit van you spotted on the CCTV footage...'

'Right...' Murdoch's analytical mind was already working, connecting dots.

'So just out of interest, do you think I'm stupid or are you completely mental?' She scowled at him, her voice dropping to an urgent whisper.

'And what happens when Munro finds out you're STILL investigating behind his back?'

'I'm not!' Balfour grinned. The fact this is the only independent bookie in the area that hasn't been robbed needs following up...' He gestured towards the expensive security cameras mounted around the shopfront. 'And you have to follow the evidence, even when it leads somewhere inconvenient.'

He shrugged with studied innocence. 'You're here strictly as back up, but you could find out about the van you spotted on the Heriot Row CCTV sweep and check on Douglas Kemp's alibi while we're here. Kill two birds with one stone.'

Murdoch stared at him, recognition and resignation on her face. 'Fucking hell, Balfour. You actually think there could be a connection?'

'Well, we won't know there isn't until we ask'

Even by the low expectations set by its exterior, the interior of Menzies Bookmakers was a significant letdown. Reeking of stale cigarettes and desperation, fruit machines lined its yellowed walls, their electronic jingles masking the conversations between punters hunched like beggars over racing forms, faces lit by the blue glow of television screens showing an array of odds.

Behind reinforced glass sat Jojo Menzies - thin, sharp-eyed, with the calculating gaze of someone who measured every interaction in terms of profit and loss. While not quite casting the physical presence you'd expect of a man rumoured to have a personal hand in a decent chunk of Edinburgh's crime statistics, he had the look of a predator who could smell vulnerability a city mile away, and reeked of danger.

'Police Scotland,' Balfour announced, producing his warrant card. 'DC Balfour, DC Murdoch. We need to verify someone's whereabouts.'

Menzies barely glanced at their credentials, already dismissing the threat level they represented. 'Are you aye? Who?'

'Douglas Kemp. Tuesday evening, around nine-thirty to eleven.'

'Douglas? Aye, he was here. Came in around half-nine, stayed till after eleven. Regular as clockwork, that one.' Menzies's voice carried the bored tone of someone reciting routine information. 'Good customer, and he pays his debts... eventually.'

'We also need to ask about a white transit van registered to this address,' Murdoch added, making notes. 'Can you tell us why it was on Heriot Row the same evening?'

'Business vehicle,' Menzies shrugged nonchalantly. 'It gets used for various things, but I usually let one of the lads borrow it in the evenings if they need it, so it'll probably just have been someone dodging traffic and taking a short cut through to the west end.

'Why?'

Ignoring the question, Balfour studied the shop's layout, noting the expensive security cameras and reinforced fixtures that seemed incongruous with its tired exterior.

'Speaking of business Mr Menzies - I see you've managed to avoid the recent wave of robberies. There have been six shops hit in the area over the past four months, but not yours.'

'Aye, well I've got good security. Word gets around about which places are more trouble than they're worth.'

'Must be expensive though, security like this?' Murdoch observed, nodding towards the array of cameras and reinforced glass.

'You get what you pay for in this business.' Menzies's smile was thin. 'Cheaper than getting robbed.'

Balfour's attention was caught by what appeared to be a high-end tactical flashlight sitting casually on the shelf behind the counter, its black aluminium body gleaming under the fluorescent lights.

'That's interesting,' he said, pointing to the device. 'Premium bit of kit. Mind if I have a look?'

Menzies eyes widened for a second, but he shrugged and reached for the device without concern. 'Some punter left a torch in the toilets last week. I was planning on handing it in to Lost & Found sooner or later, but you know how it is.'

Turning the device in his hands, Balfour shot Menzies a sharp look as he examined it.

'Interesting torch...' He grinned, indicating its crenellated bezel with its twin metal contacts. 'Contact points for electrical discharge and a two-stage trigger system? Hardly standard issue.'

'I hope this doesn't shock you too deeply, Mr Menzies.' Balfour's voice took on an unmistakable edge, 'but this isn't a torch - it's a taser. Probably a modified Czech or Russian model and definitely very, very illegal.

'Like I said, someone left it behind.' Menzies's voice remained steady as he smiled back, though his eyes had sharpened with interest. 'Second one this month.'

'Well, we'll save you the trouble of handing it in,' Balfour said with heavy sarcasm, pocketing the device. 'Unless you want to claim possession? That might get complicated though - it's a Section 5 firearms offence.'

The effect was visible but controlled. Menzies's expression hardened, his relaxed mask slipping slightly to reveal something colder underneath.

'Look, I run a legitimate business here,' he said with a warning edge. 'No drugs, no violence, no trouble. Whatever that thing is, it's not mine.'

'Course it's not,' Balfour replied mildly. 'It's amazing how often this sort of thing gets left lying around, isn't it?'

***

The briefing was not going quite how Mulholland had expected.

After he'd told a delighted Munro that Gavin James' second alibi was unreliable - the word of a whore - he'd been anticipating praise, perhaps even a pat on the back for cracking the case wide open.

Instead, Balfour had calmly produced the security footage from Catherine Stewart's Morningside flat, and now the room felt like a deflating balloon.

'So let me get this straight,' Munro said, his voice dangerously quiet as he stared at the tablet screen. 'James enters the flat Monday afternoon, stays put through the entire murder window, and you're telling me this footage is genuine?'

'High-definition, timestamped, covers every room,' Campbell confirmed. 'Tech analysis confirms it hasn't been tampered with. James was physically incapable of being at Heriot Row when his wife was killed.'

Munro stared at the tablet, his jaw working silently. 'Could be faked. Deep fake technology, AI editing software... CSI shit.'

'Sir, the metadata checks out,' Campbell said diplomatically. 'And the content... James was genuinely distraught. You can't fake that level of breakdown for eighteen hours straight.'

'Maybe he's a better actor than we thought,' Munro muttered, but even he didn't sound convinced.

Murdoch cleared her throat. 'Actually sir, I've been looking deeper into the financial side. James's losses are real enough, but there's more complexity to the family finances than we initially thought.'

She consulted her tablet. 'He's by no means short of money, but George Cockburn's investments have also been struggling. He's been associated with multiple failed ventures and he's made some large cash settlements through his lawyers to three different women, so he's been burning through money almost as fast as James.'

'So they're both fuck-ups,' McGinty observed. 'That doesn't change James's motive.'

'But it does give Cockburn one too,' Balfour said quietly. 'Especially when you consider who actually controls the family trust.'

Munro's resistance was immediate. 'Hold on. One piece of footage doesn't clear James completely. It could be manipulation or it could be timing - we just haven't figured it out yet.'

'Sir, with respect, the evidence is pretty conclusive,' Campbell said.

'Evidence can be misleading,' Munro shot back. 'James still had the strongest motive. His wife was about to sign papers that would have bankrupted him.'

'But Cockburn had motive too,' Balfour said carefully. 'When Rowena died, overall control of the trust passed directly to him, not to her husband.'

'And he might have had opportunity,' Murdoch added, consulting her notes. According to airport records, he took the last flight home the evening before, which was delayed. The airline put him up in a hotel, and he checked in at 1:30am, but that still gives him an unaccounted window.'

Campbell leaned in. 'How big a window?'

'Several hours. Certainly enough time to visit Heriot Row and return before checking out to meet James in town.'

McGinty's stony expression glinted. 'Cockburn... aye, well I've heard stories that would fit with that.'

'What kind of stories?' Murdoch asked, pen poised.

'The kind you don't write down if you don't have proof,' McGinty said grimly. 'But the word is he's got tastes that run to the violent side.'

Mulholland squirmed in his chair. This wasn't how the investigation was supposed to work. You followed procedure, arrested the obvious suspect, closed the case, got the credit and walked off into the sunset with a girl on your arm.

'But this is all speculation,' he said desperately. 'James had motive, means, opportunity...'

'James has debt problems,' Balfour corrected. 'Cockburn has control issues. When Rowena threatened to cut off the family money, who had more to lose?'

Campbell consulted her notes. 'According to what he told us in his interview, when Rowena died control passed directly to George. Not to her husband.'

Munro stared at the evidence board, his knuckles white where they gripped the edge of the conference table. The case he'd been so confident about was disintegrating before his eyes.

'So what do you want us to do, sir?' Campbell asked diplomatically. 'Ignore the evidence because it's inconvenient?'

Munro stared at the evidence, his internal struggle visible. Career preservation warred with mounting evidence, political pressure battled against the facts laid out before him.

'This is still largely circumstantial,' he said finally, but the fight had gone out of his voice. 'But... I suppose we can't ignore the alibi footage. Or the trust implications.'

He turned to Mulholland with resignation rather than anger. 'James, you'll work with the team on the Cockburn investigation. Murdoch's coordinating, so you'll take direction from her. And you can support Balfour on the betting shop investigation if he needs it.'

The words hit Mulholland like a slap. Support Balfour. Take direction from Murdoch. Just as he could almost taste it, his moment of triumph had turned to shit.

'Yes sir,' he managed, his voice steady despite the burning in his chest.

Munro smiled weakly, his tone reeking of reluctant fairness. 'Your work on the alibi was solid son. We needed to know the truth - even if it wasn't what we wanted.'

As the team began to disperse, Mulholland caught Balfour's eye across the room. There was something there he couldn't quite recognise. It wasn't triumph. It wasn't mockery. Maybe it was understanding. Perhaps even sympathy.

But somehow that only made it worse.

The last thing he wanted was pity from David fucking Balfour.

***

The canteen coffee smelt like burnt disappointment, but maybe that was just the bitter aftertaste.

Anyway, Mulholland needed something to do with his hands as he watched Balfour and Murdoch through the glass partition, their heads bent together over case files like they were planning the invasion of fucking Normandy.

Three hours since the briefing, and he still felt radioactive. Campbell had given him busy work - cross-referencing CCTV timestamps, checking vehicle registrations, the kind of tasks you assigned to probationers.

Meanwhile, Balfour was building a case that would probably make his career.

'Fuck,' he muttered, stirring sugar into a drink that really didn't deserve the effort.

The thing that really burned wasn't just the demotion. Three months ago, he'd been lead detective on a domestic violence case - open and shut, husband clearly guilty. But the defence lawyer had torn apart his interview technique, questioning his methods, his note-taking, even suggesting he'd led the witness. The case collapsed, the bastard walked free, and suddenly Mulholland was "lacking attention to detail."

Meanwhile, Balfour waltzes in with his posh accent and perfect paperwork, making everyone else look sloppy by comparison.

It wasn't even Munro's patronising 'your work was solid, son' bullshit that bothered him. It was the look in Balfour's eyes - that flash of recognition, maybe even sympathy. Like he understood exactly what Mulholland was going through.

Because of course he fucking did.

It must be close to twenty years since those Highland holidays, but Mulholland could still picture it clearly: the dishevelled lochside B&B, the peeling wallpaper in the breakfast room and Mrs Balfour bustling about with forced cheerfulness while her son helped with the washing up, thin as a whip, quiet as a mouse, but always watching.

Because while his school friends went to Benidorm, James Mulholland trudged through Scottish glens being lectured about heritage and character building, part of his endless campaign to elevate the family above their working-class roots.

Already marked out for being neither properly working-class nor affluent enough to be middle-class. Those holidays had made Mulholland a target back at school.

'Weird poof,' they'd said.

He'd learned to say nothing. To play the game, coast along as part of the mob, then - whenever he got the chance - fight with every underhanded tactic - every shred of aggression, every fist, every weapon that fell to hand and felt safe to use.

It was a lesson that had served him well in the police force.

Until it hadn't.

The move to MIT 13 had been billed as 'gaining experience with complex cases' but he knew the truth. Too many complaints about his interview techniques. Too many snowflakes who felt 'pressured' or 'intimidated.' Too many statements that had been 'clarified' in ways that helped the prosecution case.

The final straw had been a seventeen-year-old suspect who'd reminded him too much of his school tormentors - cocky, working-class, full of attitude. Mulholland had kicked the living shit out of him.

Nothing was ever proven, but he was banished to MIT 13: where careers went to die..

The irony was toxic. Mulholland had applied himself - scraped through university, joined the police, climbed the ladder rung by bloody rung. And where had it got him? Taking orders from a man who'd somehow been transformed from a skint Highland kid into Edinburgh's landed gentry.

Mulholland had spent years perfecting his own middle-class performance, learning the right accent, the proper mannerisms, the kind of casual confidence that opened doors. But Balfour wore it like a second skin, completely natural.

Through the glass, he watched as Murdoch laughed at something Balfour had said. Easy camaraderie, the kind Mulholland had never managed with anyone .

Even McGinty - the flinty bastard - seemed to respect Balfour in a way he hardly ever showed for anyone else.

It wasn't fair. Mulholland had followed the rules, kissed arse and done everything right. He'd earned his place through merit while Balfour had simply inherited his way into relevance.

His mobile buzzed. Another fucking text from Campbell: 'Need those vehicle checks completed ASAP. Meeting at 4.'

Busy work. Shovel up all that shite over there and put it in a pile over here. Fill your eight hours and try hard not fuck anything up. Strictly categorised as the kind of assignment that said 'we don't trust you with anything important' in the politest possible way.

Mulholland drained his coffee and headed back to his desk, jaw clenched with determination. The question was simple.

Did he want to spend the rest of his career watching from the sidelines while David fucking Balfour hoovered up the credit? Or did he have the balls to fight him for top spot?

Because everyone had secrets, didn't they? Everyone had weaknesses. And, well, accidents happened to everyone, eventually.

Even golden boys with perfect timing and mysterious trust funds.

Especially them.

Chapter 21

The Manse, Callander, 1860

The morning sun cast angular shards of light across the polished mahogany table where Amelia Sterling had arranged her collection of apparatus with methodical precision for a fulminating audience.

Glass slides, magnifying instruments, and small vials of fine powder formed a peculiar still life against the traditional furnishings, whilst her leather-bound notebook lay open beside them, its pages covered with detailed sketches that would have puzzled any casual observer and most informed ones too.

Gathered around the table in various states of bewilderment tinged with a faint sense of disapproval, the assembled worthies of Callander regarded the young schoolteacher's preparations with expressions ranging from curiosity to outright alarm. The Reverend MacLeod's visage had adopted its familiar cast of perpetual moral indignation, whilst Dr Geddes—professional interest warring with social caution—shuffled forward, dripping in unwilling enthusiasm.

'Gentlemen,' Amelia began, lifting her head to survey her skeptical audience, 'what I propose to demonstrate this morning may challenge your preconceptions about the nature of evidence, but I assure you that the principles I shall outline are founded upon the most rigorous scientific methodology.'

She lifted one of the glass slides, holding it to catch the light so that the assembled men, peering closely, could observe the intricate whorls and ridges etched upon its surface.

'Sir William Herschel's recent work in Bengal has demonstrated conclusively that human fingerprint patterns are unique to each individual, as distinctive as their handwriting and infinitely more difficult to forge. Hence his use of finger-marks on contracts over the past two years as the most reliable way to identify individuals.'

Dr Geddes, his medical training compelling him toward intellectual honesty despite his social reservations, cleared his throat cautiously.

'Miss Sterling, whilst your enthusiasm for Colonial innovations is... admirable, surely you cannot suggest that administrative practices from India could assist in criminal investigation here?'

'On the contrary, Doctor,' Amelia replied with patient firmness, selecting a magnifying apparatus and positioning it carefully above one of her specimens. 'What I propose is precisely that. If fingerprint patterns are truly unique, then the axe used to murder Janet Henderson should bear the distinctive marks of whoever wielded it.'

The silence that followed carried the weight of generations, each man wrestling with implications that stretched the limits of their respective imaginary horizons.

MacLeod's fingers drummed against the tabletop whilst Arbuthnot polished his spectacles, apparently lost in thought.

'Miss Sterling,' the Reverend began, doubt and confusion spreading across his face in equal proportions, 'whilst I would not question the ingenuity of Colonial administration, surely we must consider the broader implications of such... innovation. What precedent does this set? Are we to abandon the wisdom of centuries, the tried methods of Christian justice, in favour of foreign customs and scientific apparatus?'

Young, who had been observing the proceedings with the bluff, open curiosity he applied to every novel development, pitched in with growing interest as he considered the possibilities. 'Miss Sterling, assuming your scientific principles are sound, how precisely would such an examination proceed?'

With the efficiency of someone who had clearly rehearsed her demonstration, Amelia produced a small vial of dark powder and began dusting one of the glass slides with delicate precision.

'By applying fine graphite powder to suspected surfaces, latent fingerprints become visible under magnification. The patterns revealed can then be compared systematically with those of known individuals.'

She gestured toward her notebook, its pages covered with carefully annotated drawings.

'I have already documented the basic pattern types - loops, whorls, arches - and established my methodology for systematic comparison. By mapping any two marks on an object and comparing them, we should be able to prove conclusively whether a particular individual handled a specific object.'

Arbuthnot's legal training asserted itself with customary precision. 'Even assuming the validity of these foreign theories, such evidence could carry no weight whatsoever in a Scottish court of law. Our legal system recognises witness testimony, physical evidence of established types, and moral character - not speculative interpretations of skin markings.'

'But surely, Mr Arbuthnot,' Balfour interjected quietly from his position near the window, 'truth remains truth regardless of whether our legal system has learned to recognise it? If scientific methodology can demonstrate innocence or guilt with mathematical certainty, should we not at least examine such evidence?'

The question hung in the morning air like incense, whilst outside the sounds of village life continued their familiar rhythm.

'The implications are... disturbing,' muttered MacLeod, pressing his fingertips against his temples as if to repel an onrush of dangerous thinking. 'If mere mortals can read guilt or innocence in the patterns of human flesh, what becomes of faith in Divine judgment? What becomes of the established order that has served society for centuries?'

His words, as though caught up by the swirling winds of progress that were beginning to blow through his era, went unheard.

Dr Geddes, the battle between scientific curiosity and social conformity now clearly won, studied the apparatus with barely concealed fascination.

'It would certainly help ease Henderson's mind to see this matter finally disposed of. Miss Sterling, assuming we were to proceed with such an examination - hypothetically, you understand - what exactly would we expect to discover?'

'Two sets of fingerprints upon the axe handle,' Amelia replied with clinical precision. 'Janet Henderson's, and those of her killer.'

***

As the days had passed since the murder, the Mount Stewart farmhouse kitchen had slowly taken on the quality of a grotesque museum exhibit.

Despite some clumsy attempts at restoration, dark stains still marked the flagstone floor where Janet Henderson had died, while the whitewashed walls bore their mute testimony in sprays of russet brown that it seemed no amount of scrubbing could entirely erase.

Upon the scoured oak table, arranged with the precision of a surgical theatre, lay Amelia Sterling's collection of scientific apparatus - magnifying glasses of varying strengths, sheets of fine paper, measuring instruments, and several small glass vials containing powders caught the afternoon light.

At the centre of this methodical display rested the bloodied axe, its blade cleaned but its handle still stained by its terrible story.

'Gentlemen,' Amelia announced, her voice crisp and authoritative, 'before we proceed, I must insist that no one touch anything on this table unless by my express direction. The effectiveness of this technique depends enormously upon maintaining the evidence in its current state.'

Blowing a stray curl away from her face, she moved over the table with confident efficiency, her dark dress rustling against the rough flagstones as she got to work. Drawing what appeared to be a lady's powder compact from a small leather case, and opening it to reveal the fine dark substance within.

'When fingers touch any surface, they leave behind traces of natural oils and perspiration that, when properly revealed, display distinctive ridge patterns that cannot be duplicated,' she explained, applying the powder to a soft brush with delicate movements. 'Each individual possesses unique markings that can be systematically compared and identified.'

Young, fascinated, edged in as close as he dared. 'But surely such... remnants would have been destroyed by the cleaning process?'

'On the contrary, Mr Young. The oils penetrate more deeply into wood grain, and despite having been roughly wiped, the axe handle shows clear evidence of multiple handprints.'

Her brush moved across the worn wood with systematic precision, the dark powder adhering to invisible traces. Working with methodical care, she pressed sheets of fine paper against the dusted surfaces, transferring the revealed patterns with gentle pressure before lifting them away to examine under her magnifying glass.

'Capital!' she grinned, looking up from the transferred impressions with obvious satisfaction. 'The prints have been captured beautifully.'

As she fanned the papers out across the table, Shaw, who had been watching the proceedings with the fascination of a man witnessing genuine sorcery, exhaled deeply.

'Bloody hell,' he breathed, his unedifying countenance lighting up like a schoolboy's. 'Begging your pardon miss, but that's proper magic.'

'Not magic, Mr Shaw - merely science applied with appropriate precision and, if I may say so myself, a certain amount of style.'

Amelia's magnifying glass moved systematically across the transferred patterns, her concentration absolute as she examined the intricate whorls and ridges now visible on paper. 'These smaller impressions taken largely from the middle of the shaft are smaller and more delicate ridge patterns consistent with normal kitchen use - most likely Miss Henderson's own.'

'Telegraphed instructions to Dr Littlejohn in Edinburgh should help us confirm that easily enough,' Balfour offered encouragingly. 'And the larger impressions?'

'These prints, positioned at the end of the handle, where one would grip it for a full swing, tell quite a different story.' Amelia's voice carried a note of grim satisfaction as she indicated the clear patterns with her magnifying glass. 'Unavoidably broader and different in various ways - these belong to a man.'

From her leather case, she withdrew the sheet of paper bearing Crichton's fingerprints - reluctantly provided earlier at her insistence despite his protests - arranging it beside the newly identified marks for side by side comparison.

'The ridge patterns are entirely different,' she announced with certainty, pointing between the two sets of prints. 'Mr Crichton's thumb pattern bears no resemblance whatsoever to the impression left on this weapon. Moreover, observe this distinctive whorl formation here - completely absent from his natural markings.'

The silence that followed was broken only by the whisper of wind through the bare birches outside and Young's sharp intake of breath as the implications began to crystalise.

'We must examine other surfaces,' Amelia continued, moving purposefully toward the kitchen door.

Her brush and powder revealed the same two sets of prints upon the iron latch - Henderson's delicate marks overlaid by the same masculine hand that had gripped the murder weapon, while embedded in the wood grain near the latch mechanism were tiny fibres - dark strands she extracted with a pair of fine tweezers and deposited them in a small glass vial.

She paused, studying the find with her magnifying glass briefly as her brow furrowed in concentration.

'These bear further investigation, but in any case, the conclusion is inescapable,' she declared, returning to face Balfour and Young.

'John Crichton never touched this murder weapon.'

***

To give him his due, Arbuthnot was masterful in his destruction of the evidence, systematically dismantling Amelia's revolutionary techniques with the methodical precision of a man demolishing a house of cards.

'Gentlemen,' he had begun, his hastily procured commission as acting Justice of the Peace for the district lending legal weight to what might otherwise have been just another provincial parlour gathering. 'We find ourselves confronted with methods entirely unknown to Scottish jurisprudence, techniques that have neither been tested in our courts nor sanctioned by our legal tradition.'

As the excitement of their discovery gave way to a sinking feeling in the pit of his stomach, Young had felt the familiar weight of legal conservatism settling upon the proceedings like a chain around his neck, knowing that new ideas moved with glacial slowness through courts still governed by procedures established when being beheaded in front of a baying mob was considered a proportionate penalty for petty theft.

Standing before the assembled worthies while the grey morning haar pressed against the Manse windows, Arbuthnot had approached Amelia's scientific work with that special brand of distrust the law reserved for any departure from established precedent, his confidence boosted by the full authority of centuries of judicial tradition.

'Miss Sterling's methods may possess merit in foreign circles,' he had continued in a patronising tone that made even the middle-of-the-road Young's jaw clench with suppressed frustration, 'but Scots law requires more than theoretical possibility - it demands proof tested through generations of legal practice, evidence that can withstand the scrutiny of learned judges rather than simply matching the pet theories of provincial investigators.'

The young Procurator Fiscal had watched helplessly as his carefully constructed case crumbled beneath an assault that was both legally sound and morally bankrupt, each procedural objection delivered with the confidence of a man whose authority derived not from expertise but from institutional momentum.

'These patterns and measurements,' Arbuthnot had declared, indicating Amelia's meticulous diagrams with dismissive gestures, 'however cleverly presented, remain unproven novelties that no Scottish court has ever recognised - techniques that might satisfy colonial traders but surely cannot overturn the sworn testimony of respectable witnesses.'

Dr Geddes, his instinctive deference to the established order, had ultimately retreated into professional caution, vaguely murmuring his agreement while working hard not to meet Amelia's frosty gaze.

Never one to be perturbed by a lack of jurisdiction, meanwhile, the Reverend MacLeod had provided the moral framework for rejection, offering judgments unfettered by understanding as he helped cast doubt on methods that not only threatened legal procedure but the established order itself.

'The testimony of honest Christian witnesses,' he had thundered, 'cannot be overturned by marks virtually invisible to the naked eye, patterns that might mean anything or nothing according to the fancy of whoever examines them.'

Young had known his cause was lost from the moment Arbuthnot produced his commission, the machinery of justice grinding forward with unstoppable momentum.

The ultimate decision, supported by a telegram from the Sheriff himself, had been rendered with bureaucratic finality: 'Prisoner transmission to circuit court stands. Novel evidence lacking legal precedent cannot suspend established procedure.'

Through the manse windows, Young had watched the prison van lumber through the village in the soft grey light, its iron-bound wheels sparking against the cobblestones as they carried an innocent man towards his appointment with capital justice.

Standing behind him at the cold fireplace, her scientific diagrams returned to their leather satchel, Amelia Sterling's dark eyes blazed with barely contained fury.

Chapter 22

MIT-13 Office, Edinburgh, 2025

Eyes blazing with barely contained delight, DCI Munro swept into the incident room like a conquering general, brandishing a steaming coffee mug alongside what appeared to be the printouts from a conspiracy theorist's fever dream.

The perpetual disorder of MIT-13's cramped headquarters shifted into defensive mode as the team hastily concluded their morning routines, weaving through the collection of sealed removal boxes that appeared to have been dumped into the office overnight as they gathered around their makeshift incident-room table for morning briefing.

Most of the team assumed the careful look of bomb disposal experts who'd just spotted a suspicious package. McGinty simmered behind his customary newspaper. Mulholland—practically levitating from his chair with anticipation—perked up noticeably, his reptile brain sensing an opportunity to claw his way back into favour.

'Right then, people!' Munro boomed, slapping his papers down on the table with enough force to send the usual collection of mismatched coffee mugs dancing across its scarred surface.

'I've cracked it. Completely bloody cracked it. This is what separates the real detectives from the amateur hour brigade - when faced with the impossible, you ask the right bloody questions!'

Around the table, heads dipped in the familiar ritual of bracing for impact as Munro launched into full bombastic mode, his confidence radiating like heat from a blast furnace.

'We've been thinking too small, too conventional,' he continued, warming to his theme as he spread out reams of what looked like a selection of drone and aerial photography shots printed out from the web. 'You lot have been fixated on locked rooms and camera blind spots, but we're dealing with a twenty-first century crime here, not some Agatha bloody Christie parlour game!'

Campbell, brow furrowed. 'Sir, what exactly are you suggesting?'

Munro grinned maniacally as he jabbed at the aerial photographs. 'Drone delivery, Detective Inspector. Our killer never entered the building at all. He used an unmanned aerial vehicle to deliver the murder weapon directly through Rowena James's study window, then retrieved it the same way. No cameras, no witnesses, no physical presence required.'

The silence that followed was broken only by the rattle of the building's fast deteriorating ventilation system and something that sounded distinctly like McGinty grinding his teeth.

'Think about it!' Munro pressed on, oblivious to his team's stunned expressions. 'George Cockburn's been haemorrhaging money on tech investments for years; it's all there in Murdoch's financial analysis. What if he was actually acquiring specialist equipment for this exact purpose?'

Murdoch consulted her notes. 'Sir, his investments were primarily in agricultural technology and renewable energy startups. There's no evidence of drone purchases or...'

'Agricultural technology!' Munro interrupted triumphantly. 'Crop spraying drones, delivery systems, precision targeting equipment. All perfectly legitimate business expenses that could easily be adapted for our purposes.'

Sensing that it was his turn to enter the fray, Balfour cleared his throat. 'Sir, with respect, the physics of delivering sufficient force through a window to cause those head injuries would require...'

'Don't lecture me about fucking physics, Balfour,' Munro cut him off with a sudden flash of venom. 'I've already thought about that. A weighted projectile or a spring-loaded mechanism, possibly even explosive charges, the technology exists, it's commercially available, and it explains every bloody inconsistency in this case.'

Campbell tried again, her tone measured. 'The resource allocation for investigating aerial delivery methods would be considerable, sir. Perhaps we should consider...'

'Considerable but necessary,' Munro declared, throwing himself down into a chair and surveying his team with evident satisfaction. 'This is exactly the sort of innovative thinking that separates MIT-13 from the plodding masses. While everyone else is still checking door handles and interviewing neighbours, we'll be solving murders from the bloody stratosphere!'

Practically whooping in delight, Mulholland seized his moment with enthusiasm. 'Brilliant analysis, boss! I mean, it explains everything, doesn't it? The impossible entry, the lack of witnesses, the precision of the attack.

'Classic case of thinking outside the box to achieve maximum operational efficiency.'

McGinty's newspaper crackled ominously as his grip tightened.

'Right then,' Munro continued, consulting what appeared to be a hastily scribbled action plan. 'Mulholland, you're coordinating with the Civil Aviation Authority - I want flight records, drone registrations, anything that puts an unmanned vehicle over Heriot Row during our window. Campbell, liaise with the tech boys about trajectory analysis and impact calculations.

'McGinty, pull together a reexamination of the CCTV from surrounding streets to see what you've missed, and while you're at it - pay a visit to these tech startups of his and find out what they're really up to.'

***

The drive to the commercial development took them through Edinburgh's less picturesque quarters, slipping past the endless array of the greying concrete and harling constructions that had seemed like a good idea in the 1970s.

Since the city's planning authorities had learned that scattering a couple of fake turrets around any new development helped soften the blow and blend in a little with the old town's medieval heart, but out here it looked like the place where architecture came to die.

Shifting gear without exactly speeding, McGinty piloted the ageing pool car through narrow streets with the grim efficiency of someone who'd spent decades learning every rat run in the city, while Balfour consulted his tablet for addresses of Cockburn's tech investments.

'That's the Civil Aviation Authority done,' he muttered, checking his phone as it buzzed. 'Mulholland's already been on to them. No unauthorised flights recorded anywhere in the country during our window.'

'I'm sure we're all deeply fucking shocked.'

Balfour's phone chimed with a WhatsApp message from Murdoch: 'CCTV analysis complete. Guess what? Zero aerial objects detected in a 48-hour window around murder. Absolutely nothing airborne except pigeons and one dodgy looking seagull.'

'Right,' McGinty said, pulling into a potholed car park beside a collection of low-rise units that looked like they'd been assembled from a particularly uninspiring set of industrial off-brand Lego. Environmental consultancy's Unit 15. Agricultural tech's Unit 23. Which poisoned chalice do you fancy first?'

They went with the agricultural consultancy, finding a bemused rosy cheeked countrywoman who confirmed that yes, Cockburn was one of the biggest investors in their precision fertiliser system, but that no, it couldn't possibly deliver anything heavier than grass seed with any accuracy beyond about fifty metres.

'Farming equipment isn't really designed for shooting projectiles about the place,' she grinned. 'We've got plenty of equipment that would take your arm off and turn it into mincemeat, if you fancy having a look at that?'

The environmental consultancy proved marginally more promising. The owner - a bearded enthusiast called Semple who looked like he'd stepped out of a renewable energy brochure - actually understood drone technology.

'Aye, we use them for site surveys, wind farm inspections, that sort of thing,' he confirmed, leading them through an office cluttered with charts showing wind patterns and solar radiation data. 'Amazon's been experimenting with delivery drones for years now, but anything with the power you're describing would need to be the size of a large suitcase. Not exactly subtle.'

McGinty's phone buzzed again, this time with a text from Mulholland: 'Air traffic control confirmed zero drone activity over central Edinburgh yesterday. Also checked military flight paths. Nothing.'

'What about delivery systems?' Balfour asked, as McGinty closed his eyes and massaged the bridge of his nose. 'Could a drone precisely drop and retrieve objects inside a building?'

Semple laughed. 'In a perfect world, with GPS targeting and no wind, you might theoretically be able to do that, but in real conditions? You'd be lucky to hit the right street. And that's assuming you could lift whatever weight you're trying to drop in the first place. Our survey drones max out at about two kilos, and that's really pushing it.'

Balfour nodded. 'And how involved is Mr Cockburn in your day-to-day operations?'

'Not at all really. I mean technically he's our landlord - he owns this whole development and subsidised rent is part of the standard investment package he offers companies - but apart from that we send him an annual report and he sends a lawyer to the AGM. That's as far as it goes.'

As they walked back to the car, McGinty's phone rang. Campbell's name blinking up on the screen.

'How's the wild goose chase proceeding?' she asked without preamble.

'Exactly as expected,' McGinty replied, his voice flat but clearly simmering. 'A total waste of fucking time.

'Boss, no drone could do what Munro is suggesting. You don't have to be an expert in engineering to see that. It's basic bloody common sense.'

Campbell sighed deeply. 'I thought as much. The tech boys are trying to be diplomatic about it, but they're essentially saying the same thing. What's your ETA back?'

McGinty checked his watch. 'Twenty minutes. Assuming Munro hasn't invented a new theory involving trained pigeons by the time we get there.'

'Don't give him ideas.'

As McGinty ended the call with a hollow laugh, Balfour studied the commercial development with fresh eyes.
'Interesting how Cockburn's investments work. Reduced rent in exchange for equity stakes. Makes any losses more palatable when you're not paying full commercial rates.'

'Aye,' McGinty replied, starting the engine. 'But the big question now is… will our illustrious leader listen when we try to explain that his brilliant drone theory is a steaming pile of shite.'

As they pulled out of the car park, a white transit van approached from the opposite direction. Balfour recognised the two men in the front seats - Tam and Eddie, the pair who'd made Douglas Kemp nervous at the betting shop.

'Those two seem to get everywhere,' he observed quietly as the van turned into the development behind them.

***

The incident room seemed a lot less roomy when McGinty was angry.

It wasn't that he showed it in any obvious way. There was no raised voice, no dramatic gestures, no furniture being thrown about, but something critical had shifted in the atmosphere since the team had reassembled from their futile errands, a subtle electrical crackle that made everyone speak a little more quietly and move a little more carefully around the taciturn Highlander.

'Right then,' Munro announced with undiminished enthusiasm, apparently oblivious to the gathering storm. 'I've been thinking about trajectory analysis while you lot have been out playing with gadgets. The drone theory explains everything - we just need to refine the technical parameters.'

Campbell cast an eye over her notes and butted in. 'Sir, the Civil Aviation Authority confirms no unauthorised flights. CCTV shows no aerial objects. The tech consultants say the payload requirements would make it impossible to operate covertly.'

'Technical consultants,' Munro waved dismissively. 'Probably never investigated a real crime in their lives. We need to think like criminals, not engineers. Mulholland, what did you get from the aviation boys?'

'They were tossers boss,' Mulholland chirped. 'A complete dead end. They couldn't find any drone registrations in Cockburn's name, any flight plans or radar contacts. Nothing.'

McGinty sat perfectly still at his desk, his silence gaining weight.

'Obviously he wouldn't register it in his own name,' Munro pressed on. 'Shell companies, false identities, criminal networks. We need to dig deeper, think laterally. This is exactly the sort of sophisticated operation that requires proper detective work.'

'Is it fuck.'

The words dropped into the room with a heart-stopping thud, quiet but unmistakable. McGinty hadn't moved from his chair, hadn't raised his voice above conversational level, but every person present felt the change in atmospheric pressure.

'I'm sorry?' Munro blinked, caught off guard.

McGinty looked up slowly, his pale eyes fixing on his superior.

'I said, is it fuck… sir.' His voice remained perfectly level, but had taken on an extra sibilance as his diction sharpened.

'Twenty-three years I've been doing this job. Seen every sort of murder, every sort of copper and every sort of arsehole with every sort of excuse. Got to tell you though - this drone bollocks is the biggest load of shite I've encountered yet.'

The silence tautened. Mulholland looked like he wanted to hide under the table. Campbell's pen stopped moving. Balfour and Murdoch tensed and, in the midst of one of its rare moments of functionality, even the ventilation system seemed to hold its breath.

'DS McGinty,' Munro began, the warning note in his voice somehow impeded by an unmistakable sense of hesitation, 'I think you need to remember who you're talking to.'

'Oh, I know exactly who I'm talking to,' McGinty replied, rising from his chair with deliberate slowness. 'I'm talking to a DCI who's so desperate to avoid admitting he's on the wrong track that he'd rather waste police resources than change his fucking mind.'

He moved closer to Munro's desk, each step measured and purposeful.

'So maybe you need to remember who you're talking to, sunshine. You must ken why I was sent here right? Because I've left bigger men than you needing dental work after… um… expressing my professional disagreement.'

McGinty's voice lowered as he hovered within inches of Munro's face, leaving the rest of the team struggling to hear.

'Fuck this up and I'll fucking enjoy doing it to you.'

'Now,' McGinty continued, stepping back slightly, 'We could explain again why the drone theory won't work, we could detail the resource implications of continuing this investigation, or we could try to estimate the scale of the professional embarrassment we'll all face when the press - or anybody else - gets hold of this.'

His pale eyes never left Munro's face.

'Or you could save us all a lot of time and aggravation by admitting that you've backed the wrong horse, and we can get on with some actual police work.

'Your choice, sir.'

His face unusually pale, Munro cleared his throat and looked away, apparently finding something fascinating in his computer screen.

'Well,' he said finally, his voice lacking its usual bluster. 'I'm… ah… not ruling out alternative theories, and obviously we need to explore all avenues thoroughly before drawing conclusions. That goes without saying.'

McGinty nodded slowly, the ghost of a smile playing at the corners of his mouth.

'Aye,' he said quietly. 'That we do.'

He collected his jacket from the back of his chair, picked up his newspaper with unhurried calm, nodded politely to Campbell, and walked toward the door.

'I'll be in the canteen if anyone needs me.'

'Christ,' Murdoch whispered. 'What was that about?'

Campbell glanced around, then leaned closer to Murdoch and Balfour. 'Old history,' she said, lowering her voice.

'It didn't end well for either of them.'

Chapter 23

Railway Carriage, Carse of Stirling, 1860

The morning train wound its way southward through the heartland of Scotland, cutting through the ancient Carse of Stirling as the Highland heights gave way to the gentler slopes and broad valley floors that marked the journey into lowland civilisation.

Seated in their first-class compartment as the carriage swayed with the familiar rhythm of iron on steel, Young consulted his pocket watch yet again, as if the action could somehow spirit them into the city's heart more quickly than the hissing, spitting locomotive was already endeavouring to do.

'The authorities in Edinburgh will require some convincing, Balfour,' he said, his breath forming small clouds in the compartment's chill air as he gazed across the frost-covered fields of the approaching lowlands.

'The Sheriff may have approved Fox's interview, but questioning him and investigating the circumstances of his arrest while outside our jurisdiction will require delicate handling - particularly as it involves procedures that some might consider irregular.'

Opposite him, Balfour watched the changing landscape with careful attention, quietly observing the scattered Highland crofts as they gave way to substantial stone farmhouses. Surrounded by enclosed fields, they spoke of progress and polish, while alongside the chattering rails, gleaming new telegraph poles marched southward like soldiers carrying news at the speed of light.

'The timing troubles me most,' he replied, absently polishing the crystal of his pocket watch as he spoke. 'Fox was arrested for illegal rail travel from Callander the day after the murder, suggesting he departed the area immediately following Janet Henderson's death - yet he'd been observed near Mount Stewart Farm during the precise window when the crime was committed.'

'While I'm perfectly prepared to believe that this crime was not his, his presence nearby is entirely too coincidental for my liking.'

Shaw, hunched in the corner seat with his battered greatcoat wrapped around him like armour against the encroaching civility of the first class carriage, looked up from his brooding contemplation of the passing countryside.

'Aye, well that's because it's no' a coincidence sir. In years of dealing with vagrants and petty thieves and all round villains, I've never known one to change his habits so dramatically without powerful motivation,' he growled.

'Fox has been following the same seasonal pattern for years - stealing just enough to survive, moving from bothy to bothy, never straying far from familiar territory. Yet something drove him to change the habits of a lifetime on the very day that poor lassie was killed and race back to the city.'

'Coincidence my arse.'

With all that he needed to say succinctly and definitively said, Shaw rose from his seat and left the compartment, intent on catching up with an acquaintance in the guards' van before reaching Edinburgh, leaving Balfour and Young to consider the task ahead.

The train began its descent toward the smoking chimneys and blackened spires of Scotland's capital, the rural tranquillity of the Highlands replaced by a city where coal smoke and brewery stank mixed with sea air to create an atmosphere thick with ambition and commerce. The soot-flecked windows revealing the medieval towers of Edinburgh Castle as they emerged through the haze like a gothic sentinel guarding the bustling streets below.

'Shaw has business elsewhere, but my townhouse in Heriot Row should accommodate the two of us comfortably,' Balfour offered as the train's whistle announced their approach to Waverley Station. 'The housekeeper I hired has been expecting our arrival since yesterday evening, and the proximity to the legal district will I'm sure save time in our investigations.'

Young nodded his appreciation, though his expression remained troubled as he gathered his papers and prepared for their arrival in a city built on ancient power and dynastic reputations.

'Shaw has a rather… forthright approach to his opinions, but I confess that I also find myself uneasy about Fox's sudden flight and arrest,' he admitted. 'A guilty man runs, but then so too do the innocent, and why has he been detained for an offense that carries a maximum fine of forty shillings?'

'Certainly it was not due to my request - it was sheer luck that I learned from a colleague that he was being held at all. We have either been the very fortunate beneficiaries of administrative incompetence, my dear Balfour, or there is someone of influence with their own interest in Jon Fox.'

'If that is the case, they may not appreciate our interference.'

Balfour smiled. 'Well, as I'm sure the estimable Shaw would say, if they've got nothing to hide, they'll have nothing to fear from our questions. And if they have got something to hide…'

He left the implication hanging in the smoky air as Edinburgh's maze of wynds and closes rose around them and the train ground to a halt beneath the soaring glass roof of Waverley Station. In less than twenty-four hours they would know whether the mysterious Fox represented the missing piece of their

Highland puzzle, or merely another red herring in a case that seemed determined to confound every assumption.

***

A granite fortress set against the afternoon sky, the Edinburgh Gaol rose from Calton Hill, its imposing neoclassical facade dappled by a strengthening spring sunlight that conspired to mask the misery behind its walls.

As Balfour and Young climbed the steep approach that led to its iron gates, built barely forty years earlier to replace the ancient Tolbooth, the prison's modern style might have spoken to its progressive ideals and reforming spirit, but the air around its entrance seemed thick with accumulated desperation.

For the thousands who had passed through its doors since 1817, hope had been extinguished just as efficiently as it would have been by the medieval dungeons it had replaced.

'Fox, Jon. Charged with travelling on the railway without having previously paid the fare, contrary to the provisions of the Railways Clauses Consolidation Act, 1845,' the turnkey intoned, consulting his ledger with methodical indifference. 'Aye, we've got him. Been here for days now, though there's been some interest in his case from unexpected quarters.'

His keys jangled against his belt as he led them deeper into the building's bowels.

'What sort of interest?' Young enquired, his legal instincts immediately alert to any irregularities in the prisoner's treatment.

'Gentleman came by yesterday evening, well-dressed sort, asking about the specifics of his charges and when he might be released,' the turnkey replied with a shrug that suggested such inquiries were not entirely unusual. 'Didn't give his name, but he wasn't the sort of gentleman you ask questions about, if you catch my meaning, sir.'

They found Fox hunched on a straw pallet in a cell barely large enough to contain a man of average height, his angular frame folded into the available space. Black marks clung to his unkempt clothing despite the prison's perfunctory attempts at cleanliness, while his eyes darted between each of the new entrants as he strained to rapidly size them up.

'Jon Fox?' Balfour began, settling onto the single wooden stool provided while Young remained standing near the cell door. 'I'm Balfour, Justice of the Peace, and this is Mr Young, Procurator Fiscal for Perthshire. We need to speak with you about your recent movements in the Callander district.'

'Most particularly on The Old Military Road to Strathyre.'

Fox's reaction was guarded but telling - his body tensed briefly as the cornered animal inside him calculated the distance to the nearest escape route, but cunning quickly took over, and he adopted a hastily manufactured air of innocence, his gaze flicking between the two men.

'I never done nothing wrong in Callander,' he smirked, his tone wheedling. 'Just passing through, I was. A man's got to travel, hasn't he?'

'Indeed he has,' Young agreed mildly. 'But you were observed near Mount Stewart Farm on Tuesday afternoon - the same day that Miss Janet Henderson was murdered in her own kitchen. Quite a remarkable coincidence, wouldn't you say?'

For all of his affected confidence, Fox recoiled as the statement landed, his face draining of what little colour it possessed.

'Murder? I never... I wouldn't... Christ almighty, I never touched nobody!' he stammered, his voice rising to a shrill vibrato that echoed off the prison's stone interior. 'I was just looking about, seeing if there was anything worth... I mean, I was just passing by like!'

Balfour pressed a little harder, persistent. 'Looking about for what, exactly? You were seen covered in what looked like coal dust, Jon, and Mount Stewart has a coal cellar with an outside door…

'Were you in there Jon? Perhaps looking for a way in?'

'I never went inside!' Fox protested. 'Maybe I had a look at the outside, maybe I thought there might be something left about that nobody would miss, but I never went into the house itself. I swear it on my mother's grave!'

Young stepped closer, pressing home the advantage. 'But you did see something, didn't you? Something that frightened you enough to abandon your usual hunting ground and flee immediately to Edinburgh.

'So what was it man? What exactly did you see at Mount Stewart Farm?'

The question hung in the air momentarily as Fox's eyes darted frantically between his interrogators, seeking some escape from the trap he sensed was slowly closing around him.

'If there was ever a time to be a good man, this is yours Mr Fox,' Balfour observed quietly. 'An innocent woman is dead and a man sits in Perth jail awaiting trial for a crime he didn't commit. Whatever the circumstances or the… ah… complexities of your situation, you must know that you need to speak the truth.'

Fox's eyes flickered briefly as he stared at Balfour, but before he could respond, the sound of heavy footsteps echoed through the corridor, accompanied by the turnkey's voice raised in apparent surprise.

'Gentlemen, I'm afraid I must interrupt your interview,' the warder announced, his expression vaguely bewildered as he approached the cell.

'Mr Fox is to be released immediately - his fare has been paid in full and all charges dismissed. It's all most irregular, but the orders came directly from the Sheriff's office.'

Fox's demeanour shifted immediately from cornered rat to calculating opportunism, his eyes brightening as he grasped the implications of unexpected freedom.

'Released? All charges dropped?' he repeated, scrambling to his feet with renewed energy. 'Well, I'm not one to look a gift horse in the mouth, am I?'

His earlier panic evaporated like morning mist, replaced by the cheerful pragmatism.

'Don't suppose you gentlemen know who my benefactor might be?' he chirped, winking. 'Always pays to know who your friends are, doesn't it?'

But the turnkey was already unlocking the cell door, the legal machinery set in motion, and as Fox gathered his few possessions with obvious glee, whistling tunelessly as he embraced his unexpected good fortune, Balfour watched with growing unease.

'Fox,' he said quietly as the vagrant prepared to follow the turnkey toward freedom, 'Be careful - men who pay strangers' debts rarely do so from pure charity.'

The warning fell on deaf ears.

As Fox disappeared down the corridor, already planning how to celebrate his liberation in Edinburgh's countless taverns, Young turned to Balfour with troubled eyes as the sound of his footsteps faded into the prison's depths.

'I know you would have preferred to learn whatever he's keeping secret, Balfour,' he observed grimly. 'But I fear we may have just watched a man walk out the frying pan and directly into the fire.'

***

The narrow closes and wynds that tumbled down from the Royal Mile toward the Cowgate like burns cutting through its rocky slopes seemed to swallow sound itself, muffling their footsteps as Shaw led Balfour and Young through Edinburgh's ancient arteries with the quick movements of a man navigating familiar territory.

Here, in the shadow of the Old Town's towering tenements, the city's medieval bones poked through the veneer of progress, each twisting passageway telling a unique story wrought of centuries of use.

'This way, gentlemen,' Shaw announced, turning into a close so narrow that the upper floors of the buildings on either side nearly touched overhead, creating a tunnel of grimy stone that blocked out most of the early evening light.

'We'll find what we need to know in The Grassmarket, but it pays to approach these matters with proper preparation.'

As they descended the uneven worn steps, Young found himself increasingly uncomfortable with their surroundings. The respectable world of legal chambers and courthouse arbitration that he'd frequented since leaving the army seemed a universe away from this labyrinth of dark turns, questionable commerce and dubious characters.

'I don't doubt your expertise in these matters, Shaw,' he began, navigating around a pool of something unpleasant gathered in one doorway. 'But I confess to being a tad uncertain about the wisdom of pursuing our investigation through such... informal channels.

'Should matters take an unfortunate turn, the legal implications of associating with the criminal elements could prove most damaging to our standing.'

Shaw paused at the mouth of another close, his gnarled features creasing into something that might have been amusement as he regarded the distinguished Procurator Fiscal.

'Aye, well, there's law enough in your courts, wi' wigs and Latin words, but there's another kind that keeps a man breathing when he's cold and starving in the closes. You'll not find it written down, but it rules just the same.

'If you mean to see justice done, laddie, you'd best learn a bit of both.'

He gestured toward the bustling activity visible at the close's end, where the broader expanse of the Grassmarket opened before them - a stage set for Edinburgh's earthier dramas.

'Your Fox is running scared across my Edinburgh now - through the sort of places that don't ask questions or keep records. If we want to find him, we need to think like he does.'

The Grassmarket spread before them, its cobblestones worn smooth by centuries of life, villainy and commerce. Costomongers roared, market stalls competed for space with rough taverns and shadowy figures conducted business in doorways as life in Edinburgh flowed past in a chaotic tumult, a stark contrast to the refined facade the city worked hard to display in the refined Georgian splendour fanning out on the other side of the Castle Rock.

Elbowing his way expertly through the crowds, Shaw led them directly to a public house called The Black Bull, its faded sign apparently a beacon to Edinburgh's more enterprising citizens. Its interior thick with pipe smoke and whispered conversations.

'Solomon Shaw!'

The greeting came from a burly man behind the bar with arms like tree trunks and a face formed by the accumulated evidence of a lifetime's disagreements. 'What in the name of Christ brings you back to civilisation?'

'Business, Tam,' Shaw replied, accepting the offered hand with genuine warmth. 'These are my associates - Mr

Balfour and Mr Young, both respectable gentlemen despite their present company.'

Young, resolute but uncomfortably aware of the many calculating eyes turned in their direction and assessing whether these well-dressed strangers represented opportunity or threat, touched his hat brim in silent greeting. Balfour - seemingly entirely at ease in the rough surroundings - offered a smile and a handshake, his dark eyes drinking in every detail.

'We're looking for information about a Flash man named Jon Fox,' Shaw continued, lowering his voice as he leaned across the scarred wooden counter top.

'Released from The Calton this afternoon because someone wi' more siller than us paid his sentence and had the charges dropped, and we need tae ken who and why.'

Tam's expression grew thoughtful as he considered this intelligence, his scarred knuckles drumming against an empty tankard while he weighed the implications.

'Fox? You're not the first to be asking questions about a lad wi' that name.' He paused, glancing around the crowded taproom before continuing. 'A professional sort came in less than an hour ago looking for him. Very free with his coin he was. Might be connected to your man's sudden good fortune.'

'What sort of questions?' Balfour asked quietly.

'Locations, habits, who he associates with, where he kips,' Tam replied with a shrug. 'And there's more money available for anyone who can provide current information about your man's whereabouts.'

'Then we'd best find him first,' said Shaw, stepping back from the bar with a grim nod. 'I doubt that anyone paying those prices is going to have to wait long for an answer.'

As they prepared to leave, Tam called Shaw aside for a brief private conversation, their voices too low to be overheard and their expressions deeply conspiratorial.

'Well?' Young asked as they emerged into the Grassmarket's bustling evening activity.

'There's three places Fox is likely to head,' Shaw replied, pausing briefly to get his bearings as they walked back onto the throbbing marketplace. 'We can check them tonight, but we'll need to move quickly.'

Chapter 24

MIT-13 Interview Suite, Edinburgh, 2025

'The time is 14:22 hours,' Campbell announced, her voice crisp and professional as she checked the twin-deck recording machine positioned on the scratched metal table.

The old CD recorder – still standard equipment in the outdated wing MIT-13 had been relegated to – hummed quietly beneath the yellow fluorescent light.

'Present are Detective Inspector Fiona Campbell, Detective Constable David Balfour, Mr George Cockburn, and representing Mr Cockburn, Patricia Fraser KC.'

While his KC sat with predatory stillness beside him, George Cockburn, by contrast, possessed the relaxed confidence of a man who had never doubted his own superiority and saw no reason to start now.

It was a very rare thing for a suspect to exude control once locked away in these rooms, but Cockburn reeked of privilege. Everything about him – from his perfectly tailored suit to the way he arranged his manicured hands on the table – spoke of someone accustomed to controlling every situation he had ever found himself in.

From his position beside Campbell, Balfour searched their quarry's face carefully for any hint of discomfort but found only detached disinterest. Apparently indifferent to everyone present, he basked in the harsh overhead light, radiating an aura of casual menace.

'Mr Cockburn,' Campbell began, opening her folder, 'thank you for coming in voluntarily. We'd like to discuss your relationship with your late sister.'

'Of course,' Cockburn replied, his cultured Edinburgh accent carrying just enough boredom to make his bored disdain abundantly clear. 'Though I must say, Detective Inspector, that after your colleagues' earlier rather... amateur performance, I hope you've prepared a more sophisticated line of questioning.'

Fraser's expensive pen scratched urgently across her legal pad, while Cockburn smiled over the table with leering confidence.

'How would you characterise your relationship with Rowena?' Campbell continued, ignoring the slight.

Cockburn's smile carried all the warmth of a winter morning. 'I was very much her protector.'

'Rowena was weak. Always drawn to damaged things – broken toys, stray animals and hopeless causes. She had this pathetic need to nurture things that weren't worth fixing.'

His tongue flicked briefly across his lower lip as he spoke. 'I learned early that the world sorts itself into predators and prey, Detective Inspector. Rowena never understood which category she truly belonged in.'

Balfour noted Fraser's brief pause, a slight twitching of a muscle in her cheek as her client's personality laid itself bare, but it was momentary, and she continued without comment.

'And which category do you place yourself in, Mr Cockburn?'

'Which do you think?' Cockburn replied, his pale eyes fixed on Campbell with unwavering intensity. 'I find most people tedious, and I don't suffer fools gladly. Would you like me to apologise for that? Or should I pretend otherwise to ensure that nobody's feelings get hurt?

'And before you ask, I include my late sister's pathetic husband in that number. The man was exactly what I expected Rowena to choose – weak, needy and completely... submissive.'

The way he lingered over the final word was laden with implication but again, an unruffled Campbell maintained her composure.

'You didn't approve of their marriage?'

'Approve?' Cockburn's laugh was sharp and humourless. 'Rowena had an unerring instinct for collecting damaged strays. I suppose James fitted the pattern – another broken thing for her to try and repair.'

His fingers drummed slowly against the table surface, each tap deliberate and measured. 'She never understood that some people actually enjoy being broken – or that the entire process can be deeply educational.'

Balfour, reflecting that sometimes it seemed a pity that obnoxious behaviour and disturbing attitudes didn't constitute actual criminal behaviour, joined in.

'What do you mean by educational, Mr Cockburn?'

'I mean that Rowena wasted time trying to help the hopeless, while I focused on understanding how power actually works.' His smile broadened slightly, revealing perfectly maintained teeth. 'Who's strong, who's weak, who can be… persuaded. It's remarkable what people will accept when they understand their proper place.'

Fraser cleared her throat, but Cockburn continued regardless, apparently enjoying the effect his words were having on the assembled company.

'My sister believed in fairness, kindness, all those tedious middle-class virtues that make life so unnecessarily dishonest. That was her fatal flaw. I was always more direct in my approach to getting what I wanted.'

Balfour remained focused, studying Cockburn's micro-expressions with intensity, as Campbell seized on the comment.

'Fatal flaw?' she asked, her voice remaining steady, her grip on her pen tightening almost imperceptibly.

'A poor choice of words perhaps,' Cockburn conceded with a wave of theatrical regret that fooled nobody. 'But accurate nonetheless.'

Campbell made careful notes, her expression revealing nothing as she absorbed the casual cruelty.

'And your childhood together? Were you close?'

'Close?' Cockburn's eyes reflected the lighting like chips of ice. 'We got on well enough, rubbed along together but Rowena was sentimental. I was more… pragmatic.'

'What do you mean by pragmatic, Mr Cockburn?'

'I mean I understood power from an early age. Like I said – who is strong, and who is weak. That's all that really matters.'

The temperature in the room seemed to drop several degrees as the implications of Cockburn's worldview settled over it.

Campbell's next question carried a subtle edge that suggested her professional composure was being tested by her subject's complete lack of empathy.

'And how does murdering your sister fit into that philosophy, Mr Cockburn?'

***

It is often said in Edinburgh's most polite circles that considerable fees can be expected to buy impeccable results.

So when it came, Fraser's intervention – announced by the deliberately expensive snap of her briefcase clasps – arrived with a sense of polish and aplomb that sent a sick, queasy feeling in the pit of the detectives' stomachs.

'My client anticipated your interest in his movements,' the KC smiled smoothly, withdrawing a meticulously organised folder that looked like it had been prepared by a small army of forensic accountants. 'And so we took the liberty of documenting his journey in considerable detail.'

The folder's contents spilled across the metal table surface: hotel receipts, boarding passes, CCTV stills, witness statements, even a passenger manifest highlighted in fluorescent yellow where Cockburn's name appeared amongst the delayed travellers.

'Flight BA327 to Edinburgh was delayed three hours due to air traffic control strikes in London,' she explained with the satisfaction of someone unveiling a royal flush. 'We will of course share digital copies but here's the passenger manifest, baggage claim receipts, gate announcements and CCTV footage showing Mr Cockburn was trapped in Heathrow until past midnight.'

Campbell examined the documentation swiftly, her trained eye checking timestamps and cross-referencing details while Balfour studied the precision of a timeline within which every minute seemed to have been accounted for.

'The Hilton,' she continued, producing another sheaf of papers. 'Checked in at 1:47 AM – here's the key card data, CCTV from the lobby, room service order at 2:15 AM for a whisky and sandwiches. The night porter remembers my client quite distinctly.'

Behind the two way glass in the observation room, Murdoch was already pulling up the hotel's security database on her tablet, cross-referencing the timestamps while McGinty scowled in grim concentration.

'Breakfast at the hotel restaurant, 8:30 AM,' Fraser pressed on relentlessly. 'Receipt, CCTV, waitress remembers Mr Cockburn's complaint about the coffee being cold. Then the taxi to meet Mr James in Charlotte Square – driver's details included, naturally.'

The alibi was watertight. More than watertight – it was professionally constructed with the kind of obsessive detail that suggested either genuine innocence or remarkable preparation.

'It's... um... convenient how everything's documented,' Campbell managed to respond, her usual calm professionalism briefly deflated by the sheer weight of corroborating evidence.

'Convenient?' Cockburn's eyebrows rose disdainfully.

His gaze fixed on each detective in turn with amusement. 'My father taught me that truth is what you can prove, not what you believe. Everything I do, everywhere I go, everyone I meet – it's all recorded, filed, and cross-referenced.'

Campbell flipped through the hotel security stills, noting the timestamps that placed Cockburn in the Hilton's lobby at precisely the time Rowena James was being murdered in her Heriot Row study.

'Your timeline accounts for every hour,' she observed with grudging respect.

'Every minute,' Cockburn corrected smoothly. 'I learned early that details matter, Detective Inspector. When you live as I do, it pays to take frequent... precautions.'

'What do you mean by that, Mr Cockburn?' Balfour asked.

'I mean that wealth attracts accusations, Detective Constable. The more successful you become, the more people wish to take it from you by any means necessary – hence the importance of maintaining comprehensive records.'

He looked slowly around the room once more, dripping with contempt.

'Come now detectives. You must know better than anyone that the law isn't about what people think, or feel, or how they believe things should be – the only thing that matters is what they can prove.'

Cockburn leaned back in his chair, stretching with affected boredom. 'You see, gentlemen, unlike my late sister's husband, I actually plan ahead.

'James stumbled through life expecting others to clean up his messes. I ensure they didn't seep out in the first place.'

Watching on, Murdoch looked up from her tablet with visible reluctance. 'Hotel CCTV confirms his presence throughout the night. Phone location data shows his mobile never left the Caledonian premises. Credit card transactions match his stated timeline perfectly.'

'Of course they do,' McGinty growled, grinding his teeth.

As Cockburn's smile grew wider, the detectives' silence broken only by the hum of obsolete recording equipment, Fraser began returning the documentation to her briefcase with brisk finality. 'I trust this resolves any questions about my client's whereabouts during the relevant period.

'Now, shall we move on – or would you like to take a short break first?'

***

The break lasted exactly 10 minutes – long enough for Campbell to splash cold water on her face and for the team to briefly regroup in the corridor for an urgent whispered consultation about their evaporating case.

When they reconvened, Cockburn was examining his manicured fingernails with the detached interest of someone attending a particularly tedious board meeting, while Fraser consulted her watch with choreographed impatience.

'Let's discuss your household arrangements,' Campbell began, settling back into her chair with renewed focus. 'We understand that Douglas Kemp works as your caretaker?'

'He's a sort of family retainer,' Cockburn replied with casual dismissiveness. 'His parents worked for us for years – mother was housekeeper, father the chauffeur – and then when they died, Rowena bloody insisted we keep him on. So he lives in the old servants' quarters and does a bit of maintenance work around the place.'

'He receives wages for his work?'

'I don't concern myself with the details but I believe disability benefits cover most of his needs. It's charity, really.' His eyes flickered with something that might have been amusement. 'My sister's bleeding heart couldn't bear the thought of turning him out.'

'You mentioned he has disabilities?' Balfour asked, consulting his notes.

'A childhood accident when we were children,' Cockburn replied with a shrug. 'I was the one who found him actually – unconscious and bleeding amongst an avalanche of heavy items in the old family collection room.

'They rushed him into hospital but he suffered brain damage from the head injuries, and has never been quite right since.'

'The room where Kemp was injured,' Balfour probed. 'Is it still in use?'

'The family museum, really. It used to house my Great Grandfather's collection of maritime artefacts but most of that is in storage somewhere now. I suppose it was all very educational, but it was just a pile of rusty junk to me.'

'What was he doing in there?' Campbell asked.

Cockburn smiled. 'Some children wander where they shouldn't be and suffer consequences as a result. Who can tell? Probably fell climbing the shelves, but he told everyone he couldn't remember what happened so I guess nobody will ever really know.'

Unblinking, Cockburn checked his watch ostentatiously before looking up again and gazing at the detectives expectantly.

'Now. Is there anything else you need, or can I go about my day?'

'Just a few more questions please Mr Cockburn,' Campbell continued. 'How was Kemp's relationship with your sister?'

'Rowena was soft on him,' Cockburn responded, his distaste obvious. 'She treated him like an extra brother. Constantly bailing him out of trouble, always gave him advances on his allowance, covering his debts, making excuses for his failures. Pathetic sentimentality.'

His composure flickered with irritation.

'She'd lecture me endlessly about our "duty of care" after his accident, as if a servant's childhood mishap made us responsible for him forever.'

'And on the evening of the murder – you mentioned he was out?' Balfour asked.

'At the bookmakers, naturally, blowing what little he has.' Cockburn's smile was icy.

'Menzies is actually one of my tenants. He rents a unit in my commercial development, and came to me a few months ago to speak about the money Kemp owed him as a result of spending every evening on those moronic machines.'

Campbell leaned forward. 'So that you could pay his debts?'

'So that I could tell him to sort it out by any means necessary,' he scoffed.

'Menzies wanted to talk to me before applying pressure as a professional courtesy. He didn't want any… unpleasantness spoiling the ongoing business relationship.'

Balfour remembered Kemp's reaction when they'd mentioned Menzies during their interview – the way he'd paled when Jojo's accomplices were mentioned – and shuddered inwardly.

'You gave a loan shark permission to intimidate your employee?' Campbell's voice carried an unaccustomed edge.

'I gave a tenant my blessing to collect what he was owed. Menzies runs a respectable operation – just asks for payment with a bit more… enthusiasm than the high street banks.' Cockburn's smile broadened.

'In exchange for his occasional services collecting debts and ensuring my tenants understand their obligations, the colourful Mr Menzies pays reduced rent on his own premises. It's a mutually beneficial arrangement – I get reliable payments, he gets cheap premises – and I was not about to endanger that simply because Douglas hasn't learned the value of fiscal responsibility.'

'You'd profit from his suffering?'

'Only from teaching him about consequences. Kemp needed to understand that actions have results for his own sake. The gambling debts simply provided an educational opportunity, and I understand he became remarkably more motivated after his conversation with Menzies' colleagues.'

'Is it possible Mr Kemp could have nursed a grudge against your sister?' Balfour interjected. 'Perhaps even blamed her for his circumstances?'

The suggestion seemed to genuinely amuse Cockburn, his laughter immediate and unrestrained. 'Little Dougie? Hold a grudge against Rowena? That's hilarious, Detective Constable. As I'm sure I told you before the man worshipped her – followed her around like a devoted spaniel, grateful for every scrap of attention she threw his way.'

His eyes glittered. 'No, if anything, he'd have thrown himself in front of a bus to protect her. The poor fool simply doesn't have the courage or the capacity for violence.'

Campbell closed her folder with deliberate precision. 'Thank you for your cooperation, Mr Cockburn. We may have further questions.'

'Of course,' he replied, rising from his chair with fluid grace. 'I'll be staying in Callander until the house is free of grubby policemen, but you'll find my documentation remains quite comprehensive. Whatever happened to poor Rowena, you'll need to look elsewhere for your culprit.'

Chapter 25

The Cowgate, Edinburgh, 1860

The abandoned cellars beneath the collapsed tenement had revealed nothing beyond an acrid stench, rats, and disappointment.

Emerging from his search empty-handed, brushing dust from his coat as he made his way back through Edinburgh's labyrinthine Old Town, Balfour was plunged into deep thought as he trudged back towards the arranged meeting point near the Lawnmarket.

Several hours had passed since Shaw's contact at The Black Bull had sent them racing through different corners of the city's underworld, each taking one of the three locations where Fox might seek refuge. The warren of derelict buildings and forgotten spaces that honeycombed the area below the Royal Mile had seemed a promising lead, but Fox - if he had ever been there - was long gone.

Gas lamps flickered weakly in the evening mist as Balfour navigated the steep climb back towards respectability, his footsteps echoing upwards.

The close he chose for his ascent was little more than a crack between buildings, so narrow that the upper storeys nearly touched overhead, creating a tunnel of grimy masonry that blocked out most of the remaining daylight. Lit only by the weak light flickering through small windows at irregular intervals, the stink of coal smoke, unwashed bodies, and something indefinably rotten hung heavy in the nighttime air.

It was here, in this desperate urban gulley, that they emerged. Three men stepping out from darkened doorways with unmistakable intent.

The first, a thick-set man with the hunched shoulders of a dock worker and hands like slabs of meat, stood in the path ahead, while behind Balfour two more figures materialised - one tall and lean with the quick movements of a street fighter, the other shorter, but carrying a murderous looking cudgel.

'You're wandering where you're no' welcome, fancy man.'

The thick-set man, his accent betraying a lifetime spent on the harsh edge of the Cowgate's rougher quarters, stepped forward, blocking the narrow passage completely.

'Perhaps I should choose a different route,' Balfour replied, his hand moving smoothly into the pocket of his heavy tweed coat. 'But I suspect that really wouldn't make any difference to you gentlemen now, would it?'

The thick-set man's grin revealed teeth that had seen better decades. 'Nothing personal, ken. Just business.'

For what he'd taken as a random coalition of street thugs, they moved with surprising efficiency, closing the distance from three directions simultaneously. Expressions fixed, weapons drawn, odds very much in their favour.

Arriving in a flash of instinct and repetition, Balfour's military training served him well.

Sidestepping the lead attacker's rush, he delivered a precise blow to the man's solar plexus that sent him staggering backward, gasping for breath.

So far so good. But the narrow confines of the close worked against him, limiting his movement and preventing him from using the space he needed to handle multiple opponents.

The tall man came at him with surprising speed, hands reaching for Balfour's throat, and with a twist of his hips, the detective used the attacker's momentum to spin him crashing into the stone.

Two down. But even as his second opponent leaned dazed against the walls, the third man's cudgel was already swinging in a vicious arc aimed at Balfour's skull.

Only reflexes honed in the chaos of India saved him. He ducked under the blow and heard the wooden club strike the stone close to where his head had been, watching as the thick-set thug recovered from their first exchange and began advancing again, this time with a blade glinting in his fist.

For a moment that stretched like eternity, Balfour found himself pressed back against the wall of the close, facing two armed men in a space barely wider than a coffin, with nowhere to retreat and no room to manoeuvre.

So, reaching into his coat pocket, he withdrew something that appeared to be a heavy black metallic tube, with a crenellated bezel and twin contact points...

The device discharged with a sharp crack that echoed off the stone walls like a pistol shot and the thick-set man convulsed and dropped, his blade skittering across the cobblestones as electrical current seized his muscles, while his companion with the cudgel paused, eyes wide with confusion and sudden fear.

That hesitation cost him. Balfour stepped forward and delivered a precise blow to his wrist that sent the weapon clattering away, followed by an uppercut that lifted the attacker off his feet and deposited him on the cobbles.

Breathing hard, Balfour quickly retrieved the taser and concealed it again, checking the groaning forms sprawled around him. Eyeing his attackers as they recovered, he snatched up the dropped cudgel and backed into a doorway, poised for a second attack.

And then Solomon Shaw arrived, exploding up the winding close like a particularly ugly avenging angel wrapped in a ball of fury.

Pausing only briefly for a quick professional assessment of the scene, Shaw launched himself at the tall attacker who was struggling to regain his feet and delivered his first catastrophic blow.

What followed was not so much a fight as a master class in street violence. Shaw's fists, glinting with brass knuckledusters, found their targets with surgical precision while his boots delivered kicks that sent his opponents rolling across the cobblestones like scattered leaves.

The remaining conscious attackers discovered that whatever reputation they might have enjoyed in Edinburgh's criminal underworld counted for nothing against a man like Shaw, and within moments, all three were reduced to coughing, teeth-spitting, semi-conscious heaps scattered across the close.

Shaw stood over them with grim satisfaction, flexing his knuckles as he surveyed his handiwork. 'Well now,' he said, breathing only slightly harder than usual. 'Your man there seemed to go down a bit quick for a lad his size.'

He gestured toward the thick-set attacker, still twitching slightly from the electrical aftereffects, and his eyes, sparking with intelligence, held a question that Balfour pretended not to notice.

'Perhaps he has a weak constitution,' Balfour suggested mildly, stepping carefully around the evidence of their brief but decisive battle. 'Some men simply lack the stamina for conflict.'

Shaw, shooting him a sharp glance, merely grunted.

***

'They were professional work, those lads,' Shaw observed as they picked their way through the narrow close toward the broader thoroughfare.

'Street ruffians looking to roll a gent for his purse - that's to be expected Mr Balfour. Boys will be boys and all that. But those there were a different calibre of fellow altogether. If I was a wagering man, I'd warrant that they'd been waiting for you in particular.'

The gaslight from the main street cast long shadows between the ancient tenements as they emerged from the cramped passage, crossing the Royal Mile to sweep down into the New Town, Edinburgh's medieval silhouette stark against the cloudless night sky behind them.

Balfour, his strides lengthening as they took the downhill slope, barely acknowledged Shaw's observation, nodding vaguely as he squinted down at the vista before them, still deep in thought.

'Speaking of professional matters,' he said eventually, shaking his head clear of cluttering thoughts. 'I'm guessing that you didn't have any luck finding our quarry either?'

Shaw grinned. 'Aye, well. I was wondering when you'd ask about that.'

'He was nowhere to be found at the first place I tried, but I passed a few coppers around the local bairns, and they soon tracked him down in a doss house off the Canongate, drunk as a lord on somebody else's coin.'

'What did he tell you?' Balfour asked, tipping his hat at a passing couple as he adjusted to the respectable streets of the New Town.

'Nothing at first,' Shaw reminisced with grim satisfaction. 'Your man Fox is a slippery wee bugger, but to be fair he was extremely cooperative once we'd had a private conversation and I explained his situation properly.'

Balfour, reasoning that some details were better unknown, said nothing, and waited for Shaw to continue.

'The way he tells it, he'd been watching Mount Stewart since the Monday morning, waiting for his chance. He saw Crichton working a distant field and knew Miller was sacked, so when the house looked empty, he risked slipping down to the coal cellar.'

Shaw's voice trailed off briefly as he rummaged within the voluminous folds of his disreputable coat, before producing a leather document portfolio with a grim flourish.

'Soon as he got through the cellar, he found this lying on the floor near the door into the house - like someone had dropped it. Fox thought it might be valuable, so he scooped it up.'

'And then?'

'That's when he decided to have a quick look round the kitchen door to see if the coast was clear. Saw the poor lassie's body sprawled there in her own blood.'

Shaw's expression darkened as he considered the scene. 'It near scared him out of his wits. He panicked and scrambled back through the coal cellar like a madman, falling over himself getting out, and then ran like the wind. Didn't stop until he was back on the Old Military Road.'

Balfour leafed through the portfolio, its brass corners gleaming dully in the streetlight. It appeared unremarkable, just Henderson's private correspondence and business papers, but perhaps further examination would bring more to light.

'And did Fox see the killer?'

'He claims he didn't,' said Shaw, 'and I believe him.'

Shaw's eyes glittered with dark knowledge. 'But I keep hearing someone's been asking questions about Fox in the taverns, offering serious coin for information about his whereabouts. The same someone who paid for his release, I'd wager.'

'That would seem to suggest that he knows something worth paying for,' Balfour mused, tucking the portfolio inside his coat as they turned into Heriot Row.

'Aye,' Shaw replied grimly. "Either that or someone thinks he does.'

***

Its polished mahogany and gleaming brass fittings glowing in the comfortable warmth, the drawing room of Balfour's Heriot Row townhouse provided a stark contrast to the violence they'd left behind.

Balfour winced as Young examined the cuts across his knuckles by the light of a crystal oil lamp.

'Hold still, you stubborn fool,' his friend scolded with easy familiarity, dabbing at the wounds with practised efficiency. 'These are clean breaks and you'll heal quickly enough, although by all accounts we're fortunate - that was a closer call than I'd like.'

As he worked, Young's trained eye catalogued the fresh damage with professional concern, noting how Balfour had instinctively protected himself with the defensive techniques they'd both learned in the heat of a toxic colonial war.

'I'll take Shaw's word as gospel that these weren't common street thieves, Balfour. The way they moved, their coordination - this was something else.'

'I found nothing but rats and rotting barrels, whilst you were fighting for your life. We really should have stayed close and searched together - three men would have made those thugs think twice about an ambush.'

Young applied a clean bandage with steady hands and gazed into the middle distance as recollection called.

'Takes me back to that night outside Lucknow. Do you remember? When we walked into that ambush.'

'At least tonight we both walked away,' Balfour replied, flexing his bandaged fingers. 'Unlike Havildar Singh.'

'Aye, God rest him.' Young's expression grew sombre as they recalled an evil night in another time, a long way away. 'Though I notice you've still got the same reflexes that kept us alive then. Some habits die hard, don't they old friend?'

Young poured two generous measures of whisky, handing one to his friend as he recalled the blistering hot summer of 1857.

'You pulled the same trick at Cawnpore - waited until they thought they had you cornered, then turned the tables completely. To this day I'd swear it - it was like you had the advantage all along. By God man. I'll never forget their faces as they ran that day.'

Balfour accepted the glass with a slight smile. 'Experience teaches a man to use whatever tools come to hand.'

'Indeed it does. And speaking of experience...' Young settled back in his chair, idly flicking through the portfolio. 'You've always had a knack for finding the truth in impossible situations. That business with the forged contracts in Perth last year, the Aberfoyle poisoning case - you see patterns others miss, Balfour, and you'll see through this one too.'

Balfour shrugged as he held his glass up to the light, watching the beams catch in its fiery depths. 'Sometimes I wonder if we're simply good at spotting lies because we've lived with so many of our own.'

'Speak for yourself,' Young replied with dry humour. 'My lies are purely to either preserve others' feelings or from professional necessity.'

Piercing his melancholy, Balfour's smile lit up as he regarded Young with warmth. 'You know what John? I'd stake everything I have to wager that is absolutely true. You're too decent for the world we walk in.'

Reaching out and taking the portfolio from his friend's hand, Balfour placed it on the table top and flicked open the cover.

'If what Fox says is true, it seems likely that whoever dropped it was either Janet Henderson, or her killer.'

Young joined him at the table, noting the neat bundles of documents tied with ribbon. 'Henderson's private papers, by the look of it. Just business correspondence and financial records I imagine.'

'Any cash that was in here would already have been poured down Fox's throat,' Balfour mused, 'but it certainly doesn't look like anything worth dying for.'

'I suppose few things ever do.'

He selected the first bundle of papers, pausing briefly as he untangled the ribbon. 'Although sometimes John - I honestly believe we're just playing parts in stories that were written long before we arrived.'

'Philosophical tonight, aren't we old chap?' Young observed, his tone gentle. 'Is that the whisky talking?'

'Perhaps.' Balfour grinned, spreading the first few documents across the table between them. 'But either way, it seems that someone has at least taken notice of our narrative.'

Chapter 26

MIT-13 Office, Edinburgh, 2025

'It's never just about the final act. Every narrative is built entirely on the chapters that came before it.'

Stretching in his chair, Balfour blinked under the flickering light and suppressed a yawn. It had seemed like a good idea when he'd first suggested to Murdoch that they'd delved further back into the CCTV archives to flush out any clues about Rowena James' death in the days and weeks running up to her murder. Now, at 2:30am in a cold and empty incident room, not so much.

Balfour rubbed his eyes and leaned back in his chair, feeling the familiar ache between his shoulder blades that came from hours hunched over computer screens, watching endless loops of surveillance footage blurring into a monotonous parade of empty corridors and unremarkable comings and goings.

Beside him, Murdoch was systematically working through another stack of CCTV files, black lines under her eyes as she methodically catalogued timestamps and cross-referenced them against the timeline they'd been building for weeks leading up to Rowena James's killing

She glanced up from her screen, where frame after frame of the street entrance flickered past in fast-forward motion. 'I know Munro thinks it's a waste of time and resources - that we should concentrate on the financial aspects. But you're right - we've been so focused on the day itself that we've ignored the story that was building for months beforehand.'

She paused the footage and rubbed her temples. In the wee small hours, the incident room possessed a peculiar quality of suspended reality, where the fluorescent strip lighting cast everything in harsh, unforgiving detail while the world beyond slept peacefully in its bed.

'Christ,' she said suddenly, her frustration showing. 'This whole place is mental, isn't it? Nobody talks about anything that matters.'

She gestured at the empty chairs around them. 'What was that about the other day? I mean, a DS basically threatens a DCI and that's it - nothing more said?'

A pause. The whiteboard still bore Munro's confident notes on his hired killer theory, but the enthusiasm that had driven those theories had dissipated rapidly after a day that had seen the entire team fruitlessly combing the city for any suggestion that Gavin James had hired a professional to dispatch his wealthy wife.

'Anyway… McGinty's sources came back with nothing on the hired killer angle,' Murdoch observed, glancing at the stack of witness statements dumped on the side of her desk earlier that afternoon. 'He's unearthed a laundry list of prostitutes and rent boys who know Cockburn only too well, but no one's heard a whisper about any professional hits.'

'They're all too wrapped up in the Bowes-Carrick feud,' responded Balfour, referring to the escalating conflict between two rival crime clans that had enveloped central Scotland in an explosion of arson attacks, assaults and contract killings in recent months.

'The entire underworld is watching its back right now and the usual suspects are either in hiding or dead. If someone tried to hire someone… or even attempted to import talent for the job, they'd be red hot.'

And so they ploughed on.

The process was mind-numbing in its repetitive tedium, hour after hour of watching identical camera angles playing back the mundane details of life at 22 Heriot Row - delivery vans arriving with groceries, postmen making their rounds, Kemp intermittently flitting in and out of shot to empty bins or tend to some minor matter of maintenance. Most of the footage revealed nothing more significant than the changing weather.

'There,' Murdoch said suddenly, her finger hovering over the pause button as a familiar white transit van appeared in the corner of the frame. 'That's the third time in a week I've spotted that registration. Same van we saw on Heriot Row the day of the murder, same one that's been flagged in connection with the betting shop robberies.'

Balfour, shaking off his drowsiness, studied the timestamp. 'Two weeks before the murder. And look there -' He pointed to two figures leaving the van and descending the steps to the basement flat. Even at the grainy distance offered by the city's street-level footage, Big Eddie Wallace and Tam Ferguson were unmistakable.

'So… it looks Wallace and Ferguson have been visiting Kemp's flat regularly,' Murdoch observed, jotting down notes. She scrolled back through the footage, marking timestamps where the white van appeared. 'Always during specific time windows - mid afternoon when the main house would be quiet, never staying longer than 20 minutes

Fingers flying across the keyboard, she expertly captured stills of each arrival and departure, always featuring the two thugs, sometimes carrying something bundled under their arms, and on one solitary shot, an indistinct view of Kemp's face staring up at their retreating backs.

It was hard to tell at that distance, but he looked terrified.

***

The staccato rap on the incident room door came just after half past seven, jolting Balfour from the semiconscious state he'd drifted into and causing Murdoch, asleep face down on her desk, to jolt suddenly awake and sit up with a start.

Dr Randolph Cliff stood in the doorway, looking uncharacteristically benign as the sounds of the morning shift beginning to trickle in resonated up through the lonely corridor behind him.

'Good morning Mr Balfour. I hope I'm not interrupting anything crucial,' the pathologist smiled. 'I was on my way in for an early post-mortem and thought I might catch you before the circus starts.'

Murdoch, untangling the post-it note that had somehow got entwined in her tangled hair, looked up surprised. Forget the six months working in MIT-13, since her first posting to CID she'd never known Cliff to make personal visits to an incident room - the chief pathologist typically summoned detectives to his domain in the Cowgate mortuary for exposition, not the other way around.

'Dr Cliff,' Balfour said, standing and hastily clearing files from a nearby chair. 'What can we do for you?'

'Actually, it's more what I might be able to do for you.' Cliff approached their workstation, his eyes inevitably drawn to the CCTV footage still playing on Murdoch's monitor. 'I've received the results back from the lab and I've got a partial update on your murder weapon.'

Murdoch paused the footage she'd left running on her monitor when exhaustion had finally won her over, but not before Cliff caught a glimpse of the sequence they'd been reviewing. Eyes narrowed, he immediately focused on the figure in the middle of the screen - Douglas Kemp, moving with his characteristic unsteady gait.

'Good lord,' he said quietly, leaning closer to study the frozen frame. 'Has he been in a car crash?'

'That's the caretaker from our murder scene,' Balfour responded. 'And not that I know of. As I understand it he's had a long-standing disability since childhood.'

Cliff's expression shifted from casual interest to professional focus as he watched Kemp's posture and movement patterns. 'May I?' He gestured toward Murdoch's chair.

She moved aside, allowing the pathologist to scroll through several sequences showing Kemp's comings and goings. Cliff watched with the focused attention of someone trained to read the story that bodies tell, his brow furrowing as he observed Kemp's uneven gait, the way he favoured his left side, the subtle protective positioning of his shoulders.

'Fascinating,' Cliff murmured, pausing on a particularly clear shot of Kemp ascending the basement steps. 'That man moves like someone carrying multiple injuries. Chronic damage, by the look of it.

'See how he compensates for weakness in his left leg? And there - the way he holds his head suggests possible hearing loss or balance issues on that side.'

Murdoch shook her head. 'You can tell all that from CCTV footage?'

'Thirty years of forensic pathology teaches you to read bodies like books,' Cliff replied. 'The human body never lies - even years after the fact. Clearly this man has sustained significant head injuries at some point - probably as a child, given the compensatory patterns that have developed.'

Balfour exchanged glances with Murdoch. 'Cockburn mentioned in his interview that Kemp had been injured in a childhood accident. Some sort of fall in the family museum.'

'A fall?' Cliff's tone sharpened as he studied the footage again. 'I'd be very curious to see the medical records from that incident. His movement patterns scream trauma consistent with multiple impact injuries - not the sort of thing you'd expect from a single fall.'

The pathologist sat back in the chair, his expression thoughtful. 'Which brings me to the actual reason for my visit. The lab have sent through the additional test results I requested on the trace evidence from Rowena James's wounds.'

He reached into his jacket pocket and withdrew a manila envelope, extracting several photographs of microscopic analysis results. 'The murder weapon was definitely something heavy and spherical - I'd estimate at least fifteen to twenty pounds, with a rough, pitted surface. The injury patterns are quite distinctive.'

Balfour studied the enhanced images. 'Any idea what could cause that sort of damage?'

'Something round, cast iron, and roughly six to eight inches in diameter? To me it suggests that you're looking for a cannonball, however bizarre that seems,' said Cliff with a shrug. 'Certainly the surface pitting and rust traces would be consistent with something like that.'

Balfour made a note about the weapon description, his expression briefly perplexed. 'A cannonball. Well, I suppose we did ask...'

'I'm sure that doesn't feel like it helps at the moment, but the forensic evidence doesn't lie,' Cliff said, standing to leave.

'Whatever was used to kill her, it was heavy, spherical and old. The rust analysis suggests significant age - decades at minimum, possibly much longer, but we couldn't tell in greater detail without hiring an archaeometallurgist.

'And if you decide to submit a budget request for that, I'd very much like to be at the meeting when Munro hears about it.'

He paused at the door, his expression uncharacteristically serious. 'Seriously though, be careful with this one. I've seen enough victims of long-term abuse to recognise the signs, and I'd bet my last pound on that man carrying more than just physical scars. Whatever happened to him as a child, the damage will go well beyond anything you can see.'

As Cliff's footsteps faded down the corridor, Balfour sat in contemplative silence, surrounded by evidence and a growing feeling that the investigation was about to take a very different direction from the one Munro had been pursuing so desperately.

'We need to talk to Kemp again,' he said finally. 'But this time, we ask the right questions.'

***

Balfour had suggested they conduct the interview in Kemp's basement flat rather than at the station, recognising that the caretaker would be far more relaxed in familiar surroundings and an informal context.

The sitting room was small, tidy, and judging by the decades-old furniture and personal touches, had been last decorated by his mother. From the figurines arranged carefully on the cast iron mantelpiece to the ancient small television and the well-thumbed paperback novels stacked on the alcove shelves, it hinted at a time, many years ago, when Douglas had been a happy little boy.

'We're not here to cause you any trouble, Douglas,' Balfour said from his position on the small sofa, while Murdoch sat nearby with her notebook. They'd decided against formal recording equipment, hoping the more casual approach would encourage honesty. 'We just need to understand a few things better about those visitors you had. Is that alright?'

Kemp nodded from his familiar armchair, noticeably more relaxed than he'd been during their previous encounters.

'Good. Now, we've been looking at the CCTV footage from the weeks before Mrs James died, and we noticed you had some visitors at your flat. Two men in a white van - Eddie

Wallace and Tam Ferguson. Do you remember them coming to see you?'

The change was immediate and startling. Kemp's already pale complexion turned ashen, and a tremor ran through his hands as he goggled back at Balfour.

'I... I don't...' he stammered, his voice barely above a whisper. 'They said I wasn't supposed to talk about them coming round.'

'They can't hurt you here, Douglas,' Murdoch said softly. 'You're safe. We just need to know what they wanted.'

Kemp's eyes darted between the two detectives, his internal struggle playing out visibly. 'They said... they said I owed them money. From the machines at Jojo's.'

'How much did they say you owed?' Balfour asked.

'Lots. I couldn't understand it all - the numbers got confused in my head.' Kemp's voice cracked with the effort of remembering. 'But Eddie said it was alright. He said I could give them things from the house that nobody would miss.'

'What sort of things?' Murdoch asked gently.

'Silver photo frames from the drawing room. Some of Mrs James's old jewellery. Vases and things from the big storage room downstairs.' Kemp's distress was evident as he continued.

'They said it wasn't really stealing because the family wouldn't notice. They said I was just paying off what I owed fair and square and that's a good thing.

He sniffed, childlike. 'And they said if I was a good pal, they'd let me come and play in the big room.'

Balfour's attention sharpened. 'What big room?'

'At Jojo's. There's a room upstairs where the men all go - not just the fruit machines downstairs. They play card games with lots of money and have special machines. Eddie and Tam bring the things in their van so they can say I'm allowed to go too.'

'And what did they say would happen if you didn't give them things Douglas?'

For the first time since they'd arrived, Kemp relaxed, and looked back at them unblinkingly as he responded in a clear, calm voice.

'They said they'd hurt me. Really bad.'

Balfour, exchanging glances with Murdoch, switched tack.

'Douglas… Mr Cockburn said that when you were a boy, something happened in the big house and you were hurt.'

Kemp's gaze dropped to his lap, shoulders curling in. 'I wasn't supposed to be in the big room, but Mr George said it was the best hiding place and no one would find me.'

Murdoch, her eyes directly holding his, patted his knee encouragingly. 'What kind of room was it?'

'The one with the ships and the shelves all the way up.' His words faltered, and he shook his head violently. 'I wasn't meant to climb but he got angry and said I had to go up. And I don't remember but something fell, and then I was lying on the ground and Mr George said the chain thing had hit me on the head.'

Balfour glanced at Murdoch before asking gently, 'And what did George do then?'

Kemp's eyes glazed as he struggled to remember. 'He watched me. There was shouting and people running up and down the stairs, but he stayed and watched.'

The detectives let the silence breathe for a moment until Murdoch, her voice quiet but steady, pressed gently forward. "And after, how did he treat you?"

Kemp's expression shifted, a strange smile pulling at his mouth. 'Brought sweets. Toys. Nice things. He says I'm broken, so he has to keep me safe. I can't do money or things like that, so he decides for me.'

He swallowed hard. 'Sometimes… sometimes he gets angry. If I forget things. Or do them wrong. Then he has to show me what happens if you are bad and you don't listen, but that's all my fault.'

Balfour felt a chill settle in his gut. 'Thank you for being so honest with us, Douglas. You've been very helpful.'

As they prepared to leave, Kemp looked up with an expression of genuine confusion. 'Am I in trouble? For taking those things? They said it was the same as paying money.'

'No, you're not in trouble for any of that Douglas,' Balfour assured him, a determined set to his jaw. 'But I know some people who are.'

Chapter 27

Heriot Row, Edinburgh, 1860

Stretching in a long line from the mahogany table to the opposite wall, the contents of Henderson's recovered portfolio trailed across Balfour's drawing room, lengths of string pilfered from the basement butler's pantry looping through a forest of decanters and furniture to link significant documents as the parade of paperwork marched beneath the gas light.

The familiar weight of revelation settling upon his shoulders, Balfour scrutinised the spread before him in silence as an early spring gale rattled at the windows. Even ensconced within the sanctuary his townhouse had become, its fire burning low in the grate and two glasses of whisky forgotten beside the stacks of correspondence, an uncomfortable suspicion was beginning to play in the outer recesses of his mind.

'These aren't the routine farm records I was expecting,' Young observed, exhausted from hours of combing carefully through the documentation. 'Railway company certificates, investment correspondence, letters from concerned parties...' He trailed off, examining the elaborate seals and expensive paper stock with growing interest.

Balfour selected a particularly thick certificate bearing an elaborate seal, its expensive paper stock and formal engraving screaming respectability and financial stability.

'Royal Mauritanian Railway Company,' he read aloud, his voice carrying the same tone he might use to identify a particularly virulent disease. 'Promising exceptional returns through the development of mining operations and transportation infrastructure in the African colonies —

operations that would require immediate capital investment from Scottish gentlemen seeking profitable ventures in expanding imperial territories'.

'Railway speculation', Young murmured grimly, recognising the pattern even as his friend continued examining the growing collection of similar certificates. 'I won't deny that many have made their fortunes from these colonial companies, Balfour, but it can be the devil's own job to sort the wheat from the chaff.

'After the crisis of 1857, a good half of these supposedly solid investment opportunities proved to be nothing more than elaborate confidence schemes designed to separate gullible investors from what remained of their capital.'

Running his finger along the formal letterhead of an Edinburgh investment house, Balfour's contemplative scowl deepened as yet another inconsistency emerged from the piles before them.

The dates on various correspondence didn't align properly with the supposed development timeline, several of the referenced mining concessions appeared to overlap in impossible ways, and most tellingly, the promised quarterly reports to investors seemed to have been delayed indefinitely while the Royal Mauritanian Railway Company continued to solicit additional capital from new sources.

He would need to wait until he was alone to conduct his final research, but the conclusion he could feel gnawing at the back of his brain was beginning to feel inevitable.

'Look at these letters from investors,' Young said as he held several pages up to the lamplight. 'Widows seeking safe harbour for their late husbands' savings, retired military officers looking to supplement their pensions and country parsons hoping to provide better futures for their children — Henderson seems to have awoken great hope amongst some of the more… financially vulnerable members of polite society.'

Balfour examined a letter dated eighteen months earlier, noting how the correspondent expressed complete confidence in the venture based on 'Miss Henderson's personal assurance of her brother's integrity and business acumen', and felt the familiar cold anger clutch him in its grip once more.

Janet Henderson's reputation for moral rectitude and careful household management had clearly been exploited as validation for her brother's enterprise, her good name serving as collateral for investments that, at best, represented a significant gamble for anyone involved.

'The scale of this operation is remarkable,' he said quietly, spreading out correspondence that showed enquiries from potential investors across Scotland and Northern England. 'How could even a well-to-do farmer create an entire financial architecture like this? Running a prosperous farm in the Trossachs is one thing, but building a railway across the Sahara? That's a different kettle of fish altogether.'

Young poured himself another measure of whisky, his hands steady as the full implications of what they were reading began to settle. 'It's even more unlikely than that, old chap. If these documents are to be relied upon, Henderson lost almost the entirety of his family's assets in the crash of '57, and yet seems to have recovered within a matter of months.

'Certainly, the Henderson household maintained an expensive lifestyle throughout,' Balfour muttered, skimming through the proffered household accounts. 'No ordinary investor was making substantial profits during those years, but somehow Henderson continued to afford servants, fine clothing, quality horses, and all the trappings of a successful gentleman farmer.'

Noting a curious architectural symbol - a five pointed star - embossed faintly in the corner of several letterheads, Balfour turned his attention back to the correspondence.

'We've been told that Janet managed every aspect of her brother's domestic affairs, and yet... I wonder how much she knew - or what she thought of such high-stakes endeavours.'

For a moment, the parlour fell silent except for the soft ticking of the mantel clock and the occasional dying crackle from the fire.

'Whatever the conclusion, our friend Henderson has questions to answer', Balfour said finally. 'These discrepancies won't explain themselves.'

'Agreed,' Young replied. 'Though I suspect we'll need to move carefully. Henderson has too many friends for my liking.'

Nodding thoughtfully, Balfour began to gather the scattered papers with methodical precision as the embers settled lower in the grate.

'We'll take the first train back to Callander tomorrow.'

***

Shaw's carriage clattered up through the cobbled streets of the New Town as the first pale light of dawn struggled through Edinburgh's perpetual shroud of coal smoke, the familiar rhythm of iron-shod wheels against stone providing counterpoint to the rumble of activity emanating from the direction of the train Station.

'You'll be wanting third class, I imagine?' Shaw enquired, poker-faced, as they approached the terminus, his tone carrying the same gruff courtesy as always, though Balfour noticed the man's eyes lingered a fraction longer on their faces than was entirely necessary.

Shaw's features retained their usual scowling impassiveness as he helped them down from the carriage, but Balfour could have sworn that something had shifted in his manner - a quality of attention that suggested the events of the previous evening had sparked more than passing interest in them both.

The great iron and glass cathedral of the railway terminus swallowed them in clouds of steam and the organised chaos of morning departures, porters weaving between mountains of luggage whilst passengers clutched their tickets and peered anxiously at the departure boards through the haze.

'Stirling service, platform four,' the booking clerk announced without looking up from his ledger. 'Departing in twenty minutes, gentlemen. Change there for the Doune line, but mind the express from Glasgow - she comes through fast.'

As they made their way toward the platform, a stocky figure in working clothes emerged from behind a stack of mail bags, breaking into a wide grin of recognition as he spotted Shaw.

'Cousin Solomon!' The man's voice carried the same Highland cadence as Shaw's, though roughened by years of city work. 'Ready to return my pair then? How did they serve you?'

Shaw nodded, leading him toward where the horses and carriage waited beyond the station entrance. 'Well enough, Hamish. Fine beasts.' He counted out coins from his purse, pressing them into his cousin's calloused palm. 'Fair payment for the hire.'

'Much obliged,' Hamish replied, pocketing the coins whilst taking the reins of his animals. 'Though I had grim news about that Jon Fox fellow you were asking after. He was found beaten to death in Arthur Place this morning.'

Young's hand paused halfway to his ticket pocket, but Shaw remained carefully impassive.

'When did this happen?'

'Early hours, by the look of it', Hamish shrugged. 'The polis had me cart the body to the mortuary. He took a real beating, though the footpads who handed him out must have been disturbed in their work - the fools left his purse behind.'

As the carter chuckled darkly and led his horses away toward the street, Shaw shook his head slowly at his two companions.

'Unfortunate timing,' he observed quietly, his eyes fixed on the departing figure. 'A man tells his story one day, meets his end the next.'

Young purchased first-class tickets whilst Shaw - refusing all entreaties to join them - secured himself a place in third class, noting that although the premium carriage did offer certain comforts, there was a lot more life to be found in the cheap seats.

Propelled by clouds of steam and the acrid smell of coal smoke, the journey north unfolded through Scotland's industrial heartland before giving way to gentler countryside, the train's rhythm changing as they passed the belching smokestacks of the Carron Ironworks near Falkirk, then climbed toward Stirling - where the ancient castle commanded its rocky crag unmoved by the centuries.

From Stirling they transferred to the newer Dunblane line, the single-track railway that wound along the banks of the River Teith through increasingly wild country, past stone villages and patches of woodland to where the first hints of Highland grandeur began to assert themselves against the softer Lowland landscape.

'Unfortunate business about Fox,' Balfour remarked as they approached Callander's modest terminus, his tone betraying the regret he felt for any man's violent end.

'These things happen in the criminal classes, I'm afraid', Young replied absently, gathering his travelling case as the train began to slow.

'They certainly seem to', Balfour agreed simply, and said nothing more on the matter.

The single platform at Callander stretched before them as the train wheezed to a halt, its wooden buildings and modest facilities welcoming them to a community that served as both terminus and threshold - the last outpost of civilisation before the true Highlands began.

***

Shaw's carriage wound through the familiar countryside toward Mount Stewart as the afternoon light cast long shadows across the fields, the rhythmic clip of hooves on the hard-packed road providing a steady beat as they made their way towards the erstwhile murder scene.

Henderson's farmhouse appeared much as it had during their first visit, its whitewashed walls and slate roof speaking of prosperity and respectability. Although to Balfour's eye the building seemed to have lost its air of domestic comfort - as if it had been scrubbed away by the skivvy sent to clean the house before Henderson's recent return.

Henderson received them in his parlour with careful courtesy, appearing much recovered from his initial grief as he gestured toward the chairs neatly arranged around the fireplace.

'Gentlemen,' he began, his voice betraying nothing of what had gone so recently before. 'I trust your visit to Edinburgh proved fruitful? I must confess I'm not entirely certain why you felt it necessary to pursue matters so far from Callander, but I'm sure you know your business.

'Are you here to witness my formal statement regarding Crichton's guilt?'

Ignoring the question, Balfour settled himself in a chair whilst Young remained standing, the Procurator Fiscal's attention focused on removing a pile of documents from the leather satchel he'd carried inside.

'It was rather a productive trip actually,' Young began, withdrawing several of the railway certificates with a flourish.

'During which we recovered some documents that seem to have been taken from your home.'

Henderson's eyes flicked toward the pile with a speed that betrayed a flash of recognition, but his expression remained neutral as he leaned forward to examine the stack deposited with a thump on the parlour table.

'I'm not certain I understand Mr Young. These appear to be legitimate investment certificates - railway development in the African colonies, I believe? Janet took a keen interest in such ventures, certainly, though I confess the details were rather beyond my simple farming ways.'

'Were they indeed?' Balfour interjected, selecting one of the more recent certificates and holding it up to catch the afternoon light. 'Because the correspondence we discovered suggests that these particular investments required your rather more active involvement than debenture schemes typically demand.'

The silence that followed stretched on uncomfortably as Henderson stared at the recovered documents.

'I'm afraid I don't follow,' he said finally, though his voice had acquired a quality that suggested he understood the implication all too well. 'If Janet involved herself in correspondence regarding these investments, she did so without consulting me.

'As you know, she managed most of our household's financial affairs.'

Young opened the satchel wider, revealing the full extent of their recovered evidence. 'Mr Henderson, we have here correspondence dating back three years, detailing systematic solicitation of investment from households across Scotland - all of it conducted using your sister's reputation as validation for the venture's legitimacy.'

Henderson's hand moved instinctively toward his throat, a gesture so brief it might have been missed by less observant men.

'You must understand that poor Janet was... enthusiastic about these colonial opportunities. If she represented the investments in terms that proved overly optimistic, I fear that was simply her nature. She always believed the best of people and their ventures.'

'Including ventures that promised exceptional returns from railways that were never built?' Balfour asked. 'Operations that required constant fresh capital whilst apparently producing no tangible results for their investors?'

Henderson rose from his chair and moved toward the window overlooking his well-tended fields, keeping his back firmly to the assembled company.

'Gentlemen, I think you may have misunderstood the nature of these colonial enterprises. I am only a farmer, but I understand such ventures require patience and substantial initial investment before they begin to show returns.

The investors who committed their funds will have almost certainly done so with full understanding of the risks involved.'

'Did they?' Young's voice carried the cold precision of the courtroom now. 'Because the letters we recovered suggest they committed their funds based on assurances of your integrity and business acumen.'

Henderson turned from the window, his face haggard.

'After the crash of '57, we lost everything,' he said quietly, his voice barely above a whisper. 'The house, the farm, Janet's future - all of it would have been gone in a matter of months. I... she had to find a way to rebuild what we'd lost, to provide the security we deserved.'

'By separating innocent people from their savings?' Balfour's voice remained level.

'By creating opportunities that may still well succeed,' Henderson replied, some of his haughty spirit returning. 'I understand that in such businesses it is often simply a matter of raising sufficient capital to make the ventures viable.'

Balfour paused to examine one of the certificates speculatively, his finger tracing the elaborate letterhead. 'Many of these documents bear a common hallmark - a five-pointed star - that appears on correspondence from several different investment houses across Scotland.'

Henderson's face went very still.

'And the handwriting on these solicitation letters,' Young intoned, spreading several pages across the table between them. 'A remarkably consistent and manly hand for correspondence supposedly originating from your sister and multiple other sources, wouldn't you say?'

The silence stretched between them as Henderson stared, unblinking, at the evidence laid out before him.

Young closed the satchel with deliberate finality. 'Mr Henderson, we shall need to examine your financial records more thoroughly. These are serious allegations that require proper investigation through the appropriate legal channels.'

Henderson sank back into his chair, the fight seemingly gone out of him.

'You couldn't possibly understand the pressures,' he said finally. 'The expectations of maintaining the family's position, our standing in the community. Janet deserved better than poverty and disgrace.'

'Yes she did,' Balfour observed grimly, his gaze unblinking.

Henderson looked up at them both, offering the investigators the momentary impression of a cornered animal. 'And what of the investigation into Janet's death? Surely that takes precedence over these... supposed financial irregularities?'

Young gathered his papers with methodical calm. 'We shall be in touch regarding both matters, Mr Henderson.
'You should expect our visit soon.'

Chapter 28

Muirhouse Industrial Estate, Edinburgh, 2025

The door didn't so much crash inward as leap clean off its hinges, McGinty's bulk hitting it like a bull on amphetamines whilst armed officers poured through the breach.

After all the planning, the tactical weapons briefings, the risk assessments and the heart-pumping adrenaline production as the team prepared to go over the top, resistance was notable by its absence and the gaff was practically empty.

Well, not entirely empty.

Fifteen minutes earlier, a fleet of armed response vehicles, unmarked police cars and forensic vans had slipped into the uninspiring commercial development. Beneath a sky that promised rain without delivering it, they'd surrounded Unit 47B with choreographed efficiency of professionals who'd done this dance countless times before.

McGinty had crouched behind the lead vehicle, radio in one hand, his face set in the grim expression of someone preparing for the kind of confrontation that usually ended with hospitalisations and a paperwork trail that would follow you for years. While armed response units flanked the target building, poised and ready for action, uniformed constables sealed off the distant perimeter to keep innocent civilians at bay.

'Right, listen up!' Although trying to keep it low, McGinty's voice carried all the authority of someone who'd kicked down more doors than he cared to remember.

'No heroics, no cock-ups, and absolutely no fucking about. Intelligence suggests professional equipment, possible armed resistance, and a bunch of bastards that have been running circles around us for months. So we go in hard, we go in fast, and we come out with everything that isn't nailed down,' he hissed.

'Everybody got that? Good. Now. On my mark… three… two… one…'

And now here they were, the assembled might of Police Scotland's finest staring at a unit whose door had been unlocked the entire time, its contents laid out with deliberate care, as if someone had been expecting visitors and had thoughtfully prepared for their arrival.

Two men stood with their hands raised in the classic position. A pair of experienced bams who knew the drill, their expressions carrying the resignation of people who'd been caught red-handed and weren't particularly surprised about it - Eddie Wallace and Tam Ferguson.

'Right then,' McGinty observed, surveying the scene whilst tactical officers lowered their weapons with expressions of profound disappointment, 'that was fucking underwhelming.'

The interior revealing itself in the harsh glare of portable lighting was a professional criminal's wet dream. Electronic jamming devices sat in neat rows along makeshift shelving, their sleek black casings marked with Cyrillic characters and technical specifications, while modified tasers occupied their own section, tactical housings stripped and rebuilt with contact points that would drop a grown man in seconds.

Professional surveillance equipment, signal intercept devices, and what appeared to be military-grade night vision goggles completed the inventory of a criminal operation that had moved well beyond opportunistic theft into something approaching paramilitary efficiency.

'Christ almighty,' muttered one of the tactical officers, holstering his weapon as he stared at the array of professional criminal tools. 'This lot could take down half the city's security systems.'

Balfour, stepping forward as uniformed constables moved in to secure the prisoners, took in the scene with a sweeping glance.

'Eddie Wallace, Tam Ferguson, you're both under arrest on suspicion of robbery, conspiracy to commit robbery, and possession of prohibited weapons. You do not have to say anything, but it may harm your defence if you do not mention when questioned something which you later rely on in court.'

'Aye,' added McGinty. 'And it's also likely I'll knock your fucking teeth out, so don't piss us about.'

They began systematically cataloguing each item, mentally calculating a shopping list of prison sentences and connecting dots between the equipment and the pattern of betting shop robberies that had been plaguing the city. The dramatic entry might have been an anticlimax, but the evidential horde went far beyond anything they'd anticipated.

McGinty's mobile buzzed.

'This is Campbell,' came the voice from the phone's speaker, tinged with frustration. 'Our search of the betting shop has yielded minimal results. Just standard gambling operation stuff - cash tills, odds computers, paperwork. The CCTV might reveal more, but Menzies is in custody and he's bloody furious.'

'Och, is the poor wee darling not happy?' McGinty grinned, winking at Balfour as they watched the scene of crime techs begin to load the evidence into vans. 'Wondering how you can do this to such an upstanding member of society?'

'Something like that. Keeps mentioning how he pays his taxes and contributes to the community - as if we don't. 'Campbell's voice sounded weary. 'He seems to think that buys him protection and keeps asking when his lawyer's arriving, like he's been expecting this.'

Balfour surveyed the organised array of criminal tools surrounding him, each piece representing months of planning and significant financial investment. A criminal enterprise -

operating with quality equipment and systematic methodology - wrapped up neatly and tied with a bow marked "Exhibit A".

'Well, he can expect his lawyer all he wants,' he replied, lifting a particularly sophisticated electronic device that looked like it belonged in a spy thriller. 'Because what we've got here is enough to send them down for a decade.'

***

If the custody suite at Fettes Avenue possessed all the charm of a Victorian workhouse rebuilt by blind accountants, Big Eddie Wallace did nothing to improve its ambience.

Handcuffed to the metal table with the resigned expression of a man who'd played this game before and knew exactly how it ended, he seemed almost at home in the sickly atmosphere of its medicine-yellow walls and fluorescent lighting. Apparently unintimidated by McGinty's baleful glare, he winked at the young solicitor by his side as the DS spread a phalanx of evidence out before him.

'Right then, Eddie,' McGinty smiled, consulting his notes. 'Let's start with the easy bit. Your prints are all over that gear we found in the lock-up. The modified tasers, the electronic jammers, the surveillance equipment - everything.'

'Care to explain how that happened?'

Wallace studied the evidence photographs spread across the table, his expression transparently calculating as he processed the overwhelming case against him. 'Aye, well. You've got us cold, haven't you?'

'Aye, we have. Six robberies, professional equipment, CCTV footage, forensic evidence. You're looking at ten to fifteen years unless you start helping yourself.'

'What kind of deal are we talking about?' Wallace leaned forward, bravado evaporating as reality set in. 'Full confession, guilty plea, what's that worth?'

'Depends what you give us. But it's the difference between a decade inside and getting out while you can still remember what the missus looks like.'

Glancing at his brief, Wallace nodded slowly. 'Right... fair game, chief. Yeah, we did the robberies. Me, Tam, the whole thing. Planned it, did it, spent it, the works.'

'Good start. Now tell me about Jojo Menzies.'

The shutters came down immediately, Wallace's smile hardening.

'Mr Menzies just employs us as casual doormen for busy nights. He's got nothing to do with this.'

McGinty raised an eyebrow. 'Eddie, son, are you forgetting we found all this gear in his lock-up?'

'Nah. We've been subletting storage space from him, that's all. He hasn't set foot in the place for years. Jojo never had a clue what we were storing there.'

In the adjacent interview room, where Balfour was simultaneously facing Tam Ferguson across an identical metal table, an uncannily similar scene was playing out.

'So what you're saying, Tam, is that you planned and executed all six robberies together, taking full responsibility for the operation,' he said, his tone conversational rather than confrontational. 'And that in return for a reduced sentence, you'll give us a full confession and a guilty plea. Is that right?'

'Right. Yeah, that's... that's accurate.' Ferguson slumped back in his chair. 'We did it all ourselves. Our planning, our gear, our operation.'

'And what was Jojo Menzies' involvement?'

Ferguson's response was immediate, defensive, and clearly rehearsed. 'Jojo's got nothing to do with any of this. He just runs the betting shop, which is a legitimate business, and we rented storage space from him. He was unaware of our intentions.'

Balfour shook his head. 'So you're telling me two bams from Niddrie independently acquired military-grade electronic jamming equipment and modified tactical weapons?'

'Aye. We... eh... we saved up. Bought the gear through a guy on the dark web.' Ferguson's voice carried the familiar quality of someone who had come with a prepared story and was sticking to it.

'And what about Jamie Sinclair?'

Ferguson's voice dropped, a genuine hint of remorse. 'Kid's only nineteen, you know? Naive as they come. We needed someone clean to move some stuff between locations, and we knew him from around the scheme. Knew he was looking for work.'

'What did you tell him?'

'We said we needed someone to move stock about and do deliveries for a legit electronics supplier - specialist stuff for telecoms systems and that. Told him it was high-end gear and we needed someone straight to do the driving and keep it secure.' Ferguson ran his hands through his hair.

'The daft laddie believed everything we told him. Genuinely thought he was earning honest money and a shot at a full-time job.'

Fighting back the rising anger, Balfour pressed on. 'And when you needed a scapegoat?'

'That was... look, we never meant for Jamie to get hurt. But when the police started getting close, someone put in an anonymous tip about the kid. Next thing we know, he's arrested with marked notes from the McKenzie job. We didn't even ken he had any. Honest.'

'So who made that call, Tam? Who's the grass?'

As Ferguson's silence stretched between them, Balfour didn't bother to ask again - he was fairly certain who the concerned citizen had been .

'Right then, Tam. Let's talk about Douglas Kemp.'

Although clearly surprised by the question, Ferguson's demeanor rapidly switched to the defensive. 'Look, the debt collection was legitimate. Douglas owed Jojo money from the machines, fair and square. We get paid to collect.'

'How much money?'

'Thousands. That boy couldn't keep away from the fruit machines, and Jojo let him go until he owed serious money.'

Balfour made careful notes, purposely remaining silent as the silence gained weight, only the whir of the recording equipment marking the passing seconds until finally, the pressure on Ferguson to fill the gap became irresistible.

'Kemp's not even the only one. Cockburn's dozens of tenants like him all over Edinburgh. Half of them work for him too, and when they need to borrow cash they end up getting pointed at Jojo,' Ferguson said with a shrug.

'Wee Douglas is just one of many. When they can't pay cash, we'll take stuff from them. Silver frames, jewelry, whatever they can get their hands on. We get paid and Cockburn doesn't give a fuck either way. End of story.'

As he left Ferguson to confer with his lawyer, Balfour found McGinty in the corridor, reading something on his phone.

'It's a message from Campbell. She says Munro wants results yesterday. We're to wrap up the case by end of shift or face a disciplinary.'

'Charming.'

'Aye, he is that,' grunted McGinty. 'Wallace's going down for the robberies, but no way he's going to give up Menzies. How about Ferguson?'

Balfour sighed with exasperation. 'Same. He'll plead guilty all the way but won't say a word about Jojo.'

"Well you've got to hand it to them, they're taking it like pros.' shrugged McGinty. 'Smart. Plead guilty for the lighter sentence. Jojo looks after you while you're away. Get parole and walk back out into a ready-made gig and a pile of cash once you've served half your sentence.'

'Munro's not going to be too happy about Menzies walking.'

'Och he won't care, so long as it looks like everyone went down for the bookie jobs he can add it to the "solved" pile and keep his head down. That's all that matters to that balloon. Did you get anything else?'

'Ferguson did open when I mentioned Jamie Sinclair,' Balfour replied. 'I know he's been caught red-handed but it turns out the entire thing was a set up from the beginning. He actually thought it was his big break.'

McGinty looked concerned. 'Wallace told me nothing about that. Said Sinclair was just a driver. But... shite... his statement and the evidence the boy was caught with would be enough to send young Jamie down for a five stretch if the brass or the fiscal push for it.'

'Will they?'

McGinty's expression darkened. 'Not if I can fucking help it.'

***

Murdoch rubbed her eyes and reached for what had to be her sixth cup of coffee, pushing aside the empty takeaway containers and towers of printouts that had been accumulating for weeks. For some reason the cleaning crew seemed to have stopped coming to this side of the building and - aided and abetted by the pair of broken vending machines that had been wheeled into the corner sometime during the last 24 hours - the clutter was starting to get out of hand.

'Fucking hell,' she muttered, scrolling through yet another database with the focused intensity of someone who'd found something significant and wasn't entirely sure what to do about it.

'You know,' she said without looking up, 'when you asked me to dig into Cockburn's employment records, I told you it was a bad idea. That we'd be crossing lines we shouldn't cross.'

She gestured at the screens displaying employment records, tax documents, and insurance claims stretching back over two decades. 'I said if I did this, I'd have to access employment records without warrants, cross-reference private medical data, use police databases for unauthorized background checks. Break about six different data protection laws and probably commit several Privacy Act violations.'

Balfour, shaking the rain off his overcoat, placed a steaming takeaway bag on the desktop. 'And did you?'

'Of course I did.'

Balfour settled into the chair beside her, noting the methodical way she'd organised the information into a dynamic collage - timelines, cross-references, highlighted patterns that painted a disturbing picture of them all.

'What have you found?'

With a deep intake of breath, Murdoch whizzed through the details on screen. 'I looked into Douglas Kemp first and you were right. There's no record of him receiving any income or paying any tax for his caretaker role. He doesn't have a bank account and he's never sat a driving test or applied for a passport.'

'So I worked through a list of Cockburn's buildings and guess what I found?'

Balfour shook his head. He had a bad feeling that what she was about to reveal would not be a surprise, but after the shift she had pulled, and the lengths she had gone to, he wouldn't have said so for all the world.

'Eighteen different vulnerable adults employed across Cockburn's various properties over the past twenty years,' Murdoch spat, every detail checked and double-checked. 'All of them fitting the same profile - learning difficulties, social isolation, minimal family support. All of them living in accommodation tied to their employment.'

She angrily clicked through a series of documents, each telling a similar story.

'Look at this pattern. It's absolutely fucking blatant.

'They get employed as caretakers, cleaners, general maintenance. Low wages, but free accommodation in basement flats or converted outbuildings. Completely dependent on their employer for housing, income, everything.

'All of them, David. Every fucking one following the same trajectory. Employment, dependency, debt, exploitation.' She pulled up medical records that made Balfour's stomach turn. 'And look at the injury patterns.'

Hospital admissions for falls, accidents, unexplained bruising. No questions asked. A trail of human suffering nobody had cared enough about to spot.

'Jesus Christ,' Balfour muttered, scanning the systematic documentation. 'I thought it was just bullying and exploitation - this is more like slavery.'

'That's what I thought. So I went deeper.' Murdoch's voice carried a note of apprehension as she opened another set of documents. 'And that's where we have a problem.'

She turned to face him directly, her expression serious. 'Balfour, to get this information, I've done everything I warned you about and more - unauthorized database access, privacy violations, the works.'

'How bad is it, procedurally?'

'Career-ending bad - for both of us. If anyone finds out I was doing this research and you knew about it, everything I've found could be ruled inadmissible.

Worse, it would probably screw up any hope of an authorised investigation into Cockburn's activities in the future.'

Balfour studied the evidence spread across multiple screens - a comprehensive picture of systematic exploitation that demanded action, obtained through methods that made action legally impossible.

'But if we ignore this, eighteen people suffer while their abuser operates with complete impunity,' he said.

'Exactly. On the plus side we have clear evidence of systematic abuse. On the negative - we can't use it without destroying our careers and letting the bad guy - who is a complete prick - get away with it.'

Shite.

'There has to be a way to get this information legitimately,' Balfour said finally. 'Anonymous tips, concerned social workers, employment tribunal complaints. Someone official who could request this data through proper channels.'

'Maybe. But that would take months, maybe years. And in the meantime, people like Douglas Kemp continue to suffer.' Murdoch gestured at the screens helplessly. 'How many more of them will there be in that time?'

'Then we find another way. Because ignoring this is not an option.'

Murdoch nodded. She paused for a moment as she wandered into a thought, then lifted her head and gave Balfour a quizzical look.

'We need to go to DI Campbell. She was a heavyweight in Organised Crime & Counter-Terrorism before she got sent here - maybe she can pull strings, speak to friends in high places - that sort of thing.'

Balfour, nodding his assent, sat down and, rifling in the plastic bag, removed a rapidly cooling fast food container and handed it to Murdoch.

'There'll be no coming back from this,' she said, accepting the uninviting snack. What happens if she turns us in?'

Raking around the bag for his own sorry supper, Balfour's dark eyes sparkled as he flashed her a broad grin.

'Then the Professional Standards Department will be forced to look into it while they're pulling apart our lives.'

Chapter 29

Lawyer Arbuthnot's Office, Callander, 1860

Watching the tendrils of morning mist threading through the village from the Teith's murky banks had done little to counter Balfour's growing unease, and as he walked with Young towards Arbuthnot's law office, each step felt like another stride towards the executioner's block.

Starched, pressed and polished, Arbuthnot was standing behind his leather-topped desk as they entered, the morning's correspondence spread before him in neat rows.

'Ah, Balfour, Young - excellent timing,' the solicitor boomed as the two men entered, apparently oblivious to the fact that the appointment had been arranged - via messages carried between the Manse by a small and grubby hand - for precisely this moment. 'The news from Perth confirms what we've long suspected - justice can indeed move swiftly when necessity demands it.'

Young settled into his customary chair whilst Balfour remained standing, studying how Arbuthnot's demeanour had transformed from his usual reptilian stillness to barely contained triumphalism.

'You've received news from Perth about Crichton's case?' Balfour enquired, though the answer was already evident.

'Indeed - my friends there inform me that an early place on the diet has become available for next Tuesday, and the Sheriff-Depute saw fit to advance Crichton's case immediately,' Arbuthnot replied, brandishing a copy of that morning's telegram with evident glee. 'The charges are clear, the evidence overwhelming, and the community's need for resolution urgent - all factors that favour expeditious proceedings.'

'Next week?' Young frowned. 'But surely the defence has barely had time to prepare?'

'A minor inconvenience, I'm sure, as the case against Crichton is quite irrefutable,' Arbuthnot responded, his glasses glinting.

'I notarised Mrs MacPherson's sworn affidavit myself, placing him directly in conspiracy with Miller. She witnessed him handing the girl a bundle that clinked - a sound we agreed was unmistakably the noise of metal keys striking coins - mere hours before Miller's flight from the district.

'The physical evidence supports this witness account perfectly,' he continued, warming to his theme. 'The arresting constables found three pounds, two shillings on Miller's person when she was apprehended after fleeing, and where else would people of that class find such a sum - other than in Henderson's strongbox?'

Young nodded grimly whilst Balfour remained silent, recognising how such evidence would appear to any jury seeking straightforward explanations for inexplicable crimes, the chain of culpability apparently stretching from Crichton's hands to Janet Henderson's brutal death.

'Add to this Crichton's established motive - his repeated public threats against the Henderson family, witnessed by half the district over recent months, and his documented grievances over wages that had clearly festered into murderous resentment,' Arbuthnot declared, as he paced the floor behind his desk.

'Then consider his intimate knowledge of household routines through his work on the property, his access to all areas of the farm, and his demonstrated capacity for violence - as evidenced by his assault upon PC Buchan during his arrest.

'Gentlemen - the man has provided a complete confession through his own actions.'

Young shifted uncomfortably in his chair as he watched the country lawyer pace back and forth. 'And what of Fox, Arbuthnot? His presence near the property on the day of the murder might have provided alternative testimony, perhaps casting doubt on the tale as you tell it...'

'Fox?' Arbuthnot dismissed that with a sweep of his hand. 'He is dead, so sadly not in a position to testify. On its own, his presence near the property proves nothing - vagrants by their very nature wander everywhere.

'And in any case, gentlemen, the physical evidence against Crichton would surely outweigh anything Fox might have offered up.'

Shaking his head in mock despair, the solicitor continued.

'The prosecution's theory is elegantly simple and completely convincing,' he concluded. 'Crichton murdered Janet Henderson after she caught him in the very act of robbery, stole the money, and somehow locked and bolted the house, presumably using the keys he stole weeks earlier.

'Doubtless motivated by the desire to remove the evidence of his adultery, he then passed the booty to Miller with the insistence that she immediately run away, but her flight was discovered and the damning evidence found - a perfect sequence of crime, conspiracy, and capture.'

Balfour exchanged a meaningful glance with Young.

'All circumstantial, of course,' he observed, 'Hardly incontrovertible, and certainly not a great deal to gamble a man's life on.'

Arbuthnot tried, and failed, to hide his irritation.

'Circumstantial perhaps, but overwhelming in its cumulative weight - no reasonable jury could examine such evidence and reach any conclusion other than guilt. Quite frankly, Mr Balfour, I would also add that the community deserves closure, rather than endless speculation regarding theoretical alternatives.'

Rising from his chair with deliberate slowness, Balfour moved toward the window where he could observe the morning's commerce in the street below, carters and merchants conducting their business in a tuneless cacophony.

'Curious. While we seek justice for one woman, the fortunes of another have become the foundation for everything that followed,' he remarked, his brooding attention seemingly focused on the passing traffic.

'I envy you your sense of certainty, Mr Arbuthnot, but this case began with Christina Miller, and unless I'm very much mistaken it will end with her too.'

***

As they returned to the manse for lunch following a stroll along the Teith in a spring sun busily burning off the morning haar, Balfour and Young were surprised by Reverend MacLeod, whom they found waiting in ambush by the door.

'Ah, gentlemen,' MacLeod yelped with forced joviality as they approached, 'excellent timing. We have visitors waiting in the parlour.'

Ushered into the familiar comfort of the parlour, they found Dr Geddes and Arbuthnot assembled within, their glasses charged with port from the minister's sideboard and their conversation abruptly cut short.

Young glanced questioningly at Balfour, who moved to the window overlooking the garden and turned to cast an inquiring gaze over the assembled company, while the subjects of his attention shuffled slightly and exchanged conspiratorial looks.

Arbuthnot cleared his throat and stepped forward. 'We felt it necessary to address certain... irregularities in your recent conduct, Mr Balfour. The community has observed your investigations with growing concern.'

'All of them?' smiled Balfour, 'or just a representative few?'

Ignoring the question, MacLeod joined his friend. 'Your approach has become somewhat erratic, Mr Balfour. One moment you're fighting tooth and nail to exonerate Christina Miller, and the next... well, Mr Arbuthnot reports that you now insist she remains central to the entire case.'

'Most confusing for a community seeking clear answers,' Dr Geddes chimed in. 'And as to poor Henderson - his nerves simply cannot withstand much more.'

Balfour, hands clasped behind his back, shook his head firmly. 'Miller's innocence in no way precludes her importance to understanding what actually occurred. She has always been central to our story, and without her we can never know the whole truth.'

'But to what end?' Arbuthnot demanded shrilly. 'Crichton faces trial next week with overwhelming evidence against him. The case is resolved, society is satisfied, and Henderson's recovery can finally begin. What possible purpose can this continued speculation serve?'

'Beyond unsettling my already traumatised parishioners and prolonging Henderson's suffering unnecessarily,' MacLeod interjected, 'we understand from the poor fellow that many of his influential friends in Edinburgh also share our concerns.'

'I'm sure your methods are very modern,' Dr Geddes observed, 'but first you allow Miss Sterling to play chemistry at the murder scene, then this business with the servant girl... it hardly inspires confidence in your conclusions.'

'Particularly,' Arbuthnot added thin-lipped, 'when those conclusions seem entirely designed to overturn the logical and reasonable conclusion - that Crichton's guilt is manifest and that he should and will hang.'

The parlour fell into tense silence, and in the vacuum of their assembly, the world seemed to halt for a moment.

'Gentlemen,' Balfour said finally, his voice steely, 'I understand your desire for closure. But justice requires following evidence wherever it leads, not merely where it proves most convenient.'

MacLeod's certainty was absolute. 'The evidence leads to John Crichton man. Everything else is speculation that serves no purpose save to prolong Henderson's agony and unsettle proper order.'

'The case is closed,' Arbuthnot declared firmly. 'Further investigation benefits no one, and I will ensure that my friends in high office are aware of that, Balfour. Very aware.'

As the men rose to depart, Dr Geddes paused at the door and looked back.

'Henderson cannot endure much more of this uncertainty, Mr Balfour. For his health, if for nothing else, perhaps it's time to accept that your questions have been answered as thoroughly as they're ever likely to be.'

***

The air was still cool as they walked along the banks of the Teith towards the Meadows, but it carried with it the fresh scent of thawed earth and the promise of spring as the river ran by fast and bright.

It was Young, finally, who broke the contemplative silence that had reigned over the friends since stepping out of the Manse to clear their minds with a brisk walk.

'I know Arbuthnot is a terrible prig, old man, but he does rather have a point. We've both seen men convicted on slimmer evidence than Crichton is facing… Miller has been cleared… and it certainly would help ease the public's mind to know there isn't a murderer loose in the county.

'Why are you still not satisfied?'

Balfour paused beside a cluster of rowan trees along the bank and watched the water - swollen by the snowmelt from the high hills beyond - flow over the stones. 'Because there are still too many questions that haven't been answered.

'Who gave Miller the money to flee? Who fathered her child? Where are those missing keys? And what else could she tell us about the goings-on in that household?

'On one hand I grant you these could simply be a collection of loose ends, red herrings and coincidences, but on the other - they could change everything.'

'Or they could be exactly what they appear to be,' Young replied as they resumed walking. 'A frightened girl sent away by a violent brute, shameful intimate secrets that have nothing to do with the case, a set of keys thrown away to hide evidence of one crime or more.

'I am your greatest champion Balfour, but sometimes the straightforward answer is the correct one.'

'Perhaps,' Balfour said as they followed the river path. 'But then there's Henderson's financial irregularities, and Janet's implication in them - there are just too many threads we haven't followed to their conclusion.'

A heron rose from the shallows and flew up river as they rounded the bend, its fishing disturbed by their advance. 'Financial irregularities, yes. But since the crash you'd be hard pressed to find a gentleman anywhere in the country that has not suffered reverses in the investment market,' countered Young.

'You said that Miller's innocence of the murder does not rule out a role in solving it. By the same token, even if Henderson is guilty of fraud that doesn't automatically implicate him in anything else. There are just too many missing pieces.'

'Precisely why we need Miller,' Balfour said. 'There are questions only she can answer.'

Young studied his friend as they walked on, recognising the familiar determination. 'And if she refuses to speak? The girl's already been through arrest, questioning and public shame, but still hasn't breathed a word on any of the issues you've raised.'

'Then we will never know whether the man on the gallows was guilty or not,' Balfour replied. 'Irrespective of whether anybody's influential friends like it or not, I'd rather not spend the rest of my days wondering if we got it wrong.'

They walked in contemplative silence for several minutes, Ben Ledi's peak clearly visible in the distance for what felt like the first time in months.

'What do you propose?' Young asked finally, though he was fairly confident he already knew the answer.

'One final approach,' Balfour replied. 'Amelia is absolute in her belief that the girl has a good and honest nature. Let us see if she can appeal to that. At least then we'll have done everything we can.'

'Whatever it is, the truth lies with Christina Miller - we need to unlock it before time runs out entirely.'

Young stopped walking, turning to face his friend directly. 'I know you're as stubborn as a mule when your mind is set, but MacLeod's threats about Henderson's influential connections may not be entirely idle - there are powerful men who want this matter concluded.'

'All the more reason to persevere,' Balfour grinned. 'When people ask you to hurry along, I generally find it's because they don't want you lingering around the things they'd rather you didn't see.'

Chapter 30

MIT 13 Office, Edinburgh, 2025

In Modern policing, walking into your boss's office and finding the Superintendent already waiting for you is rarely considered a good thing. To discover that now - mere hours since driving a horse and cart through the rule book - left Balfour feeling like he'd just been punched in the chest.

'Right then, sunshine,' Munro leered from his position standing behind Detective Superintendent Richardson. 'Time for a proper chat about your recent performance.'

Balfour settled into the uncomfortable plastic chair across from Munro's desk, his attention flicking between the two men as he tried to gauge the temperature of the room. The spark in the DCI's eye told him all he needed to know, but the steel-haired senior officer remained inscrutable as he glanced through the folder in front of him.

Through the rain-streaked window behind Munro's head, the grey Edinburgh morning remained a wet blur, while out of the corner of his eye he could see a smirking Mulholland making no effort to hide his satisfaction at Balfour's predicament.

He braced himself for a savage tirade on the consequences of crossing every procedural line imaginable, but instead, Richardson opened the manila folder and began reading from what appeared to be a completely different set of accusations altogether.

'DC Balfour, you were assigned to the betting shop robberies by DCI Munro here,' Richardson said, his voice carrying the measured authority. 'Instead, he tells me that you pursued unauthorized inquiries, conducted house-to-house interviews outside your remit, and even abandoned a scheduled forensic sweep to follow your own agenda - all of which has had a detrimental effect on the resolution of the James case.'

The relief that washed through Balfour was quickly followed by irritation as he realised what was actually happening. Munro needed someone to blame for his own investigative failures, so he'd thrown him under the bus.

'Sir, the inquiries into Kemp's movements were simply as a by-product of visiting the Elm Row bookies during the robbery —' he began, but Munro cut him off with a theatrical wave of his hand.

'Were you or were you not specifically instructed to focus on the betting shop investigation and only that?' he interrupted with a growl. 'And correct me if I'm wrong, but were you not also told that the James case had sufficient resources allocated to it without your interference?'

Through the glass partition separating Munro's office from the main squadroom, Balfour caught sight of Campbell and Murdoch entering together, their heads bent in quiet conversation as they moved toward their desks. Murdoch glanced toward the office, caught his eye through the glass, and gave him the subtlest of thumbs-up signals.

'The house-to-house interviews hadn't been completed because one of the team was... otherwise engaged, and it did yield significant intelligence sir,' Balfour replied evenly. 'Intelligence that directly supported the broader investigation into the James murder.'

'Intelligence that ultimately changed nothing,' Munro interjected, his voice loaded with rehearsed indignation. 'Your freelancing has held up progress on a high-profile case, wasted resources, and undermined team discipline.'

Richardson made a note in the file, his expression unreadable. 'And the forensic sweep you were scheduled to assist? The one that had to be delayed because you'd decided to pursue other goals without clearance?'

'I believed that once we'd established the original door between the basement and main house was sealed, I could provide more immediate investigative value by—'

'You believed,' Munro mimicked, dripping with mock amazement. 'Well there's the problem right there, isn't it? Since when do detective constables get to decide what they believe is more important than a direct fucking order from their supervisor?'

Outside, the rain had intensified, drumming against the windows with increasing urgency as if Balfour awaited his fate.

Richardson closed the file with a snap and fixed Balfour with the steady gaze of years of experience. For what seemed an age he considered the folder in his hands, then stood and stepped deliberately to the shredder beside Munro's desk, pressing the folio into its jaws and watching as they whirred into life.

Clearly this conversation had never officially taken place.

'I think we'll keep this one off the books,' he said, blithely ignoring Munro's furious scowl behind him and returning to his seat. 'You're a promising young officer, Balfour, but you need to learn to navigate more carefully.'

He straightened his jacket, his expression mixing professional concern with something that might have been a glimmer of amusement.

'Good detective work means nothing if you're not around to see it through son. Only fight the battles you can actually win.'

***

'Close the door behind you, Kirk,' Richardson said as Balfour departed, in a tone that suggested the real conversation was about to begin. 'And take a seat.'

Munro, still clearly deflated by the disciplinary meeting's unexpected conclusion, settled heavily into the chair Balfour had just vacated while Richardson remained standing, his hands clasped behind his back as he gazed out at the soaked car park below.

'Interesting complaint,' Richardson observed eventually, turning from the window to fix Munro with the steady regard that had made him a formidable interviewer during his own years on the street. 'Very detailed. Very specific about dates and times and procedural violations. I can barely imagine how you found the time to pull it together, considering your current workload.'

'Well, sir, when it comes to maintaining discipline and chain of command—' Munro began, but Richardson cut him off with a raise of his hand.

'Tell me, Kirk, how's the James case progressing? Any arrests imminent? Breakthrough evidence? Solid leads the fiscal can work with?'

The questions smacked home, and Munro shifted uncomfortably as he groped for a response.

'We're... uh... we're pursuing several avenues of inquiry, sir. These things take time, especially when team members aren't following proper protocols and undermining the investigation with unauthorised—'

'Unauthorised inquiries that apparently yielded useful intelligence,' Richardson interrupted. 'For fuck's sake, Kirk. Spare me the bullshit.'

Munro's face flushed with defensive indignation. 'Sir, with respect, Balfour's freelancing has been disruptive to team morale and operational efficiency. DC Mulholland expressed serious concerns about—'

'Ah yes, Mulholland,' Richardson scoffed. 'I remember his name from your file. Gave testimony about Balfour's supposed insubordination in quite unusual detail. Usually I'd expect my DCs to have each other's backs, but then you've always had an unusual approach to team building, haven't you Kirk?'

'Sir, I'm simply trying to maintain proper standards of professional conduct within the team,' Munro spluttered. 'When junior officers start thinking they can ignore direct orders and pursue their own agendas... well, then it'll be chaos.'

Richardson bent to pick up his briefcase but paused, placing it on the desk and drumming it with his fingers as he drifted off in thought.

'I knew Balfour's father,' he said simply. 'Good detective. Brilliant, actually. Had a talent for seeing patterns others missed - for making connections that weren't immediately obvious.'

He chuckled, shaking his head at the reminiscence. 'You couldn't shake him off. Once he got his teeth into a case he was like a dog with a bone.'

Munro frowned. 'His father's disappearance left quite a black mark though, didn't it sir? There's a lot of speculation about what really happened, and what he was into that could have made him just vanish like that. That's why the lad's been posted here, isn't it? In case he's tarred with the same brush?'

Richardson's expression hardened. 'Be careful who you listen to Kirk. That might be why some people wanted him here, but his record and performance have been outstanding since he joined up.'

He paused, shaking his head in mild disbelief. 'No, he's here because of some minor procedural bullshit. When he got posted to CID some data entry grunt in HR found a snafu in the paperwork, and MIT-13 seemed like the ideal holding pen to keep him busy while the bureaucrats sort it out.

'You know what HR are like - once they've got a box to tick they won't budge an inch until it's done, no matter how stupid.'

'So what's the problem?'

'Nothing really. He joined under the graduate scheme, and his degree is listed in the Edinburgh University roll, but someone over there screwed up his graduation date and typed it into the database as 1855,' Richardson shrugged. 'So he's here until they find a way of sorting that out.'

Richardson frowned. 'Although between you and me, Kirk, there's something bloody strange about that. Makes you wonder what kind of administrative cock-up could produce something that ridiculous.'

He stood, scanned the incident room outside the office, and fixed Munro with a baleful stare.

'What I won't tolerate, however,' he said finally, his voice darkening, 'is colleagues being sacrificed as scapegoats for failures at a senior level. I've seen that pattern too many times, Kirk. Case isn't developing as quickly as the brass would like? Throw a junior officer under the bus and hope they move on.'

He loomed in closer, his gaze never leaving Munro's face. 'Is that what's happening here? Because if it is, you and I are going to have a much longer conversation about leadership standards and professional accountability.'

Munro swallowed hard, his earlier confidence completely evaporated. 'No sir. Of course not.'

'Good,' Richardson smiled thinly, satisfied he'd made his point. 'Because I'd hate to think you were more interested in protecting your own position than in actually solving cases.'

Typical, Munro thought, Twenty-three years climbing the ranks, playing the game, kissing the right arses, and here comes some university boy to hoover up the glory while I'm left holding the shitty end of the stick.

Richardson's praise for Balfour's "investigative thinking" was barely coded criticism of his own methods. Worse, the kid seemed genuinely unimpressed by authority - the kind of copper who'd follow evidence wherever it led, regardless of who it hurt.

That made him dangerous.

Richardson moved toward the door, then paused with his hand on the handle.

'So two notes for you Kirk. First, young Balfour's showing real promise - reminds me a lot of his father - brilliant, stubborn, and completely allergic to leaving well enough alone. His father's curiosity eventually got him into trouble that even I couldn't help him out of. Don't let history repeat itself.

'Make sure he gets the support and guidance he needs to develop that potential or you'll answer to me personally.

'Second—get me a result on the James case fast.'

He let the silence hang a beat too long, then added:

'I won't ask again.'

***

Murdoch sat cross-legged on the Persian rug before the fireplace in Balfour's study, surrounded by case files and photographs that she'd spread across the floor in a pattern only she could decipher.

Her laptop balanced precariously on a stack of forensic reports as she cross-referenced witness statements with CCTV timestamps for the umpteenth time, her copper mane cascading down around her shoulders as she combed the details for something - anything - that could lead to a breakthrough Rowena James' impossible murder.

'So Old Man Richardson's on side then?' she asked without looking up from the crime scene photographs, still focused unflinchingly on the puzzle at hand.

'More than I expected,' Balfour replied, sitting back in his favourite chair and gazing across the familiar proportions of his study at the modest collection of curios and photographs that represented what little he had of his own history. 'Something about the way he handled it made me think... I think he might have known my father. Can't be sure, but there was something familiar about him.

'Either way, I'm more concerned that Campbell has agreed to help out with the Cockburn data. I've not been in the job long enough to lose it yet.'

The room's atmosphere seemed to wrap around them, the lamplight dancing across walls lined with the odd collection of antique and contemporary legal texts, police procedural manuals and almanacs that Balfour had gathered through the years. Outside the tall windows, the evening rain continued its gusty assault on the Georgian glass.

Murdoch held up two photographs side by side, frowning at some detail that had caught her attention. 'Apparently there's a hundred ways to do it if you've got the willpower. If a social worker happens to raise a concern, or a journalist happens to sniff around... well, then we've got cause.

'Campbell's got contacts in Social Services who can request the employment records legitimately, and a friend in HMRC who could order an investigation into the tax side of things. She said it would take a few days to set up, but in the meantime we're to keep our heads down - whatever happens, it didn't come from us.'

'Not that any of it gets us any closer to proving who killed Rowena James,' Balfour sighed, rising from his chair and moving to examine the room more closely, his dark eyes taking in details he'd seen thousands of times but never really considered in context.

'The problem is that Munro has been right all along.'
'What?'

'Oh, I know he's run us all ragged chasing rainbows on this case, but there's one thing that he's been spot on about from the beginning - this is a classic locked room mystery. If we can solve the how we'll find the who.'

'That's been the problem with this entire bloody case,' he said, pacing the polished floorboards. 'Every time we think we've found the answer, the physical evidence contradicts the obvious explanation.'

Murdoch looked up from her photographs with interest. 'How d'you mean?'

'CCTV shows nobody entering the study, but someone clearly did. The door was locked from the inside, but the killer obviously got out. We keep assuming that someone's lying or the evidence is wrong, but what if we're missing something fundamental about the physical space itself?'

He paused, his analytical mind working through the contradictions that had plagued the investigation from the beginning, while something nagged at the edge of his memory - a detail that felt important but remained frustratingly elusive.

Murdoch gathered the photographs into a neat pile and stretched. 'But we looked into that, didn't we? When we confirmed that the entrance from the basement was permanently sealed?

'Maybe we're overthinking it. Maybe the answer's simpler than we're making out and is right in front of our faces.'

Balfour turned to gesture toward the full width of his study, then stopped abruptly as something about its dimensions registered with sudden, startling clarity.

'Christ,' he muttered, the pieces finally clicking into place. 'Murdoch, look at this room. Really look at it.'

She followed his gaze, taking in the generous proportions of the townhouse study with its high ceilings and elegant symmetry. 'It's lovely, but I don't see—'

'The width,' Balfour interrupted, his excitement building. 'You've been in the Cockburn study. This room - built in the same period, by the same builder, in the same style, to the same proportions - is significantly wider than theirs.'

Murdoch frowned, looking round as she considered the comparison. 'But why would that matter?'

'Because Georgian houses were built on symmetry. This whole row of houses is meant to be identical,' Balfour said, his mind racing as fragments of memory began to coalesce into something approaching understanding.

He remembered a visit to the Cockburn house at number 22 in another time - watching the servants appear and disappear as if by magic, never seeing them use the main corridors, never hearing footsteps on the main stairs. A building specifically designed to keep the domestic staff invisible to the family and their guests.

'One didn't wish to see servants constantly traipsing through the main rooms, after all,' he whispered mostly to himself.

The realisation hit them both simultaneously, Murdoch's eyes widening as she grasped the implications.

'Hidden servant passages,' she breathed. 'Built into the wall space.'

'Exactly! The aristocratic obsession with making their domestic staff invisible,' Balfour grinned, his mood gaining momentum as the breakthrough took shape. 'Narrow staircases and corridors behind the main rooms, allowing servants to move through the house without ever being seen by the family or their guests.'

He gestured toward where the passage would run within his own walls. 'That's why their study is narrower than mine - the space was sacrificed for something else.'

Murdoch was already opening her laptop, her excitement palpable. 'So someone could have entered the locked study completely undetected. Not through any door or window we were watching…'

'But through a servant staircase that has probably been almost completely forgotten for decades,' Balfour chimed. 'Bypassing every security camera, every supposed witness, every piece of evidence that convinced us the room was sealed.'

The implications galloped through his mind with gathering force: the locked room mystery solved, the invisible killer explained, the means of access that had eluded them from the beginning established and staring them in the face.

'And now,' he said quietly, settling back into his chair as the pieces aligned, 'it gives us a very specific question to ask: who could have known those passages still existed?'

He felt a surge of satisfaction at finally cracking the puzzle that had baffled them for weeks. 'Christ, we've been going round in circles thinking someone would have to be Houdini to get through all those locks on the front door and back out again without being seen.'

Murdoch laughed, closing her laptop with a snap. 'Aye, you'd need to be working with a pretty old lock to pull that sort of trick off.'

'Hmmmm,' Balfour murmured, drifting into thought as somewhere, a long way away, a connection sparked.

Chapter 31

Crag Cottage, Callander, 1860

'Execution?' Her voice cracked like kindling, dark eyes growing wide with horror. 'John Crichton? But surely... they cannot mean... I never thought it would come to...'

Sinking heavily into the worn wooden chair beside the midwife's hearth, her face draining of what little colour pregnancy had given her pale cheeks, there was no hiding Christina Miller's true feelings as her dark eyes grew wide—hands instinctively moving to protect the swell of her belly as if protecting the child within from the terrible news

The drive to the midwife's cottage had been tense with unspoken urgency, Shaw urging his beasts on in white-knuckled determination as the carriage lurched over the rough track that wound towards Morag Morrison's isolated dwelling. Balfour and Amelia sat in strained silence, each lost in contemplation as they approached the cramped sanctuary to which the girl had fled to escape a storm of accusation and speculation.

Now, squeezed together into the low-ceilinged cottage, they watched the young woman's composure waver as the full weight of Crichton's predicament finally struck her.

'There can be no doubt,' Balfour said gently. 'The tide of opinion has moved against him, and without new revelations, John Crichton will hang.'

The silence that followed stretched like a held breath, while somewhere in the distance a curlew called across the loch.

'You must understand,' Amelia said from her perch on the cottage's simple wooden settle, 'that we are not here to judge or condemn. We seek only the truth, whatever that might be, but time grows short Christina, and if you have anything to say, now is the time to say it.'

She straightened her shoulders and met their eyes with the defiant spark that had marked their first encounter in the Crichton cottage.

'You think I'm a wicked creature, don't you?' she said, her voice gaining strength, the old fire kindling. 'Well, maybe I am, and maybe I did get myself into trouble. But I never hurt anyone, and I never stole anything either, no matter what you think of me.'

She straightened in her chair, chin lifting with stubborn pride, and held their gaze unflinchingly.

'What I think,' Amelia replied firmly, 'is that you are a young woman in an impossible situation, trying to protect everyone but yourself, whether they deserve it or not.'

They waited for a moment, breathless as the weight of one young girl's impossible predicament hung across all their shoulders.

'There are questions we must have answers to Miss Miller,' Balfour interrupted, soft but urgent. 'The money… the keys… the man who–'

'Just tell us what you know,' Amelia said simply, placing a single gloved hand on Balfour's arm to silence him. 'If you do that honestly, then you have done all you can do, and then you can leave here, and face life without fear.'

Miller closed her eyes and drew a deep, exhausted breath. 'Henderson… he gave me money. Three pounds and some silver to help me get away, to start fresh somewhere no one would know about…' She gestured helplessly at her condition.

'It was the afternoon after… after they found Miss Janet. He came to me on the road in the doctor's gig, said the scandal would follow me everywhere if I stayed, that it would be better for everyone if I just… disappeared.'

Amelia caught the inconsistency before Balfour could speak. 'But Christina, if Mr Henderson was so concerned for your welfare, why didn't he provide this assistance when you were first dismissed?'

'I don't know. He said he'd thought about it and that it would ruin us both if certain things came to light. He said he'd make sure nobody bothered me again if I promised to just go and to keep quiet about... about everything.'

'Everything?' Amelia pressed gently.

Christina's voice dropped to barely a whisper. 'The baby... it's his. Mr Henderson is the father.'

Christina's eyes darted between her questioners, the weight of months of deception finally off her shoulders, while Balfour worked hard to suppress any hint of surprise, nodding slowly as he skipped the obvious questions and kept the conversation moving, fearful that Miller might refuse to speak again.

'I believe you,' he said. 'But there are still witnesses who told us that Crichton handed you a bundle containing the coins and keys at the inn.'

Christina shook her head vigorously, tears flowing freely now but her voice gaining strength with anger. 'John tried to make me stay, but when I wouldn't he brought me some bread, cheese and a knife, spoon and tankard wrapped in an old tablecloth for the journey.

'That's all he did. Try to be the only man who was ever truly kind to me. Who never beat me, or was cruel, or who wanted me to... do anything.'

'But what about the keys?' Balfour asked carefully, 'was it him who stole them?'

'There were never any stolen keys, sir. That was just another of Mr Henderson's lies.'

She wiped her eyes with the back of her hand, gathering strength from finally speaking truths she had carried alone for so long. 'I skivvied for that man for two years, and every evening, after supper, he had his regular routine - he'd sit at his desk in the parlour and lay out his portfolio of papers, his cash box and his ring of keys while he tallied the accounts.

'Then one night Miss Janet asked for the key to the strongbox and he said they were gone - just like that. I said I'd swear I'd seen them on the table like usual but he gave me a look and I shut my mouth.'

Miller's voice grew steadier as she continued. 'There was a right to-do. He said he could have a spare set made up but Miss Janet wouldn't let it lie, and while she went to hunt in the kitchen he grabbed me and said he'd tell everyone I did it.

'But then Miss Janet realised I was with child and sent me away herself and Henderson switched his story - started saying it must have been Crichton who stole them, but I swear those keys were never lost.'

'He told me that if I ever breathed a word about what I knew - about anything - he would see to it terrible things happened to me,' she shuddered as her voice grew fierce. That people would believe whatever he told them about a nobody… a lying servant girl.'

Her eyes blazed with sudden fury. 'Well, he was right about that much, wasn't he? Everyone was quick enough to believe I was a thief and a murderer. But he was wrong about one thing—I may be nobody, but I ain't scared of him.'

***

The afternoon was crisp and clear as they stood at the entrance to Mount Stewart Farm, the early light slanting low through bare branches to create a tracery of shadows across the farmyard flagstones, as Shaw disappeared back down the road towards Callander.

His instructions were clear: to call at Dr Geddes' house and request in the strongest possible terms that Mr Henderson return with him immediately. Shaw, a rare glint of humour in his eye, cheerfully agreed.

'We have perhaps an hour and a half,' Amelia announced, dumping her familiar leather satchel on the stone step. 'But I believe it will only take a few moments of that time to prove my theory.'

She withdrew a length of fine string from her bag, then moved purposefully toward the kitchen door where Janet Henderson had died such a violent death only weeks before.

'Observe the latch mechanism carefully, gentlemen,' she continued, indicating the simple iron handle. 'Note the clearance – sufficient space for a string of appropriate gauge to pass through when the door is closed, but not so generous as to compromise security.'

With Balfour and Young looking on, brows furrowed, she demonstrated it step by step.

'First,' she explained, positioning the string around the latch mechanism whilst holding both ends from the exterior side of the door, 'the murderer secures the string in such a fashion that pulling it taut will cause the latch to engage from the inside, creating the appearance of internal securing whilst the perpetrator remains safely outside.'

The latch clicked into place with mechanical certainty as she demonstrated the principle, the sound echoing across the farmyard with startling clarity in the still afternoon air.

'Then,' she continued, indicating the length of string that extended beneath the door gap, 'by maintaining tension on the exterior end whilst closing the door, the murderer ensures the internal mechanism remains engaged, creating an apparently impossible situation – a room secured from within, yet with no occupant save the victim.'

Young edged closer. 'But surely any such arrangement would have been immediately visible to whoever discovered the body?'

'On the contrary, Mr Young,' Amelia replied, threading the string around the latch with movements so precise they seemed almost surgical. 'The genius of this method lies not in its complexity but in its simplicity – after the murderer's departure, he simply pulls the string free of its arrangement, leaving no trace of the mechanism save for...'

She gestured toward the door frame with obvious satisfaction. 'These tiny fibres embedded in the wood grain around the latch mechanism – fragments of the string itself, torn away by friction during the mechanical operation.'

She withdrew the small glass vial containing the dark strands she had extracted from the door frame during their earlier investigation, holding it up for their inspection. 'These fibres originated from a string of very specific composition which should not be hard to compare, should we find a match.'

As she spoke Amelia stepped into the house and led them to a polished walnut sewing box on a stand by the parlour window. She lifted the lid and sitting on top of the arrayed coloured silks, sat a reel of pale, lustrous cord.

Holding it beside the vial, she allowed the tiny fibres within to catch the glow. 'You see, gentlemen,' she beamed, 'Not very hard to compare at all.'

Young stared at the vial, then Amelia, then the vial again - momentarily speechless. 'Good God, Miss Sterling. This... this changes everything.'

'It changes everything, but also nothing,' Balfour interjected, rapidly working through the implications. 'Amelia has already used science to prove that Crichton never touched the murder weapon and he's still awaiting trial. Using it to prove that Henderson is guilty is going to be no easier.

He stopped, gazing at the clock mounted on the kitchen wall as the events of the last few days swirled around his mind, a carousel of people, places and promises that gradually slowed, crystallised, and eventually arrived with a bump in the form of a conclusion.

'Right,' he said, grinning as he buttoned his jacket and straightened his tie. 'We've uncovered the how - now it's high time we caught the who.'

***

As the sun descended behind Ben Ledi's slopes through its windows, the farmhouse kitchen where Janet Henderson had met her violent end now served as the impromptu stage on which Balfour would play his final hand.

Henderson stormed through the kitchen door with barely contained fury, his face flushed with indignation. 'This is intolerable! Summoning me from my business like some common criminal! Your man here,' he gestured angrily at Shaw, 'is an impudent oaf!'

'He didnae want to come,' explained Shaw with a cherubic grin. 'He was having tea at the manse… so I brought the lot of them.'

Dr Geddes, Arbuthnot, and the Reverend MacLeod, coloured various shades of outrage at Shaw's handling, stood in the doorway while Amelia smoothly took their coats in an uncustomary bout of domesticity. Henderson shrugged out of his heavy woollen coat with continued irritation, his attention focused on Balfour and Young rather than Amelia as she deftly removed the garment from his hand.

'Gentlemen,' Henderson began with a studied effort to regain his authority. 'I trust you don't object to my having witnesses to this outrage?'

'On the contrary,' Balfour replied, his voice carrying that dangerous quietness his companions had learned to recognise. 'I'd very much appreciate their opinion on some new evidence that has come to light following our most recent conversation with Miss Miller.'

'This again, Balfour?' Arbuthnot interjected. 'Whatever she might claim now, the word of a pregnant girl with a grudge against her former employer can scarcely be considered reliable.'

'Actually, I rather think that in this case it can, Mr Arbuthnot,' Balfour said as Henderson's three supporters stared in growing bewilderment. 'Miss Miller has also provided a complete account of the funds Mr Henderson gave her to facilitate her departure - when her continued presence might prove inconvenient.

'What's more,' he continued, 'she has also provided a complete account of your relationship with her and the circumstances of her dismissal.'

Henderson, sweating slightly despite the coolness of the air, merely spluttered. 'Lies! The girl was a thief - you found the money in her quarters yourselves!'

'Careful now Henderson,' intoned Balfour smoothly. 'That is no way to speak about the mother of your child.'

The silence was deafening.

'This is madness!' Dr Geddes protested weakly, his habitual confidence evaporating as he watched his comfortable assumptions slowly begin to unravel before his eyes. 'Henderson, tell them this is all some terrible misunderstanding!'

Henderson, shaking his head in disbelief, said nothing. The shift in his expression was barely perceptible - a tightening around the eyes, a slight stiffening of his shoulders - but Balfour caught it, and continued to press home the advantage.

'Did Janet find out about the girl? Is that what happened, Mr Henderson? Or was it Mauritania? Was she going to expose you for what you've done?'

Henderson's lips moved wordlessly as he struggled to comprehend, before exploding in rage. 'This is preposterous! The ravings of a slut and the fantasies of amateurs! I demand that you leave my property immediately!'

Arbuthnot's brow furrowed as he attempted to rally to his friend's defence. 'Gentlemen, whatever accusations you may level, Mr Henderson remains a man of standing in this community, and I must insist that proper legal procedures-'

'Enough!' Balfour interrupted. 'The time for niceties is over. The man you have been determined to defend since the beginning has in fact got far greater motive than any other to commit this crime, while the reputation you seem so content to take as a guarantee of his innocence is built on a tissue of lies.

'Janet knew that, didn't she, Mr Henderson? Is that why you killed her?'

The Reverend MacLeod, recovering his voice, interjected. 'Surely you're forgetting the simple fact that I was with Henderson when he discovered poor Janet? The door was locked from within. I tried it myself.

'It couldn't have been Henderson.'

'Precisely! The killer must have somehow used the stolen keys,' protested Arbuthnot.

Balfour caught Amelia's eye for a moment and nodded before continuing. 'Ah yes - the keys. So much attention has been focused on them, yet they are and have always been completely irrelevant. Indeed, they were never stolen in the first place.'

Ignoring the protestations from his audience, he strode across the room to the door. 'You created that fiction as a simple diversion - first to ward off your sister's suspicions, second to compel Miller's silence, and third to help convince your friends that Crichton must be the guilty party.

'It was a clever device. But not as clever as the method you used to latch the door after your sister's murder.'

On cue, Amelia stepped forward with Henderson's coat and, sliding her hand into his pocket, withdrew a length of silken cord.

'Shall I show them how, Mr Henderson?'

That was the breaking point - the enormity of his exposure clearly written across the gentleman farmer's features.

Rising abruptly from his position beside the table, eyes darting frantically between his accusers and the door, he jabbed an accusatory finger at Balfour.

'That doesn't... you can't... you don't understand!' he screamed, his voice cracking with emotion. 'She was willing to destroy it all! The investments, the reputation, the family name! It would all have come out...'

He stopped abruptly. Horrifically aware of how completely he had betrayed himself, whilst his former allies stared in appalled silence.

For one frozen moment, the kitchen was suspended in perfect silence, and then Henderson lunged desperately toward the door and made his escape.

It might even have succeeded had it not been for Solomon Shaw, who stood waiting on the cobblestones.

The collision was brief and decisive - Henderson's desperate charge meeting Shaw's solid forearm with a crunching impact that sent the murderer sprawling. A weatherbeaten hand grasped him roughly by the collar, and within seconds he had been dragged back through the kitchen doorway and unceremoniously deposited back into his chair.

Balfour, indicating that the others should take a seat, leaned against the empty fireplace and trapped his quarry in an unblinking gaze.

'Now then, Mr Henderson. Shall we begin again?'

Chapter 32

Heriot Row, Edinburgh, 2025

If it could have stood witness, the drawing room of number 22 Heriot Row would undoubtedly be able to tell many tales collected over two centuries of opulent existence, but few of them would have been as black as the story Detective Constable Balfour was preparing to unfold.

A fitful light played through the tall windows overlooking the street where Rowena James had lived and died, while her bereaved family sat in various states, running from boredom to fear, their expensive legal counsel flanking them like a pair of well-tailored bodyguards.

Campbell positioned herself opposite them in a single armchair beside a mahogany side table where her digital recorder sat next to a tablet containing the files that would reshape several lives before teatime. Murdoch and Mulholland stood behind, while McGinty leaned against the door frame, hands in pockets.

'Thank you, everyone, for joining us today', Balfour began, standing at the apex of the rough circle the assembly was arranged in, 'I realise that some of you might have been alarmed by the urgency of my call, but we're here because this family's secrets have finally caught up with them, and it's time we discussed what kind of men these really are.'

George Cockburn's pale eyes flashed with aristocratic outrage as he straightened in his chair. 'This is outrageous! I will not be lectured by some jumped-up constable!'

'Is it?' Balfour's dark gaze fixed on him with unwavering intensity. 'Let us examine the evidence, shall we? Mr James…

eight point three million pounds in personal guarantees. What kind of husband allows his wife to shoulder a burden like that - and then still conducts an affair behind her back?'

As Gavin James's face drained of colour, his lawyer's pen hovered warningly over his notes. 'Detective Constable, my client's personal—'

'While your wife was working eighteen-hour days to save your failing business', Balfour continued relentlessly, 'you were with your mistress. Multiple failed ventures, contractor disputes, weather delays, protest campaigns - every problem that could destroy a property development, and still she stood by you. Still guaranteed your debts. Still protected your worthless hide.'

'That's enough—' James began, but Balfour, backed by a warning growl from McGinty, was not about to budge.

'And you, Mr Cockburn. Scores of failed investments, bleeding the family trust dry; several legal settlements with women who couldn't fight back; multiple counts of assault on the vulnerable man who serves as your caretaker and a long, long list of sex workers with credible tales they're too scared to make official.

'You used your family position to escape the consequences at every turn, until your sister threatened to intervene...'

James shifted uncomfortably in his chair. 'Getting a bit personal, isn't it?' he muttered, though his voice lacked any of his brother-in-law's sneering confidence.

'Personal?' Balfour's voice carried a clap of thunder with it. 'A woman is dead because of the toxic family dynamic you two cowards created. Your idea of marriage, Mr James, is letting your wife guarantee your debts while you're shagging your mistress. And your concept of proper conduct, Mr Cockburn, is beneath contempt.'

Again, Cockburn's QC moved to interrupt, but Campbell headed her off. 'DC Balfour is establishing character and credibility, ladies and gentlemen. I suggest we allow him to proceed.'

'Cowards, the pair of you', Balfour continued, his assessment landing like a slap across his audience's face. 'Worthless, rotten cowards without a trace of moral backbone - and now someone's dead because of it.'

He moved to Campbell's evidence table, picking up the waiting tablet. 'But let's examine what the evidence actually tells us about your guilt or innocence, shall we?'

He hit the first file prepared by Murdoch, the screen reflecting against crystal decanters as CCTV footage began to play. 'Mr James, the security cameras place you in Catherine Stewart's Morningside flat from Monday afternoon through the entire murder window. Eighteen hours of high-definition footage showing you physically incapable of being at Heriot Row when your wife was killed.'

James's solicitor leaned forward judiciously as the timestamps scrolled past. 'My client's movements are fully documented—'

'Indeed they are', Balfour agreed. 'Documented conducting an extramarital affair while his wife worked to save his failing business. Undeniable evidence that Gavin James is morally reprehensible and financially reckless, but not a murderer.'

He turned his attention to George, whose eyes had narrowed. 'Mr Cockburn, the records show your delayed flight from London and your hotel check-in at 1:30am, leaving several unaccounted hours that could potentially have provided opportunity. You had knowledge of family routines, security systems, and access to the house.'

'My client has explained his travel arrangements—' Patricia Fraser began.

'He has', Balfour nodded. 'And while those arrangements might have shown it was unlikely that you could have committed the murder, but they also helped unlock your fundamental character.'

He scrolled through to a second piece of CCTV footage, this time showing two scantily dressed women walking through a hotel lobby. 'The testimony of the escorts you arranged to come to your hotel room that night does indeed provide a watertight alibi, but also, unfortunately, paints a lurid portrait of a man who exploits the weak - a bully who gets his kicks maltreating people too vulnerable to fight back.'

Campbell consulted her notes with professional neutrality. 'Both suspects had motives - James to avoid financial ruin, Cockburn to gain control of the family trust. Both had some degree of motive and opportunity.'

'But neither possessed the strength of character for murder', Balfour said quietly, 'or for honesty.'

'Make no mistake: both of you contributed to the toxic family dynamic that made this tragedy inevitable. And both of you are morally culpable for creating the circumstances that led to Rowena James's death - even if neither of you wielded the weapon.'

* * *

The silence that followed Balfour's exposition was profound. It enveloped the room as he slowly regarded each of the assembled company in turn, then remained unbroken as he stood by the fireplace wall, his fingers gently fluttering over the immaculate Georgian panelling.

'The question that's plagued this investigation from the very beginning', he said, his audience's attention locked into his every word, 'is how someone entered a locked room without being seen by cameras covering every approach. We've checked every entrance, every corridor, every possible route to this study - and yet we've found nothing.

'It has been - in every respect - an impossible crime.'

Mulholland, standing with lip curled in the background as he watched Balfour's exposition, glanced at the doorway where McGinty had been standing minutes before. He'd vanished, unnoticed, but before he could comment a rap of Balfour's knuckles against the wall snapped back his attention.

'The answer', the dark eyed DC continued, his hand resting on the elegant wainscoting, 'lies not in what we could see - but in what we were never meant to see at all.'

Noiselessly, a section of panelling beside him swung softly inward on hidden hinges. There was a momentary pause, and then McGinty appeared in the dark aperture, stepping into the drawing room like a magician's assistant.

'Scottish engineering at its finest', he announced with professional satisfaction. 'Takes you straight down to the old servants' quarters in the basement - or up to the study, opening immediately behind the desk.'

Cockburn's composure cracked, a look of genuine surprise finally piercing his carefully maintained demeanour as he gripped the arm of his chair. James, meanwhile, his stomach lurching, looked like he could picture it all too clearly: a door sighing open behind the great desk, someone stepping silently into the study...

Murdoch gestured towards the security cameras covering the windows and doorway. 'The CCTV coverage was perfect for anyone using normal routes through the house, but this staircase bypasses every camera in the building'

'This passage was designed so the family would never have to see their servants', Balfour continued. 'Built shortly after the house was constructed by an inveterate snob, it allowed the family's staff to move between floors without disturbing their betters. The perfect infrastructure for keeping people invisible.'

George Cockburn's voice wavered for the first time since the interview had begun. 'That's… that passage… surely sealed for decades—'

'On the contrary', Balfour interrupted, his voice steady, 'it's been in regular use by someone who's known it for their entire life.'

Patricia Fraser, brow furrowed, raised a tentative hand. 'Are you suggesting—'

'I'm suggesting that someone had his own way in', Balfour said quietly. 'The same route his family had used for decades before him. The same architectural anomaly that had enabled generations of snobbery, ignorance and exploitation.'

Campbell studied the hidden entrance, the light dawning in her eyes. 'He could access the study at any time without being seen on security cameras?'

'More than that', Balfour replied, his voice carrying the weight of absolute certainty. 'He could move through this house like a ghost. She may not have known it, but Rowena's family has been hiding its servants for generations. Last Monday night, someone used that same system to hide from her.'

Across the room, a pair of eyes flicked instinctively toward the yawning gap behind the panelling, then away again just as quickly. The movement was so small it might have been missed, yet it carried the weight of someone who knew all too well what Balfour was describing.

* * *

'When Dr Cliff first examined the crime scene, he observed that whoever did this must have really hated Rowena James. The violence was so savage, so personal, that it felt like only hatred could explain it.'

Balfour paused, a look of profound sadness clouding his face. 'But he was wrong. This murder wasn't about hate, or greed, or any of the base emotions that lie beneath ninety-nine out of a hundred of the horrible things that people do.

'This was about love. Real, honest, unquestioning love - and the terrible cloying fear it creates when you think you may lose it.'

As the revelation sunk into the silence that followed, Balfour's eyes turned towards the hunched figure in the corner. Hands trembling with mounting terror as he stared at the figure of McGinty, standing in the entrance to the house's open secret.

'Douglas', Balfour he said gently, the scalding tone he'd used to eviscerate James and Cockburn only minutes before noticeably absent, 'would you like to tell us what happened?'

Kemp remained silent, his head bowed for what seemed like an age, before finally looking up with the desperate eyes of a child caught in an unforgivable act. 'She... she wanted to speak to me', he whispered, his voice hoarse through the tears. 'She said she knew about the missing things and we needed to have a chat.'

Murdoch, handed the tablet by Balfour, scrolled through the crime scene photographs until she found what she was looking for and held it up. 'One of the windows open on Mrs James's computer screen was a household inventory. She'd been cataloguing missing items for weeks.'

'The silver frames, the jewellery, the things from downstairs', Kemp continued, his confession tumbling out in broken fragments. ' Eddie and Tam said it wasn't stealing because I was just giving them stuff to pay what I owed. But then Rowena said that it made her sad… I didn't know what to do.'

Campbell, compassionate but coolly professional, encouraged him. 'So what did you do Douglas?'

'I thought...' Kemp's voice broke entirely now, tears streaming down his cheeks as the weight of what he'd done overwhelmed him. 'I thought she'd send me away. Mr George always said she would. He said she said she was getting tired of having me around.

'But I don't have anywhere to go…'

The pathetic simplicity of it was sickening. A brain-damaged man, exploited by loan sharks, terrorised by his supposed protector, had killed the one person who showed him kindness because he couldn't cope with the prospect of losing her.

'Didn't you think she would be kind - that she'd help you like always?' Balfour asked quietly. 'If you just talked to her?'

'She was disappointed!' Kemp sobbed. 'I never… I can't… I wouldn't do that!

'I'm not bad and she shouldn't have wanted to send me away, and Mr George says you must always make people understand when they are wrong - even if it hurts.

'When she said she wanted to talk to me about the missing things, I went upstairs through the old passage my mum and dad used to use. I wasn't going to hurt her very much. Just enough so that she said I could stay.'

'The heavy thing', Murdoch said gently. 'Where is it?'

Kemp's eyes flickered with shame toward the wall. 'It's at the bottom of the passage with the other old thing. I remembered it from my accident, and I... I couldn't think.'

The irony was devastating. The tragedy complete. Yet George Cockburn's eyes glittered with barely concealed satisfaction as the confession unfolded before him.

'Terrible case', George murmured with a feigned note of sympathy that fooled no one. 'Poor Douglas clearly couldn't handle the pressure of his debts. One does what one can for people like him, but some individuals simply can't be helped, can they?'

The casual cruelty of the comment hit home, causing even his battle-hardened QC to reveal the briefest flash of contempt while McGinty, glowering, gripped the doorframe beside him. Balfour and Murdoch remained impassive, sharing only the briefest of glances.

'Douglas Kemp', Campbell said rising from her chair, the weight of inevitability settling over the elegant room, 'I'm arresting you for the murder of Rowena James. You do not have to say anything, but it may harm your defence if you do not mention when questioned something which you later rely on in court.'

As the formal caution continued, Kemp sat vacant and uncomprehending, barely capable of understanding the charges being laid against him. Their murderer had been unmasked, but in the circumstances, it didn't feel a lot like justice.

George Cockburn straightened his expensive suit jacket and checked his watch, nodding to the QC beside him as he stretched luxuriantly and smiled at the faces staring across the room at him.

'If there's nothing else', Patricia Fraser said as she placed her notebook back into her briefcase, 'my client has been most cooperative throughout this difficult process. As I understand it the only accusation remaining against him is common assault, and given the circumstances of your only witness against him, I don't believe he will have much of a case to answer.'

As Mulholland shouldered his way to the front and moved to escort a handcuffed Douglas Kemp from the room, Cockburn casually pulled out his phone, scrolling through messages as if the tragic confession had been nothing more than a mildly entertaining show.

'Patricia', he said to his solicitor with aristocratic ease, 'could you recommend someone reliable to have the house cleaned professionally? I'm thinking of redecorating - may even move into the master bedroom… now that it's available.'

Chapter 33

Mount Stewart Farm, Callander, 1860

Slumped in the chair where he'd been deposited, in the very spot where his crimes had reached their bloody crescendo, Henderson's face was ashen and his hands trembling as he faced the courtroom that had once been his home, shrinking beneath the accusatory glare of those who had once been his friends.

'Now then, Mr Henderson,' Balfour said levelly, settling himself in the chair opposite as Young withdrew his notebook. 'Shall we begin with the truth this time?'

'Why don't you tell me about the railways?'

Henderson buried his face in his hands, exhaling deeply, before finally accepting the nature of his current position and raising his head to speak. 'Some of the African ventures were real - investors had been receiving healthy returns in the beginning - but the Royal Mauritanian Railway Company... it never existed.'

Arbuthnot silenced Dr Geddes's strangled note of protest with a sharp gesture as Henderson continued, curtly nodding at his acquaintance to continue as the words began tumbling out.

'After the crash of fifty-seven, we lost everything. The farm had been mortgaged to sink funds into American securities, and when the London market froze we were left beyond recovery, Janet's future prospects destroyed, our family's position in the community hanging by the thinnest thread,' he said, his voice gathering strength as he justified his actions to himself if nobody else.

'But then, when it seemed all was lost, one of my connections in finance made me aware of how we could... create opportunities where none existed.'

Young's pen scratched steadily across the paper as Henderson described the elaborate fraud in methodical detail - the carefully forged correspondence from non-existent railway companies, the strategic endorsements by established brokers to create credibility for the nascent enterprise - and the systematic targeting of vulnerable investors across Scotland.

Widows seeking security, retired military officers hoping to supplement modest pensions, country parsons dreaming of better futures for their children - all drawn into the web by a sheen of commercial rectitude and financial prudence.

'And Janet's involvement? How did that come about?'

Henderson shook his head in resignation. 'It may surprise you to learn that I have not always been... well liked. I do not suffer fools, sir, and have never hesitated to give my opinion when I found others lacking. From the outset I knew that Janet's softer approach would make engaging others in such correspondence simpler, more natural and welcome.

'At first I used her name judiciously, but soon every letter of solicitation, every progress report and every dividend notice—all written in my hand—bearing her signatures, promising returns from railways that would never be built.'

Somehow, Henderson's voice still carried a faintly triumphal ring. 'But the money was real enough. Thousands of pounds from people who trusted my... her... good name.'

'And Janet discovered this?' Balfour pressed.

Henderson's composure cracked. 'It started with a letter sent directly to her by a cousin in Aberfeldy that I was unable to intercept. She began asking uncomfortable questions about the investments, wondering why the promised returns never materialised, why the reports from Africa seemed... inconsistent. I started hiding the keys to the strongbox, claiming they'd been stolen, anything to keep her from accessing the documents.' He laughed bitterly. 'But Janet was thorough in everything she did. She found where I'd hidden them, opened the box, and confronted me that evening.'

The kitchen held its breath as Henderson described that fatal evening - Janet's moral certainty colliding with his desperate justifications, her refusal to be complicit in defrauding innocent people, his growing rage as he realised she would never be swayed from exposing the truth.

'She had every letter, every promise, wrapped up in the folio demanding explanations for each of them.' Henderson's face grew stormy. 'I tried everything, but the daft lassie was immovable. She said that she would write to every investor immediately, contact the authorities, and expose everything.'

'She retired to the kitchen, said she needed time to think, to plan how to make restitution to the people I'd cheated.' His hands trembled. 'After a few hours, I followed her there, desperate to find some way to change her mind, to protect the farm, our position, the respect of the community—all of it slipping away because of her bloody moral certainty.'

Henderson's voice dropped to barely a whisper. 'She always maintained that work steadied her thoughts, and I found her stooped at the hearth, humming low over her task, so intent on it that she scarcely marked my step.

'I stood a while, watching her prepare to lay waste to all I'd built, and the rage… it rose like a fever. The axe she used for kindling lay close at hand, so I took it up and…' his voice broke. 'By Heaven - she never so much as turned her head. In my mercy she had no notion. Not a whit.'

Young continued documenting as Henderson provided the mechanical details of murder and deception - the repeated blows that silenced his sister's voice forever, the string mechanism that created the locked room illusion, his calculated absence to forge an alibi whilst Janet's body lay undiscovered. Then came the systematic framing of the innocent.

'Then came the necessity of deflecting suspicion. I had already told Janet my keys were stolen and had planned to use them against Miller, but after the murder it was a simple matter to claim Crichton must have taken them,' said Henderson, now in unstoppable flow.

'The man had always been surly, resistant to proper authority. So it was easy enough to encourage witnesses to see his complaints as murderous threats.'

'And the money found in Miller's possession?' Young asked, his face barely containing the fury burning within his honest countryman's soul.

'It would have been convenient if she and her bastard child had disappeared quietly, but I knew it would be found if she was apprehended.' Henderson's cold pragmatism was chilling. 'The same reason I hid money and Janet's jewelry in her old room - my childhood bedroom - as evidence of theft that would implicate both her and perhaps even Crichton in a conspiracy.'

'Two birds with one stone,' Young muttered, his disgust evident. 'Frame them both and at least one hangs in your stead.'

Henderson shrugged. 'It would have been… convenient. A solution that protected what truly mattered.'

'And Christina Miller?' Amelia asked quietly.

Henderson seemed indifferent. 'The child is mine. Janet discovered that as well - said it was the final proof of my complete moral corruption...'

'She was right, of course. About everything.'

'One last thing,' interjected Balfour. 'Several of the letters and documents recovered carry the embossed watermark of a five pointed star. What does that refer to?'

Henderson's face froze, and he seemed to immediately retreat back into caution.

'My railway schemes, Mr Young, were not entirely my own creation. There are gentlemen in Edinburgh, in London, who provided… guidance. Expertise. Capital. Did you really think a farmer could construct such an elaborate financial architecture without assistance? Without protection?

'That five pointed star, as you call it, is proof that my associations extend far beyond Callander. That there are people in positions of considerable influence who have a vested interest in this affair - and that you would be wise to rush to judgement less hastily.'

His patience at an end, Young abruptly stood and addressed the transformed character before him. 'No more! The evidence laid before me is clear and conclusive. You, sir, stand accused by your own admission of the murder of Janet Henderson, and of gross fraud upon investors throughout Scotland.

'By the authority vested in the office of the Procurator Fiscal, you shall be committed forthwith to the custody of the Sheriff, there to await your trial before the High Court of Justiciary.

'You are undone, and the law will have its reckoning.'

The guilty man, his composure apparently restored, shrugged carelessly as he returned Young's gaze, unflinching.

'Oh, I think you'll find the matter rather more complicated than that.'

***

A morning that was meant to begin with the trial and despatch of John Crichton instead exploded in a welter of clerical activity as Henderson's confession finally set the machinery of justice grinding into motion.

Arriving that morning with his captive in tow, Young had established himself in the Sheriff's Perth chambers with the satisfaction of a man who had returned from battle not only with his shield, but with all the spoils of victory piled on top of it. Spreading Henderson's witnessed confession, Miller's exonerating testimony, and Amelia's scientific notes across the polished oak table, he grinned broadly as the long-serving judge read with growing astonishment.

'It's as clear-cut a case as I've seen,' declared Sheriff Fergusson, reviewing the evidence with evident admiration. 'Murder, systematic fraud, conspiracy - everything required for prosecution without room for hesitation or doubt.

'Young. Mr Balfour. I commend you. But for this intervention I would have sent an innocent man to the gallows before the week was out.'

He wasted no time, within hours Crichton had been released from custody amid public acclaim, whilst arrangements were put in place to ensure Miller's complete exoneration. Meanwhile the village elders that had once rushed to condemn the innocent were now falling over themselves to send congratulatory telegrams praising Young's thoroughness in exposing the real villain.

'The High Court will want this expedited,' Fergusson noted, initialing documents. 'Such systematic criminality demands swift justice, and the evidence is overwhelming.'

The hammer, when it fell, came in the hand of a young clerk, barely out of his teens, his voice wobbling as he interrupted the meeting with a nervous tap on the door and placed an urgent package - delivered that morning - on the sheriff's desk.

A set of notarised documents bearing unfamiliar seals and processed through channels Young didn't recognise—spilled out.

'This is most irregular,' Fergusson frowned. 'These papers appear to be in order, but I have never seen anything like them before. Who authorised an inquiry into the prisoner's state of mind, and on what grounds?'

The nervous clerk could only shrug. 'Orders came by special courier, sir. From the Crown Office in Edinburgh—or so the envelope was marked. But the routing… is unclear.'

Glancing at Young, Balfour felt the first stirring of alarm. The language was correct, the seals authentic, but the entire proceeding felt at odds with the natural running of such matters.

He was right to be concerned.

By afternoon, what had begun as a straightforward prosecution had become a complex administrative maze. It seemed as if additional evaluations were being ordered every hour, with requests from a litany of offices being delivered to the Perth Court by a cavalcade of special couriers as every legal authority in the country somehow found themselves dragged into a many-fronted battle for jurisdiction.

'My clerks have had three telegraphed enquiries about Henderson's mental state,' Fergusson reported with bewilderment. 'From Edinburgh practitioners I've never heard of, all asking identical questions about his fitness for trial.'

The Sheriff's irritation mounted as complications multiplied. 'In thirty years, I've never seen such irregular interest in a straightforward criminal matter. Half of Edinburgh seems suddenly concerned for this beggar's welfare.'

Young, meanwhile, studied the multiplying paperwork with growing unease. Each document bore a forest of seals, stamps, and co-signatories - all of them demonstrably genuine, but in such numbers that they apparently transcended the usual run of government process.

'Look at this,' he murmured to Balfour, indicating the rising visible markings. 'I don't know about you, old chap, but I've got rather a bad feeling about this.'

***

The final act played out later that afternoon, with curiously little fanfare, as Young sat in Sheriff Fergusson's chambers surrounded by the debris of what had begun as straightforward prosecution and had transformed into something resembling a bureaucratic siege.

The desk was strewn with documents, their vellum crowded by a rash of seals he knew well and many he did not, counter-signed by authorities whose names were foreign to him, and marked with routing codes that appeared to not so much sneak around the usual channels but stamp across them.

'I've been Sheriff in this district since time began,' Fergusson muttered, examining the latest batch of paperwork with the bewildered expression of a man watching his professional world rearrange itself according to rules he didn't recognize. 'Never seen anything like this. These orders appear to carry the highest legal authority, but they're implementing procedures I've never encountered in an entire life of service.'

The decisive document had arrived an hour earlier, carried by yet another special courier whose credentials seemed to outrank everyone present.

'William Henderson, having been assessed by competent medical authority as suffering from acute mental distress resulting from recent traumatic events, is hereby committed to private medical care for treatment of psychological instability,' Young read aloud, his voice carrying flat and exhausted.

'The routing stamps show this passed through at least six different administrative offices before reaching us,' Balfour observed, tracing the bureaucratic trail with his finger. 'Its authenticity is beyond doubt.'

Sheriff Fergusson nodded grimly as he initialed the final documents. 'The medical opinion supporting this commitment comes from practitioners I've never heard of, citing assessments conducted without my knowledge or approval. Yet every seal, every signature, every procedural step appears completely legitimate.'

'Because it is legitimate,' came a cultured voice from the chamber doorway, where a stranger in plain but expensive travelling clothes stood examining the proceedings, a small silver cinquefoil gleaming from his buttonhole.
'The Crown has determined that Mr Henderson's case requires… alternative handling, on account of considerations that reach far beyond this chamber.'
He stepped inside with measured assurance, a flustered clerk trailing at his heels.
'Gentlemen, I am here to see these arrangements executed without hindrance,' the stranger went on, his smile precisely judged. 'In the frenzy of his derangement, Mr Henderson utters accusations which, if given credence, would cast grave aspersions upon certain persons of influence. Their honour and station must not be imperilled by the incoherent fancies of a disordered mind.
'It has therefore been resolved that justice, and indeed the national interest, would be better served by placing him under treatment for his affliction. Should his reason be restored, inquiry may then be made into the truth of his allegations, but until such a time, we must regard them as nothing more than the imaginings of a lunatic.'
And just like that it was over. The decision made, the history wrote. All hopes of restitution gone forever.
Within the hour, Henderson had been loaded into a carriage bound for a private medical facility whose location they were told would remain undisclosed.
'The arrangement provides treatment rather than punishment,' the distinguished stranger had explained with a smile. 'A more… compassionate resolution than the public

spectacle of a trial, and one that serves the interests of all parties.'

Balfour, studying the papers strewn across the Sheriff's desk, was left feeling empty - astonished at how one man's guilt had thrown the whole edifice of justice into disarray. Whether it was by accident or design he could not tell; but from where he sat, it left nothing but a host of unanswered questions.

And he really didn't like questions without answers.

Chapter 34

Procurator Fiscal's Office, Edinburgh, 2025

The weather outside the Procurator Fiscal's office window seemed to be undecided whether to continue the previous night's downpour or push forwards into the spring as Balfour and Campbell settled into their chairs, bound copies of the expedited psychiatric reports placed on the mahogany table for review.

Medical terminology, tea and biscuits—the proper progression of the Scottish procedural process—delivered lukewarm in a chipped cup on a mismatched saucer.

Procurator Fiscal Margaret Blair adjusted her reading glasses as she scanned the final page of the assessment, brow furrowed and pen in hand as she balanced the competing demands of justice, public safety, and individual protection.

'Well, the medical evidence is quite clear,' she began, glancing up from the page to address the assembled company.

'Both Dr Robertson and Dr Williams have reached identical conclusions regarding Mr Kemp's capacity to participate in criminal proceedings.'

Campbell sat poised, her notebook open to a page dense with procedural notes and case references, while across the table, Dr Randolph Cliff, the pathologist whose initial observations had helped establish the medical foundation for today's decision—nodded gravely as the Fiscal continued.

'Under the Criminal Procedure Scotland Act 1995, the test is straightforward but demanding,' Blair explained, selecting a highlighted passage from the psychiatric evaluation.

'Is the defendant capable, by reason of mental or physical condition, of participating effectively in a trial? Dr Robertson's assessment demonstrates conclusively that Mr Kemp cannot understand the proceedings, cannot instruct legal representatives, and cannot meaningfully follow the court process.'

The emotional gulf between the clinical language demanded by the legislation and the reality of Douglas Kemp's decades of abuse felt enormously wide, but Balfour recognised the legal precision and the need for it. To the victims, crime is a deeply emotional, wholly personal phenomenon. To the legal system, it is a clinical exercise, stripped of human feeling and determined by the precise dictionary definition of the word of law.

It is a deeply satisfying, wholly unsympathetic thing, but utterly necessary to ensure that the true nature of justice is upheld.

Mostly.

'The historical brain injury identified during the investigation and documented by Dr Robertson provides crucial context,' Cliff interjected, his medical expertise lending weight to the psychiatric conclusions. 'The neurological damage from his childhood accident, combined with years of untreated trauma, has left him with the cognitive capacity of a child—entirely unable to comprehend the complexities of criminal proceedings.'

Blair nodded, making a notation in her legal pad and indicating the second report. 'Dr Williams concurs that Mr Kemp represents a clear case where prosecution would serve neither justice nor the public interest. The court's recognition of him as a victim rather than purely perpetrator reflects the reality that his actions—while tragic—occurred within a context of systematic exploitation by individuals who deliberately targeted his vulnerability.'

The irony was not lost on Balfour that after a lifetime of faithful service and helpless victimhood, it was ultimately only by becoming the perpetrator that the system had stepped in to provide him with protection and patience he truly needed.

'So what will your recommendation be?' Campbell asked, drilling quickly down to the nub of the matter.

Blair tapped her pen on the pad in front of her for a few moments, as if conducting a rapid internal check on the assembled thinking, before nodding with certainty. 'The Crown will not be proceeding with prosecution. We'll invite the court to impose a hospital order under the Mental Health Act, and I'm certain it will concur.

'What that will actually mean to Mr Kemp, and to what extent he can ultimately hope for complete rehabilitation I cannot say,' she continued. 'But what we can say, at least, is that he will receive appropriate medical and psychiatric treatment, not to mention protection from anyone who might seek to exploit his condition.'

'For the first time in his adult life,' muttered Balfour.

With a sympathetic nod, Scotland's top public prosecutor assembled the psychiatric reports into a neat pile, casting Campbell a quick glance. 'I understand that there may be broader implications here and that a multi-agency investigation is underway, but for now, I'd regard the case as closed.'

As they gathered their papers and prepared to leave, Balfour couldn't help reflecting on the anticlimactic conclusion to his first major case.

Outside the Fiscal's office, the afternoon light had a different quality—cleaner, brighter, with the first real warmth of the year beginning to soften the city's stone edges.

Today hadn't done much to quell the sick feeling in his gut, but perhaps this was what real justice looked like when it functioned properly—not in cinematic vengeance or slick retribution but in protection for the vulnerable and a gentle rebalancing of the scales.

***

Between yesterday's broken vending machines and this morning's delivery of surplus office furniture—a collection of mismatched filing cabinets and water-damaged desk chairs that had been unceremoniously dumped near the windows—the incident room was beginning to resemble a storage facility more than a functioning police department.

None of that seemed to bother DCI Kirk Munro, legend in his own lunchtime. He swept a shovel-sized hand toward the briefing board, its grid of mugshots, evidence photos and connecting lines now dominated by bright orange post-its stamped "CLOSED!" across the faces of Menzies, Wallace, Ferguson and Kemp.

'And that, DI Campbell, is effective leadership. Modern policing at its very best," he beamed, rocking back and forth on his heels.

'So—let's wrap up this betting shop business one last time. Four arrests, solid evidence, part of the stolen cash recovered, and significant stash of illegal equipment taken off the streets—exactly the kind of result that keeps the brass happy and a real feather in my cap.'

Campbell exchanged a glance with Murdoch, both recognising the familiar pattern of their DCI rewriting history to suit his preferred narrative, while across the room McGinty slouched against the wall, arms folded across his chest.

'For starters, Big Eddie Wallace and his crew are looking at serious time,' Munro continued, tapping the relevant photographs with obvious satisfaction. 'Multiple counts of armed robbery, intimidation, the whole package. Wallace's already accepted a guilty plea in exchange for a reduced sentence—he's taking responsibility for the entire operation.'

Balfour frowned slightly. 'What about Menzies, sir?'

'Aye, it would have been nice to take down Jojo, but Big Eddie claims he personally organised the whole thing himself—bought the kit, hired the industrial unit, planned every job and even recruited Ferguson. Unless he changes his tune we've got nothing, so the Fiscal says that the slippery bugger has to walk.'

Murdoch shrugged. 'Well, Wallace's position has certainly been consistent, sir. He's been taking full responsibility and protecting Menzies right from his first interview. The only problem with that is that it's complete and total bollocks.'

McGinty stirred from his position against the wall with a grunt. 'Aye, well, say what you like about scumbags, but they know the rules and they protect their mates. Not something you can say for everybody.'

Munro's expression hardened slightly. 'Well, the important thing is we've got confessions, we've got evidence, and we've got convictions. Job done.'

He glanced around the room, quelling any further discussion on the topic.

'That just leaves Jamie Sinclair. The big man was curiously quiet about him too. McGinty—you were following up on that, yes?'

McGinty, exchanging a look with Balfour, gave a noncommittal shrug. 'Seems there was a procedural error on that front... sir. The Crown spotted a chain of custody issue with the main piece of evidence against him and decided not to proceed.'

'Aye, the exhibit log's missing a signature," he said, turning to address the whole room. 'Must've been one of the uniforms on scene—someone scribbled something you can't read, and by the time it came back through the chain, it was too late to pin down who.

The matter-of-fact delivery couldn't quite disguise the hint of satisfaction in McGinty's voice, but the veteran detective remained impassive as he returned to his customary silence.

'I suppose these things happen on a busy op,' Munro observed philosophically, scratching the stubble on his chin as he refused to catch McGinty's eye. 'Can't win them all. The important thing is we've cleared the board, protected the public, and shown we can deliver results when it matters.'

Mulholland, who'd sat sulking at his desk throughout the briefing, waggled his notebook theatrically. 'Great work boss... a real team effort. I bet the Super will be kissing your arse over this. Just to check: I'll still be recorded as lead detective on the final reports yeah?'

Campbell and Murdoch didn't bother to conceal their eye-rolls while McGinty's expression suggested he was contemplating violence. Balfour just grinned more broadly than he had done in months.

'Noted,' Munro replied with a beam. 'We'll sort out the paperwork later but there's plenty of credit for the both of us, son.'

***

'I've got to tell you, George, that things really aren't looking good. In fact, I'd say that you're so deep in the shit that we'll need to call in the underwater search team to even find you.'

If his face had fallen at the unaccustomed contempt laced through her opening line, it did nothing to prepare him for what was to come.

'Mr Cockburn," Campbell continued, sliding a thick manila folder across the metal table to his QC. 'You are the subject of a comprehensive multi-agency investigation into systematic modern slavery, abuse and the financial exploitation of thirty-four vulnerable adults spanning the past two decades.

'The pattern is always the same—isolation, dependency, escalating abuse. What's remarkable about it is just how predictable men like you are.'

The first flicker of uncertainty crossed Cockburn's features as he registered the scope of the charges, his usual smug grin disappearing as his QC ran through the documentation with a sense of growing alarm.

'The investigation involved Police Scotland, HMRC, the Department for Work and Pensions, Social Services, and the Modern Slavery Unit,' Murdoch continued methodically. 'We have employment records showing no legitimate wages paid to vulnerable workers, tax documents revealing systematic benefit fraud, medical records documenting patterns of injury consistent with systematic abuse, and witness statements from seventeen former employees.'

Cockburn's face had begun to drain of colour as the weight of evidence mounted, his entitled composure cracking visibly as Fraser continued to speed-read page after page.

'We've frozen your assets pending proceeds of crime proceedings,' Murdoch added neutrally. 'All personal bank accounts, property portfolios, investment funds—the lot. The current financial analysis suggests approximately three million pounds in unpaid wages, benefits fraud totalling eight hundred thousand pounds and a pattern of endemic tax evasion throughout.'

'This is... this is quite impossible,' Cockburn stammered. 'These... they... are just private employment arrangements...'

Patricia Fraser silenced him with a sharp bark of warning, pinning him to his seat with a warning glare, before turning to Campbell with practiced efficiency. 'My client would naturally be willing to provide full cooperation in exchange for appropriate consideration regarding sentencing.

'A guilty plea, complete disclosure of financial arrangements, assistance with identifying other potential victims... it's all on the table.'

The shift from confident denial to plea bargaining happened so quickly that Cockburn stared at his lawyer in obvious disbelief as the reality of his situation finally penetrated his privileged worldview.

'Full cooperation?' he repeated weakly. 'But surely...'

'Would you like to avoid a life sentence George?' Fraser snapped back, slamming her palm down on the folder of evidence. 'Our priority now is damage limitation, so please—shut up and let me do the talking.'

For several moments Cockburn sat in stunned silence, but gradually his expression began to change as his initial panic gave way to anger.

'Is that the best you bitches can do?' he snarled across the interview table, flecks of saliva dotting its stainless steel surface.

'Do you really think a pair of guttersnipe whores can hurt me with your jealous little lies?

Take my money—you can't touch the family trust and that's worth way more. And do you think a man like me—with my money, and my influence, and my stomach for violence—won't make the very most of whatever prison you send me to?

'Stupid fucking sluts,' he spat. 'There's nothing you can do that will change anything. When I get out will I be poor? No. Will I struggle to reintegrate with society? No. Will there be anything to stop me doing anything I fucking want? No there won't.

'Will I be "rehabilitated"? Absolutely fucking not.'

He laughed. 'By the time I walk out of those gates, you'll still be slaving away every day like morons, still striving to pay the mortgages on the ghastly little boxes you live in—still being good little worker bees doing as you're told.

'But me? I'll still have wealth, and power, and a name that still means something wherever you go in this city.

'I'll still be a Cockburn, and everything that the name means.'

As their suspect sneered, Murdoch gathered the evidence files, a barely noticeable smile playing at the corners of her mouth as they escorted him from the interview room.

Cockburn had regained much of his composure, already planning his adaptation to temporary circumstances. But as they reached the corridor, he stopped short at the sight of Balfour waiting with another figure.

'Fancy bumping into you here, Mr Cockburn,' Balfour said cheerfully, 'Have you met Sarah Mitchell, chief reporter for BBC Scotland's evening news show?'

Chapter 35

The Manse, Callander, 1860

Not for the first time, Young reached for MacLeod's brandy decanter and applied it to his glass with enthusiasm, continuing to nurse the quiet fury that two previous visits and an entire day's journey back from Perth had failed to dissipate.

'So Henderson disappears into private care,' he said finally, his voice carrying the flat precision of a man reciting the details of his own defeat. 'Location undisclosed, practitioners unspecified, condition unexamined - but the paperwork immaculate and the procedures technically flawless.

'After all that - all our work - he just walks away.'

Shaw, still wrapped in the dissolute folds of his greatcoat, grunted in agreement - spitting into the fire with sufficient venom to produce an angry hiss.

'Not walks away,' Balfour corrected from the window, where he had been studying the slowly warming day. 'Vanishes. You saw the paperwork—this was something instigated at the very highest levels, through high offices it beggars belief to think might have been within Henderson's social circle.

'I think there can be little doubt that the closer he stepped towards the hangman's noose, the looser his tongue would have become, and who can tell what—or who—might have been revealed? The answers to that particular question lie somewhere in the details of the Mauritanian share scandal, I'm sure, but we're unlikely to discover anything now.'

Amelia Sterling, who'd remained silent throughout Balfour and Young's exposition of the events in Perth, finally spoke from her examination of MacLeod's theological text collection.

'What strikes me most is how remarkably swiftly the process was undertaken. If it takes three weeks to get a simple marriage license, whoever was responsible for the intervention certainly managed to persuade the official channels to move with remarkable speed.

'Precisely how does someone accomplish that? Surely there are only three possibilities: that a plan was in place to address Henderson's specific circumstance all along, that the order came from the very highest levels of government, or that it has been done many, many times before.'

'Or a combination of all three,' Balfour nodded in agreement.

Young, who despite himself could not harbour black moods for long, swirled his brandy thoughtfully and raised it to both the assembled company and no one in particular.

'Och well. Both Crichton and Miller are exonerated and free. Two innocent souls saved, and live to fight another day—that is something is it not?

'As for myself, I've been offered a Justice of the Peace appointment in Edinburgh and this sorry affair has convinced me that it's time for a change of scene—not to mention a different perspective on how justice might be pursued.'

He grimaced, a glint of the old military fire in his eye as he looked around at the disparate group and gestured to indicate the world around him.

'Because this is not enough. Had we—all four of us here—not taken the time to ask the question, two—three—blameless people would be dead, and the truth swept under the carpet. And if that happened here and now, it must surely happen everywhere, all the time.'

'No. The country needs protection—a battalion to stand guard against these... these bandits—who laugh in the face of decency and make a mockery of fair play.'

"What? Sodgers? Like the Black Watch do you mean?' Shaw, brow furrowed.

'No,' laughed Balfour. 'Not like them.'

'The Black Watch are the muscle of the system—legitimacy in a uniform. What John is talking about is something else: a watch upon the Watch, the people who operate between the lines, who take notice when truth and justice are not aligned.'

'The Grey Watch,' Amelia murmured.

***

After Young had gone to clear his head, and with one eye on the clock before the farewell dinner to be hosted for them both by the Reverend MacLeod, Balfour turned to settle one of the two burning questions still at the forefront of his mind.

'Actually, Solomon,' he said, 'I have something of a proposal for you, if you'd consider it. My townhouse in Edinburgh requires proper management, and I find myself in need of someone I can trust absolutely to run the establishment - particularly whenever I am absent for extended periods.'

Shaw raised an impressive eyebrow. 'Are you offering me employment, Mr Balfour?'

'I am indeed—as a general factotum, to take on day-to-day running, maintenance, and driving as required,' he smiled. 'Mrs Shaw could take on the housekeeping duties, if she's willing, and you could have the entire basement and first floor as quarters, should you wish.'

Shaw pulled his pipe from the depths of his greatcoat and began filling it from his tobacco pouch, considering the offer as he struck a match against the hearth.

'My cousin's been after taking over the carriage trade for years,' he mused, applying the flame to the bowl with methodical precision. 'He's got the horses and the knowledge, just needed the opportunity. As for Edinburgh, well, it's no stranger to me. Mrs Shaw's sister lives in Stockbridge - works as housekeeper to some professor at the university. Been after us to visit for years, so she'd be pleased to have family nearby.'

He paused for thought. 'And what about you, Mr Balfour? Where would you be in this arrangement?'

'On the second floor, when I'm in residence. Though I should warn you that my business often requires extended absences—sometimes for weeks at a time. You'd be managing the place independently during those periods, but my rooms will always be sealed when I'm away, so you would only have to concern yourself with the normal running of the house.

Balfour paused thoughtfully. 'There's no issue if you need to come back to The Trossachs occasionally. I've been considering the purchase of a couple of properties here myself—and will need someone to keep an eye on them from time to time.'

Shaw nodded slowly. 'Sounds like a practical arrangement for all concerned. Mrs Shaw would enjoy having proper accommodation, and I... I have some unfinished business there, so I do.'

Producing a battered pewter flask from somewhere within his clothing, Shaw raised it and took two rapid gulps.

'Right then,' he announced with a flourish. 'If you're heading to Edinburgh, Mr Balfour, and Young here's taking up his appointment, I suppose I'd better come along too.'

With a grunt, he wrapped his greatcoat around himself. 'Right then, I'd best get back to see the horses,' he said, pausing at the door, touching his cap in a brief salute. 'Good evening.'

As Shaw's heavy footsteps faded down the corridor, Amelia Sterling rose from her position beside the bookshelf, smoothing her skirts and following him with her expression set.

'If you'll excuse me,' she said over her shoulder to Balfour, 'I believe I should have a quick word with Solomon and Mrs Shaw before they retire for the evening.'

***

'To our distinguished guests,' the Reverend MacLeod declared, raising his glass, 'and to their safe journey to Edinburgh, where no doubt their talents will find... appropriate scope.'

While the sense of relief in their host's tone might have been a touch more obvious than courtesy generally demanded, in truth it was an emotion equally shared by his fellow members of the village's civic elite. Dr Geddes, Arbuthnot and the host all wearing expressions of barely concealed delight at the prospect of a welcome return to normal order as soon as their guests could be ushered out.

'Gentlemen,' MacLeod began, clearing his throat. 'We felt it appropriate to express our gratitude for your... thorough investigation into the Henderson matter. My parishioners' peace of mind has been greatly restored by the resolution of this unfortunate business.'

Arbuthnot nodded, his face forming into something that resembled a smile. 'Seconded! Justice has been served, and the community need not endure the spectacle of a public trial. A most satisfactory result.'

'Quite so,' Dr Geddes chimed in. 'The poor man's obvious mental distress made prosecution impossible, but his removal from society provides the protection the public requires.'

'Does it?' Balfour, who had been studying the three worthies with the detached interest, finally spoke. 'It certainly protects Henderson. I'm not so sure who else.'

The temperature in the room seemed to drop momentarily.

'Really, Mr Balfour,' MacLeod protested with wounded dignity, 'surely proper medical intervention in a case of obvious mental disturbance is simple Christian compassion?'

'Quite probably Reverend,' Amelia Sterling interjected from behind them. 'But would that abundance of empathy still be flowing if Christina Miller or John Crichton were the guilty party?'

The minister's raven-haired bete noir stood grinning in the doorway, one permanently wayward lock tumbling over her shoulder. One hand leaned casually against the frame, the other carrying a sealed envelope by her side.

Cutting off her host's stuttered protestations, she hurled a devastating smile at the company before continuing.

'Come now gentlemen. Let us not pretend. Had Crichton been found guilty, you would have toasted his demise without a thought - not for him, nor for his wife and children.'

Arbuthnot cleared his throat to respond, but again she cut him off.

'Do not deny who you are, sir. I come from a family that considers itself something of a cut above the rest of humanity—raised at a table where, frankly, the practitioners of trades like sawbones and scribe would not have been welcome.

'So I know how easily some look over the heads of others. I understand how intoxicating it is to regard yourself - irrespective of the evidence - as somehow better than the next man.'

She paused, plucking a glass of claret from the immobile hand of Dr Geddes before continuing to address an audience stunned into silence.

'That misplaced conviction was all that was required to drag innocent people to the very brink with barely a thought. A simple, lazy, slovenly lack of regard that came within a whisker of leaving one man dead—and the rest of you damned.'

MacLeod, recovering, said weakly: 'But, Miss Sterling, as your host and guardian I—'

'Ah yes,' Amelia interrupted. 'About that...'

'As you may or may not be aware, I have spent the past month corresponding with practitioners in Edinburgh regarding my work in the science of detection. Now a friend of my father has requested my assistance in cataloguing a collection of medical jurisprudence for the keeper of the Advocates' Library. Hardly work for a lady of breeding, of course—but I believe I shall be very much at home there.'

'Edinburgh?' MacLeod managed faintly.

'Edinburgh,' Amelia confirmed with serene satisfaction. 'Mrs Shaw has kindly agreed to offer me lodgings there - under proper chaperonage - to allow me to both pursue my research and maintain appropriate propriety.'

She placed the envelope she'd been carrying gently into the palm of the minister's hand.

'My resignation, sir. Gentlemen, it has been... educational serving this community as a teacher. I trust that my replacement will find the children eager to learn, the parents appropriately grateful, and the trustees duly enthusiastic with regards to her instruction.'

Stepping back through the door with fluid grace, Amelia Sterling paused, tucked a disobedient curl behind her ear, and nodded her farewell.

'Good day, gentlemen. I trust you'll find the future... illuminating.'

Chapter 36

MIT 13 Office, Edinburgh, 2025

'Gather round for what will be one of the shortest, but also probably the most important briefings of your careers.'

Beaming from between the two stacks of empty plastic crates that had somehow materialised overnight, DCI Munro towered over his assembled team as they hunched at their keyboards, finalising the productions—each exhibit from the two cases sealed, labelled, and readied for trial, the last task before drawing a line under both inquiries.

'They say you can't slip anything past a real detective. Well, I'm here to tell you what I've just told Superintendent Richardson - they're spot on, because that's a fucking fact.

He tapped the side of his nose with a mysterious finger. 'Now... for a few weeks now I've been picking up subtle clues - tiny hints that most people wouldn't notice, but that a master of the art can use to reveal what others can't see.

'Get ready for the big time folks. We're moving.'

A flurry of glances flitted between the team. It had been hard not to notice the gradual build up of activity as a variety of items had been wheeled in and out of the office in recent weeks, while McGinty had been told by Maureen from the canteen two days previously that something was afoot.

'There's boxes everywhere, boss,' Mulholland observed helpfully. 'Are we finally getting moved somewhere decent?'

Munro's grin widened to encompass his entire face, radiating unbridled confidence.

'James, my boy, I think you'll find that when you consistently deliver results like I have with the Rowena James case and the bookie heists, certain people in positions of authority begin to take notice,' he declared, rocking back on his heels.

'My... our recent successes haven't gone unnoticed at the highest levels and...'

He paused, taking a moment to look at each of them in turn as the suspense mounted.

'Gartcosh,' he continued, rolling the word around his tongue like he was savouring a fine wine. 'The Scottish Crime Campus. State-of-the-art facilities, proper resources, the sort of investigative environment where real police work gets done by real detectives.'

He gestured expansively at the collection of mismatched furniture, temperamental computers, and general institutional shabbiness that constituted their current working environment.

'No more making do with hand-me-down equipment and surplus office space. No more squeezing five detectives into accommodation designed for three. We're talking about purpose-built incident rooms, dedicated forensics support, and - perhaps most importantly - the recognition that MIT-13 has finally proved itself worthy of serious consideration.'

'Has this been confirmed officially, Sir?' Campbell asked, one eyebrow subtly arched as she looked up from her screen.

'There hasn't been time, but I popped my head into the Super's office and let's just say he complimented me on my skills as a detective.'

'That's brilliant news, boss,' Mulholland enthused, practically vibrating with excitement at the prospect of associating himself with what appeared to be genuine advancement. 'When do we move?'

'Patience, son,' Munro replied, enjoying his moment. 'These things take time to arrange properly. But I've been led to understand that the wheels are already in motion, and it's simply a matter of crossing the t's and dotting the i's before we pack our bags.'

He paused dramatically, clearly enjoying the attention.

'I think it's fair to say that all of you contributed to resolving two very problematic cases, and you should know that I recognise your efforts. Sometimes, it takes a strong leader to bring out the best in their team, and I'm particularly proud of how I've managed to develop this squad over these past months.'

The silence that followed was pregnant with unspoken responses, but Munro remained oblivious. Munro's grin widened as he surveyed his domain with obvious satisfaction.

'Efficiency, cost-effectiveness, and results. Cases closed quickly and cleanly without expensive deviations or wasted time - focusing resources where they deliver maximum operational impact.

'That's Munro's Law.'

***

Over the course of a storied career, Detective Superintendent Gordon Richardson QPM had built a reputation as both a formidable street detective and a shrewd political operator. Known across the ranks as "The Old Man", he could fill a room simply by stepping into it.

This time was no different.

His appearance in the doorway cut through the prevailing atmosphere in a heartbeat, instantly transforming the room's energy from manic optimism to hushed expectation—his steel-grey hair and measured bearing radiating authority.

'Superintendent,' Munro greeted, faltering slightly at the unexpected arrival. 'I was just bringing the team up to speed on our recent successes… and the upcoming transition arrangements.'

Stepping nimbly into the incident room—past the collection of removal boxes, hastily organised case files, and the team's carefully neutral expressions—Richardson gave a nod of greeting to Campbell before speaking.

'Yes, I thought it might be useful to discuss those successes in a bit more detail,' he said. 'Particularly given the thoroughness of the reports I've been reviewing about both investigations.'

He moved further into the room, positioning himself where he could observe both Munro and the team simultaneously, his attention briefly settling on each officer before returning to the DCI.

'The betting shop robberies, for instance. Quite an impressive result - almost the entire operation wrapped up with enough evidence to secure maximum convictions. Equipment seizures, financial intelligence, the works—it's undeniably solid work.'

Munro's grin widened. 'Thank you sir. And credit where credit is due - the team responded well to my strategic direction.'

'Indeed,' Richardson continued, consulting the folder he carried. 'Though I can't help noticing that the breakthrough came from some rather traditional police work, really. Door-to-door inquiries, pattern recognition, following the evidence wherever it led rather than jumping to obvious conclusions.

'Sterling stuff.'

'Well, sir, as I'm always telling this lot - it takes strong leadership to coordinate investigative strands into a coherent strategy,' Munro replied, 'but at the end of the day we're just one big effective team.'

'Quite right,' Richardson agreed, his expression deadpan. 'And of course, that leadership also means ensuring that credit for good work reaches the officers who earned it.'

For a moment Balfour and Murdoch could have sworn that the Superintendent winked in their direction, but the thought was fleeting, and quickly vanished as Munro barged on.

'Naturally, sir. I believe in recognising talent and developing it appropriately,' Munro boomed. 'In fact, I'm particularly proud of how I've managed to develop young Balfour's investigative instincts. Sometimes it takes experience to spot potential and nurture it.'

He paused, glancing in Mulholland's direction. 'James here was my formal lead on the bookmaker jobs, of course, and Murdoch helped too.

Richardson's expression remained unchanged.

'Balfour,' Richardson mused, glancing at his folder again. 'And Murdoch. Yes, their work has certainly been noted. Thorough, methodical, willing to pursue lines of inquiry that others might have overlooked.

'The sort of detective work that gets results.'

He looked up from his notes, his gaze settling on Balfour.

'Sometimes the best thing you can do is simply get out of the way and let good officers do what they do best.'

***

As the sudden bright sunshine of early spring cut through the window blinds, sending shafts of light and shadow across the room, Richardson turned his attention fully to Balfour, his expression softening almost imperceptibly as he addressed the younger officer directly.

'David, I've been reviewing your work on both investigations, and I have to say I'm impressed with what I've seen. The way you've connected patterns others had missed, followed through on seemingly minor details, and refused to accept the first answer you were given - that's the sort of investigative thinking we need more of in the modern force.

He paused, nodding to Munro before continuing. 'Which is why I'd like to formally invite you to begin preparing for your sergeant's examinations.'

The silence that followed was electric. Mulholland looked like he might throw up, while Munro's expression shifted rapidly from surprise to something approaching panic.

'Sir, that's... that's very ... I appreciate the confidence you're showing in my abilities,' Balfour replied, caught off guard.

'It's not confidence, son - it's recognition of demonstrated competence,' Richardson said firmly. 'The sort of work you've been doing deserves to be rewarded with increased responsibility and appropriate rank. And DC Murdoch... don't imagine for a moment that I've forgotten you.'

Murdoch caught Balfour's eye across the room and flashed him a smile of excitement, while Campbell nodded approvingly from her desk. Even McGinty looked up from his newspaper with what might have been the ghost of a grin.

'However,' Richardson continued, his tone shifting slightly as he abruptly switched tacks, 'there are also some administrative matters we need to address regarding MIT-13's current accommodation arrangements.'

The mood in the room shifted as he recaptured their attention.

'It won't come as much of a surprise to hear that the ongoing renovation work here in Fettes has been putting pressure on resources, nor that this means we need to relocate you - temporarily - while the facilities are being upgraded.

'The good news, however, is that we've secured alternative accommodation that should more than meet your operational requirements.'

Munro leaned forward eagerly, his optimism renewed. 'Gartcosh sir? The Crime Campus facilities would certainly provide us with the sort of professional environment that—'

'Callander,' Richardson interrupted smoothly. 'We've arranged surplus council accommodation in the town centre. Basic but functional office space that should serve your needs adequately while the renovations are completed.'

Munro's face went through a remarkable series of expressions - confusion, disbelief, and finally crushing disappointment, as the reality became clear.

'Callander?' Mulholland echoed weakly. 'In the... in the Trossachs?'

'That's right constable - top marks for geographical knowledge. Stirling MIT needs extra cover but have assured me they don't have the room to accommodate you. Fortunately, your new facilities are available immediately, and the location should provide you with a quiet environment while you adapt to your new caseload.'

So much for being promoted to the big leagues.

As Richardson left, and the team began to absorb the implications of their new posting, Munro approached Balfour with a smile on his face and undisguised loathing in his eyes.

'Well done on the sergeant's opportunity, son,' he said quietly, drawing him to the side and positioning himself close enough that only Balfour could hear his words clearly. 'Of course, you'll need to remember that promotions like this require ongoing support from senior officers who understand your potential.'

Taking a grip on the lapel of the young detective's coat and pulling him in close, his vast frame looming, Munro's voice dropped to barely above a whisper, delivered through his teeth with an unmistakable edge.

'I'll be keeping you tight from now on, son. Close supervision, regular progress reviews, making sure you remember exactly who helped develop your career and who can still break it if you don't keep them sweet.'

The threat was delivered with a trademark smile, but there was no mistaking the underlying message.

'Now then, Davey boy. Be a good lad and go and get me a fucking coffee.'

Epilogue

A confident spring sunshine illuminated the scene as Balfour reached the top of the crags, each footfall steady and deliberate on the weathered stone path as he stood on the precipice and looked down on the town below.

To his right, the great shoulders of Highland Perthshire rose in ancient majesty, their greening flanks beckoning up to the shimmering loch beyond. To his left, the great Carse of Stirling stretched away towards the distant cities, smoking with modernity and fertile opportunity.

Only here, on this high place, could he see both paths clearly. Sitting in the warming sun, in a soft wind laden with the scent of growing things, thinking less about what had been accomplished and more about what lay ahead.

He knew he couldn't maintain this existence forever - this careful balance between worlds, identities, loyalties and obligations. The strain was already showing, the questions already being asked, the inconsistencies already glaring for anyone sharp enough to notice them.

And yet the concept of home seemed to have taken on a new meaning - as if it offered a possibility of belonging that he'd always felt was out of his reach, but now... now he'd found people worth caring about. Causes worth fighting for. Wrongs that were worthy of redress.

The battles ahead would be different, but perhaps that was the point. Perhaps that was the reason he'd been given this extraordinary gift.

A buzzard circled overhead, riding the thermals with effortless grace, and he watched it for a long moment before turning his attention back to the landscape below. The town was fully awake now, people moving about their business, beginning another day in the long chain of days that connected past to future, one generation to the next.

The sun climbed higher, warming his face and casting sharp shadows on the path below. Time to go. Time to return to whichever world was calling him today. Time to pick up the threads of whichever life needed his attention.

He rose slowly, brushing dust from his clothes, and took one last look at the view spread out before him. Tomorrow would bring new challenges, new mysteries and new opportunities, but then so had yesterday, so that was alright.

The path down the crag was easier than the climb up had been, and he took it like a man who knew exactly where he was going, even if he wasn't entirely sure exactly when he'd get there.

Behind him, the mountains kept their eternal watch. Before him, the world waited.

Acknowledgements

First and foremost, thank you for reading Blood and Birthright. As an independent author, every reader matters enormously, and I'm genuinely grateful you chose to spend your time with David Balfour.

Thank you for taking the time—the most valuable thing we possess—and also for having the patience to overlook any mistakes, bungles, errors or plain tomfoolery.

If you enjoyed this book, please consider leaving a review on Amazon, Goodreads, or your preferred platform. Reviews are absolutely vital for helping other readers discover the series, and even a few sentences about what you liked can make all the difference. Your recommendation to friends, family, or book clubs is equally valuable - word of mouth remains the best way for books like this to find their audience.

Now, to the many people who helped bring this story to life:

To my wife, who not only encouraged this project from the beginning but endured countless dinner conversations about it all with remarkable patience.

To the staff and volunteers of Scotland's libraries, museums, and cultural institutions, whose unknowing expertise has proved invaluable in recreating 1860s Edinburgh with some degree of historical accuracy. Any remaining errors are entirely my own.

To Mackers, Doug, Tony and Willie—who've helped more than they could possibly know.

And finally, to Robert Louis Stevenson, whose David Balfour inspired this homage across the centuries. I hope I've done justice to the name.

The Callander Murders

The Second Balfour Investigation

In the shadow of the Trossachs, death follows a calendar.

Every month, on the same date, another body appears in Callander and the surrounding highlands. Each victim is found staged beneath a source of light—streetlamps, car headlights, the glow of a mobile phone. The pattern is precise, ritualistic, and utterly baffling.

DC David Balfour finds himself drawn into a case that seems to echo across time itself. As the investigation deepens, fragments surface of a forgotten Victorian scandal: children who vanished from Edinburgh's gaslit streets in 1860, lured by a mysterious lamplighter into the darkness of the Old Town's wynds and closes.

The parallels are impossible to ignore. In both eras, the powerful seem determined to bury the truth. In both eras, light itself has become a weapon.

But as Balfour delves into the connection between past and present, he begins to suspect that what appears to be the work of a single obsessed killer may be something far more complex—and far more dangerous.

Someone is using the old stories as camouflage. Someone with their own agenda.

In the Trossachs, where ancient stones mark the landscape and history runs deep as the lochs, some patterns refuse to stay buried. And some lights lead only to darkness.

From the author of *Blood and Birthright* comes another atmospheric dual-timeline mystery.

- Due December 2025

Author's Note

Blood and Birthright grew from a simple question: does justice transcend time?

The Edinburgh of 1860 was a city of stark contrasts—gleaming New Town elegance built on Old Town squalor, where social reform battled entrenched privilege. But this tension felt remarkably contemporary as I researched the novel, and realised that many of the issues David Balfour faces - corruption, class bias, institutional power protecting the wealthy - remain depressingly relevant.

The time travel element of The Balfour Investigations is meant to serve the mystery rather than dominate it. These are not science fiction stories or tales of the supernatural - simply dual timeline mysteries where the primary investigator happens to be the same guy.

The intention with both timelines is to follow realistic investigative procedures. The nineteenth-century sections draw heavily on contemporary police reports and forensic practices, while the modern chapters reflect current Scottish police protocols.

Readers familiar with Stevenson's original David Balfour will recognise certain character names and Scottish settings, but this is very much its own story. I've tried to capture the spirit of adventure and moral clarity that made Stevenson's work so enduring, whilst addressing themes that speak to contemporary readers.

Discussion Questions

(For book clubs and readers)

1. How does the dual-timeline structure affect your reading experience? Were you more invested in the historical or contemporary mystery?
2. David Balfour uses his time-travel ability to pursue justice. Do you think he's justified in interfering with both timelines? What are the ethical implications?
3. Both murders involve family members killing to protect reputation and financial interests. What does this suggest about how little - or how much - has changed across 160 years?
4. The novel explores themes of class, privilege, and institutional corruption. How do these issues manifest differently in 1866 versus 2025?
5. Which supporting character did you find most compelling - Solomon Shaw, Amelia Sterling, or DCI Munro? What did they bring to the story?
6. How does Edinburgh itself function as a character in the novel? Would the story work as well in another city?
7. David's investigation methods differ significantly between time periods. How do the limitations and advantages of each era affect his detective work?
8. The novel ends with David establishing allies in both timelines. What kind of cases would you like to see him investigate next?

About The Author

James Black lives in the Trossachs with his wife, a fluctuating population of their nomadic offspring, and an increasingly demanding collection of animals. A former journalist, he discovered his passion for crime fiction during a career spent travelling the globe and witnessing stories you couldn't make up.

When not writing, he can be found swearing under his breath while tackling a wide variety of tasks from repairing paddock fences to wrestling wayward sheep. Remarkably, he chooses to do this.

This is his debut novel.

Stay Connected

Sign up for James Black's newsletter to receive:

- **Exclusive short stories** featuring David Balfour & MIT-13
- **Early access** to new book announcements
- **Behind-the-scenes** research notes and historical photographs
- **Updates** on the writing process and upcoming releases

Sign up at: www.jamesblackauthor.com

- **Website**: www.jamesblackauthor.com
- **Twitter**: @JamesBlackBooks
- **Facebook**: JamesBlackAuthor
- **Instagram**: @jamesblackauthor
- **Amazon**: https://www.amazon.com/author/james-black

Review and Recommend

If you enjoyed *Blood and Birthright*, please consider:

- **Leaving a review** on Amazon, Goodreads, or your preferred platform [ASIN: B0FMLKHF54 - Reviews]
- **Recommending** to your book club or reading group
- **Sharing** on social media with #BloodAndBirthright

Your support helps independent authors reach new readers!

Printed in Dunstable, United Kingdom